The King of the Vile

by David Dalglish

BOOKS BY DAVID DALGLISH

THE HALF-ORC SERIES
The Weight of Blood
The Cost of Betrayal
The Death of Promises
The Shadows of Grace
A Sliver of Redemption
The Prison of Angels
The King of the Vile

THE SHADOWDANCE SERIES
Cloak and Spider (novella)
A Dance of Cloaks
A Dance of Blades
A Dance of Mirrors
A Dance of Shadows
A Dance of Ghosts
A Dance of Chaos

THE PALADINS
Night of Wolves
Clash of Faiths
The Old Ways
The Broken Pieces

THE BREAKING WORLD
Dawn of Swords
Wrath of Lions
Blood of Gods

David Dalglish

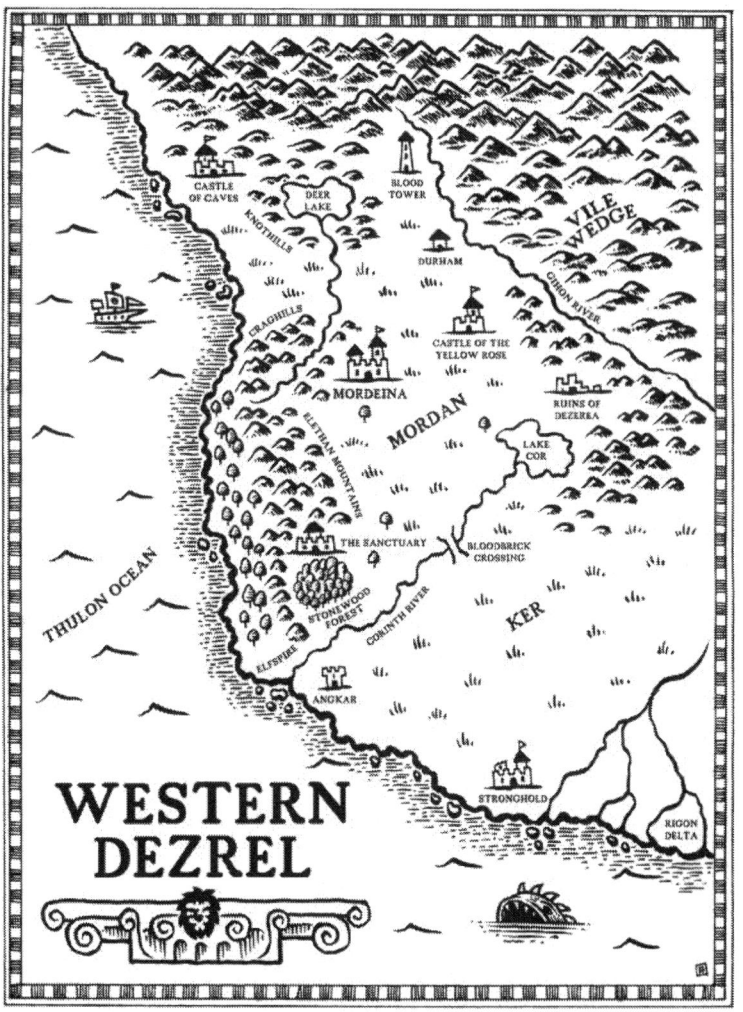

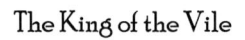

The King of the Vile

Prologue

Alric Perry awoke gasping for air, his arms pushing against the heavy blanket atop him.

"What is it?" his wife Rosemary asked as she rolled to face him. "Is it that dream again?"

Shifting so his back was to her, Alric stared at the bare wood wall, unable to close his eyes. Too much risk of falling asleep. Too much risk of returning to the dreaming world.

"No," he lied.

He lay there until morning, enduring the bleak hours as the moon faded and the sun rose. When the first hint of light slipped beneath the cracks of their heavy curtain, Alric rose out of bed and splashed water across his face from the washbasin they kept in the adjacent room. Glad he couldn't see the redness of his eyes, he ran his fingers through his long black hair, trying to straighten it into something manageable.

"Is this what you want?" Alric whispered into the silence. "Is it really?"

Rosemary stirred at the same time he heard the first of his two sons walking across the creaking wood floors to the kitchen. Alric smiled a bitter smile. Rosemary always seemed to know when the kids would wake. There were crops to be tended, his work in the fields slacking as of late, but he didn't go out, nor did he make himself something to eat. He stood there, waiting for his wife to get out of bed. Her hair a mess, she glanced at him as she slid off the hay mattress.

"You should have gone back to sleep," she said, easily reading his red eyes. "It's only a dream."

Alric grunted, said nothing. Still in her shift, Rosemary passed through the kitchen on her way out the front door, pausing to rustle the hair of their eldest, Bartholomew. Alric found it hard to breathe as he watched. He was going to do it. He was actually going to do it.

Having finished relieving herself, Rosemary came back inside to change her clothes. When she saw him standing there, unmoving, she frowned.

"What is it?" she asked.

"I'm going," he told her.

She froze. "No, you're not," she told him.

He shook his head, unsure of what else to say. It was crazy. He knew that. She knew that, too.

"Damn it," Rosemary said, storming toward him. "It's a dream, Alric, a stupid dream. You can't leave me here, you can't…"

He tried to wrap his arms around her, but she pushed him away, her eyes widening.

"Don't," she said. "You can't leave us like this. The harvest starts next week, and we're short on hands as it is."

"We've a spare bed, and good food," Alric said. "There's plenty of boys in town who'll work for both."

"But what if you don't come back? You know what everyone's been saying. The angels are killing everyone they pardoned. Everyone. You're safe here in Ker, but there…"

"It was only one night," Alric insisted. "And it doesn't matter. I still have to go."

His wife's lower lip quivered, but she steeled herself. She'd always been a tough woman. It's what attracted Alric to her in the first place.

"You think this is what Ashhur wants you to do?" she asked him. "He wants you to abandon your wife? Your kids? Does that sound like the right thing to do?"

Again he shook his head, helpless against her. How could he explain it? There was no way to show her, no way to convince her. The dreams had come for months now, their clarity and strength increasing tenfold over the past week.

"Please stop," he said. He caught their two little boys watching from the kitchen, pretending not to see, and it made his heart ache. "Rose…I can't sleep. I can barely eat. Whatever this is, it's tearing me apart. I need to do something."

Rosemary looked away, crossed her arms.

"Come on boys," she said, suddenly hurrying into the kitchen. "Your father needs some time alone. Dress yourselves so we can go to grandpappy's house."

Alric stayed in their bedroom, coming out only when they were leaving. He knelt so he could hug his sons, kiss the tops of their heads, and say goodbye. Rosemary spoke without words, her message instead conveyed by the severity of the slamming door. It rattled the house and left Alric with shaking hands and watery eyes.

Packing his supplies took little time. They'd had many prosperous harvests the past few years, so the jars he stuffed into his rucksack would not be missed. He brought only a single change of clothes, knowing any more than that would be a luxury he couldn't afford to carry. It was a long walk to Mordeina, after all. He did pack a second pair of boots, new ones he'd purchased a week ago. He'd argued with Rosemary that it hadn't been because of his dreams. Holding them in his hands, running his fingers over the leather, he wasn't sure if it'd been a lie or not.

He filled two waterskins at the stream running through the back of their land, then hoisted his rucksack over his shoulders. The weight was heavier than he expected, and he grunted. *So what?* he told himself. If he could endure the dreams, he could endure a sore back and blistered feet. With no other delay, he began walking down the long worn path leading north from their property. He didn't even risk a look back at their house. It wasn't that he expected to never return. It was that he knew the slightest glance behind might cost him his courage.

Waiting for him at the crossroad leading to town was Rosemary's father, Jacob.

"I can't say I'm surprised," Jacob said. He was a wealthy man, his clothes fine but well-worn. His hands and face were weathered from countless hours in the fields. Hard blue eyes bore into Alric, and there was little sympathy in them.

"Just doing what I think is right," Alric said.

The King of the Vile

"I'm sure you are." Jacob looked back toward his own lands, the largest surrounding the little village of Greenbrook. "She won't be waiting for you. I'll make sure of that. She needs a man to take care of her, one who won't run off because of childish nonsense."

Alric bit his tongue to hold back his anger. He'd known this would happen if he left. His marriage had always been rocky, and Jacob never truly approved. To him, Alric was just an outsider, a foreigner. To go now, to abandon his family...

"You do what you think is best," Alric said, dipping his head in respect. Putting his back to his father-in-law, to the entire village of Greenbrook, Alric started walking northeast.

Not far off the worn path was a well-maintained road leading to the Bloodbrick Bridge. He followed it, the rucksack feeling heavier than ever. This was it. The miles steadily passing beneath his feet, he tried to feel some optimism. He was doing what his god wanted, after all. Why should he not rejoice? He sang some songs the traveling priests had taught him, and they cheered his heart a little. It never lasted. Such cheer, such thoughts, never lasted when the after-images of the dreams flashed before his eyes.

No, whatever Ashhur wanted him to do, it wouldn't be easy. It wouldn't be safe. He was far too fearful a man to rejoice in what, deep in his heart, he felt was a death sentence.

It was five miles to the Bloodbrick, and he was not alone as he traveled. Several times he had to shift off the road so wagons could pass him by, all heading the opposite direction. After a few hours, a wagon rolled along from behind him, driven by an elderly man.

"Headed to the bridge?" the man asked. His teeth and hair were missing, but his eyes were lively.

"I am," Alric said.

"Hop on. Could always use someone to listen to my prattling."

Alric tossed his rucksack into the tiny wagon, which was stuffed with bags of flour, and climbed aboard.

"Soldiers got to eat," the old man explained, having caught Alric's wandering eyes.

"Of course," Alric said. Before spurring the donkeys onward, the old man reached to his belt and pulled a long dagger halfway out of its sheath.

"Don't be getting any funny ideas," he said. "Been on the road longer than you've been alive, so keep your hands off me, and off my shit, and we'll get along swell."

"Understood," Alric said. "I'm only glad to rest my feet for a little while."

"How far you been walking?"

"Since Greenbrook."

"Hah!" The trader set the wagon to rolling. "You're sore from that? I once had to walk all the way from Angkar to Angelport. Let me tell you something, when you're walking that long a journey, sore feet's the easiest of your problems..."

He continued on, and Alric only half-heartedly listened. He kept his focus on the bridge coming into view. The Bloodbrick was the only major way across the Corinth River, which formed the border for the nations of Ker and Mordan. If Alric wanted to get to Mordeina, Mordan's capital, he'd need to cross, but he doubted that'd happen without incident based on what he saw.

Thousands of soldiers lined the river, their gathering of tents so thick he could barely see across to the other side. Multiple barricades were set up before the bridge, constantly patrolled. Alric felt his heart thud in his chest at the sight of it all. There were so many people, not just soldiers, but traders, camp followers, even some children and animals lurking around the edges. It was like one swelling, shifting organism, and the thought of being inside it made Alric sick. He'd never done well with crowds, hated merely having friends over too long in his house. To go through that many...

"Well, here we are," the trader said. "You looking for someone?"

"No," Alric said, hopping off the wagon and reaching for his rucksack. "I'm hoping to cross."

The elderly man's laughter followed him as he approached the soldiers. He stayed on the road, his arms crossed over his chest for protection. From both sides of the road came shouts, some joyful, some not. One of the camp followers, a pretty miss with fiery red hair, made a move toward him until she saw his simple farmer's clothing. Her face remained pleasant, but Alric saw the dismissal in her eyes, and it made his stomach twist.

At last he reached the barricades, and was ordered to halt by the guards stationed there.

"What's your business?" the man in charge asked him as another roughly yanked the rucksack off his back and began searching through his things. A third soldier patted him down for weapons. He found none.

"Travel," Alric said. "Not business. I wish to visit Mordeina."

"You a member of any trading guilds?"

He shook his head.

"Are you a servant of a noble lord, or of any noble lineage?"

"No," Alric said, again shaking his head. "I'm a farmer. That's all."

The second soldier shoved the rucksack back into his arms and nodded to the others.

"The border's closed," the soldier said. "I'm sorry, but if you aren't nobility, and aren't a merchant, you're not crossing."

For a brief moment Alric felt relief. He could go home. He could abandon this stupid notion that he was somehow important. That relief was met with shame, and the stubbornness Alric had carried with him all his life.

"You don't understand," he said. "I have to cross."

"I'm sure you do," the soldier said, motioning to the other two. "But it don't matter."

They pushed him back, making way for the next in line to be checked. Alric watched, feeling as if the entire world were shrinking in around him. He had to cross. He had to.

Making his way back down the road, he walked until the commotion around the Bloodbrick was but a murmur on the wind. Telling himself it'd be all right, that Ashhur would protect him, he veered off the road and into the field beyond. The bridge was the only way to cross the Corinth for wagons and horses, but any river could be crossed if one could swim it. Soldiers patrolled the water's edge, but once he was a mile out from the bridge Alric found a safe space to cross. By then night had fallen, and coming with it was a chill hinting at the approach of autumn. Alric stared across the wide, murky water, focusing on the dry land on the other side.

"Please," he prayed to Ashhur. "Please, I'm doing this for you, so...don't let me die. Is that a fair enough request?"

One of the priests he'd met in Greenbrook had told him to never pray for something he wasn't prepared to have granted. If going on living was something he wasn't prepared for, he hoped the river swept him away into the night. Tightening the straps to his rucksack, he took a step.

"Damn that's cold," he said, jerking his foot back out. Hopping up and down, he berated his childish hesitation. The water was cold? What did he expect, a bubbling hot spring?

"Here we go," he said, and then before anything like reason or sanity could take hold, he dashed into the water. His entrance was clumsy, desperate, and within moments he felt the water pulling on him. At first he thought he'd be fine, but when his feet lost touch with the bottom, he flailed his arms and kicked his legs. It was less of a swim and more of a lunge that pushed him toward the other side. The rucksack was heavy on his back, too heavy. Each time his head dipped below the water he found himself struggling a little bit harder to push back to the surface.

Minutes passed, and his lungs began to burn from the struggle. The darkness made it difficult to tell, but he swore the far side was coming no closer. He was lost in the center of the river, dragged along with its current. Panic struck him, and at last he let go of his pack. With its weight gone, he frantically swam toward the other side.

Cold and wet, he crawled onto the wet earth and collapsed. He felt the mud curling beneath his fingers, and he dared not think of what bugs and leeches might be sinking into his flesh for a meal. Shivers followed, and he closed his eyes and let the sobs begin. He cried for his family, his wife, his home, the loss of everything. And for what?

For what?

A sudden warmth came over him. He looked up, feeling dread but not understanding why. He wasn't at the river anymore, and his clothes were dry. A growing rumble met his ears, and he realized he was in the midst of a crowd. The sun had risen, and on either side of the street were towering buildings made of crystal and glass. Thousands upon thousands streamed deeper into the elegant, otherworldly city.

Confused, Alric followed, feeling compelled to join the crowd. At the end of the road he came upon a castle, which faded away to reveal a great throne. The seat was carved of gold, sitting atop a red dais covered with fine silk. Just staring at it made Alric feel afraid. And then from the sky came a man of shadow, his features barren, his eyes empty white spaces. With shoulders hunched as if carrying a great burden, he sat upon the throne. A heavy crown formed upon his head, coated with jewels and bathed in silver. Half the crowd cheered, the other half cried in terror. Not understanding either, Alric watched in rapt awe.

The shadows of this king deepened. The red dais flowed, the silk turning to blood. The gold of the throne peeled away, revealing washed bone. The jewels of the crown became eyes, the silver their moving tears. Louder the crowd screamed as the shadow king lifted a scepter. The ground rumbled. The crystal buildings shattered and fell. The sun and moon danced in the sky, the sun rising in the west and setting in the east. Through it all the people screamed, and Alric found himself screaming with them.

Like a flood came the fire, washing over the people, pooling around the throne and lifting it into the air. The liquid flame burned away Alric's flesh, left his hands blackened husks. Nostrils filled with the stench of burning meat, eyes flooded with smoke, Alric looked upon the shadow king and opened his mouth to speak.

Like always, he could not hear the words. As the dream fled him, and his eyes snapped open, he felt overwhelmed with a single emotion, an emotion that left his muscles clenched and his hands shaking.

Rage.

"If I must," Alric said, struggling to his feet and staggering over the riverbank. "Ashhur help me, if I must."

Tired, lost, and alone beneath a great blanket of stars, Alric walked north. Into Mordan. Into the land of angels.

1

He was burning, but the voices didn't seem to care, nor their owners deign to stop it. Couldn't they see? Was his pain not obvious? The fire, it lashed his face, his hands, licked away his robes, left him naked and...

Tarlak's eyes snapped open and frantically surveyed his surroundings. He was in a small room with an ornate cabinet on one end and a plain chair at the other. The walls were decorated with paintings, their frames carved gold. The lone door showed no visible hand or knob. A lone man stood over Tarlak, his clothes a uniform red. Something about the way he surveyed him like a dissected carcass spurred Tarlak into action. He tried to sit up, to form the first motions of a spell, but he found himself bound. His head slammed back down against the bed he lay upon, and he let out a scream of pain. His sudden movement awakened a thousand needles stabbing across his body.

"Where?" he muttered with a tongue so dry it felt made of sand. "Where am I?"

"The Apprentices' Tower," said the man in red. "Now lay still. I haven't finished putting on today's ointments."

Tarlak tried to concentrate, but it felt like a fog had settled over his mind. *One thing at a time*, he told himself. *Focus on one thing at a time.* He started with the restraints. Two cords of leather, one around his neck, the other his forehead. Together they kept his head pinned to the bed. More buckles locked down his elbows and wrists, limiting his range of movements. Worst were his fingers, all ten inside individual loops of iron screwed to a metal inset in the bed, preventing them from even twitching. Last were a few more simple cords around his knees and ankles, thoroughly imprisoning him.

The King of the Vile

Casting a spell was out, Tarlak decided. Dread swelled in his chest, but he fought it down. Think, he told himself. He was in the apprentices' tower, which meant the Council of Mages had spared him after their treacherous assault on King Antonil and his weary army. Remembrance of that ambush sparked a fire in his chest, and he strained once more against the buckles and cords.

"Why am I here?" he asked.

"Because the Lord of the Council decided you would live," said his caretaker. "For now."

The man held up his bucket and dipped his hand inside. When he pulled it out it was caked with a thick white cream. Its similarity to soured milk did not help Tarlak's queasy stomach. Without any attempt at tenderness, the apprentice rubbed it on Tarlak's right leg. A cool sensation spread upon contact, dulling the pain. Seeing him apply the medicine made Tarlak aware of his nakedness, with only a simple cloth to cover his loins. Not that Tarlak was particularly shy, but it allowed him to see the extent of his burns. What he saw was disturbing enough that he looked away and focused on the ceiling instead.

"What's your name?" he asked.

"Why do you care?"

"If I'm to be tied down half-naked in a room with another man, I'd prefer to know his name."

The man grabbed another clump of the white goo, frowned at him.

"Cecil."

"Just Cecil?"

"Cecil Towerborn, if you must know."

Tarlak grunted. Well, that was interesting, if he could call such a factoid interesting amid horrible pain in his arms, legs, and face. The moniker 'Towerborn' was given to those dumped at the steps of the Apprentices' Tower by mothers and fathers too poor, or too terrible, to raise their own children. Those tested and shown to contain significant magical potential were kept. Those found lacking, well, those types of stories were Tarlak's favorites to tell when the night was young and he had an audience he wanted to mentally scar.

Speaking of scars…

"Well, Cecil," Tarlak said, forcing himself to talk. Each moment he was awake he found the fog lifting, and in its place came raging, fiery pain. "Would you care to tell me how badly you scoundrels burned me?"

Cecil hesitated, then resumed spreading the cream. His robes were red, signifying him as an apprentice, but he looked to be in his thirties. Faint lines surrounded pale blue eyes, and the boyish cut of his blond hair seemed almost comical. Tarlak wondered what had kept him stalled for so long, unable to transition over to the Masters' Tower. That he'd survived at all as a Towerborn meant he had some measure of prowess.

"Not as terrible as it should have been," Cecil said. "The dead king protected you from much of it, and your meager protection spell prevented the burns from going as deep as they would have otherwise."

"Yes, I get it, I should have died," Tarlak said, groaning despite himself. "Tell me things I don't know."

Cecil set down the bucket and wiped his hand with a towel.

"Very well. Your legs sustained some burns, but should heal fine, especially with our care. Your arms, though, will bear scars for the rest of your life, however long that is. As for your face, that is where it is most erratic, due to a failing in your defenses, no doubt. The burns are in small blotches, and also likely to scar."

Tarlak let out a sigh. That explained the constant itch in his arms and fingers. No doubt that itch was subdued pain he'd feel in due time. Not that they didn't already hurt. They did. He just knew they were capable of hurting worse.

A knock came from the door, and Cecil turned to go.

"Wait," Tarlak said. "I have one more question."

Cecil turned, clearly impatient.

"What?" he asked.

Tarlak swallowed, braced himself.

"Did the fire burn off all my hair?"

Cecil blinked, and it took him a second to collect himself.

"Yes," he said. "You're as bald as a baby's ass."

"Bastards," Tarlak said, letting out a sigh as he relaxed back into the bed. "Cruel, heartless bastards."

The King of the Vile

Cecil opened the door, bowed to whoever had knocked, and stepped out. With not much else to look at, Tarlak stared at the ceiling. A cursory glance at the paintings showed them replications of forests, rivers, and mountains. Free things, he realized. Things to remind him of how isolated and alone he was, chained in that tiny little room. Or maybe it was to trick him into thinking he was freer than he actually was? Too bad his mind didn't work like that. Or maybe subliminal messages couldn't work on someone half-burned to death and strapped down to a bed.

Tarlak heard the door close, footsteps on the hard stone, and then his new visitor stepped into his peripheral vision. Tarlak started, instinctively trying to form a protection spell despite his locked down fingers. The visitor was a tall man, his robe a deep black that reflected red when the light from the windows hit it just right. His angular face was clean shaven. Long straight hair fell down around his neck, and the softest of movements caused red, orange, and yellow ripples to cascade outward, like a fire burned deep within every dark strand. Unlike the fire of his hair, his eyebrows were bushy and bright gold. There was only one person who would dare dress in such a manner, and use magic to showcase his reputation in his chosen specialization: Roand the Flame, Lord of the Council.

Roand stood over him, hands at the edge of the bed. His irises, a gradient of color going from red in the center to yellow at the far edges, narrowed as he stared down.

"Your name," he said. "What is it?"

"Tarlak Eschaton," Tarlak said, smiling his widest smile. "At your service."

Roand didn't bat an eye.

"Do you have proof you are who you say you are?"

"That depends. Did my robes survive?"

"Parts of them did."

"Good," Tarlak said, letting out a chuckle. "They were yellow, weren't they? Would anyone else in the whole damn world wear those same robes? Of course not. I'm Tarlak Eschaton, hero of the free world; you're Roand the Flame, the psychopathic murderer of thousands of soldiers, and right now we'll just have to trust one another to be who we say we are. Well, not that you've said anything, but it's pretty obvious. I can't imagine anyone crazy enough to dress like *you*, either."

"Such a fiery spirit," Roand said, reaching out and grabbing Tarlak's arm. His fingers scraped away healing cream, taking blackened flesh with it.

"I'd have chosen a different term," Tarlak said, closing his eyes and fighting the pain. "People might fear you were making a pun."

Roand scraped along Tarlak's arm a second time, his well-manicured nails digging. Tarlak could hear the tearing of his skin, and it made him want to vomit.

"Still your tongue," the master wizard said. "Humor is how you handle difficult situations, but you let it wander into insult and childishness. In my presence you will behave yourself in a manner more befitting a wizard of your skill."

Joking was actually his way of ignoring the rapidly increasing pain, but Tarlak didn't feel like arguing the point.

"And if I don't?" he asked.

"Then I will make the rest of your body look like your arms, and I promise you, I will not let you die afterward. You'll lie here and suffer for an age. You know who I am, and where you are. Time itself can be manipulated in this tower, and in those moments, as the fire peels away your flesh, you'll feel seconds pass like years."

Tarlak opened his eyes, winked. "Yes, sir," he said.

Roand took the lone chair from the corner, set it beside the bed, and sat down. He leaned closer to Tarlak, his hands rubbing together.

"I want you to be fully aware of your situation," Roand said. "I believe we, as human beings, always benefit the more information we have. With understanding comes wisdom, and with wisdom comes a better life. In your case, a longer life. The reason you were not executed on the battlefield is simple, Tarlak. And no, it is not because of your claim on a spot of the Council by defeating your former master, Madral."

Tarlak kept his face impassive as best he could.

"You know about that, eh?" he asked. "I always wondered."

The King of the Vile

"Of course we do," Roand said. "As we know of much of your exploits. You've never actively worked against the Council, and your killing of our assassins in your younger days impressed us more than annoyed us. Your reputation, while a bit foolish, is still one of high regard. These things enhanced my decision, but they were not the deciding factor. No, the reason you are still alive is a simple one: your blood."

Tarlak raised an eyebrow, wondering if he even had an eyebrow left to raise.

"My...blood?"

"For a man of jokes, you think so literally," Roand said. "Your bloodline, if you must force me to be precise. The Eschaton were once known as the Escheton, and it was Turock Escheton who placed the first stone of these towers and wrote the laws we still abide by today. Simply put, you are descended from the finest, most brilliant mind to ever grace these walls. To have you die so pitifully before our very doorstep would have been an insult to his name."

Tarlak tried to wrap his head around this new development. He'd heard the name, of course, but his interest in family history had never been very high, and he'd not connected the two. Part of him wondered if he'd been better off with his great-great-great-grandfather being a random fisherman instead of an ancient wizard. Then he might be dead instead of in massive amounts of hurt.

"Fascinating," Tarlak said. "So does that mean you'll heal me up and send me on my way?"

The fire in Roand's eyes pulsed. Tarlak had a feeling it was the closest the man ever came to laughing.

"Not quite," he said. "You have consistently practiced the art of magic while simultaneously spurning requests to join our ranks. The Council will convene to determine your fate, Tarlak Eschaton. If we deem your insults against us too severe, we will have you executed."

Tarlak let out a cough, and despite the pain, he couldn't help but laugh at the absurdity. They were keeping him alive...so they could kill him?

"I thought you didn't want to insult my dear ancestor's memory?" he asked.

Roand smiled at him.

"In everything we do, we'll be following the rules given to us by Turock," he said. "In what better way could we honor his memory than that?"

Tarlak tried to shrug, found he couldn't. "By letting me live? That sounds like a good one."

Roand stood, slowly shaking his head.

"I assure you, in all that we do, none of it is arbitrary," he said. "We will judge your worth to the community of wizards, and before them, your life will be weighed. Your charm and skill will mean nothing."

"What about having saved the world?" Tarlak said as the master wizard headed for the door. His head had begun to spin, and the pain in his limbs stung with renewed vigor. "Surely that counts for something!"

Roand's look was strangely one of disappointment.

"You think you saved the world?" he asked. "Consider that another mark against you."

The wizard left, the door shut, and at its heavy echo, Tarlak closed his eyes and screamed until the pain in his arms sent him back into unconsciousness.

2

"Do you remember when I told you things couldn't get much worse?" Deathmask asked Veliana as the two huddled in the dingy basement of a vacant home.

"Yeah," Veliana said, eyes fixed on the door. They'd stacked a few planks against it, plus scattered broken stones on the floor in desperate hope of making their attackers stumble. A meager defense against the fury of an angel, but it was something.

"I've decided I was wrong."

"No shit."

Deathmask pulled out a handful of ash from a pouch pocket and tossed it into the air. A whisper of magic and it froze, hovering like a cloud obscuring his masked face. Deathmask wasn't entirely sure if the angels could know fear or not, but it made him feel marginally better. He was the dark specter, the man in the shadows manipulating the events of the city. He wouldn't be undone by a glorified turkey wielding a sword.

"They shouldn't be able to find us here," Veliana said, twirling a dagger in her left hand. They were alone in the dark, able to see only because of spells he'd cast upon them, hiding behind an overturned table, its rotting wood their only protection against whoever might attack. And they would be attacked. Deathmask was certain of that. With him carrying the supposed guilt of sending Avlimar crashing to the ground, there would be no respite.

"They found us before," he said. "As they did the hideout before that. It's like they're getting help."

"The whole bloody city is out looking for us," Veliana said. "Of course they're getting help."

"I meant competent help."

"True, that is a rarer luxury."

A creak from the other side of the door silenced them. Deathmask clenched a fist, steeling his mind for combat. He would not die here, not like some cornered rat. Not for a crime he never committed. If he were to die in such a way, at least it should be for a crime he *did* commit.

The door shook once, then shattered inward. Two soldiers with heavy mauls backed away from the exposed entrance as daylight streamed inside. More soldiers poured through the broken entrance, their shields raised before them, their naked blades reflecting the daylight. As their plated boots kicked aside the rocks, Veliana spurred into action, a soft violet light shining off her daggers as she charged. Deathmask paused a moment to enjoy the sight of her spinning and weaving, her daggers lashing out for vulnerable spots in the soldiers' armor.

A special girl, he thought as fire burst across his palms. She'd ruled the Ash Guild before his arrival, and if the gods were kind, they'd let her rule it long after he died. Standing behind the table, he outstretched his hands and let loose a burst of his power. Twin lances of fire shot from his palms, melting through the chestplates of the two soldiers they struck. The fire swirled within the confines of their armor, burning flesh as the men screamed. Veliana kicked one to the ground, leapt over his body, and spun before the stunned soldier behind him. Her dagger cut a line across his throat, spilling blood to the floor.

Deathmask covered her retreat with bolts of shadow that slammed into the men like boulders. Even from a distance, he could hear their bones break from the force. Veliana summersaulted over a leg sweep, fell flat to the ground, and then rolled toward the overturned table.

"That's enough," Deathmask said, his wrists connecting as he gathered his power. White light sparked like electricity before his palms, then vanished as a ball of darkness replaced it. It grew in size, sucking in howling wind. Deathmask let it loose. It rolled through the air with a sound of thunder, the men it touched screaming as their skin turned to ash, as their life force was pulled into the rotating sphere of darkness and light. When the sphere reached the door, it detonated, flinging bodies against walls hard enough to cave in armor.

Deathmask let out the breath he'd been holding. Only ten men lay dead before him. He'd expected more.

"Just a single patrol," he said as Veliana stood and stretched her back. "Maybe they weren't sure we were here."

Rubble blasted inward, making way for an armored angel to duck into the basement. His wings curled about him to fit through the entrance, the daylight adding a golden hue to the white feathers. The angel held aloft a long blade that must have weighed more than Veliana.

"Deathmask of the Ash Guild," the angel said. "You have this one chance to surrender for trial before I am forced to kill you."

"And you have this one chance to run away before I pluck your feathers and send you back to the castle well-cooked," Deathmask countered. "Actually, change that. I'm going to do that no matter what you try."

The angel tensed, clearly not amused.

"What about me?" Veliana asked. "Can I go free?"

When the angel opened his mouth to answer, she leapt at him, both daggers thrusting. The angel's speed was incredible as he twisted his enormous blade in the way of her attack. But it'd only been a feint, for she fell short, rolled, and then back-flipped away as his sword slammed the stone. Cracks ran in all directions.

The distraction was all Deathmask needed to cast his spell, and with a bellow he unleashed his fury. Dozens of colorless spiders rose from the shadows at his feet, some scurrying along the ground, others leaping to the ceiling. They swarmed past Veliana and into the angel, whose magical blade swept side to side, failing to scatter them all. The spiders leapt upon him, sinking in their fangs. With each bite their form changed to smoke, pouring into the angel's body through the bloody openings they created. The angel dropped his sword, tore at his skin, and screamed. The veins in his body became snaking, branching black lines, rippling beneath his flesh. His scream lost power, and with a clatter of armor, he fell dead to the ground.

Frowning, Veliana walked over to the body and tapped it with her foot.

"That's a new one," she said.

"I don't like to use it," Deathmask said, clutching the table to steady himself. "One slip of concentration, and those spiders go wild, biting at anything nearby."

Veliana lifted her lone good eyebrow at him. "I'd prefer you not use those spells when I'm in the way of the target," she said.

"My precious Vel, when have I ever lost my concentration?"

She rolled her eyes but said nothing. Deathmask grinned, using his apparent carelessness to hide how much the spell had taken out of him. It would have been wiser to use something else, but his mood was foul, and he'd wanted the angel to suffer. Once his breath returned, Deathmask headed for the basement's exit.

"We'll need to move again," he said.

"There's nowhere left."

"There's always somewhere. We just have to find it. Besides, it's not like we can stay here."

Veliana seemed in no hurry. She stood over the angel, staring down at his delicate features and grimacing.

"Why does the Council want you dead so badly?" she asked.

"Perhaps they don't like how well I've done without them," Deathmask said, stepping over corpses. "Maybe they're tired of me acting outside their jurisdiction. For Karak's sake, maybe they're just bored. It doesn't matter."

"So what *does* matter? Proving our innocence?"

Deathmask reached the door and glanced up the stairs to make sure no soldiers waited at the top. He laughed as he did.

"Innocent?" he said. "We'll never prove ourselves innocent. The frame is too beautiful. The very witnesses to our supposed crime are angels, and the assassins that tried for King Gregory's life looked all too similar to myself. No, innocence is not what we're after, Vel. What we're after is vengeance for the ones responsible."

"Assuming we live that long."

Deathmask turned toward her and offered his hand.

"Is that not always the case with us?" he asked.

She took it, and he pulled her toward him.

"I let the Council meddle," he said, holding her close. "And this is the price we pay for my foolishness. Whatever game they're playing here, I don't want to play it any longer. Avlimar is in ruins, and amid its carcass rises the earthbound city. If there's to be any stopping it, we need to win some allies in high places, and fast."

"I thought there'd be no proving our innocence?" Veliana asked, roughly pushing him away.

"There won't," he said. "Not in any court that matters. But we can convince Harruq, or at least his wife. That's a start."

"How?"

"When a man is murdered, and you don't know how, what do you do?"

"You check the body."

"Exactly."

Deathmask winked at her, then dashed up the stairs. They exited out into the quiet streets of Mordeina, and from there they ran to the nearest alleyway, heading for the hidden places, the crowded mazes and underground veins beneath the city. The whole nation might believe he was the destroyer of Avlimar, but such a feat was beyond even him. But the Council? No, that was an enemy to fear, an enemy clever enough, and ruthless enough, to do whatever necessary to get what it wanted. Deathmask had no doubt they were the ones responsible for the eternal city's fall. However, knowing it and proving it were two very different things, and right now he hadn't the slightest shred of evidence.

Come nightfall, though, he'd find it. He banished the ash from his face, pulled aside his mask, and hurried faster along the narrowing streets. Come nightfall, he'd take his first step toward vengeance against the organization that had banished him and stripped him of everything, even his name. Just as amusing to him, he'd do it while hiding in the one place the angels would never think to look.

High above the angels flew, and as they ran, Deathmask kept one eye on the sky at all times. In that way, he doubted he was any different from the rest of the city's inhabitants.

Harruq Tun stared upon the ruins of Avlimar from a high castle balcony, the people searching through the remains tiny specks at such a distance.

"We've had to increase our patrols, and even they are not enough," Azariah said, standing beside him and sharing the view. The angel's soft hands, smooth and unblemished, gently tapped the railing. Despite the fading of Ashhur's magic, he still wore his white priestly robes, and he kept his brown hair cut short around the neck. "The allure of gold and silver is too much. The people scavenge the remains of our great city, and when we turn them away, they come back mere hours later."

"I can spare a few soldiers to help out," Harruq said, containing his sigh. "Not many, but every little bit helps, right?"

"We don't need soldiers," Azariah insisted. "We need law. The sinful will resist any punishment so long as they continue to draw breath. Declare theft from our fallen city punishable by death. That is the only thing these base creatures will fear."

"Death?" Harruq said, lifting an eyebrow. "Little harsh, isn't it?"

In answer, Azariah gestured to the sky, where the city of Avlimar once floated.

"What we had was a piece of eternity itself," the angel said. "Our remembrance of beauty and perfection. Now the city has fallen, and though we try to rebuild, we cannot. Every brick and stone is taken under the cover of night, smuggled to thieves' dens and underground markets. The promise of eternity, now bartered and traded like a bit of food or scrap of metal. We must stop it. I defer this to you only in respect to Ahaesarus's wishes. We must have peace with mankind if we are to perform our required duties."

Harruq stared at the ruins, which lay scattered across the green fields stretching out beyond the walls of Mordeina. Even from such a distance, the sunlight glinted off the gold, silver, and pearls.

"Theft is theft," he said at last. "Avlimar's remains belong to the angels, and any who take them must be punished as the thieves they are. Consider it law. I'll discuss it with the scribes later today, get it made public, but remember, *my* soldiers carry out the sentence, not angels. Got it?"

Without waiting for an answer, Harruq left the balcony and trudged down the cold halls of the castle.

"There is more we must discuss," Azariah said, following after him. "Much more. Avlimar's fall is a sign from Ashhur, and only fools would dare ignore it."

"I thought Deathmask and his guild were responsible?" Harruq said, eyeing him sidelong.

"Even darkness can be made to serve the light. It is our failures that led to the collapse, and we must study those failures, and from them learn how we may evolve this world into something better."

"Fascinating," Harruq muttered. "What does this have to do with me?"

"Because we need your help in making amends."

Much as he liked the sound of the angels making amends, the half-orc still felt uneasy about what Azariah was trying to get at. He bought himself some time by descending a set of stairs. With the angel's wide wings, there was no way they could walk side by side, and Harruq dashed down ahead of him. Reaching the bottom, he gnawed his lip and wondered.

Deathmask, guilty of destroying Avlimar? Deathmask, allying with Kevin Maryll in his failed attempt to overthrow the angels and usurp the throne? It didn't make sense. It wasn't like him. It was too…obvious. Too destined for failure. But over a dozen angels reported seeing him flee the ruins immediately after Avlimar's collapse, and several others swore they had seen him sneaking about the floating city days before its destruction, eluding pursuers. Even now, Harruq had angels leading squads of soldiers about the city, arresting members of his guild and searching for any hint of the powerful wizard. Doubtful as it was, he hoped to capture Deathmask alive. He'd love to have some answers.

Harruq's brief escape from Azariah proved fruitless, for as he stepped into the grand hall before the throne room he found several lords gathered together, waiting for him.

"Greetings, Steward," the first to notice him said. He was a chubby man with a lengthy black mustache. His blue clothes were tight fitted, his breeches held up with an enormous leather belt. "We'd worried you'd caught ill, so long was your absence."

Harruq rolled his eyes. He'd fled to his room for an hour so he might have a break from courtly proceedings, and when he'd gone to the balcony for the fresh air, Azariah had spotted him and landed. Caught ill? He wished. Then he could stay in his room all day and night. If he'd been wise, he'd have turned down Antonil's request to serve as temporary ruler in his absence. Harruq belonged on a battlefield, not a throne room.

"Healthy as ever," Harruq said, trying to move past them toward the exit. The chubby man blocked his way.

"Please, I'm sure you're busy doing whatever it is you're doing, but we must have an audience," he said. The other lords nodded. Harruq let out a sigh, and wondered what he'd done to Ashhur to deserve such punishment. Behind him, Azariah stepped into the room, and a noticeable chill followed. Harruq was hardly surprised. If anyone resented the rise of angel authority, it was the lords who had seen much of their power in punishing and policing their serfs stripped away. They could no longer act above the law either. There was no bribing an angel, nor lying their way out of sticky situations.

Harruq frowned at the chubby lord, trying to pull up a name to match the face. He failed.

"Who are you again?" he asked.

"Lord Richard Aerling, ruler of the southern lands," said the lord. If he was offended at not being known, he didn't show it. "With me are Lord Typh, Baron Usun, and Baron Foster."

Harruq nodded to each as they were introduced, forgetting their faces and names moments after seeing and hearing them. Gods, he was not meant to be a politician. Azariah took up position behind him, respectfully waiting for a chance to resume his conversation.

"Nice to meet you all," Harruq said, trying not to be impatient. "So...what is it you want?"

"We've come from the south with dire news," Richard said. "As all four of us own lands bordering Ker, we thought it best if we approached you together when we told you."

Harruq rubbed his eyes, the man's high-pitched voice giving him a headache.

"Told me what?"

"It's very simple," Richard said. "King Bram has already begun his invasion of Mordan."

The words struck Harruq like a brick to the forehead.

"That's, that's...no," he said. "I've got men stationed at the Bloodbrick, and they haven't reported any new activity from Ker in weeks."

"Invasions can be preceded in many ways," said the other lord, Typh or whatever. The man was incredibly tall, but his mustache wasn't quite as long as Richard's.

"Indeed," Richard insisted. "And the damage a small group of men can do to an unprotected home is equal to a full army. A village under my care by the name of Norstrom has been completely annihilated."

This time Harruq had no idea what to say. He glanced back at Azariah, found the angel frozen stiff, a frown locked on his face.

"Are you certain it was men from Ker?" Azariah asked.

"Who else could it be?" Richard asked. "Hundreds of people dead. Not a one escaped. That's a portent of invasion, and we must act accordingly! We've begun mustering our soldiers, but we lost many of our troops in King Antonil's second campaign, may Ashhur rest his soul."

An invasion? War? Harruq forced himself out of his stunned shell, forced his mind to work.

"Troops?" he said. "What troops do you think we have to spare? Have you not already read the summons I sent you? The North is under attack, and needs every man we can spare."

"Mere rumors of a few aggressive animal packs are nothing compared to an organized army," Richard insisted. "The North will endure, but will we? We must strike at Bram before he realizes we've discovered his cowardly tactic."

"You have no proof," Harruq insisted. "Did you find a banner? A witness? Tracks you could follow? What if Norstrom were attacked by bandits instead?"

The chubby man's confidence wavered, but only a little.

"I assure you, Steward, my lands are free of any such bandits, something that cannot be said for the North. Believe me, King Bram's soldiers will be crossing the Bloodbrick any day now, and all you have to stop them are a pitifully few number of men. The time to act is now. All we ask for is a formal declaration of war against the nation of Ker."

That was it. He couldn't take anymore.

"Out," he said. "Get out, all of you. I'm not declaring war, not now, not until Bram marches his army into our lands. When that happens you may send your soldiers to fight, but until then I want your men here. If the rumors of the North are true, we'll need every last one of them."

Richard opened his mouth to respond, but Harruq would have none of it.

"I. Said. *Out*."

He stepped closer with every word, his hand reaching for a sword buckled to his belt. The southern lords left, openly glaring at him. Harruq glared right back.

"Gods damn it all," Harruq said, blushing when he realized Azariah was still staring at him.

"It does feel like that at times," Azariah said. "But we're not abandoned, Harruq. You must have patience. We are here, Ashhur's angels, and we will protect the innocents with our lives."

"What about that business in Norstrom?" he asked. "Do you think he's right?"

A shadow crossed the angel's face.

"I will look into it," he said. "Give me time."

"I'm not sure time is something we…"

The doors, which had been opened partway to let the lords and barons out, suddenly burst open completely. Harruq's jaw dropped as a white horse flew into the hall, her great wings beating to slow her progress. Harruq drew his sword, but quickly realized that would not be necessary. He recognized the beast as Sonowin, faithful steed of Scoutmaster Dieredon. Except it wasn't the wily elf riding Sonowin, but a slender man with gray hair who stepped off on unsteady feet.

"Welcome?" Harruq said, baffled.

The man approached Harruq, saluted.

"Sir Daniel Coldmine, at your service," he said. "Forgive me for such a brazen entrance, but there is no time. The entire Vile Wedge has crossed the Gihon. Blood Tower has fallen, as has the rest of the Wall. At least twenty thousand strong of all manner of creatures march through our northern lands, destroying everything. I come at Lord Arthur Hemman's behest, to plead for aid. He cannot hold them off on his own."

Just when Harruq thought the day couldn't get any worse...

"Twenty thousand?" he said, feeling dumb as he asked.

"If not more."

His mind reeled, thinking of the men he'd need to summon, the vast stretches of land that'd need to be protected, the effect it'd have on trade. Above all, he imagined the thousands that'd be dying as they scrambled to react.

"Then we have no choice," he said shaking his head. "Azariah, get Ahaesarus in here. It's time we formed ourselves an army."

3

The night was young, the stars a bright field above, when Jessilynn heard the first sounds of the monsters' approach. *They're here*, she thought, her entire body stiffening. *Keep me calm, Ashhur. I can't afford to fail.*

It wasn't her life she feared for as the bird-men stalked the outer edges of the quaint home, but the thirty villagers hiding in the cellar, relying on her to save them. Jessilynn lay flat on her stomach atop the thatched roof, careful not to move. Her bow lay to her right, and she kept a hand on it at all times. Its touch comforted her, reminding her she wasn't helpless, nor alone. Ashhur was with her...and with her arrows.

The soft hoot of an owl sounded. Jess flicked her eyes over to where Dieredon crouched on another rooftop, his wicked-looking bow leaning against his shoulder. His dark green and brown clothes camouflaged him well, and the cloak wrapped around his body seemed to darken, matching the color of the thatched roof. The elf pointed two fingers at his eyes then gestured to the tall grasslands forming the village's border not far to Jessilynn's right. She nodded, letting him know she'd seen them. In response, the elf clutched his hand into a fist and shook his head. Not yet, he was telling her. They still must wait.

Jessilynn crouched lower and stared at the tall grass. Its stalks shook and waved as the bird-men passed through them, sickening caricatures of human life. Their faces were long and slender, their mouths contorted into beaks strong enough to puncture metal. Colorful feathers, pointless remnants of the animals they'd once been, covered their arms. Their arms had long feathers, pointless remnants of their bestial heritage, for they could not fly. Where most men would have fingers, these creatures had long, hooked

The King of the Vile

claws capable of shredding flesh with ease. For the past several days, she and Dieredon had stayed ahead of an entire pack of such creatures, warning villages so they might flee to safety.

Assuming anywhere was safe.

When they'd reached their current village several hours ago, they decided the bird-men would need beaten back if the villagers were to have a chance to flee. So they'd prepared their ambush, gathered all villagers into the cellars of the two homes, thirty in hers, another twenty in Dieredon's, and waited.

"It won't take them long to discover the hiding place," Dieredon had told her. "Fifty men, women, and children cowering in fear will release a strong scent they'll track with ease."

"Why not spread them out?" Jessilynn had asked, which earned her a shake of the elf's head.

"I want the people gathered together," he'd said. "Because then our foes will do the same. When we hit them, hit them fast and hard. The fewer who survive, the fewer we must face another day."

The grass continued to shift, and Jessilynn watched with steadily growing worry. Something was wrong. Twice before, she and Dieredon had fended off attacks by the creatures, and a third time they'd stumbled upon a raid in progress. All three times, the bird-men had rushed in with reckless speed, hoping to overwhelm any potential defenses before surprise wore off. Yet now they continued to circle, heads low, arms tucked to their bodies, their yellow eyes peering out with caution.

They know something's wrong, she thought. *Everywhere else, the people have been asleep in their homes, yet here they're hiding together.*

She glanced once more at Dieredon. So far his attention remained on the tall grass, and if he was worried about the creature's caution, he didn't show it. His face was perfectly calm, brown eyes alert, muscles tensed and ready to act. Jessilynn tried to match her teacher's demeanor. She had to be ready. Even the slightest delay might cost lives, and she'd seen enough death to last her a lifetime. Sadly it seemed she would see far more before the night was done.

Jessilynn's eyes narrowed as she watched the grass steadily sway from the bird-men's movements. Something about it seemed...unnatural. Staged, even. They were walking back and forth, back and forth, without ever stepping foot beyond relative safety. This went beyond caution. Grabbing her bow, she slowly rolled over so she could look the other way. Just as she feared, over a dozen of the beasts rushed down the road from the opposite direction. Panic spiked in her heart before she could fight it down. The bird-men had sensed the ambush, and formed one of their own.

You think you have us trapped? thought Jessilynn as she pulled an arrow from the quiver strapped to her back. A smile flitted across her lips. She was a paladin of Ashhur, and these creatures were about to witness the fury of her god. Rising up on one knee, she lifted her bow, nocked an arrow, and aimed at the nearest of the bird-men. The metal arrowhead shone a soft blue-white, pulsing as if a star were trapped inside. There'd be no hiding after she let loose, and given the number of enemies they faced, every shot must count. Breathing out slowly, and taking extra care with her aim, she finally released her arrow.

Like a falling star it streaked through the night, leaving behind a trail of silver. When it struck the bird-man in the chest, it blasted him backward as if he'd been swatted by a giant. The body rolled, smoke rising from the giant hole in its ribcage.

The creatures squawked and shrieked with ear-piercing volume. From all sides they rushed, crooked legs dashing, clawed fingers flexing. Jessilynn stood, no longer needing to hide. Across the road, Dieredon did the same. With speed she couldn't hope to match, the elf fired arrow after arrow into the tall grass, dropping several beasts before they could come barreling toward the homes. Jessilynn protected the other way, pausing the briefest moment before each shot to steady her aim. She shot center of mass, trusting the power of her god-blessed arrows. Dieredon might be able to spear an orc through the eye from a thousand yards, but she didn't need such accuracy when a hit to the chest could shatter ribs and break spines.

"All sides!" she heard Dieredon shout as she dropped a fourth creature with an arrow that hit its stomach and tore out the other side of its body. "Focus on all sides!"

The King of the Vile

She turned and quickly understood her teacher's warning. While she wasn't looking, the bird-men had swarmed from all directions. She increased her firing speed despite the risks to her aim. They were so many, at least fifty by her count, and moving with such speed! She shot down two, missed a third, and then spun left, to where a trio of bird-men had almost reached the side of the home. Jessilynn killed one, but the other two vanished beneath the rooftop. She took a step, hoping to fire straight down, but her foot punched right through the thatched roof. Her leg vanished up to the knee when she fell.

"Dieredon!" she screamed, but the beasts had reached his home as well, and he could not spare a single shot. Jessilynn heard incessant scraping as the bird-men's sharp claws dug into the home's wooden sides. They were climbing up.

Jessilynn fell to her back, leg still awkwardly trapped. Her bow lay atop her, and she hoisted it with her left hand while grabbing the drawstring. There was no way she could draw an arrow in time as two of the vile creatures clutched the roof and pulled themselves up, but she didn't need to. Ashhur was with her. At her touch, an arrow materialized itself, nocked and ready. It shone a pale white, with blue mist curling off its translucent feathers. Jessilynn released, and before the string had even finished snapping forward she was already reaching for it to fire again. The first arrow blasted its target into the air. Chunks of rooftop flew with it, ripped free by the force of impact. The second bird-man leapt toward her, but another blessed arrow struck it, vaporizing its skull.

The headless corpse tumbled backwards, hit the rooftop's edge, and then tumbled over. Jessilynn tilted her head, saw another trying to flank her. Twisting her body, her trapped knee wrenching painfully, she brought her bow to bear. The angle was awkward, and she could barely pull the string back halfway, but the arrow flew true, sparking with power as it ripped through the beast's feathered stomach and knocked it off the rooftop to die in the street below. Jessilynn spun about, looking for more, but it seemed they'd abandoned the climb. Confused, she sat up and glanced at Dieredon. The elf had dropped from the rooftop, his bow slung over his back. He wielded two long daggers, dancing and weaving through the creatures as they tried, and failed, to surround him.

A sudden flurry of scratching, coupled with a cracking sound as wood broke, tore her attention back to her own home. *The cellar,* Jessilynn realized. The creatures were tearing open the door in search of easier prey.

Jessilynn dropped her bow and yanked upward as hard as she could to free her trapped knee. Sharp pieces of wood tore into her skin, but she grit her teeth against the pain and ignored it. A little pain and blood didn't matter. The people trapped beneath her, the people who had trusted her to keep them safe, were the only ones who did. Grabbing her bow, she limped closer to the roof's edge, stepping carefully despite her hurry. She'd be of no use to anyone stuck in another hole.

The cellar door was fronted with thick stone and had been barred from the inside, but that protection meant little as Jessilynn watched three of the creatures rip enormous chunks of wood free with each scrape. Jessilynn felt her throat constrict. If they could do that to wood, what might they do to soft, human flesh?

She didn't want to find out. Refusing to draw a regular arrow, she pulled back the empty string, trusting Ashhur to grant her an arrow of far more power. Her first shot blasted the leg off one of the creatures; her second removed its arm and left it to bleed to death. One looked up at her and screeched, the sound so loud it made her nauseous. She put an arrow down its throat as a reward. The creature's innards liquefied, the arrow tearing out its lower back with an explosion of gore.

Gross, thought Jessilynn as she turned to the last of the creatures. She'd thought it'd try to dodge, or perhaps run, but instead it ripped into the broken remains of the cellar door. Panicking, she rushed her shot, but the bird-man didn't dive inside. Instead it grabbed one of the broken pieces and hurled it straight up at her. Her arrow missed wide, punching a crater into the grass, while the hurled plank cracked against her forehead. Jessilynn stumbled, her whole world spinning from the blow. The pain was sudden and vicious, and she felt blood trickling between her eyes and down her nose. Focus, she had to focus. Her left

The King of the Vile

hand clutched her bow tightly as she fought down a sudden urge to vomit.

Forcing herself back to her knees, she looked down to where several more of the creatures had rushed into the cellar. From within she heard the sound of fighting, coupled with loud, terrible screams. People were dying. Her charges were dying. With no way to help them, Jessilynn did the only thing that made sense to her woozy mind at the time: she rolled off the rooftop.

She didn't scream when she hit the ground, which Jessilynn considered a victory. The impact bruised her arm and stung her neck as her head whipped up and down. The instinct to vomit went from a mild urge to a sudden, unstoppable need. Even as her stomach heaved, and bile splashed across her knees, she rose to her feet and lifted her bow. The three bird-men hadn't seen her, instead hustling through the narrow cellar door, desperate for their meal.

Hustling through in a nice, even line.

Jessilynn drew back the drawstring, felt an arrow materialize between her fingers. Bits of her earlier meal clung to the string, the smell of vomit and blood overwhelming to her nose. Begging Ashhur to keep her aim steady, she took in a deep breath, let it out, and released. The light arrow shot through the cellar door, and with its passing she heard the sound of bones shattering. All three bird-men collapsed, gaping holes in their chests.

Jessilynn turned and saw Dieredon approaching with blood coating, none of it appearing his. The villagers slowly exited the cellars, stepping around the many feathered corpses.

"They safe?" Jessilynn asked, still feeling like her balance was yet to return.

"For now," Dieredon said. He glanced toward the grasslands, where several of the bird-men fled in the far distance, and frowned.

"Good," Jessilynn said, and then she vomited all over his fine, elven boots.

An hour later, Jessilynn lay beside a small fire, the upper half of her body wrapped in a blanket. They camped in the heart of the village. The place was empty, since Dieredon had urged the people to gather their things and head south, toward the Castle of the Yellow Rose. Behind the walls protected by Lord Arthur, they might have a chance.

"We don't need to stay here," Jessilynn said as Dieredon carefully tended the fire. She could tell he was anxious. No doubt he wanted to be many miles from here, warning another village instead of taking care of her.

"I've seen such a reaction before," the elf said, tossing a small stick into the fire's center and then crouching low, chin resting on his fist. "That blow to your head was worse than you let on. Have the headaches started?"

She nodded.

"I thought so," Dieredon said. "I must warn you, Jess, the bruise on your forehead will heal far faster than the hidden damage. This next week will be difficult for you. Daylight will be uncomfortable on your eyes, as will any loud noises."

"I'll suffer through," Jessilynn said. "We don't have time to be sick. The creatures are still moving, and so must we."

Dieredon shook his head. "Tonight you rest." His brown eyes flicked up from the fire to hers. "Unless...can you heal yourself using Ashhur's power?"

Jessilynn huddled tighter underneath her blanket. Healing? There'd been no occasion to try at the Citadel, with both Lathaar and Jerico insisting they'd focus more on that subject once the students were older. She knew the rudimentary prayers, the concepts behind it, but to perform such an act, and on herself?

"I don't know," she admitted.

Across the fire, the elf shrugged his shoulders.

"That's fine," he said. "But surely there's no harm in trying?"

Jessilynn let out a soft chuckle. "I guess not." She sat up straight and let the blanket fall into her lap. The movement sent a spike of pain from the back of her head down her spine, and she hissed as she clenched her teeth. She felt so foolish, so pathetic. A simple block, that's all it'd taken. Jerico had endured an onslaught of thousands of undead, yet a humanoid bird hurling a chunk of wood had her down and suffering. If there was ever an epic retelling of her journey with Dieredon, she hoped this part would be mercifully left out.

The King of the Vile

Telling herself a dose of humility was always welcome, she put her right hand on her bruised forehead and closed her eyes. The damage was hidden, Dieredon had told her, and so she tried to focus on the pain deep inside her head. Calming herself with a deep breath, she began the prayer as best as she could remember Lathaar teaching it.

"Through your power, not mine, let this wound be healed," she whispered. Exactly as she expected, nothing happened. Jessilynn let out a sigh.

"It was worth the attempt," Dieredon said. "This will slow down our travels significantly."

"I'm sorry," Jessilynn said, crouching as if to make herself as small as possible. The elf stared at her, and she wondered what he could possibly be thinking behind that careful, guarded stare.

"Perhaps you should consider wearing a helmet like many of your brethren," Dieredon suggested.

"You don't wear a helmet."

"I also would have dodged the throw."

Jessilynn laughed despite the hurt it caused.

"Of course you would have," she said. "And if you find a helmet around here that fits me, I'll wear it, but I'm not holding my breath."

Silence settled between them. Jessilynn shifted closer to the fire, warming her toes. For several long minutes there was silence. Bored, Jessilynn tapped her fingers on Darius's sword, lying beside her in the grass. She'd kept it strapped to her back throughout all their travels, putting it aside only when they were to battle. Dieredon frowned at the blade often, but to her appreciation, he never questioned her need to bring it with her.

"We do too little," he said, his voice a whisper, the words a guilty confession. "Killing handfuls of the creatures? Saving scattered villages? We're like flies biting at the side of a horse."

"What else are we to do?" Jessilynn asked.

The elf turned her way, and the intensity in his eyes was frightening.

"You said two wolf-men led this horde."

"Moonslayer and Manfeaster," she said. "I killed Moonslayer during my escape."

"Then Manfeaster must die, and soon," Dieredon said. "We retreat from the vile beasts' numbers when instead we should be racing right into their heart. With their leader dead, all cooperation between the races dies with him."

"Then you shouldn't have sent Sonowin away, because how are we to make it through the hordes of monsters between Manfeaster and us?"

"My skills in stealth are more than sufficient," Dieredon said.

Jessilynn winced against a sudden pain in her skull. "Yes, *yours* are. I on the other hand..." She fell silent, and when the elf said nothing, she sighed. "I'm holding you back, aren't I, Dieredon? Just go. This is too important, so leave me and take down Manfeaster on your own."

Dieredon stared at her across the fire, and it seemed his hard visage softened.

"I'm not leaving you," he said. "And never suggest I do so again."

The elf wrapped his own blanket about himself and lay down beside the fire with his back to her. Jessilynn stared at him, feeling strangely guilty.

He may never leave me, she thought, *but it doesn't mean I'm not holding him back.*

As the headache assaulted her, she gritted her teeth and reflected on her first attempt to heal herself. She'd expected it to fail, thought such an injury clearly beyond her power. But why did she still consider herself so limited? By the mere touch of her bowstring, she could summon Ashhur's presence in the form of an arrow. She wasn't some little girl. She wasn't a helpless trainee.

Putting her fingers back to her forehead, she closed her eyes, once more falling into prayer. This time she didn't meekly request healing, nor doubt its granting. This time, she demanded it.

You are with me, she prayed silently. *Through your power, banish this pain. Your power, not mine, and so it shall always be.*

She heard the ringing of distant bells. When she opened her eyes, the light of the fire did not hurt her, and the aching waves of the headache were already receding. Jessilynn smiled as she lay down to sleep for the night. Her hand reached out, touching the long blade of Darius's sword.

"Not forgotten," she whispered, repeating the words the deceased paladin had spoken in her time of need. "Not abandoned, not unloved."

Her fingers brushed across the steel, fingertips leaving an afterimage of shimmering blue light, that glow calming her heart and allowing her to sleep.

4

As King Henley's honored guest, Qurrah could have slept in the enormous tent at the heart of the camp, but instead he preferred the far outskirts beside the Corinth River, where the people were few and the soft flow of the water and the chirp of the crickets could drown out the human noises. Neither him nor Tessanna had been comfortable with crowds all their lives, and since gaining their labels as the Betrayer and the Bride, solitude had grown all the more alluring. They had no tent, only a large padded bedroll and a shared blanket.

"They march for war soon," Tessanna said, sitting up and staring at the distant campfires of thousands of men.

"I know," Qurrah whispered.

"Harruq will fight them when they do."

Qurrah sighed. "I know."

Her hand wrapped around his, and he turned to look upon her. She was pale, thin, her long dark hair a shroud falling down around her hunched, diminutive form. Her face was turned away from him, staring at the army. Qurrah didn't need to see her expression to know she was worried. But it wasn't the army that troubled her, he knew that. It was the frightful future.

"My days of fighting Harruq are done," Qurrah said. "If we march into Mordan, we do so to overthrow the growing tyranny of the angels, not wage war against my brother and the boy king."

"A distinction few will make."

Qurrah sat up, the blanket falling down about his waist.

"Is that what's bothering you?" he asked. "Are you afraid this will somehow come between me and Harruq?"

"No," she said. "What bothers me is the impending disaster Mother wished me to prevent."

The King of the Vile

"What disaster?" he asked, wishing he could glimpse the visions Celestia haunted her with. "What happens that is so terrible?"

"I see it no longer," Tess said, and she sounded so sad, so defeated. "I only know my chance to stop it is passed. We must suffer through the bloodshed until its end, Qurrah. Suffer through, and bury the dead."

Qurrah took her hand and gently pulled her toward him. "Come to bed," he said. "And try not to worry."

His wife finally turned his way. Tears were in her black eyes despite the smile on her face.

"Without worry, I'm only sadness," she said.

"You're more than that and you know it."

She leaned in to kiss his lips.

"If you insist, I'll believe," she said, then lay down beside him to sleep.

Qurrah kept to himself the next morning as he ate his breakfast. He needed time to think, for Tessanna's words were a warning he needed to accept. If he marched at the side of King Bram Henley and his soldiers, and Harruq joined Mordan's troops to fight back, then to many people it'd seem like the second Gods' War never ended. But it *had* ended. In their own ways, both Harruq and Qurrah now followed Ashhur's teachings. They were no longer enemies, nor the brother gods' avatars to battle each other in their place, and Qurrah would do everything he could to keep it that way.

But the specter of the angels hovered over everything, tainting so much of what Ashhur had preached. Something had to be done, Qurrah felt it in his bones. Dezrel's freedom was teetering on a knife, and it put a bitter taste in his mouth realizing how similar that'd be to the world Karak desired to create.

"I'll be back in a bit," Qurrah told Tess as he put aside his plate half-finished.

"You won't get yourself in trouble, will you?" she asked. Her worry sounded genuine, a bit of the childlike persona Tessanna had steadily moved away from. Other than during the conflict with the angels, when her madness nearly tore her apart, it seemed the various pieces of his wife's mind were unevenly knitting back together again. She might never be anyone's definition of 'normal', but Qurrah prayed she never reverted into the beautiful, wounded, dangerous creature she'd been when he first met her.

"No trouble," Qurrah promised. "Just talk."

"Talk tends to cause the most trouble."

Qurrah chuckled.

"Not this time."

Tessanna nodded, then suddenly rose to her feet.

"I'll be bathing in the river," she said, tossing aside the blanket.

Qurrah lifted an eyebrow.

"Isn't it a little cold for that?" he asked.

His wife snickered.

"Then you'll need to hurry back to warm me up, won't you, Qurrah?"

She stripped off her dress, tossed it atop her blankets, and walked naked toward the riverbank. Qurrah stared, momentarily debated warming her up prior to her dip in the water, then shook his head. *Keep focused,* he told himself even as he stared at her pale skin and the curve of her sides. *She wants you to stay, and she's far too evil and clever to just ask.*

Adjusting his breeches, Qurrah marched into the center of King Bram's gathered soldiers. They numbered seven thousand at least, not counting the many traders, craftsmen, and camp followers that mingled all along the exterior. The tents spread out across either side of the road that lead up to the Bloodbrick, with soldiers blocking off the bridge entrance so they might first scan anyone coming in or out of the country. Qurrah endured guarded looks as he weaved through their numbers. To many, he was still the bedtime-story monster, the downfall of nearly half the continent. But they'd also seen him stand against the angels that had attacked their king's castle. While no doubt plenty still blamed him for that as well, at least there'd be a sliver of doubt, a sliver that hopefully grew into something meaningful. Qurrah had no desire to play the villain, not anymore.

In the heart of the camp was King Bram's giant pavilion, its sides fluttering in the soft morning breeze. A ring of soldiers

The King of the Vile

protected it at all times, but they recognized Qurrah and let him pass without question. Qurrah pulled open the flap the tiniest bit so he might speak to those within.

"Might I come in, your highness?" he asked.

"You're always welcome here," came Bram's voice, and with permission given, Qurrah slipped inside.

The pavilion was actually smaller than it appeared from the outside. Immediately beside Qurrah were two desks, each stacked with parchments, a few blank, most covered with numbers, dates, and costs. A dormant fire pit was in the very center, carefully crafted with rectangular stone bricks. A thin curtain hung from the top of the pavilion, sectioning off the bed chambers. King Bram sat on the only other piece of furniture, an old rocking chair that faced the fire. The king nodded at Qurrah's entrance, and he feigned a smile.

"Good to see you again, Qurrah," said Bram. "You should visit me more often. Intelligent minds are a rarity these days."

Qurrah bit down an initial desire to ask if the king was feeling all right. The past months had aged him terribly; strands of gray peeked through his long dark hair. A scar ran from above his right eye all the way down to his chin, a family mark rulers of Ker had supposedly adopted since the very first king. While it might have once added a bit of danger and dashing to the man's looks, now it was decidedly ugly, the skin above and below the eye starting to crack, the pale color almost yellow compared to Bram's normally tanned skin.

The pressures of ruling a kingdom, Qurrah thought. *Even the strong can wear down over time.*

Through subterfuge and deception, Bram had managed to spare his kingdom much of the destruction the second Gods' War had wrought upon Dezrel, followed by earning their full independence from Mordan. But such victories meant no relaxation for their king, only a fanatical need to protect his borders from the encroaching angels who, only weeks earlier, had come flying over in an attempt to execute Qurrah for his previously forgiven crimes.

"Where is Loreina?" Qurrah asked.

"The queen is out getting fresh air," Bram said. "It's the stench and the noise of all these people. Sometimes she needs to escape it to feel like herself again."

Qurrah nodded. Honestly, he was happy not to have her there. It'd make a potentially rocky conversation at least slightly easier, since Loreina was far hungrier for war than her husband.

"I come hoping for answers to a few nagging questions," Qurrah said, trying to keep his tone light. Despite a few misgivings, he held great respect for King Bram and wished to prevent adding to his burdens if he could.

"Go ahead," Bram said, steadily rocking in his chair. "It seems every hour I have men and women asking things of me, but I trust you to accept answers you might not wish to hear. If only the same could be said of my lesser subjects…"

Qurrah chuckled. "You praise me unjustly. I would not consider myself one who has responded well to being told 'no' in the past."

"I handle it no better," Bram said. "But you and I, we do things to solve such problems, not whine and complain like children. The great men of history remain defiant to those who would deny them. The forgotten whimper and lower their eyes, bitter in their helplessness. Now what is it you wish to ask me, Qurrah?"

The half-orc took in a deep breath. He almost let the matter drop. Almost.

"My wife fears you will soon invade Mordan," he said. "If that happens, I am reluctant to remain visible as your ally. I'm sure you understand why."

"Your brother," Bram said. He planted his feet and stopped the chair from rocking.

"Yes," Qurrah said. "I will not face him on the battlefield, and any talk of such already upsets me deeply. Our conflicts are in the past, and I would wish them to remain buried."

"But the past never stays buried," Bram said, rising to his feet. "It resurfaces without fail, for it is a rare man who is willing to let go of the past. What is it you are truly afraid of, my friend? A little gossip? No, you're stronger than that. *Fiercer* than that. Tell me honestly. We have no need for pretenses here."

Qurrah stared at the man in his fine robes lined with silver, the symbol of Ker, a clenched fist in the center of a shield, sewn onto his chest. Could he make such an admission? Did he even know the truth himself?

"I have harmed my brother enough," he said softly. "I will not march at your side if it will harm him further."

Bram crossed the small space to put his hands on Qurrah's shoulders. His stern gaze locked him in place, every word dripping with pained honesty.

"It isn't your brother we march against," Bram said. "It isn't even the boy king. It's the angels, Qurrah. It's always been the angels. They are beings of another world, another life, not this one. They have no place here, not if we are to be free. Whether he would admit it or not, Harruq is a prisoner like everyone else. If my men can overthrow such tyranny, if we can prevent the end of our sovereignty, then it is worth all the spilled blood in the world. This must be done. I've seen your power, and I know how important you are to this campaign. When we march into Mordan, I need your and your wife at my side. When you kill, it will not be in the name of Karak or Ashhur. It will be in the name of freedom."

"When," Qurrah said, hands curling into fists. "Not if, but *when* we march into Mordan? Then it is already decided?"

Bram sighed. "We are simply waiting for the opportune time, but yes, Qurrah, I consider this inevitable. The angels came for you, and one day, they will come for all of us. Best it be when we are prepared, and at a time of *our* choosing instead of theirs."

Qurrah thought of how broken Tessanna had been from killing the angels. How might she react in knowing the entire goal of their campaign was to repeat that on a grander scale? Qurrah had a feeling it wouldn't go over well.

"What if we work with my brother to scale down the angels' authority?" Qurrah suggested, thinking maybe, just maybe, a diplomatic solution was still possible. "I could go speak with him. It's not too late to—"

"It *is* too late, Qurrah," said Bram. "Death warrants are out for your head, did you not know that?"

Qurrah took a step back as if slapped.

"Issued by who?"

"Your brother," Bram said, looking pained as he said it. "I'm sorry. I didn't want to tell you."

Qurrah shook his head. It couldn't be right. Harruq wouldn't issue such an order. When Judarius came to kill him, Ahaesarus had insisted it'd been a mistake, something that would never happen again. But for Harruq to issue a warrant for his capture and execution, for him to be so determined to keep him out of Mordan...

He's lying, Qurrah decided as he stared at the tired king. *I don't know why exactly, but he is lying. I trust you more than that, Harruq.*

Despite all the sins he'd committed, despite the death of Harruq's own daughter, Harruq had forgiven him. No angel could convince him to issue a death warrant. His brother was too stubborn, too proud, to ever do such a thing.

But if Bram was telling the truth...

"Your highness," said a voice outside the tent. Qurrah turned aside so they both could look at the man pulling open the tent flap.

"Yes, Ian?" Bram asked.

The older knight hesitated a moment, as if trying to figure out how to work his jaw. "Your highness, we have guests I feel you should come greet personally."

Bram and Qurrah shared a look.

"Guests?" Bram asked.

"Guests," Ian said, nodding. "From the Stronghold."

At the mention of Karak's last lingering foothold in all of Dezrel, Qurrah felt his stomach twist into knots. Guests from the Stronghold? That meant one thing. After years of laying low in the fortified building, protected by Ker's strict borders, the dark paladins had finally emerged. The question was why.

Given Bram's goal of killing angels, Qurrah decided that might not be such a difficult question after all.

"Considering your...history...I would understand if you'd like to go elsewhere," Bram said, noting Qurrah's unease.

"If you'll allow me, I'm staying," Qurrah said. "Whatever they've come to say, I'd like to hear it for myself."

Bram nodded.

The King of the Vile

"Then let's go."

The two exited the pavilion and followed Sir Ian toward the southern portion of the camp. Spotting the dark paladins was easy enough, for it seemed no one wanted to remain close to their group of ten. Seeing that black armor, even at a distance, covered Qurrah's neck with a cold sweat and made his hands start to shake. He'd not seen one of their kind since Thulos's defeat in Avlimar. The very sight of the lion crest carved into their chestplates flashed a hundred memories through his mind, and none of them good. For a time, Qurrah had marched alongside Velixar and an army full of priests and paladins of Karak. Looking back on it now, he could hardly believe he'd endured such a trial willingly.

"Whatever they want, it will be nothing good," Qurrah told the king.

"We'll see about that," Bram muttered, then louder to the paladins, "Greetings, my friends, and welcome to my camp."

The ten lifted their right arms, fists pressed against their chests in respect. Qurrah felt a strong desire to slink away, to watch from the crowd, but he berated his cowardice as he stood at the side of the king with his head held high. His eyes flitted over the paladins, taking stock of them. They were young, all of them. Had they been trainees left behind at the Stronghold during the war, perhaps? Or maybe their age had allowed them to flee unnoticed in the chaos of that final battle at Mordeina?

The oldest of them stepped forward, and he bowed to Bram amid a rattle of platemail. His skin was the deep black of the majority of Ker's people, his hair a dark brown that fell loose around his face and neck. A smile creased his lips, revealing startlingly white teeth. Upon seeing Qurrah, his violet eyes seemed to sparkle.

"Greetings, king of Ker and protector of Angkar," the man said. "My name is Xarl, master of the remnants of the Lion. Word of the angels' attack on your subjects reached our ears, and we have come to offer our aid. Our swords and axes are yours, King Bram, if you would accept them."

So his guess had been right. When presented with an opportunity to kill angels of Ashhur, Karak's pathetic scum had come crawling out from their hole, eager for blood. Qurrah glanced at Bram, certain the king would send the paladins home, but instead the king opened his arms and smiled wide at his new guests.

"If you would bear arms to defend the freedom of our people, you are welcome," he said. "Sir Ian here will find you a tent to rest in, as well as ensure you are full on supplies."

"You are most gracious, your highness," Xarl said.

Ian cleared his throat. "This way," the older knight said, leading them off the path and into the mazelike array of tents. Qurrah watched them leave with steadily burning rage.

"Your highness," he began, but the king cut him off.

"Save it," Bram said. "Karak is no threat to my kingdom's sovereignty. Ashhur is. We currently share a common enemy, so I expect you to behave while they remain my ally, is that understood, half-orc?"

Qurrah accepted the berating silently, and as the king marched away without waiting for an answer, he ground his teeth together. Whatever hope he had for peace was done. Karak's paladins would make sure of that.

Fuming, he returned to his small camp beside the river. Tessanna spotted his approach, and she emerged naked from the water. Her lips were blue, her pale skin somehow even paler, as she wrapped a thick blanket about herself.

"What's wrong?" she asked, immediately sensing his discomfort.

Qurrah wasn't sure how to tell her. If she knew of the paladins' arrival, would she even stay with the army?

"There's...some new recruits," he said.

"So?" she asked. Water dripped from her long hair. Her lips quivered from the cold she pretended not to feel.

Qurrah tried to find a way to broach the subject gently, but it seemed that was a pointless hope, for Tess's eyes widened as she stared over his shoulder. Qurrah turned to see Xarl approaching. Clenching his hand into a fist, Qurrah imagined summoning a roaring inferno to consume the bastard. It'd certainly be satisfying, but he remained calm as the dark paladin stopped before them, a maddening smile on his face.

The King of the Vile

"Qurrah Tun," Xarl said. "I'd hoped to speak with you before you left."

"I have nothing to say to you," Qurrah said.

Xarl stepped closer, his smile widening. It looked so false it might as well have been painted on.

"But I do have words for you," he said. "I know of your past. I know you once walked alongside the prophet. You were one of the faithful, and though you are now lost, I believe in time you will return to Karak, just as I believe a new prophet will be born unto us. Consider us friends, Qurrah. We have no need to be enemies."

"I see plenty of need," Tessanna said softly. Her shoulders hunched, the blanket wrapping tighter about her body to hide her nakedness.

"Ah, Celestia's daughter, it is wonderful to meet you as well," Xarl laughed. "Neither should you bear us ill will. Celestia has always preached balance, has she not? Well, what greater travesty to balance is there than this world Ashhur's angels have created?"

"It's still better than what Karak would have created," she said.

Xarl's eyes seemed to sparkle at that.

"Perhaps," he said. "Though the tales we read of when Karak walked the land, and the Neldar he created during such time, contradict such claims. Please, shed this animosity. My brethren and I march to free Mordan from tyrannical rule. In this, we are allies, are we not?"

Qurrah tried to bite his tongue; arguing with a paladin of Karak was about as useful as trying to throw rain back into a storm cloud. But he couldn't help himself.

"You're right," he said. "I did walk alongside his prophet. I saw the paradise you think Karak would create. It was a land of death and emptiness, of ash and stone, where only the dead march in endless order. Whatever world you think your god desires to create, it's a lie, a deception, a mockery of the true destruction he would unleash to accomplish his goals. That you think for even a moment I might give my heart back to Karak shows how painfully delusional you and your kind have become. I thank Ashhur nightly that yours is a dying breed soon to be extinct from Dezrel, because we have no need of such dangerous lunacy."

At last Xarl's smile faltered, and Qurrah considered that a solid victory.

"A dying breed," the paladin said, tone low and cold. "There was a time when Ashhur's paladins and priests were the dying breed, and now his angels rule the remnants of mankind. A lot can change in a few years, Qurrah. Perhaps it'd be best for you to remember that before speaking blasphemy."

Tessanna stepped between him and Xarl, and she smiled so sweetly at the paladin.

"Leave," she said, "or I will show you how great a blasphemy I can perform on your corpse."

Xarl bowed low, flashed them one last mocking smile, and trudged back to the camp. Tessanna stood frozen as she watched him leave. Qurrah shifted his weight from foot to foot, feeling strangely guilty.

"Tess," he said, "if you want to return home, I..."

His wife spun around, and he was shocked by the anger burning in her wide eyes.

"We're staying," she said. "Whatever Karak's paladins are planning, I want to know what it is, and I want to stop it." She looked over her shoulder, her stare boring holes into the distant man's armor. "I won't let them survive. They don't get to come back, Qurrah. They don't get to burn the world then pretend to be its saviors."

5

Life was hardly pleasant, given the itchy healing of his burns and the painful way he'd been strapped down, head fixed, fingers locked to prevent spellcasting, but the boredom drove Tarlak mad the most. Hour after hour he stared at the few nature paintings, unable to move, forced to shit and piss into a pan. They wouldn't give him anything to read, and even if they did, he had no way of holding a book or turning its pages. With such terrible conditions, this left Tarlak with one single avenue of entertainment: annoying the Abyss out of his assigned caretaker, Cecil Towerborn.

"Surely you've thought about why your parents dumped you at the tower's doorstep," he said as the man steadily scrubbed Tarlak's leg with a damp cloth. "Too poor to raise you, perhaps? Doubtful, I say. Even the poorest of the poor tend to find ways to feed and clothe their young. Hoping for a better life? Maybe, if your parents didn't realize what would happen to you if you failed to show any magical affinity. Seems a bit of a stretch. Ooh, I've got it. You were an extremely *ugly* baby, and..."

"Shut up!" Cecil shouted, flinging the cloth onto the bed in frustration. "Just shut up already! Gods curse me, Dezrel has endured plagues that were less annoying than you."

Tarlak lifted his head the highest his restraints would allow, and he winked at the man.

"You're not done yet," he said. "You still need to clean my ass."

Cecil's glare made Tarlak wonder if he'd finally gone too far. If there were any sharp objects in the vicinity, they'd already be lodged in his throat. Cecil clutched the side of the bed, fingers digging into the mattress. His teeth clenched. His eyes widened.

"One more word," Cecil said. "Say one more word, and I will kill you and claim you were trying to escape."

"They'd know you were lying," Tarlak said.

"I don't care. It'd be worth it to see you die. Now have I made myself clear, you pathetic disgrace to our order?"

Tarlak clucked his tongue.

"Perfectly. Forgive me, I meant no offense. It's lonely locked in here, that's all. I promise to behave while you go about doing your duties."

"Thank you," Cecil said doubtfully. The apprentice picked up the cloth, dipped it into a bucket at his feet, and prepared to resume.

"So," Tarlak said. "Would you like to start with the left cheek, or the right?"

As Cecil flung the rag and summoned fire about his hands, Tarlak decided this was it, his moment to die, but it seemed the world had other ideas. The door to his room opened, and in stepped Roand the Flame. Cecil quickly banished the fire and spun around with a guilty look on his face.

"Cecil?" Roand asked, raising a bushy eyebrow. "Is he ready?"

"I...no, not yet," Cecil stammered.

Roand's eyes bore into the apprentice, flicking occasionally over to Tarlak's pinned body.

"Then finish up," he said. "His wounds have healed enough for his trial to finally begin. Send him to the Grand Council once he's ready."

"Yes, master," Cecil said, head bowed.

The wizard left, and Cecil let out a long sigh as the door closed.

"Trial?" Tarlak asked.

"Yes, your trial," Cecil said, picking up the rag yet again. "Followed by your well-deserved execution. By the time they're through with you, you'll wish Roand had never interrupted me."

Pleasant, thought Tarlak.

Cecil continued his daily routine, the idea of Tarlak's impending death putting a bounce in his step. Tarlak examined his burns as Cecil slowly scrubbed, surprised by how quickly they'd healed. Whatever cream they'd been putting on him had worked wonders, the burned flesh flaking off to reveal fresh pink skin underneath. Tarlak would have greatly preferred one of Ashhur's priests doing the healing instead, but at least the wizards' methods were quick and efficient. Now if only they could do something about his missing hair...

"Finished," Cecil said several minutes later. "And hopefully for the last time. Time to get you dressed."

Tarlak let out a grunt, surprised. They'd kept him covered with only a loin cloth over the past week. Tied down as he was, putting on any sort of clothing was impossible. Might he finally be released? If so, Tarlak planned on returning Cecil's attempt to burn him with a bit of fire of his own.

To Tarlak's surprise, Cecil left the room without another word. Tarlak craned his neck and stared at the closed door.

"Uh, hello?" he said.

The door opened a moment later, Cecil hurrying back inside with a pair of folded red robes in his arms. The two objects atop the robes, however, were what immediately captured Tarlak's attention. One was a loaded hand-crossbow. The other was a small black sphere covered with runes that shone a rainbow of colors. Simply being in its presence made Tarlak feel weak and strange. His connection to the weave of magical energy wavered.

A voidsphere, thought Tarlak. *Looks like escape won't be so easy after all. Couldn't these bastards slip up at least once?*

"I'm sure I don't need to tell you what this is," Cecil said as he set the voidsphere down beside the bed. "No tricks, so just behave, and try to go to your death with a shred of dignity."

"With my face as bald as it is?" said Tarlak. "I don't think that's possible."

Cecil tossed the robes onto Tarlak's bed and grabbed the crossbow in his left hand. Staying just out of reach, he steadily undid the clasps holding Tarlak's arms and legs down. Once Tarlak was completely free, Cecil retrieved the voidsphere, stepped back, and aimed the crossbow at him.

"Dress yourself," he said. "Make any attempt to escape and I put an arrow in your chest."

Tarlak grunted, and he slowly sat up on the bed. The action immediately flooded his entire body with pain. Muscles that hadn't moved weeks suddenly pulled and flexed, and it seemed every tiny shift made some part of his body ache. He let out a gasp at the sudden onslaught of pain.

Escape? he thought. *I can barely move, and he thinks I'll try to escape?*

Tarlak remained seated as he grabbed the robes and started to dress himself. They were plain enough, the fabric warm and comfortable. Lifting his arms through the sleeves unleashed a whole new wave of pain, but he bore it in silence. The last thing he wanted to do was give Cecil the satisfaction. The brat would get enough satisfaction watching Tarlak's execution.

Once the robes were over his body, he slid off the bed. Despite the pain, it felt incredibly good to be on his feet, and he slowly rolled his shoulders and stretched.

"Almost better than sex," Tarlak said, his body feeling like it was awakening from a lengthy slumber. "Not that you'd know, Cecil, so just trust me on this one."

"Cute," Cecil said. "So cute. Your death can't come soon enough."

"Careful now," Tarlak said as he stepped toward the door. "With talk like that, you're setting yourself up for disappointment."

Cecil tucked the voidsphere under his arm so he could open the door with his free hand while still pointing the crossbow at Tarlak.

"Walk," said the apprentice.

Tarlak exited the door, curious where he was. He'd never been inside either of the two towers, learning of them only through rumors and the stories his master, Madral, had told him during his training. By his guess they were in the apprentice tower, based mostly on the complete lack of ornate decorations on the bare red brick walls. A thin hallway lined with doors led to the stairs. No writing above, no markings of any kind. The floor was brick as well, and cold to his bare feet.

Cecil gestured with the crossbow. "Come along."

The King of the Vile

Tarlak shambled forward, panic rising in his chest. Stairs? He was going to have to climb *stairs?* Wincing at the anticipated pain, he flexed his legs with each step, hoping to limber up. It wouldn't be so bad, he told himself. Just a few stairs, and it wasn't like his legs were that sore.

It was that bad. They climbed up and up, the room they'd kept him in apparently as far away from their destination as possible. Tarlak leaned against the wall, bracing his weight after every step. His back was screaming, his legs so sore they burned with the tiniest movement.

They don't need to kill me, thought Tarlak. *Just make me climb up and down these stairs until I fling myself out a window.*

Not that the windows were big enough, Tarlak realized sadly. Just tiny little triangular slits that he could maybe fit his head through. It was almost like they anticipated his suicidal desire, and prevented it. Muttering to himself, Tarlak forced himself on. He'd endured worse, he told himself. Hadn't he?

"One more floor," Cecil said, and Tarlak took some satisfaction in noting how his jailor also sounded out of breath from the climb. They'd passed many exits to other floors while climbing, and Tarlak had tried to catch glimpses of what they held. Most everywhere was the same, sparse and without decoration or creature comforts. Bare floors. Plain wood furniture. They'd passed a library at one point, but cruelest was early on, when they'd passed a kitchen. The smell of warm food had awakened his dormant stomach. The only thing he'd had to eat and drink were bowls of soup, hand fed to him by the always-pleasant Cecil. This had led to many quick meals and unfinished bowls, for even hunger could not keep Tarlak's tongue under control.

Finally they exited the stairs, and Tarlak stood before a wide wooden door.

"Push it," Cecil said. "If you can."

Tarlak pressed his sore body against the door, steadily creaking it open. Once halfway, the wind caught it, yanking it further, and Tarlak stumbled out into the open air. Beneath him was a long, slender bridge spanning the gap between the two towers, the bricks a mixture of the red from the apprentice tower and the black of the masters'. To Tarlak's dismay, there wasn't a railing.

"Watch your step," Cecil said as he followed Tarlak onto the bridge. Tarlak peered over the edge to see the Rigon River flowing beneath him. The two towers were positioned on opposite sides of the river. Watch his step? He could barely move without wobbling, and while the bridge was wide, he hardly trusted his balance, and then there was the issue of the softly blowing wind. Of course, he might be able to take a certain snot-nosed apprentice tumbling over the side with him...

Cecil must have had the same thought, for he remained several feet behind Tarlak with his crossbow at the ready.

"Don't get clever," he said. "I won't be crossing until you're at the other side."

Tarlak let out a sigh. No fun at all. Turning back to the bridge, he decided that pride and dignity were already beneath him, so there was nothing left to lose. Dropping to all fours, he began crawling across the very center of the bridge. The brick hurt his knees, but he had a feeling the water below would hurt far worse if he fell. When he was halfway across, Tarlak spun on his rear and waved at Cecil.

"You coming?" he asked as if it were a cheery autumn day and they were headed for a picnic.

Tarlak chuckled and continued crawling toward the other side. Once there, he held onto the handle of the thick wooden door, used it to stand, and then flung it open. An elderly man in black robes waited for him in a small entryway, his eyes sparkling green, his beard white, the top of his head bald.

"You're finally here," the mage said. "About time. My name is Adjara. Come with me, Tarlak Eschaton. Your trial awaits."

Instead of traveling down, they immediately went up. These stairs, Tarlak noticed, were comfortably carpeted a dull crimson, and the walls were covered with paintings of former members of the Council. Mostly, they were a bunch of frowning old men.

No wonder I was never a part of this place, Tarlak thought as he slowly followed the elderly Adjara. *I swear these mages have never heard of a concept known to us regular folk as 'smiling'.*

The King of the Vile

Fifteen steps up they reached another door. Adjara opened it without ceremony, leading Tarlak into the expansive hall of the Grand Council. The domed roof stretched at least thirty feet above smooth, circular walls. The carpet alternated between various shades of red, starting in the center of the room and rippling outward as if a stone had been cast into a pond. Nine oak chairs with padded red cushions formed a circle, each one facing the center of the room. All nine were occupied, and Tarlak swallowed down his growing nervousness. Only one chair was different from the others, the one directly across from the entrance, and in that chair sat Roand the Flame.

"At last you arrive," Roand said, his deep voice echoing through the room. "Though the fault is mine in thinking Cecil could perform his tasks in a suitable amount of time."

Despite the seriousness of the situation, Tarlak chuckled, glad to know that he wasn't the only one who couldn't stand the idiot. As he stepped into the center of the room, he felt the effects of the voidsphere leaving him. It was a welcome feeling, though it wouldn't help him much. He was surrounded by nine mages, each likely an even match with himself. The slightest attempt at a spell would result in him being burned, exploded, bled from the ears, or turned into a random animal. Possibly all at once, depending on how fast each of the mages reacted.

"Greetings, men and women of the Council," Tarlak said as he slowly turned in a circle. None of the mages looked to be below middle age, and even the three women sported a few gray hairs in their carefully trimmed hair. Their faces were passive, guarded, perhaps even bored. Tarlak couldn't guess if that was good or bad.

"Or should I say Grand Council?" he added before anyone corrected him. The full Council consisted of fifty members, whereas the Grand Council consisted of the nine most powerful. From what he'd learned from Madral, the Council met at regular intervals to decide mundane matters, with the Grand Council convening only for important decisions.

Decisions like whether or not to execute a troublesome wizard who had broken their rules.

"For now, you should say nothing," Roand said. The fiery illusions cast upon his hair caused the colored flame to ripple through the strands. "You have many transgressions we must document, both against our towers as well as against Dezrel at large."

"If you'd like I can get that started for you," Tarlak said. "Let's see, I killed my master Madral when I was eighteen, turned down your invitations at least six times, operated an enterprise with significant magical involvement, my Eschaton Mercenaries to be exact, despite no written permission from your council, defeated three different assassins you sent after me, turning one into a mudskipper, one into a rabbit, and one into a frog, and last but not least, I marched alongside King Antonil Copernus during his attempt to retake the east from the orcs. That final one I don't quite understand the crime in, but since it resulted in the deaths of thousands of innocent men, I assume it's an important one."

Stunned silence greeted Tarlak when he finished. Unable to help himself, the swept an arm wide as he bowed low.

"Did I miss anything?" he asked.

"Yes," said a dour looking woman with a pointed nose and long, dangling silver earrings. "You neglected to mention your complete lack of respect toward the Grand Council during your own trial."

Tarlak smiled at her.

"That one seemed unnecessary, since you were all here to witness it."

"Enough," Roand said. A thin gold rod covered with red gems lay across his lap, and he waved it once toward Tarlak. Immediately, the air in Tarlak's lungs seemed to grow sticky and hot, and when he tried to speak, it was like trying to vomit up stone. Pulse pounding in his neck, he breathed in and out, trying to relax. The strange discomfort only affected him when trying to talk, so he kept quiet.

Roand set the rod back down. "In this room, I am master. And you will show respect, Tarlak, whether you feel it deserved or not. Your entire life you've carried a cavalier attitude toward authority, but this is one moment where you need to acknowledge the gravity of your situation."

The King of the Vile

"If he doesn't understand that now, he never will," said the dour woman. "Meaning this trial is over before it has already begun. He isn't worthy of candidacy. Cut off his hands and cast him from the bridge so we might move on to more important matters."

A portly man with a beard growing solely from his neck let out a half-hearted cheer in agreement.

"Let us not be so hasty," said a thin man with a face more resembling a hawk than a human. "Respect may be learned, whereas innate magical talents cannot."

Tarlak looked about, and he couldn't believe what he saw. They were serious. He'd walked into this trial thinking it'd be a sham, but apparently they truly did wish to debate his merits as a potential member of the Council. Tarlak wasn't sure if that meant they were less insane, or more. They'd brutally murdered his friend, Antonil, yet still thought he might be a productive member of their organization?

Tarlak opened his mouth to respond, felt his lungs harden and throat constrict. Roand saw and tapped his wand.

"You may speak," the Lord of the Council said. "And I pray you use a more appropriate tone."

His lungs loosened, and Tarlak slowly breathed out with relief. So there still might be a chance to save his life? Bizarre, but expecting sanity from this group was probably a mistake.

"I have performed many petty insults against you," he said, carefully weighing every word. "But given how long you've ignored me, I know most are not worthy of your attention. So I ask, please tell me what crime I committed against you worthy of death so I might defend myself."

"There is no single crime," the dour woman. "Only a repeated history of insult that must finally be stopped."

Tarlak turned to face her.

"If I might have the pleasure of your name, milady?" he asked.

The woman drummed her fingers across the arm of her chair, the slight movement traveling up her ramrod spine to cause her long earrings to sway.

"Anora," she said as if she were giving her name to a rodent.

"Well, Anora, I dare say every man alive may be hung until death for the total sins of their lifetime, but that's not quite how this works, is it? A punishment fitting the crime, for each crime, is that not correct? So if you want to chop off my hands and dump me into the river, I'd love to hear a good reason that may stand on its own."

"You refused us," said the hawk-faced man. "Practicing arcane magic without our approval is an executable offense in the eyes of the Council."

There it was. Tarlak had repeatedly spurned them, and it looked like they were still sore from his refusals. Well, if that's what they were upset about...

"Is that what bothers you?" Tarlak asked, and he spun about to face all nine of the Grand Council. "That I flung a few fireballs without your permission? Or that I did it for coin you received no cut of?"

"A bit of both, truthfully," said Roand, and he sounded strangely amused.

Tarlak hated what he was about to say, but he saw no other way out. Dropping handless into the freezing Rigon River was not how he wished to die.

"By killing Madral, I earned myself a spot on your Council," he said. "That's the rule, right? Fifty spots, with each spot taken only by defeating a holder in a duel. Then let me claim the position I earned years ago. Would any of you doubt my skill? My knowledge? I've dueled a god, some demons, even a daughter of balance. My abilities are beyond questioning, so let me end this farce and become one of your members like I should have always been."

The nine fell silent. Tarlak tried to read their faces. Were they surprised by his audacity? Insulted by it? Perhaps, but Roand's comment at the start had clued Tarlak into realizing the meeting wasn't truly about his execution. Joining the Council was. Execution was an unfortunate side effect if he happened to be denied.

"You might be powerful," Anora said, "but it is coupled with recklessness and crass humor. I see no reason to admit you, for what value do you bring to our community?"

The hawk-faced man cleared his throat.

"Given his involvement in the second Gods' War, his many travels with the angels, and his role in Mordan's reconstruction, his extensive experience alone might be invaluable," he said.

Tarlak didn't know his name but decided he liked him already.

"What new knowledge could we possibly learn about the angels?" asked neck-beard. "Just dump the bastard in the river so we can move on to the business with Avlimar's collapse."

Avlimar's collapse?

Tarlak kept his face passive, though it took great effort to do so. The floating city of the angels had fallen? But how? And why? What in blazes was going on in Mordeina during his absence?

Roand rose to his feet, scepter in hand.

"If you were to join us, you must obey all our laws," he said, taking a step toward him. "You will accept a position in the tower, along with all its responsibilities, and perform them without fail or refusal. You will forfeit all remnants of the life you once led, and grant the Grand Council total control over you future upon this mortal plane. Before we vote on the matter, do you accept such conditions, and vow to keep them all to the best of your abilities?"

In many ways it was a death sentence no different than the one that awaited him should they reject his offer. But at least this way he'd get to keep his hands. He swallowed down a stream of bile.

"I accept."

The Lord of the Council looked to the others and nodded.

"We are all aware of Tarlak Eschaton's accomplishments," he said, "as are we his faults and crimes committed against us. By accepting him as a member of the Council, all insults shall be forgotten, all his crimes forgiven. He will be one of us, given a new standard to follow, and a new life to lead. If you believe he is a worthy addition, and his defeating of Madral an appropriate approximation of a duel, then lift your hand now."

The nine voted, and Tarlak was surprised to see Roand raise his right hand in favor. Five others did as well, with only Anora, neck-beard, and a dark-skinned man with an elaborate mustache and beard choosing to deny him.

Unable to help himself, Tarlak lifted his own right hand, and he grinned.

"Well," he said. "That was unexpected."

Roand tapped his scepter with his hand.

"I do not yet trust you, Tarlak Eschaton, so know that certain protective measures will be enacted until we are more certain of your loyalties. I'm sure you understand."

"Perfectly," he said.

"Fine and good," said neck-beard. "Now can we move on? With Kevin Maryll's coup a colossal failure, we must forge a new plan, one that can handle the half-orc's interference."

"And his wife's," added Anora.

Tarlak's eyes widened. *Dear Ashhur, what is going on over there?*

"In time," Roand said. "For now, we have a new member who must be accommodated. Tarlak, have Cecil show you to Madral's old room, as well as the supply closet so you might obtain a proper set of robes. Once this meeting is over, I'll send for another master to begin integrating you into the tower's routine."

"As you wish," Tarlak said, maddened that he couldn't stay to listen but knowing he was already pushing his luck. He spun about, opened the door, and grinned at Cecil Towerborn, who waited patiently on the other side.

"Judgment reached," Tarlak said. "I'm now a member. Apparently you're to show me to Madral's old room. My guess is that it's about to become mine."

Cecil's eyes widened, and his nostril's flared as if he were a bull about to charge.

"Follow me," the apprentice said through clenched teeth.

Tarlak chuckled as they descended the stairs.

"Who'd have thought they'd make me a permanent member?" Tarlak said while Cecil seethed. "Hey, come to think of it, since you're still an apprentice, that gives me authority over you, right? How incredibly amusing, don't you think?"

Cecil paused mid-step, and when he glanced over his shoulder, he looked ready to commit murder. The sight put a smile on Tarlak's face. Maybe life in the towers wouldn't be entirely awful after all...

6

Harruq sat at the foot of the bed, scratching his chin.

"Hey Aurelia, if I abdicate my position, does that put you in charge?"

Aurelia hoisted Aubrienna up onto a footstool before the large oval mirror in their bedroom, letting their little girl stare at herself while her mother brushed her hair.

"An elven woman ruling from a human throne?" Aurelia said. "I think we have enough riots as it is. Let's try not to add more."

"Worth a shot," he sighed.

"Not really."

Harruq chuckled as he watched his wife loop yellow ribbons through Aubby's hair, tying them into neat bows to hold together the various curls. Harruq looked at his own beefy hands and frowned. He could hack a god to death with his swords, but those little bows would always be beyond him. It was strange how skilled he could be in one thing, and totally inept in another. Just like he could lead men to victory in battle but fail so spectacularly when he had to lead those same men with his ass stuck to a cushion in the middle of an ornate throne room.

"If I can't swing my sword, I'm useless," he mumbled. "Some great hero I am."

He caught Aurelia staring at him in the mirror, and his neck flushed.

"Sorry," he said. "Feeling a little morbid today."

"Morbid?" Aubrienna asked. Her auburn curls bounced when she turned her head. She wore a green dress with golden trim, and it made her look much older than her five years.

"It means daddy is feeling stressed and sad," Aurelia said, kissing the top of her head. "Go give him a hug and kiss. It'll make him feel better."

Aubrienna hopped down from the stool, ran the five steps to the bed, and flung herself at Harruq as if her life depended upon it. Harruq smiled as he scooped her up, grunting as if she weighed a thousand times more than her actual weight.

"Such a big girl," he said as he pulled her close.

"You're the best daddy," Aubrienna told him. "The very best, so don't be sad."

She kissed his cheek, and sure enough, it did help ease his grumpiness. Kissing her back, he put her down and stood.

"With such a blessing, how can I not conquer all who oppose me?" he asked. Aurelia winked at him as she adjusted her matching green and gold dress.

"I'm taking her and Gregory to the market," she said. "I think it'll do some good for the people to see him out and about." She turned while still in the process of putting in a long, dangling gold earring. "It might do some good for them to see *you* enjoying yourself as well. There's far too much fear in the populace, even if they don't know what they're afraid of."

"They know exactly what they're afraid of," Harruq said as he opened the door to his room. "And it's flying above them with big white wings."

Harruq shut the door, breathed in, breathed out. *You can do this,* he thought. *You defeated waves of demons. You killed a god. This? This is nothing.*

He traversed the halls to the large throne room. Only a few soldiers were inside. He heard the commotion of the people waiting to see him beyond the doors. The sound took his breath away, made his head feel light. Harruq recognized the signs of panic, but what could he do? This wasn't a battle where he could clang his swords together and drive his doubt away.

Sir Wess, captain of the guard and the man responsible for helping Harruq keep the peace, waited patiently beside the throne, his armor shining, his tabard clean and white. His role had been created upon Antonil's departure, with no intention of it being

The King of the Vile

permanent, but with Antonil's death, Sir Wess had stepped up admirably.

"You look well today," Sir Wess said. He was an older man, his mustache sprinkled with gray and his eyes surrounded by wrinkles. A surly man by any definition, but he'd steadily warmed to Harruq over time.

Harruq forced a grin and plopped down on the throne.

"That's a lie and we both know it," he said. "How many are waiting for me out there?"

The knight's face twitched.

"Over one hundred," the knight said. "Most have come to plead for mercy for those currently awaiting execution in our dungeons."

Harruq winced.

"Thieves caught trying to steal from Avlimar's ruins?" he guessed.

"Or from Devlimar," Sir Wess added. "The angels complain to me daily about the difficulty of building their earthbound city. I've grown quite good at ignoring them, but given the new law demanding punishment for such crimes, keeping a deaf ear has become rather difficult."

Harruq slumped in the throne, rubbing his eyes. Damn it, must it start already? Why could no one leave the angels be as they used the remnants of their former home to build a new one in the fields outside Mordeina?

"If that's it, send them on their way," Harruq said. "I won't listen to their pleadings. They all knew the law. It's their own damn fault for ignoring it."

The knight glanced to the floor, and he cleared his throat before speaking.

"Steward, I am not certain that is wise," he said.

"It is very wise," said a familiar voice from up above. Harruq turned to see Azariah flying in from one of the enormous windows by the ceiling. His robe fluttered as he landed, wings shaking a brief moment before folding in around his shoulders.

"The people are ready to riot," Sir Wess argued. "If we carry out these executions, I can make no guarantee to Devlimar's safety."

"The people will learn to accept our place in this world," Azariah said. "Stealing from us and pretending it is no crime only shows we are viewed as less than human in their eyes. This cannot be allowed. Until the greater population understands this, then we all must suffer growing pains."

Harruq rolled his eyes. Deep in the pit of his stomach he knew Azariah was wrong, but damned if he knew any way to articulate it, especially compared to the angel's convincing argument.

"Increase the amount of guards surrounding Devlimar," Harruq told Sir Wess. "I don't want a riot, so make sure we don't have one. We've all more important things to deal with."

"Speaking of..." Azariah pulled out a scroll from within his robe and held it out to Harruq. "New laws and regulations. Our kind have voted upon them and now seek your approval."

Harruq felt his jaw drop slightly, and he shook his head to banish his surprise.

"I meant the beast-men invasion of the North," he said. "Do you really think *now* is a good time to discuss new laws?"

The angel looked taken aback.

"We are attempting reform that will bring about the salvation of mankind," Azariah said. "It is always the proper time."

Harruq groaned.

"Fine. Sure. But I can't handle this right now, Azariah. Soldiers are gathering from all corners of Mordan, and that's going to take time, time the people in the North may not have. Why haven't the angels flown to their aid?"

Azariah stood up straight, and somehow he managed to look both indignant and condescending at the same time.

"We are convening another meeting tonight to discuss such measures," he said. "To engage this invading force will risk many lives, and involve abandoning all posts throughout Mordan. We will not do such a thing lightly, nor recklessly. Undue haste will cost more lives than it saves."

"Undue haste?" Harruq asked. "Villages are being overwhelmed, and you're worried about undue haste?"

"I do not expect you to always understand," Azariah said. "But I assure you, we have not abandoned the people." He took his rolled scroll and slid it back into a hidden pocket of his robe. "If you are not ready to read our new proposals, I will delay them for now and focus on the building of Devlimar. Good day to you Harruq."

He bowed, spread his wings, and flew back out the high window.

"He cares more about rebuilding his home than protecting people in danger," Sir Wess said after the angel's departure, and Harruq had a hard time disagreeing.

"I'm not going to pretend to understand them," he said. "We just have to remember all the good they've done for us, and trust them."

The knight let out a snort.

"Yes," he said. "The good they've done. Forgive me, Steward, but my trust was worn thin when they killed hundreds in the name of justice."

Harruq winced. That same night, they'd sent angels into the nation of Ker in hopes of killing Qurrah. Sir Wess was right. Trust in the angels was hard to come by, not just in Mordan, but all of Dezrel. Still, this didn't feel right. Drumming his fingers on the arm of the chair, he pondered, then realized Sir Wess was staring at him, waiting.

"Don't you have things to do?" he asked. "People outside my door to dismiss, perhaps?"

The knight cleared his throat again.

"I have one other matter I wished to address first," he said. "Something I preferred not to mention while in the presence of one of Ashhur's angels."

Fantastic, thought Harruq.

"Go ahead," he said, slumping even further into his chair. "What is it now?"

The knight saluted.

"Earlier this morning a man came to the castle claiming to have found the individual responsible for Avlimar's collapse."

Harruq lifted an eyebrow.

"Someone found Deathmask?" he said.

"Well, he says he did," Sir Wess continued. "He desired a reward for this knowledge, of course. Supposedly he saw

Deathmask hiding in the ruins of Avlimar, beyond the protective circle of our guards."

The ruins of Avlimar? An interesting place to choose to hide.

"The ruins? What was our witness doing there, trying to steal some souvenirs for himself?"

Sir Wess shrugged.

"What did you do with him?" muttered Harruq

"I have him in solitary confinement in one of our cells, just in case we discover him to be lying."

Harruq chuckled. "Gods, you're a cold bastard. Pay the man his a reward and then let him go under strict orders he tell no one else."

"Very good. And who shall seek out Deathmask?"

Harruq tapped the swords at his sides, thinking of his earlier frustration. Perhaps it was time to go back to doing what he did best...

"I'll handle this personally," he said.

Sir Wess hardly looked happy about it, but he bowed low anyway.

"As you wish."

As the knight marched out of the room to disperse the many gathered people, Harruq glanced at the window high above him. Everything about the angels felt off, and despite damning evidence, he still couldn't believe Deathmask brought the floating city crashing to the ground. Something else was afoot, and it was high time he did something about it.

Like hearing the truth from Deathmask's own lips.

※

An evenly spaced barricade of soldiers surrounded Avlimar's ruins, some holding torches, others with small fires burning near their feet. The night was young, and the soldiers were on edge. Harruq couldn't blame them. Two dozen men and women had either slipped past or bribed their way into the ruins, and now two dozen men and women were set to die by beheading. Harruq had stalled the executions, claiming he wanted to wait until a calmer time, but truthfully he didn't have the stomach for it. Part of him hoped he might pardon them a week or two later, sparing everyone the distasteful deed.

The King of the Vile

"Come to investigate our patrols, Godslayer?" one of the guards asked as Harruq neared. He wore his dark leather armor, and on from his hips swung the two sister blades, Salvation and Condemnation. Harruq shook his head.

"I have important matters to address," he said. "Let me pass, and say nothing of my being here."

The soldier, a young man who looked like he was maybe seventeen at most, bobbed his head.

"Of course," he said. "Lips sealed, I swear."

Harruq knew the second that man went home, or to a tavern, he'd be spreading the story everywhere. Sighing, he trudged past him, longing for the days when he might travel through cities unnoticed. At worst, he might have gotten a few frowns due to his orcish heritage, but that was it. Distaste he could endure, even anger. Celebrity, on the other hand? The half-orc tapped the hilts of his swords. Being famous could go straight into the Abyss.

The night was dark, but Harruq's eyes saw well enough in the dim light due to both his orcish and elvish blood. The moon was hidden, but a few stars shone through thin gaps in the clouds, and their light sparkled off the remnants of the shattered city. Walking through the wreckage was a bizarre experience. While the angels had taken much to the steadily growing city of Devlimar not far to the west, and looters had taken plenty more, there still remained massive crumbled structures of silver and gold. He kicked broken pearls seemingly every other step. Marble and gold spires now lay in chunks.

Sometimes, when sleep seemed so far away, Harruq wondered if Ashhur had sent the city crashing to the ground to show the angels what they themselves were in danger of becoming: things of beauty and splendor, broken by the land of Dezrel.

Let's see, thought Harruq, remembering his discussion with the lad who'd supposedly spotted Deathmask. The boy's gaunt features had matched the hunger in his eyes, though Harruq knew it wasn't food he craved, but something far shinier. *Along the far western side, just after a collapsed spire, there should be a library...*

The city's collapse had certainly been strange. Some places were thoroughly leveled, while others had merely a few broken walls. What had once been paved walkways were now broken marble, but he could still make out their original positions, give or take a few destroyed buildings along the way.

The boy had said the spire blocked the path, and while Harruq hadn't understood at first, he did when he came upon the enormous and smashed cylindrical construction of silver and gold. It was at least fifteen feet high on its side, stretching across the path and combining with the ruined buildings on either side to create an impassable barricade. Harruq grunted, and decided to climb. Up and over he went, sliding down the other side and landing before a heap of ruined paintings.

Glancing around, he spotted what he guessed was the library. It was a square structure with a collapsed roof. The windows were shattered, and piled everywhere were weather-beaten books. Harruq picked one up and inspected it. The leather cover seemed all right, but the pages were ruined. Whatever knowledge the book had contained was no more.

"Just sad," Harruq said, dropping the book next to several others and peering at one of the library windows. "Whoever did this certainly deserves what's coming to them."

"And what *is* coming to them, might I ask?"

Harruq's heart thumped in his chest, and he grinned at the welcome feeling. Exhilaration mixed with fear, the drug of battle. How he'd missed it.

"Haven't decided yet," Harruq said. "Was thinking maybe drowning or decapitation, but fire might be more fun."

He slowly turned about to greet Deathmask. The man stood atop the collapsed spire, arms crossed over his chest. A gray mask covered the bulk of his face, his long dark hair covering that which the mask didn't. His mismatched eyes, one red, one black, seemed to glow in the dim starlight. Though he'd used to wear red robes, now he dressed in the new colors of his reformed Ash Guild: a dark gray shirt and cloak, with both the pants and the shirt's sleeves colored a deep black.

"What about all three?" Deathmask asked. "Burn him, cut off his head, and then drown it in a bucket of water. Surely an appropriate fate for the bastard who would dare send this magnificent city crumbling to the ground."

The King of the Vile

Harruq's hands drifted to the hilts of his swords. So far Deathmask hadn't made any threatening move, but the man was skilled. If he wanted Harruq dead, there'd be very little time to react.

"So you admit it?" he asked.

Deathmask tsk'd at him.

"There's the catch," he said. "I didn't say it was *my* head you should do those things to. I'm not the one responsible for this. Part of me wishes I was, so at least I'd deserve the abyss you and your angels have put me through. Alas, fate is cruel, and I am innocent."

"Where is Veliana?" Harruq asked, scanning the debris. "We've captured the rest of your guild, all but her. I know she's with you."

"Just keeping an eye out for intruders," Veliana said, again from behind him. He turned to see her idly lying in the empty window of the library, hands crossed behind her head. Her dark hair was pulled back in a ponytail, and she winked with her good eye. "Can't be too careful when you're the most wanted couple in all of Dezrel."

Harruq's hands tightened on his swords. He could take Veliana in a straight fight, but not with Deathmask interfering. He'd have to play this very carefully.

"If you're not responsible, then why did so many angels see you in their city hours before it fell?" he asked.

"I was never in their city," Deathmask insisted.

"So the angels are lying?"

"Not lying," Deathmask said as he paced along the top of the spire. "Fooled. Sure, they saw me there, but that doesn't mean it was *me* they saw. It could be anyone. Illusion spells aren't the most difficult thing to acquire, you know."

"If you're not responsible, then who is?" Harruq asked, forcing himself to stay calm. Deathmask had the high ground, which meant he'd have to take on Veliana first, and hope Deathmask's concern for her safety would stop him from casting a spell.

"I know who I *think* is responsible," Deathmask said. "But you won't believe me."

Harruq glanced over his shoulder, not liking how Veliana had drawn her daggers. "Try me."

"The Council of Mages would be my guess," said Deathmask. "They're certainly powerful enough, and bear me no good will after banishing me years ago. As for *why*, well, they've never been a fan of either god, considering them unnecessary blights upon the world, and I have a feeling the war that tore Dezrel asunder did little to change that perspective."

A plausible scenario, Harruq had to admit. When the second gods' war ended, the Council had sent only the most cursory of acknowledgments. They didn't promise Antonil any wealth, or advice, or aid in rebuilding. Just a few sentences on a scrap of paper thanking him for defeating Karak's followers.

"If that's the case, turn yourselves in and plead your case," Harruq said. "All you have to do is swear you had nothing to do with it, and the angels will know immediately."

Deathmask slowly shook his head. "I will not. I don't trust them."

"Why not?"

"Because there's the chance the angels did this themselves."

Harruq froze. The angels felling their own city? That was insane...wasn't it?

"As you're probably realizing, things aren't quite as simple as you'd like to pretend," Veliana said, sliding out the window. "So just...oh shit."

Harruq tensed when he heard the sound of wings. Atop one of the crumbled buildings landed an angel of Ashhur, golden armor glittering in the starlight. He carried a long spear in one hand, a shield in the other, and he looked ready to use both.

"Deathmask and Veliana of the Ash Guild, I am Syric, Ashhur's loyal servant. Surrender yourself now for trial and judgment."

"You led them here," Deathmask said, glaring.

"Not on purpose," Harruq grumbled. He faced the angel. "Greetings, Syric. I'm Harruq, steward of the realm. I'm sure you've heard of me, maybe seen me kill Thulos, perhaps? I've got this situation under control, so, just, fly away now."

He felt maddeningly impotent making such a request. His position of power never seemed to matter when dealing with the angels. As expected, the angel only raised his spear. Harruq clutched the hilts of his swords, palms sweating. His heart hammered in his chest as a second angel landed, his enormous two-handed sword already drawn.

"Do not resist," Syric said. "Shoa and I will use force if we must."

Veliana's daggers twirled in her hands. Harruq kept an eye on Deathmask at all times, waiting to see how the dangerous man would react.

"Surrender," Harruq said, desperately hoping he'd see reason. "If you're innocent, you'll be in no danger. I give my word."

Deathmask faced each of the angels in turn, then reached up to remove his mask, revealing a face horribly scarred by fire. He stared at Harruq, almost pleading, and it was strange to see such honesty from the man.

"I fought alongside you, Harruq. I bled with you. I overthrew Melorak and his cult, I freed the people from Karak's oppression. Remember that, and trust me now. I did not destroy Avlimar."

Harruq realized the angels should have immediately sensed whether it were a lie or not, and he turned to Syric.

"Is he telling the truth?" he asked.

The two angels shared an uncomfortable look.

"Sorcery," Syric said. "He masks his involvement, or protects it with clever language. We know his guilt is as certain as the rising sun."

"So be it," Deathmask said, pulling his mask back over his face. "You two had your chance."

"No," Harruq shouted, and he drew his swords. "Syric, Shoa, both of you stand down, that is an order. Let them go unharmed."

The angels stiffened as if he'd slapped them across the face.

"Who are you to order us?" Shoa asked.

"The steward of the realm," Harruq said.

"The human realm," Syric said, and he turned to Deathmask. "This is your last chance. Surrender, or die. We will not ask again."

Deathmask laughed. "Come and try, angels. You won't be the first of your kind I burn to cinders."

With a sudden burst of wings, the two lunged from their perches, Syric charging for Deathmask, Shoa for Veliana. His mind a stream of curses, Harruq dashed toward the collapsed library. Veliana had been prepared for an attack, but she appeared caught off guard the angels' speed. She dashed to one side, only to have Shoa already veering in that direction, cutting her off while swinging his enormous blade.

Before it could slice her in half, Harruq flung himself in the way, both his blades blocking the swing. The hit jarred his arms, and he let out a growl as he dug in his feet.

"You would fight me?" Shoa asked as he pushed forward, knocking Harruq back a step. "Even after all we've done?"

"Your choice," Harruq said, ducking an attempted elbow to the face and then crossing both swords into an X to block a downward chop. "Fly away, damn it, before it's too late!"

Veliana spun around to Shoa's back, and the angel had to retreat to protect himself. His sword looped about in wide circles to keep the two of them at bay. Veliana twisted and ducked, narrowly avoiding every swing. Harruq kept his distance, waiting for the right moment to attack. He wouldn't win a match of pure strength, but if he could utilize their numbers advantage to find an opening...

Veliana dropped into a roll beneath the angel's blade, then came up striking. Shoa retreated, and that's when Harruq rushed him. Salvation and Condemnation hammered into the angel's weapon, every bit of his strength poured into each blow. No chance for the angel to recover. No way to retaliate. Veliana saw the opening and went for it, but she wasn't fast enough. With a gust of air, the angel beat his wings and soaring into the air.

"Vel!" Harruq heard Deathmask scream, and immediately the woman pulled away to race to her guildmaster's aid. Harruq spared a glance, saw the disgraced mage frantically dodging Syric's spear. The angel was bleeding from multiple wounds but still fought on unimpeded. Harruq's brought his attention back to Shoa and braced for an even harder fight. With Veliana out of the picture, the angel could face Harruq without distraction. A flap of his wings and he swooped down, crashing into Harruq. The half-orc

The King of the Vile

skidded across the walkway, refusing to back down, and once the angel landed to his feet, Harruq stole the offensive.

"Is this it?" Shoa asked as his enormous blade shifted and danced to block each and every hit. "Is this the strength of the fabled Godslayer? How could Thulos have fallen to one such as you?"

"I'm not trying to kill you, you bastard," Harruq said. "Now fly away before someone gets hurt."

Shoa swung in a wide arc, and it would have cleaved Harruq in half if he'd leapt backwards a half-second later.

"Then try harder!" the angel screamed. Harruq couldn't believe the fury he saw in Shoa's emerald eyes, the rage revealed in his sneer. Why such hatred? Did they care so deeply for Avlimar's fall, or was it merely that someone had dared challenged their authority?

The angel demanded he try harder, and so Harruq did. When the enormous sword came arcing down, Harruq met it with his own. The sound of steel hitting steel was like an explosion, but this time it was the angel who found himself overpowered. Step by step he retreated as Harruq tore into him, matching the angel's savagery. Every shred of frustration, he released. Every fear, every worry, he let fuel his swords. Godslayer, they had called him. As Harruq roared, he let himself become the furious monster that had accomplished the deed. The red light around his black blades flared with power. Shoa lifted his sword to block, but the heaven-forged blade shattered against the twin strikes.

"Surrender," Harruq said, pulling back his rage. It was a struggle, and he felt every muscle in his body trembling, but he fought down the impulse to kill. Behind him, he heard Deathmask and Veliana continue to battle Syric, and he knew if he didn't end the fight soon, they would.

"I will tell the others," Shoa said. "You drew your swords in defense of criminals. No matter your position of power, you will stand trial for such a crime."

"I have a thousand sins on my shoulders, and you would condemn me for this?" Harruq asked. Out of all the angel had done, this betrayal stung the most.

"Your people begged for blood-soaked justice," Shoa said. "Cast the blame before their feet, not mine."

Syric screamed. Shoa turned, worried for his comrade, and in that brief moment Harruq plunged Condemnation into the angel's chest. Shoa lurched forward, blood leaking from beneath his armor. His mouth opened, but no words came out. Harruq let go of the blade, and he stepped away to avoid the blood. Shoa staggered, then crumpled sideways and lay still. The noise of battle quieted, both angels defeated, and the ensuing silence was deafening.

Harruq dropped to his knees before the body, and he felt his arms go limp. Lying dead before him was one of the angels his own prayer had summoned, the saviors who had emerged from a rupture in the sky to assault Thulos's demons. An angel who had fought time and again to defend Dezrel, giving everything to war in the skies above Avlimar so Harruq might have time to defeat the war god.

An angel Harruq had murdered.

"What have I done?" Harruq asked, his voice barely a whisper.

Deathmask joined his side, and he knelt before the angel's body. Two tugs, and Condemnation slid out. Using the bottom of his cloak, Deathmask cleaned off the blood, tossed the sword to the ground.

"No one will know," he said, fire wreathing his hands. With a touch, the fire spread to the angel's corpse. "They will search for their missing, and when they find them, they will place the blame on my shoulders."

Harruq retrieved Condemnation, slid both swords into their sheaths, and slowly stood. Mouth dry, legs weak, he watched the fire consume the corpse, turning flesh to bone and cloth to ash.

"This never should have happened," he said.

Deathmask clapped him on the shoulder.

"A lot of things never should have happened, but they have, and now we're stuck with the mess. Go back to the city, Harruq. Go back, and this time keep your eyes open to what's truly happening to this world. From the lowest of rogues, to the steward of the realm, no one is safe." Deathmask snapped his fingers, extinguishing the fire. "It seems mercy's been replaced with judgment in this dark hour, and all of us suffer the cost."

Harruq watched the two vanish into the ruins of Avlimar. He tried telling himself the man was wrong, that things weren't so dire. The angels were still a force of good. They were still protectors of mankind.

The sound of wings. Harruq glanced up to see two more angels land and stare at the charred corpses in horror.

"What happened here?" one of the angels asked.

Harruq swallowed down a lump in his throat and answered with the truth.

"They found Deathmask," he said. "And because of it, they died."

The angels took to the air, calling for more of their brethren to form search parties. Harruq let them be. On his entire walk back to Mordeina, he could think of nothing but the fury in Shoa's eyes, and his utter disgust at the notion that a lowly mortal such as Harruq might give orders to an angel.

7

Despite the danger, despite the swarming hordes of vile creatures threatening every mile of their journey south, Dieredon still ensured Jessilynn trained each day with her bow. Jessilynn found the dedication both admirable and insane.

"I still miss hitting stuff standing still," she said as she walked alongside the elf. Her bow was drawn, and she held an arrow loosely to the string. "What's the point in shooting while moving?"

"Because we can't afford to stand still," Dieredon said. "Given the nature of our foes, you will find rare opportunities for clean, unhurried shots. Learning to aim while jostled and moving will prove invaluable."

They walked a dirt road surrounded by tall yellow grass leading toward the Castle of the Yellow Rose. The road continued on for several miles ahead, ending at a distant forest. They'd sent the survivors of many villages that direction, and Jessilynn was relieved they'd found no signs of an ambush. Several hundred yards away, a hollow log sat in the center of the road, and Dieredon insisted she fire at it during their approach. She'd told him it was impossible, and in reply he'd fired off a single shot, the arrow arcing through the air to strike the log dead center with a dull thunk.

"Fine," she'd murmured. "It's *almost* impossible."

Her first attempt landed painfully short, the arrow hitting the dirt and burying the point. She overcompensated on her second and sent the arrow sailing into the surrounding grass.

"You'll need to retrieve that," Dieredon said.

The King of the Vile

Groaning, Jessilynn attempted a third shot. Each step she took threw off her aim, and though she tried timing it for when the bow was calm, she still failed. The arrow shot wide.

Frustrated, Jessilynn reached for another, then decided against it. Her fingers brushed the drawstring. At her touch, an arrow of pure light appeared, and without need of an arc, she aimed straight at the log and released. The arrow flew, not once dropping toward the ground. It blasted into the center of the log, sending pieces of wood flying in all directions.

"There," she said. "I hit your log, as requested."

She didn't need to look at his face to tell he was upset, only listen to the strain his voice.

"You did," Dieredon said. "But not with an actual arrow. Now go retrieve the two you lost."

"I don't understand why," she said. "It's not like I need them."

"You do," the elf insisted. "And as long as you are training under my tutelage, you will use your regular arrows."

"Even in combat?"

The elf sighed.

"Yes, even in combat if at all possible. I do not wish to argue this matter, Jessilynn."

Jessilynn looked to the tall grass, thinking of the bugs that would be crawling on her as she searched for two stupid little arrows.

"Well I do," she said, her temper flaring. "Why are you so insistent I use real arrows? You've seen what I can do without them. Ashhur is with me. All I have to do is touch the drawstring to summon an arrow, so why bother?"

"Because one day it will fail!"

Jessilynn lowered her bow, taken aback by his sudden outburst. She froze in place there in the road.

"What do you mean by that?" she asked softly.

Dieredon crossed his arms and looked away.

"I have seen it a thousand times over," he said, "and I fear I'll see it again. Mankind contains such potential, but that potential is not just for good. For all your virtues, you also fall prey to doubt, to fear, and to confusion. It is inevitable. No man or woman goes through their life without such things."

He turned to her, and she was stunned by the compassion in his eyes.

"One day, when your life is at risk, I fear your faith will falter. And in that moment, I would have you readying a real arrow that is sure to be there no matter *what* you believe."

"Do you truly think so little of me?" she asked. "Are you so certain my faith will crumble? I am stronger than that, Dieredon. Stronger than anyone's ever given me credit for, and look how Ashhur has rewarded me for it. I won't doubt. *I won't.*"

Dieredon shook his head.

"The heroes you worship in your stories are not heroes because they never doubted, but because they doubted and still fought on to accomplish great deeds. Your confidence in your own faith in Ashhur borders on arrogance. If I wounded your pride, so be it, but better your pride than your flesh."

The elf abruptly resumed walking down the road, not waiting for a response. Jessilynn stood there holding her bow, unsure of how to react. Part of her was furious; he was doubting her faith, and insisting she would someday falter in her beliefs. But part of her, the quiet voice that never seemed to go away when she was trying to sleep, insisted he was absolutely correct. She would fail, and often. Was it so terrible for the elf to point out the inevitable?

Jessilynn followed the elf down the road. When she reached the shattered log she turned off into the grass in search of her lost arrows. The first one she found easily enough, but the second proved much more difficult. Using her bow to push grass side to side, she worked her way back and forth, steadily getting farther from the road.

Just when she was about to give up and call it hopeless, she heard something whistling through the air. She looked up to see an arrow land thirty feet to her left. Far down the road, Dieredon lowered his bow. Jessilynn following his arrow, found it sticking in the dirt right beside her own. Retrieving both, she returned to the road, putting her two into her quiver and holding Dieredon's third.

"Thanks," she said after catching up to him.

The King of the Vile

The elf nodded but said nothing.

The two traveled in unbroken silence for much of the hour, Dieredon speaking only when they arrived at where the road vanished into the forest. The trees were tall and bare, most of their leaves fallen. Dieredon peered into the forest and frowned.

"The locals call this the foxwood," Dieredon said. "We must pass through, or waste two days traveling around to its southern edge."

"Why wouldn't we pass through?" she asked.

In answer he guided her off the path and toward the forest's edge. He stopped at a tree and paused. Jessilynn wondered what his elven eyes had spotted. She then spotted four deep grooves cut into the bark high above the ground, their size and shape painfully familiar. Jessilynn's hand brushed her scarred face and winced.

"Wolf-men have been here," she said.

"They have."

"What if it was from before? Back when Darius and Jerico fought them?"

The elf shook his head.

"That was years ago, while these are a day old at most. The wolves have beaten us here, Jessilynn. The question is, did they continue on, or do they wait in ambush?"

Jessilynn shuddered. How many bones might lay among the leaves? Had any of the people they saved made it through, or had they died, mauled in the dark as they traversed the foxwood?

"We can't go around," Jessilynn said. "If the wolf-men are ahead of us, then we've wasted too much time as it is. We must go through. If they try to ambush us, well..." She grinned at the elf. "You are the legendary Dieredon, after all. They're welcome to try."

Dieredon smiled, and he looked relieved despite the potential danger. "I'm glad you are with me. You are like Jerico in many ways, including his ability to tell jokes when other men would be afraid."

"I'm flattered," she said, pulling her bow off her back. "Now lead on. We should cross as much distance as we can before dark."

"Indeed, " said Dieredon. "Come nightfall, I expect the wolves to come out to play."

They ate before heading into the forest, not expecting to have much chance to rest once they entered. The path they found was hidden under leaves but still easy to follow given how densely the trees grew together. Jessilynn had missed it at first, but Dieredon, who could spot a single arrow lost in a giant field from one hundred yards, did not.

Two hours into their travel, the sun began its descent and the first of the howls sounded, piercing through the woods and echoing all around them. Jessilynn's hands shook.

"Remember to stay calm," Dieredon whispered. Leaves crunched underneath her feet with each step, but Dieredon didn't make a sound. The fact that she was surprised by that left her feeling embarrassed.

"Calm," Jessilynn muttered. "Right. Calm."

"I mean it. They'll try to frighten you, chase you off the path. Once you're lost and afraid, it's only a matter of time before..."

He paused. When another wolf howl came from behind them, Jessilynn felt her heart rate triple. If the creatures were surrounding them, how long until they sprung their trap?

"Maybe we should hide," she said. "We can wait until daylight before crossing the rest of the way."

"They'll track us by scent," Dieredon said. "There will be no hiding from them, not in a forest. We have to keep moving. Follow the path, even by moonlight, and slay those that would stop us."

"What if there's too many?" Jessilynn asked, unable to keep herself from voicing her strongest fear. The shadows of the bare tree limbs stretched long across the path, filling the forest with dark corners. Dieredon hastily counted his arrows, a quirk she'd seen him do only a few times. It was the closest the elf ever came to admitting nervousness.

"There won't be too many," he said. "And if there are, we'll kill them until the number becomes acceptable."

The howls continued, each one closer than the last. Jessilynn pulled her bow off her back and tapped Darius's sword, hoping it might inspire some confidence. Dieredon's head remained on a swivel, constantly checking both sides of the road.

The King of the Vile

"We're already surrounded," he said softly. "I can see several in the distance, lurking."

Jessilynn tightened her grip on her bow. She searched the woods, wishing she had eyes as sharp as the elf's. So far, she saw nothing, but she trusted her teacher.

"Why don't they attack?" she asked.

"They're waiting for dark."

The continued down the path, the wolves kept howling. Jessilynn's heart beat faster and faster, a cold sweat ran down her neck. Why couldn't they just attack already? Memories of her torment at the hands of the sons of Redclaw raced through her mind, of her humiliation, her torture. The scars on her face itched as if they were freshly formed.

Calm down, she told herself. *At the river you stood your ground and killed dozens. This time you're not alone.*

Her hand brushed Darius's blade.

Not that I was ever alone.

The sun dipped lower, and Jessilynn found it increasingly hard to see. All around her the rustling of leaves grew louder, and many times she caught the glint of tawny eyes staring from deep off the path. There came another wave of howls, and she shivered.

"I hear at least fifteen," Dieredon said when the howls died down. "Maybe twenty. This might be a problem." The elf glanced her way. "Jessilynn, do you trust me?"

Nothing good ever followed such a question, but she nodded anyway.

"I'm going to leave you," he said. "I want you to run for fifteen seconds down the path, just long enough for me to hide. Once you reach fifteen, stop wherever you are and hold your ground. Don't move. Don't run."

"You want me to be bait," she said.

"If it comforts you to put it that way, yes."

"It doesn't," Jessilynn said. To her right, three pairs of eyes peered at her hungrily from behind a copse of trees. "I'll do it, Dieredon, but I'm trusting you. If I die, I swear I'll haunt you for at least a decade or two."

The elf grabbed her shoulder and squeezed.

"You're not the first to make me that promise," he said, winking. "Now run."

Jessilynn swallowed, counted to three in her head, and took off. Immediately leaves and broken twigs exploded all around her. It seemed the entire night had come alive as the prowling wolf-men gave chase. Dieredon sprinted alongside her for a moment before diving into the forest. She prayed for his safety as she heard muffled grunts and a yelp. Howls chased her, and up ahead, howls greeted her. The beasts no longer hid, their long, muscular bodies easily visible as they flanked her. The fifteen seconds passed by with agonizing slowness, but at last she planted her feet, pulled an arrow from her quiver and nocked it. Blue-white light shone from the arrowhead, and telling herself to be brave, she slowly spun in place.

"Do you think I'm afraid?" Jessilynn screamed. Her role wasn't just as bait, but as a distraction, so she played the part as best as she could. "Do you think I'm afraid of pups like you?"

Several snarled as they stood to their full height, towering a solid two feet above her. Three lumbered into the road ahead, three more blocked the road behind. Saliva dripped from their teeth, low growls rumbling in their throats.

"We remember you," the middle wolf-man blocking the road ahead of her said. "You were our prisoner. You were Moonslayer's pet."

Jessilynn grinned despite her fear.

"I killed Moonslayer," she said. "And I'll kill you too, unless you run."

The wolf-man bared its fangs as it tensed for a leap.

"Arrogant human," it said. "You will suffer as we feast."

It howled, and at its signal, the rest attacked. Jessilynn released her arrow, striking the wolf's leader in the chest. The shot blasted it off its feet, innards spilling across the road as the body rolled. She reached for another arrow, but from the corner of her eye she saw a beast lunge at her. It was too close for her to react in time, but one of Dieredon's arrows plunged into its neck, dropping it. Jessilynn breathed a sigh of relief and fired, her own target receiving an arrow in the face, shattering its skull.

The King of the Vile

She heard the whistle of more arrows, the projectiles raining down at an incredible speed from Dieredon's high perch. Jessilynn spun, spotted a wolf-man with a shaft lodged into its leg trying to flee. Pulling an arrow from her quiver, she sighted it, let loose. As the beast died, Jessilynn heard another of them cry out.

"The tree! Up in the tree!"

Jessilynn turned to see several leap onto the same sturdy trunk, their sharp claws sinking into the bark. Dieredon was on a high branch, perfectly balanced as he rained down death. Even as more wolf-men raced toward her, she trusted the elf to protect her, just as she would protect him. One after the other she killed the climbing wolf-men, her arrows ripping them off the trunk.

Despite the chaos, Jessilynn felt strangely calm. She was in control. She had the power. A wolf-man died mid-leap, its body crumpling mere feet away, yet she did not let it shake her aim. One last wolf climbed up toward the elf. Her hand reached back, found the quiver empty. Deciding Dieredon couldn't possibly mind, she grabbed her bowstring anyway, an arrow of light swirling into existence at the touch of her fingers. When she fired, it hit the wolf-man in the spine, exploding with such power it cleaved the beast in two. Both halves fell.

It was the last.

Dieredon swung his bow over his back and climbed down. Jessilynn stood among the carnage, overwhelmed by how many they'd killed. It was almost surreal. At least fifteen dead wolf-men lay all about her, and she hadn't even been scratched.

"That was incredible," she whispered.

"I wish you'd used a regular arrow on that last one," the elf said. "Either that, or left it for me."

"I was out of arrows," she said, immediately defensive. "At least I waited, like you asked."

"It's not that," the elf said, and he smiled despite their long night. "I was worried you would chop the tree in half and send me tumbling down with it."

He tousled her hair, and she accepted the gesture in a state of mild shock.

"Did you just tell a joke?" she asked.

The elf shrugged.

"Perhaps. Why?"

Jessilynn stared at the dead bodies, the blood everywhere.

"Nothing," she said, hurrying down the path, hoping to put a mile or two between the carnage and their eventual campsite. "Just...nothing."

8

It'd been two days since Alric ate when he stumbled upon the little cabin beside the forest. He'd crossed a stream the day before, and drank until his stomach ached, but the closest he'd had to a meal was a grasshopper he'd caught and crushed in his hand. He'd almost eaten it. Almost. Instead he'd tossed the filth to the ground, wiped his hand clean, and continued on. As he crossed the rolling hills, he'd begun to fantasize about that grasshopper, and the many others that had flitted about the fields on either side of the stream. If he'd known how hungry he'd become, he would have swallowed down both pride and bug.

Alric more crawled than walked to a foot-worn path that stretched from the door of the cabin to the hills beyond. Unable to go on, he dropped to his stomach and lay there, staring at the cabin. It was a nice cabin, he decided. Small. Well-cared for. If only the person inside would notice him lying there, cold and hungry. Since he'd lost his supplies in the Corinth River, he'd had to beg for every scrap of food he'd eaten from the various farms he encountered on his trek north. Like a fool, he'd avoided the main road, thinking an angel might spot him for questioning. Should they discover who he was…

"Why in Karak's hairy ass are you here?"

Alric looked up to see an older woman frowning down at him. Her hair was gray, her skin wrinkled, but her blue eyes were lively. She wore a faded dress that might have once been green before dirt and time had their way with it.

"Traveling," Alric said, as if that were a worthwhile explanation. "My…my name's Alric. I hate to be a bother, and I'm ashamed I must, but…"

"Yes, yes, you can have something to eat," the woman said, dropping to her knees so she might wrap an arm underneath him. "It's either feed you or bury you, and I know which one's easier on these old bones."

Slowly she stood, and Alric forced his limbs to work. The woman had at least twenty years on him; he would not be carried into her cabin like an invalid. Together, step by step, they approached the cabin. Alric slumped against the wall as she grabbed the door.

"You'll have to endure for a bit," she said as she shoved the door open. "I've got a stew cooking over the fire, but it's got some time before it'll be ready."

Inside was warm and cozy, a veritable paradise after Alric's last few days. An old rocking chair waited by the fire, and the woman helped him over to it. Collapsing, Alric let out a moan as he gently rocked back and forth. The heat of the fire seeped into him. The feel of heat slowly spreading throughout his body was divine after the last few cold nights. His host took a step back and frowned.

"Maybe you shouldn't wait," she said, grabbing a cloth off a simple yet sturdy table. Turning to the pot, she grabbed the ladle inside and scooped out a large chunk of potato. She wrapped it with the cloth, then handed it to Alric.

"You might want to let that cool," she said, but Alric would have none of it. He opened the cloth and tore into the potato. It was tough and slippery, but it was delicious. His mouth began to salivate as he wolfed it down. When he finished, he leaned back in his chair and tried to relax. He'd been in the grips of panic for days now, and for once he felt like himself again.

"Thank you," he said, closing his eyes. He was so tired, and that tiny bit of food in him wasn't helping him stay awake.

"Most welcome," the woman said. She started rifling through her cabinets in search of something. Alric rocked back and forth, sleep inevitable at this point.

"Your name," he said, trying to resist. "May I have your name?"

He heard a cabinet door slam shut.

"Go on and sleep," the woman said. "When you wake, you can have both my soup and my name."

Alric chuckled.

"You're too kind," he said. "Too kind..."

The fire crackled, its heat carrying him away into slumber.

※

Alric awoke to a wet cloth pressing against his forehead. He started, arms flailing. Without meaning to, he slapped the cloth out of the woman's hand.

"I'm sorry," Alric said, immediately overcome with guilt. "Please, you startled me, I didn't mean to do that."

The woman nodded, a frown etched into her tanned face.

"I believe you," she said, bending down to retrieve the cloth. "Your supper is ready if you are."

That he was. As his senses returned to him, he felt warm, alert, and ravenous. Alric joined the woman at the table, a steaming bowl already served and waiting for him. Taking a wooden spoon, he prepared to eat, but not yet.

"Your name," he said. "I won't eat until I at least know your name."

The woman stared at him, and he felt himself being analyzed. Whatever judgment she reached, good or ill, he didn't know, for she kept her weathered face far too guarded.

"Beatrice," she said. "Beatrice Utter."

"You have my thanks, Beatrice," Alric said, and then he tore into the soup. Beatrice sat opposite him, saying little and eating nothing herself. Alric assumed she'd already eaten, or would later.

"I didn't mean to wake you," Beatrice said when he was halfway through the bowl. "The way you were moaning, I was thinking you had a fever. Walking hungry and cold as you were, I'm still stunned you don't. You must have been having a terrible dream."

Alric swallowed as he tried to think of a proper response.

"I have nightmares sometimes," he said. "I don't like to talk about them."

He slurped another spoonful of stew, the broth thick and meaty. As far as he was concerned, it was divine.

"Is it about the war?" Beatrice asked. "I know a lot of younger fighting men who still have nightmares. Facing off against the dead, or that dragon the mad priest summoned, isn't something you easily forget."

Alric chuckled. Despite telling her he hadn't wanted to talk, she'd asked anyway. Stubborn woman. He had a feeling she often got what she wanted.

"No," he said. "I never fought in the war. When Thulos's army marched west, my village was close to the coast, too far from their path to be affected."

"You were one of the lucky ones, then," Beatrice said. She had a thin blanket wrapped about her shoulders, and she pulled it tighter. "Around here, we were safe from their initial raids. The call for soldiers afterward? Not so lucky then. A lot of good men joined King Antonil's march to retake Veldaren alongside the angels. That first time, I mean, not the second one when the war was done. Those men, they fought the dead, they fought demons, and when they came home, they fought the shadow dragon at Mordeina's gates. Far more than any man should endure, but endure they did, and now they wake screaming from the nightmares. Scars of the mind, I say. And just like a scar, it won't be healing soon, if ever."

Alric remembered listening to the stories after the war's end. Much of it had sounded so outlandish he'd have shrugged them off as lies if not for the angels who flew about. Having the winged men around made it a lot easier to believe stories of demons and dragons.

"Can we...can we talk about something else?" he said. For some reason, discussing the war between the brother gods made him incredibly uncomfortable.

"Sure," Beatrice said, leaning back into her chair. "Perhaps you can tell me where you're going, and why you're going there in such sorry shape."

Alric's spoon clacked against the bottom of his bowl as he thought over what to say and how truthful to be.

"Do you know of the blockade at the Bloodbrick?" he asked.

"I do," Beatrice said. "News doesn't travel often to me, but that certainly did."

"Well, I crossed the Corinth into Mordan, and I didn't do it by using the Bloodbrick. Lost all my provisions in the process. Past week I've been making my way north, relying on the kindness of strangers." He met the woman's blue eyes. "Strangers like you, to whom I am most thankful."

Beatrice's gaze made him increasingly uncomfortable.

"Must be something important for you to have done that," she said.

"By Ashhur, I hope so."

Beatrice rose from the table and gestured to the pot sitting beside the fire.

"Get some more if you'd like," she said. "And then rest up. I expect you've got no coin on you, so for now, you'll earn your keep by helping me about the place the next few days. Winter's coming, and there's lots to do to prepare."

"I'm afraid I can't stay," Alric said.

"Somewhere important to be?"

There was no way to explain without explaining everything, and Alric felt too ashamed to do so.

"I only..." he shook his head. "I'll help until I regain my strength, just a day or two at most. Will that suffice?"

Beatrice didn't look happy, but he wondered if Beatrice even *could* look happy.

"Very well then." She headed toward the cabin door. "I accept. After all, I'd hate to impose."

The door opened with a loud creak and shut with a bang. Alric winced as if expecting to be shot with an arrow.

"No wonder you live alone," he said, and immediately felt guilty. The woman had warmed him by a fire, fed him, and offered him a place to sleep. To repay that kindness with cowardly insults behind her back...

"I'm sorry, Ashhur," he said as he returned to his chair by the fire and wrapped himself in a blanket. Back and forth he rocked, his full stomach spreading sleep throughout his body. "We're all imperfect vessels, but you chose a truly cracked and dirty one for this task by choosing me."

※

Beatrice woke him early that next morning.

"Chores to do," was her only explanation.

Those chores were many, and took Alric all over the woman's land. First came milking her trio of goats. Their milk was his breakfast, along with some vegetables she'd boiled before he woke. Along the forest's edge she'd placed dozens of traps for rabbits, and they checked every single one, resetting those that needed it. Of the traps, only one had caught a rabbit, and Beatrice smoothly pulled it free, broke its neck, and handed it to Alric to carry.

While Beatrice cleaned and skinned the rabbit back at the cabin, Alric steadily chopped logs for her woodpile. The hours passed, and Alric felt himself sinking into the menial tasks. It reminded him of home, and there was something wholesome about it, a feeling of accomplishment no matter how meager the work. To the north of her cabin was a stream, and he traveled to it alone so he might bathe. Afterward he brought several filled jugs back to the cabin and stashed them inside.

"Just in time," Beatrice said. "Rabbit's ready."

She'd cooked it over the fire and seasoned it with herbs from her garden. Alric tore into the meat. It tasted even better than the stew she'd cooked the day before. When he finished, he returned to his task with the firewood. With him planning to leave the next morning, he wished to do all he could to pay her back for her generosity. If he had his way, she'd not need to split another log for the rest of the year.

Come supper, Alric felt exhausted but whole. That a day before he'd fantasized about eating grasshoppers seemed insane now, a distant past of another man. Inside the cabin, he sat on the floor beside the fire, relinquishing the rocking chair to Beatrice. He had a few pillows and a blanket, and he used them to brace his head and relax, letting the flame's heat wash over him. For a long while, the popping and crackling of the fire was the only sound in the cabin.

"You screamed last night," Beatrice said, breaking the silence. "Not loud, and not long, but it woke me. You were afraid, Alric. Mighty afraid. I almost woke you, but by then you'd stopped."

She glanced his way quickly before returning to the fire.

The King of the Vile

"What demons are you running from?" she asked. "Because it don't seem like you're running fast enough."

Alric held down a groan. The woman wouldn't let up, would she? But what was the point in telling her? She'd only mock him. A hard woman like her, she'd call him crazy, or worse.

"I'm not running," he said. "I'm...traveling to Mordeina."

"What for?"

He breathed in, let out a long sigh. To the Abyss with it. Beatrice couldn't say anything any harsher than what his wife had told him.

"Ashhur wants me to go there."

Beatrice halted her rocking for the slightest second.

"Oh really?" she said. "And what for?"

Alric turned so his back was to the fire and, conveniently enough, he could no longer see Beatrice's frown.

"I don't know."

"Then how do you know Ashhur wants you to go to Mordeina?"

"The dreams," he said. "Every night, I have the same dream. I think I'm in Avlimar. Everything around me is golden and beautiful. There's a crowd of people, and they're angry and afraid. Something is happening, an announcement, maybe a coronation. All I know is that it's important I be there."

Beatrice coughed to clear her throat.

"They're only dreams," she said. "And I can tell you right now that they're nonsense."

Alric did his best not to act defensive.

"How could you know that?" he asked.

"Because," she said, "you say you're in Avlimar? That can't be. Haven't you heard? Avlimar fell."

The news hit him like a cold slap.

"Are you certain?" he asked.

"Very. I don't go to town often, but last time I did, that's all anyone was talking about. That, and the angels. Avlimar's in ruins, so if you're going there, it's not a coronation you're seeing in your dreams, but a funeral."

Alric tried to tell himself it didn't change anything. He only partly succeeded.

"It doesn't matter," he said. "I still have to go. I still have to try."

Beatrice scratched at the side of her face and frowned at him as if he were a disobedient child.

"Look, what you're wanting to do isn't wise," she said. "Unease is spreading everywhere, reaching even my ears. This isn't a safe time to be a stranger in Mordan."

"Except I'm not a stranger here," he said. "I was born and raised in Mordan. I didn't leave until just after the angels began policing the lands."

Beatrice let out a surprised grunt.

"What made you leave?"

Alric let his mind wander into the past, faces and forgotten places flashing before his eyes.

"His name was Nick Adams," Alric said, letting his mind wander to the past. "A neighbor of mine. No one liked him. He had a weak soul, spent more time in the day drunk than sober. He couldn't be trusted to repay his debts, and unless you dragged him kicking and screaming, he wasn't one to help out even if a storm blew over your barn or a fire burned up half your crops."

Alric drummed his fingers atop the floor of the cabin.

"His wife, Susannah, she was a pretty thing. Real pretty, and deserved better than him. She deserved *me*, that's what I told myself. So if I saw her at the market, or walking by my home, I'd make sure to say hello, flirt with her a bit. Never when Nick was around, of course. I'll spare you the rest, but let's say we started sleeping with one another, until Nick found out."

He paused, remembering that moment. Alric had prepared himself for a confrontation, looked forward to it even. He'd let Nick rant and scream about how she was his wife and then throw that fact right back in his face, tear down the man, tell him if he couldn't keep his wife happy then he had no claim on her. But it didn't go down that way.

"Nick came to me when he found out," Alric said softly. "Crying like a child. 'Don't take her from me,' he kept saying. He'd change. He'd do better. Susannah was everything to him, and if I walked away, he'd make everything right with her."

"What happened then?" Beatrice asked.

The King of the Vile

Alric swallowed down his shame and continued.

"I refused. I mocked him. Insulted him to his face. Told him Susannah was mine, and if he didn't want me having her, then he better do something about it. And so he did. He swung a punch at me. Just a single, stupid punch. But while he had his fists, I had a knife, and so I..." Alric wiped away a few tears that had built in his eyes. "And so I killed him. Didn't mean to. I just wanted to win. I wanted Susannah to be mine, and I wanted this drunk oaf to get the abyss out of the way. I plunged that dagger into his stomach, and I didn't even think twice about it. Not until he was dead. Not until I realized what I had done."

Alric sat up, wrapping himself in his blanket. It'd been so long since he thought of that moment. He'd tried to block it out, pretending it'd never happened, but still he saw Nick's face right before he died. Still crying. Still heartbroken.

"The town called for an angel when they found the body," Alric continued after composing himself. "I went up to him the moment he landed and told him everything. Didn't try to hide a thing. Told him of me, and Susannah, all of it. And then the angel gave me the chance to repent. Right there. I was expecting to lose my head, but I didn't. He forgave me, declared me innocent, and flew away. A few weeks later, I packed up all I had and crossed the Corinth to make a new life in Ker."

"Did the people run you out?" Beatrice asked.

"No," Alric said. "They didn't. I wish they had. Instead they didn't care. Even Susannah, I think in time she might have moved in with me. But I couldn't stand it. I killed a man, felt his blood spill across my hands, and no one cared. No one blamed me. No one hated me for it. Nick had no other family, hardly any friends. It all felt...wrong. I guess traveling to Ker was my own little exile, and now I feel like Ashhur's called for it to end."

Beatrice resumed her rocking, the creaking of the wood seeming to carry new tension.

"I think you've got nightmares because you're letting your guilt eat you alive," she said. "You won't find anything in Mordeina, Alric. You won't find anything in Avlimar's ruins, neither. It's been a long time since I had a man around this place.

Not since Johnathan died eight years ago. So long as you're willing to work, you can stay."

She rose from her chair and put a hand on his shoulder.

"Don't waste your life fleeing nightmares. They drove you hungry and cold to my doorstep, and should you leave here, they'll strip you down to your bones as you continue running. It isn't worth it. Ashhur's not calling you nowhere. You're not a prophet or a priest, just a simple, frightened man who still hasn't forgiven himself."

She left him to sleep, not that sleep came easily, or was comforting when it did.

Alric left the next morning, carrying a basket of food and a handful of silver coins.

"You should think of coming with me," he said. "King Bram's army will march over the Bloodbrick soon. I know it in my gut. Invading soldiers don't tend to be too kind to the fields and homes they pass by."

"I'll be just fine." Beatrice told him as she stood in the doorway to her home. "It's you who needs to be careful."

She went inside and shut the door. Alric took a deep breath and took his first step west. It wasn't until Beatrice's cabin was long out of sight that he dared spare a look back.

"What in Ashhur's name am I doing?" he wondered before continuing on, telling himself the dreams left him no choice, telling himself this was right.

Telling himself, again and again, that he wasn't throwing away his entire life for nothing.

9

Qurrah knew King Bram's army would invade long before the soldier arrived bearing the news. Excitement filled the air, unlike the previous few days of dull boredom.

"Does the king wish me to be at his side?" Qurrah asked the young soldier.

"I...he did not say," the soldier answered.

Qurrah chuckled

"Thank you. Go on and join the rest in preparing."

The man saluted and dashed away from the small camp Qurrah and Tessanna shared at the army's outskirts. Qurrah turned to Tess, who sat with her head resting on her knees.

"Will we join Bram?" she asked.

"It's either us at his side, or Karak's paladins," Qurrah said, shrugging. "I'd rather it be our voice whispering in his ear instead of theirs."

"And if it's both?"

With a snap of his fingers, their fire dwindled down to embers.

"Then we'll shout instead of whisper," he said. "It isn't wise to ignore either of us, and Bram will learn that soon enough."

Tessanna rose to her feet and smoothed out her plain dress. She seemed remarkably calm given the circumstances.

"You're trying to stand in a river, reshaping its flow without being pulled along with it," she said. "You're not often a fool, Qurrah, but I worry you play the part in this game."

"Angels from Mordan tried to kill us despite vowing to never enter Ker's lands," he said, struggling to keep his anger subdued. "If we're ever to be safe, Bram needs to solidify his kingdom's independence. I don't care to stop this war, only ensure Karak is not the one who benefits. The angels have overstepped their bounds, and if Bram is right in claiming Harruq has death warrants on our heads, I wonder how much power he even holds anymore."

Tessanna listened, her expression as passive as stone. Qurrah stopped talking, and she pulled him closer by the front of his robes and kissed him. It was mechanical, lifeless, and he was glad when it ended.

"I'm sorry," she said, her voice lacking any conviction. "Do what you want. I'll be with you always."

It would have been better if she'd yelled at him, even threatened him with harm. Sighing, Qurrah wrapped his arms around her, kissed her forehead.

"I only ask that you trust me," he said softly. "The world is changing, and I'm not sure whether for good or ill. All I can do is what I think is right."

"That's all we can ever do," Tessanna whispered. "But sometimes what we think is right reveals itself to be so terribly wrong."

Qurrah knew immediately what gave her pause. Even years later, the ghost of Aullienna still haunted them both. He took his wife's hand. "Come along. I want to be there when it begins."

They hurried into the bustle of the camp. At King Bram's pavilion they found the flaps open. Bram was speaking with several of his generals as they stood over a circular table containing a map of Mordan. The queen was with them. If time and pressures of ruling had aged Bram, they seemed to have completely ignored Loreina. She was smiling, her youthful eyes seeming eager for battle. A pearl-white dress tightly clung to her slender body and her hair was carefully braided, wrapped around her neck like an ornate necklace.

"Might we join you?" Qurrah asked.

Bram looked up from the table and smiled warmly.

"You are always welcome," he said.

"Thank you," Qurrah said. He and Tess stepped inside, and he glanced at the generals. "Might we have a word alone?"

They turned to their king, who nodded.

"Go see to your men," Bram said. "We march within the hour."

They filed out, leaving only Bram and Loreina. The queen clung to his side, her arms wrapped around his. Her eyes lingered on Qurrah, and he couldn't shake his constant unease. The queen's presence unnerved him more than the dark paladins. At least Karak's followers he could understand.

"You said you'd march into Mordan when the right time presented itself," Qurrah said. "I take it that time has arrived?"

"It has," Bram said. "Are you ready?"

"We are," Tessanna answered for him. "When angels crash into your ranks from the sky, crushing your numbers with but a thought, will you be?"

Loreina squeezed her husband's arm tighter, and she grinned as if Tessanna were a little girl telling jokes.

"There will be no angels, not according to what I've learned," she said. "The creatures of the Vile Wedge have poured over the Gihon, united under a self-declared King of the Vile. They're conquering the North, with apparent plans to form themselves a nation of their own."

"Is that so?" Qurrah asked, not sure whether or not to believe such an outlandish claim.

Bram tapped the map and nodded.

"With them forced to respond to such a threat, we can march on Mordeina without resistance for days," he said. "Hard-pressed on two fronts, and with their king dead and the bulk of their armies crushed, Mordan will never be more vulnerable than she is now. We cannot afford to delay any longer. Angels crossed my border and killed my men. It's time we repay them for their crimes."

Qurrah stared at Loreina. "There are many miles between here and the North. How do you know of the beast-man invasion?"

"That's my little secret," she said with a smile. "I'm sure you have a few of your own."

"Come," Bram said. He patting Qurrah on the back. "Join me on the front lines. Let's find out just how committed Mordan's troops are in defending the Bloodbrick."

They left the queen in the pavilion and traveled north through the encampment. Soldiers saluted and bowed, eagerness on their faces. They didn't fear the coming campaign, and Qurrah could only assume it was because they'd not witnessed the ferocity of the angels firsthand. If they had, they'd realize this invasion would be met with devastating resistance no matter what their king told them. Qurrah glanced at Tess, still holding his hand. Granted, that was what they were for, wasn't it? To be equalizers? The slayer of angels so Ker might remain free?

A fool, Tess had called him, and as he stopped beside the king, he wondered if she might be correct after all.

Ahead of them was the Bloodbrick, heavily guarded by the gathered might of all of Ker. On the other side, the token force King Antonil had left behind when he'd marched east awaited. Qurrah saw two hundred, maybe three hundred soldiers at most, rushing to prepare for battle as Bram's army approached. They were so badly outnumbered. Qurrah couldn't imagine them putting up much of a fight; hopefully they'd surrender, preventing needless deaths. A beam of light then shot into the air from the center of the Mordan encampment, lingering for a few moments before fading away as if it had never been.

"Calling for angels," Bram said. Qurrah nodded. He'd used one of those magical cylinders to summon a flight so he might visit Azariah in Avlimar. "I guess I shouldn't be surprised. The entire nation is filled with coddled children expecting Ashhur's angels to do all their dirty work for them." The king smirked. "They're about to receive a painful lesson on their folly."

As the soldiers formed ranks, Qurrah spotted Xarl making his way through the crowd. He frowned, and had to bite his tongue to keep silent as the dark paladin joined King Bram's side. The remaining nine of his order lingered behind, watching. Xarl smiled wide, dipped his head in respect.

"What a beautiful day," he said. "Do we at last march to war?"

"We do," Bram said.

"Then the day only grows in beauty."

"I would expect your kind to revel in war," Tessanna said. "Will you sing songs of praise as you murder and kill?"

The King of the Vile

"In all we do, we praise Karak," Xarl said. "And why should we not take joy in the first step toward freeing Dezrel from tyranny?"

"Enough," Bram said. "I won't sit here and listen to you three bicker. Is there something you needed, paladin?"

Xarl gestured to his fellow paladins. "We come ready for battle, and I ask that you grant us the honor of leading the charge across the Bloodbrick."

Qurrah's immediate instinct was to ask Bram to deny them, but he knew such a request was pointless. The king would not let Qurrah's opinion sway him. If anything, he'd let the paladins lead just to show Qurrah his place. Clenching his jaw, Qurrah waited for an answer. Bram turned to the bridge, narrowed his eyes, and stared at the steadily forming ranks of Mordan soldiers.

"The front lines are yours," Bram said. "Though this means you are part of my army, and I expect you to obey orders. Is that acceptable?"

"More than acceptable," Xarl said, his smile somehow spreading even wider. "Your soldiers will be inspired by our bravery and skill, I assure you. With our aid, even the angels pose no threat."

That was clearly what Bram wanted to hear, and he dipped his head in respect. Shouting out a command, Xarl drew his sword and led the dark paladins toward the bridge.

"You let them take the glory for themselves," Qurrah muttered.

Bram gestured to the pitiful defenses guarding the other side.

"There is no glory here," he said. "If Karak's paladins want to bleed in place of my men, they are welcome to do so. I won't sacrifice soldiers' lives out of pride and cowardice."

Qurrah was fuming, but the argument was clearly over, so he shut his mouth. Keeping to the king's side, he watched as the paladins formed a line ten wide at the first brick of the bridge. Already they were singing, their weapons wreathed with black flame. Kerran soldiers gathered around them, laughing and shouting curses at their enemies. It was a crude display, but the rest of the army appeared to enjoy it. Anything to take away their fear, Qurrah supposed.

Sir Ian approached from the front lines, looking frazzled and nervous.

"Are we prepared?" Bram asked, clapping his old friend on the shoulder.

"We are," Sir Ian said. "All we await now is your order to begin."

Bram hesitated, the gravity of the situation finally settling in.

"There is no return, not from this," said the king. "Send forward my soldiers. It is time we pay the blood price for our freedom."

"What we do, we do for the sake of all mankind," Sir Ian said, bowing. "Whatever the price, we will pay it gladly."

The knight turned and began shouting orders. The paladins at the front heard, and they released one last cheer before stampeding across the bridge. Bram's soldiers followed in a frightening tide of armor and blades. A handful of archers from the other side fired, but their arrows a nuisance at best. The dark paladins led the way at full sprint, unafraid of the arrows, unafraid of the hundreds standing against them on the other side. Qurrah felt a naive hope that they'd be crushed, but he'd seen the power of Karak's paladins many times before, and knew exactly what would happen the second the battle began.

It took less than a heartbeat. The dark paladins arrived, heralding a flood of Kerran soldiers, and the Mordan soldiers broke. Qurrah watched the dark paladins tear into their foes, flaming weapons easily punching through the chainmail. Most of the opposing soldiers flung down their weapons and fled, and to Qurrah's relief, the paladins did not give chase. The more lives spared the better, at least in Qurrah's mind.

He glanced at the king. "It seems such a contradiction."

"How so?" Bram asked.

"To keep yourself free from the rule of gods, you ally with warriors of a god," Qurrah said, gesturing to the battlefield. "Or is it only Ashhur's rule you fear, and not Karak's?"

"It is no contradiction," he replied with a chuckle. Thankfully he didn't seem offended. "We currently have the same goal: to remain free from the control of the angels in the north. Right now the ends are all that matters. When they have served their purpose, I will cast them aside."

Qurrah watched their leader, Xarl, rally his paladins. The man lifted his enormous sword above his head, crying out victory as black fire wreathed his blade. The name of Karak echoed across the bridge.

"I do not think their kind is cast aside so easily," Qurrah said.

King Bram shook his head.

"I survived the invasion of a god. I do not fear a few of Karak's deluded followers."

Lifting his arms above his head, Bram let out a cheer, the smile on his face ear to ear. The Kerran soldiers cheered with him. Qurrah watched him as the army began to cross the bridge. Even when Karak's priests had risen to power throughout Dezrel, emboldened by Thulos's arrival, Bram had steered his nation through the dangerous waters with superb skill. With Mordan in chaos, from angels, beasts, and their dead king, it seemed Bram was destined for another skillfully earned victory. Except no matter how wise the course, Qurrah couldn't shake his mounting feeling of dread.

"Puppets," Tessanna whispered, as if her own thoughts mirrored his. "We are all puppets."

"No," Qurrah said half-heartedly. "We stopped being their puppets long ago."

"Then why do we march to war alongside Karak's faithful?"

It was a question for which he had no good answer. Sighing, he joined the thousands as they crossed the Bloodbrick. Heavy footsteps thudded on stone, armor and weaponry rattled. Qurrah felt himself swept along. When he reached the very end, he stepped aside and lingered while the remaining soldiers crossed. He stood on the very last brick of the bridge and stared west. Weeks ago, he'd entered Mordan in hopes of helping his brother solidify his rule. Now he sought to battle his brother's army and weaken his angelic allies. How had the world turned upside down so quickly?

"Forgive me, Harruq," Qurrah whispered as he stepped onto Mordan soil. "But the angels must be stopped. In time, you'll understand."

Ahead of him, Tessanna turned, face still a cold, unreadable mask.

"Qurrah?" she asked.

Qurrah did not answer, only took her hand and followed the road amid a sea of Kerran soldiers.

10

For Lord Richard Aerling's sake, it was a good thing Harruq didn't have his swords on him. If he did, he'd have already lopped off the chubby lord's head and flung it out the window, like he had with Kevin Maryll. There wouldn't have been any witnesses other than his guards, and surely he could convince them it was well-deserved justice...

"Let's try this again," Harruq said, rising from the ornate throne to tower over the lord. "We wait days and days for your men to gather here, but now that they finally have, you want to march *south?*"

Sweat dripped down Richard's face and neck, but the man admirably held his ground. It only made Harruq want to strangle him more.

"King Bram's army has crossed the Bloodbrick, heralding the invasion we already warned you was taking place," Richard said.

Harruq felt like he was talking to Aubrienna during one of her stubborn fits. No matter what he said, no matter how stupid the opposing position, nothing seemed to get through.

"Except there's already an invasion to the *north*," he shouted. "Half-human monsters of the Vile Wedge swarming across the Gihon, crushing the Wall of Towers? Slaughtering whole villages? Any of this ringing some fucking bells?"

Lord Richard tugged on his collar.

"They're just animals. Savage animals. Dangerous, yes, but they'll scatter and break as winter arrives, and they pose no real threat to the Castle of the Yellow Rose, let alone Mordeina. King Bram, however, has a true army, and a brilliant tactical mind to go along with it. We will not let them pillage our lands in the south just to make up for the failed defenses of the northern lords."

Harruq stepped down from the dais, put his face inches away from Richard's.

"I am steward of this realm," he said. "I speak for the king, and I say you, and all your little lord friends, are marching north to save who you still can. Is that clear?"

Richard entire body was shaking. He could have nodded, or shook his head no, and Harruq wouldn't have known either way. Wishing he had something he could smash, Harruq was about to retake his seat when Richard spoke up behind him.

"No."

Harruq slowly turned, staring at Richard as if the man had drawn a knife on him.

"What was that?" he asked, the air in the throne room suddenly ice cold.

Richard stood to his full height, which was still a good foot shorter than Harruq.

"I said we won't go. The others sent me here as a courtesy for you, and nothing more. Our minds are set. We're marching south, to stop King Bram before he captures our lands."

Harruq flew down the steps with a single leap and slammed his fist into the chubby lord's face. The man let out a cry as he fell to his back, blood sputtering from his nose and lips. Harruq towered over the moaning lord, hands clenched as he struggled to hold back his rage.

"You would come here and tell me to my face you plan to commit treason?" he asked. "What makes you think I will let you leave here alive?"

Richard clutched his face, blood dripping between his fingers. When he spoke, his words were muffled.

"Because you're not a fool," he said. "We're marching to defend our lands, and when we crush Bram, we'll turn our eyes to the north. But if you kill me, the rest will overthrow you and Gregory and appoint a new king of Mordan. There will be nothing you can do to stop them."

"I won't need to stop them," Harruq said. "The angels will."

Richard laughed despite his obvious pain.

"Angels fighting human soldiers in the streets? You think you can control the riots that would follow, the upheaval that would

The King of the Vile

sweep across the entire countryside?" Richard spat a wad of blood and phlegm at Harruq's feet. "Even if the angels stopped us, they'd be too few to save you. Bram would walk into Mordeina, and after such chaos, the people would throw open their arms and beg for his rule."

It was an all-too-likely a scenario. Harruq reached down, grabbed Richard by the front of his shirt, and yanked him to his feet.

"I may not be able to kill you," he said, "but I don't have to send you to your friends in one piece."

He slammed his forehead into the man's already broken nose. Richard howled like a wounded dog as blood splattered everywhere. Harruq flung him toward the door, watched him roll.

"Get out!" he screamed. "Run to your little pack of rats and get out of my damn city."

Richard staggered to his feet, still clutching his face with his right hand, and rushed out the door. The guards shoved it closed behind him.

"Wess!" Harruq shouted.

The older man had stood beside the throne during the entire encounter, and he sprung forward the moment he was called.

"Yes, steward?" he asked.

Harruq breathed heavily as he fought to calm himself down. "Send for Ahaesarus, and Sir Daniel Coldmine as well. If our armies won't protect the northern lands, we'll send angels to do it instead. In case I'm late, have them wait here for me."

"And where will you be?" Sir Wess asked.

"Washing up," Harruq said, and wiped his wet forehead, then gestured to his stained shirt and pants. "I've got some coward's blood on me."

Sir Wess bowed as Harruq exited the throne room and marched down the cramped stone hallway toward his room, fuming all the while. He'd known his power was tentative, with Gregory too young and too weakly connected to the royalty to command much respect. He'd been counting on the angels to keep the lords in line. Apparently he had guessed wrong. The angels weren't protecting him. If anything, they were pushing the lords to act even further out of line.

When Harruq flung open the door to his room, he found Aurelia reclining on their bed with a book. The front cover was in flowery elvish script and laced with gold. Old elven history mixed with elaborate stories. Aurelia had begun collecting them as Aubrienna grew older as part of a blossoming desire to teach their daughter more about her heritage.

"Is something wrong?" Aurelia asked.

Harruq paused, drinking in her beauty as golden light shone through the window and illuminated her face. He desperately wished to tear off both their clothes and just have at it, but instead he began pulling off his shirt.

"I hate being in charge," he muttered.

Aurelia set aside the book and sat up. "What's the matter now?"

"Sir Richard has informed me they're all marching south to fight King Bram," Harruq said. He used his shirt to wipe the blood from his face and then tossed it to the floor. Aurelia frowned at the bloodstained clothes.

"Did you kill him?" she asked.

Harruq chuckled.

"I wish. Just a broken nose. Ugly bastard will be even uglier, but he'll live. More than I can say for the people they've left to die up north."

Once his pants were off, Harruq rummaged through their enormous armoire for a change in clothes.

"It's not your fault," Aurelia said. She slid off the bed and wrapped her arms around him, pressed her cheek against his back. Harruq sighed and leaned into her.

"Feels like it," he said.

"Even kings cannot always control their subjects, and you're no king, only a steward. Right now, we need to make the best of the situation."

"That's what I'm hoping for."

Aurelia helped him put on a new shirt, a red one with loose and smooth fabric. Upon being named steward, she'd purchased several such shirts, hoping they would make him look more authoritative. Harruq stared down at it, wondering if his armor and weapons might have better suited him. People didn't respect him as a steward; they knew him for the power he wielded, skills honed by the Watcher and blades blessed by the gods.

"If Richard, Typh, Foster, and all the others won't help, then we'll send what we can," Harruq said. "We'll send the angels."

"Harruq, I'm not sure we can trust them to go."

Sighing, Harruq turned about to face his wife. She didn't flinch at his frustration.

"Why not?" he asked, knowing he wasn't going to like the answer.

Aurelia nervously ran her hands through her long auburn hair, pulling strands from her face. Not good. Not good at all.

"When I took Gregory and Aubby to the market," she said, "a young boy came running down the street. He couldn't have been more than thirteen, and he looked terrified. An angel chased after him. Aubby and Gregory watched him drop from the sky and spear the boy through the chest with his sword."

Harruq winced and fought down anger at the thought of his poor little girl having to see something like that.

"Why'd the angel kill him?" he asked.

Aurelia frowned. "Because the boy had stolen a piece of Avlimar's wreckage. That was it. I watched them pull a tiny chunk of gold from his pocket as he lay there, motionless. No questions. No testing of lies, or seeking forgiveness. The crowd was livid. Some threw food, others stones. The angel didn't care. He never even said a word. I don't know what happened after that. It wasn't safe, so I took Gregory and Aubby away from there as fast as I could. I thought about having the guards look into it, but decided there wasn't much point by the time I reached the castle."

Harruq rubbed his face, groaning as he tried to make sense of what he heard.

"Why didn't you tell me?" he asked.

Aurelia sat back down onto her bed, shrugged. "I didn't know what to make of it. And why give you something new to worry about if there was nothing you could do? But the more I think on it, the more uneasy I feel. Something is wrong with the angels, Harruq. I don't know what, and I don't know why, but they're not the same as they once were."

"Azariah says Ashhur no longer speaks with them," Harruq said, tugging at his shirt collar to loosen it. "Bernard Ulath confirmed the same before he traveled south to join the Sanctuary. They're frustrated and confused, still trying to figure out their place in our world. But they're still who they always were, wardens of Dezrel. They'll protect us. They'll fight for us. That's the one thing I do know."

Aurelia slowly nodded.

"I hope you're right," she said. "Because I don't know what we'll do if you're wrong."

Harruq kissed her forehead.

"I do," he said. "We'll endure. Always have, and always will."

He hurried back to the throne room, telling himself over and over that things would be all right. They might be pressed on two fronts, but if Mordan's army could crush Bram's in the south while the angels gathered together to save the North, then all would be well.

When he re-entered the throne room he found several angels waiting for him. The big three, as Harruq had begun calling them in his mind. Ahaesarus, looking tall and regal as ever, stood front and center, with Azariah and his brother Judarius on either side of him. All three wore their sparkling white tunics, with Ahaesarus and Judarius also sporting thick gilded armor and weapons strapped to their backs. Across from them, hovering near the throne, waited Sir Daniel. He looked tired and miserable, and Harruq couldn't blame him. The knight had flown into Mordeina shouting a cry for aid, and as days trickled by, no one seemed to listen.

"Looks like we're all here," Harruq said as he made his way to the throne. He didn't feel like sitting, so he paced in front of the angels as they patiently made their introductions.

"Greetings, steward," Ahaesarus said, and the other two echoed him.

"Greetings," Sir Daniel muttered from the corner.

"Greetings and welcome and all that other stuff," Harruq said. "Time is short, and we need to act now. Our friendly local lords have all decided to abandon Lord Arthur so they might instead head south to tackle King Bram's invasion." Harruq

The King of the Vile

nodded to Ahaesarus. "The North is being overrun, so gather your angels and fly to Lord Arthur's aid. Once the Castle of the Yellow Rose is secure, we can spread outward from that safe zone, hunting down the beasts wherever they've scattered."

"You speak as if we are your soldiers to order about," Ahaesarus said. He smiled at Harruq, as if that might remove the sting. It didn't.

"I'm not giving orders," Harruq said. "I'm stating the damn obvious."

"Even so, I'm not sure tackling the beast-men is the wisest course," Judarius said. "Paladins of Karak march with Bram's soldiers. With Ker having so stubbornly refused Ashhur's rule, and now allying with Karak, I fear the fallen god has found himself a new home to re-grow his following."

Harruq felt the first tinge of panic.

"It's just a few paladins," he said. "They aren't going to win a war on their own."

"Jerico and Lathaar are but two," Ahaesarus said, "yet what army would not tremble when facing their combined might? If dark paladins fight alongside Kerran soldiers, then it is a conquering force we must consider before we send our combined might in the opposite direction."

"And what of Devlimar?" Azariah added. "What assurances do we have our home will remain safe during our absence?"

Harruq wanted to scream, but the angels were not Lord Richard. There'd be no head-butting an angel, no matter how appropriate it felt.

"That's what guards are for," he said, patience straining.

"Already you give us guards, and they accomplish little."

"Then I'll station *more* guards," Harruq said. "This is insane. Is your new home really that much more important than the people dying in the north?"

"We have all seen the sacrifices you and your friends made in the defense of your homes," Azariah said. "Why are we not allowed to care for our own?"

"I did it for the people there," Harruq said, growling. "Not the damn buildings."

"The last piece of Ashhur's perfection in this world is steadily being broken down and stolen. Perhaps you cannot understand, but that loss hurts us deeply."

Harruq felt the last of his sanity breaking. The angels weren't going to help? How could they not? After everything they'd done, everything they'd sacrificed...

"Harruq is right," Ahaesarus said after a long, uncomfortable silence. "The people are what matter most. We should fly north to aid against the beasts of the Wedge."

"Karak is our enemy, not the mindless creatures of the first war," Judarius said. "I say we accompany the army south."

They all turned to Azariah, Harruq desperately hoping the angel would see reason. Whichever side the wise angel joined would be the winning argument. Those hopes died with the shaking of Azariah's head.

"Devlimar will be finished within a few days," he said. "We have spent too long bleeding and dying for those who would reject our help. For once, we must look to ourselves, and ensure our own spiritual needs have been met. We must rebuild Devlimar. We must cry up to the heavens for Ashhur to hear us and answer. Let him provide us with the proper path. Until then, we are lost sheep, and whichever way we go may be wrong."

Ahaesarus turned to the smaller angel, and Harruq was surprised by the anger he heard in his voice.

"We do not have the time to..."

"We do," Azariah insisted. "Convene a council if you must, and we will vote on the matter. Or would you tell our brethren you feel it wiser to act with haste instead of seeking Ashhur's wisdom?"

The comment must have stung Ahaesarus deeply, for the angel looked away, dismayed.

"You can't," Harruq said. "You won't, but...but why not?"

"Once the council convenes, we will inform you of our decision," Azariah said with a bow. "Until then, we have work to do."

Azariah took flight, exiting one of the enormous windows. Judarius followed. Only Ahaesarus remained, and he stared after his departed brethren. Harruq felt his legs going weak, disbelief settling in.

"I don't understand," he said.

Ahaesarus shook his head.

"Neither do I," he said softly.

With a great burst of air, the angel spread his wings and flew away. Once he was gone, Harruq lowered his head, sucked in a deep breath, and screamed as loud as he could.

"FUCK."

He dropped to his rear on the carpet, resting his head in his hands. The angels had been the one faction he thought he could rely on, the one shining beacon of sanity in an insane world. Not anymore.

Footsteps behind him reminded Harruq of Sir Daniel's presence, and he turned about, his neck and face flushing.

"Sorry about that," he said.

Sir Daniel shook his head and gestured to the window the angels had exited through. "You have nothing to apologize for. Those fools, on the other hand..."

"Not sure what else there is to do," he said. He rubbed his eyes against an oncoming headache.

"There's not," Sir Daniel said. "Which is why I'm leaving."

Harruq lifted an eyebrow. "Leaving?"

The knight offered his hand, and Harruq slowly stood and accepted it.

"I've done what I can, as have you," he said. "But if nothing can be accomplished here, then I'm going to fly Sonowin to the castle to aid Arthur. I may be only one man, but I will still do what I can."

Harruq pumped the knight's fist, then stepped back.

"Don't quit on us yet," he said. "Aid will come, I promise. Just...give me a bit more time. A whole lot of strange is going on, and I need to figure out what it is so people can start behaving like they should."

Sir Daniel nodded.

"I won't tell Arthur he's abandoned," he said. "But I won't lie to him, either. For now, we must stand on our own. Good day, Steward, and may Ashhur help you in the days to come."

"Thanks," Harruq said. "I think we're going to need it."

Sir Daniel bowed low, then marched down the carpet and out the double doors. Slowly, Harruq approached the throne as if it would eat him. He stared down at the empty seat and couldn't help but wonder if it'd be better if it *remained* empty. Tilting his head to the ceiling, he shook his head.

"Are you watching?" he whispered. "Do you see what's become of us without you?"

Harruq expected no answer, so when he felt a cold wind blow, heard a soft whisper breathe his name, it chilled him to the bone. It was a voice from his past, a voice of nightmares and loss.

I see it, my wayward son, whispered the voice of the Lion. *I see it all.*

11

Lathaar sat in his room and stared at the letter on his desk. It was a simple letter, only three sentences long, sent by a farmer from a village near the Bloodbrick.

"Damn it," Lathaar slammed a fist against the desk. "Ashhur damn it all, not again."

He grabbed the small piece of parchment and hurried from his room. He had to find Jerico, had to react before things spiraled out of control. Lathaar raced down the stairs of the Citadel two at a time. The students should've still been outside performing their morning exercises, with Jerico overseeing them to make sure no one decided to take things easy or pretend their fifth sit-up was actually their fiftieth.

When he reached ground level, he shoved open the heavy doors, climbed down the five stone steps to the ground, and rushed around to the west side of the tower. Sure enough, the thirty students were in scattered groups, performing their stretches and other assorted exercises. Jerico stood among them, looking tired and bored.

"Come to join us?" Jerico asked when he saw Lathaar approaching. "Sparring won't begin for at least half an hour, but I'm bored enough to..."

He trailed off, frowning and crossing his arms. His voice lowered. "What's wrong?"

Lathaar handed him the letter. Jerico read it, and his frown deepened.

Ker declared war on Mordan. Already crossed the Bloodbrick. Karak paladins fight alongside them.

That was it, but that was all they needed to know. Jerico lowered the letter and sighed.

"Well," he said. "It looks like things are about to get interesting, aren't they?"

"I'm not sure 'interesting' is the word I would use," Lathaar said. "What do we do?"

"What *can* we do?" Jerico asked with a glance at the students. "They're too young to fight. The two of us alone won't be enough to defeat an army, nor do we need to. The angels can handle any threat Ker poses."

Lathaar shook his head. "Karak's paladins are finally on the move. We can't ignore this. Whatever they're planning, it isn't good. We both know that."

"Jerico!" called one of the younger paladins. The boy looked deathly white as he rushed over. Lathaar frowned, wondering what could possibly have spooked him so.

"What's the matter, son?" Jerico asked.

In answer the boy pointed north, just beyond the Citadel.

"There's...there's an army coming," he said.

The two paladins exchanged a look.

"They wouldn't be coming from the north," Lathaar reasoned, cutting off the thought that Ker's army had turned their way at the dark paladins' behest.

"Then who?" Jerico asked.

Together they rushed through their ranks to the corner of the Citadel. Before they were even to the other side, Lathaar could already see what had spooked the boy: a swarming mass of creatures, at least three hundred strong. They were too far away to make out individually, only that they were a mixture of gray fur and pink flesh. They rushed southward alongside the western bank of the Gihon River. Lathaar's head grew light, the air in his lungs suddenly too thin.

First Karak's paladins, now this?

"What in the abyss is going on?" he wondered aloud.

"I don't know," Jerico said. "Get the students inside. We need those doors barred at once."

The two ran back to their students, shouting orders. Lathaar failed to keep the panic from his voice as he urged them on. In a

The King of the Vile

scattered line the students ran to the front of the Citadel, rushing up the steps and through the thick doors. Lathaar slammed them shut behind him. They'd been reinforced with battle in mind, and together he and Jerico dropped the heavy iron bar into place.

"Everyone to your rooms," Jerico called behind him. "All of you move it, right now!"

"How much time do we have?" Lathaar asked as the students filed up the stairs.

"Time enough to put our armor on in case those doors don't hold," Jerico answered.

Both had rooms on the second floor, and they helped one another strap on their platemail. With each piece, Lathaar's insides hardened. How long had it been since he'd fought in battle? Five years, closing in on six? Ever since Thulos's death, he'd done little but train and teach. The world had felt legitimately safer, but that safety was now revealed a lie.

"Ready?" Jerico asked as he slid his left arm through the buckles of his shield.

Lathaar tightened his belt, then slid his long and short swords into their respective loops. Their weight was comforting, and he wondered if he should view that as a blessing or a curse.

"Ready," Lathaar said.

They climbed to the third floor armory, which had eight windows facing all directions. Lathaar moved to the northern window, Jerico the northeast. Together they watched the small army approach, only minutes away.

"Goat-men," Jerico said. "That's new."

"It is." The creatures had humanoid arms and chests, their faces long, their nostrils flat. From their heads curled long, thick horns. Their legs were backward bent and covered with fur, much more resembling a goat's.

"What are they doing across the river?" Lathaar wondered.

"It's a small group," Jerico said. "Perhaps they sneaked past the patrols?"

"Or Tower Violet has fallen," Lathaar said, referring to the southernmost building that was part of the Wall of Towers. Hundreds of soldiers and boats patrolled the Gihon from there, ensuring no creatures of the Vile Wedge escaped to terrorize the west.

"Tower Violet," Jerico said, shaking his head. "Or the entire Wall."

"We won't find out up here," Lathaar said. He headed back for the stairs. "Let's go. The doors won't hold them forever."

Lathaar prayed to Ashhur with every step he took. At the bottom of the stairs, he leaned against the wall on one side of the door, Jerico taking position on the other. And then they waited.

And waited.

"What in the world is taking them so long?" Jerico asked. They should have easily reached the Citadel by now, yet they heard no battle cries, no *thump* against the doors. With those thick, sharp horns of theirs, they could have gorged into the wood until it broke, but so far, relative silence. After another minute, Lathaar gestured up the stairs.

"Go see what's going on," he told Jerico. "We're clearly missing something."

Jerico vanished up the stairs, returning moments later. By the confused look on his face, Lathaar could only assume the worst.

"They've surrounded us," he said. "And it looks like they're settling in. This isn't an attack. It's a siege."

Lathaar tapped his fingers against the hilts of his swords and shrugged.

"Very well then," he said. Grabbing the bolt locking the door, he yanked it open with a loud screech.

"What are you doing?" Jerico asked.

Lathaar grinned.

"I'm going to go greet our guests. Keep ready at the door. You might need to shut it very, very quickly after I come back inside."

Jerico pushed the door open.

"I always thought *I* was the reckless one."

"You've clearly rubbed off on me. Consider it your fault if I die."

Lathaar exited the Citadel to a wave of guttural cries. The goat-men raised their arms, clapping their long fingers together and shouting. They formed a solid perimeter about the Citadel,

The King of the Vile

but the majority was bunched before the door. Lathaar noticed how their skin had a leathery look to it and was covered with thin, fine hairs. Their wide eyes stared at him, most yellow, some red or orange. To his surprise, he saw many wielding crude weapons, thick clubs and sharpened stakes. Even worse were the ten near the very front, facing him while holding swords and axes. The beast-men were primitive creatures, incapable of such craftsmanship. Lathaar felt even more certain Tower Violet had fallen.

He glanced over his shoulder and saw many of their students peering down at him from the upper windows. He waved at them, smiling. If he might ease their minds with false confidence, then he was more than willing to try. That done, he turned back to the waiting goat-men. Keeping his swords sheathed, Lathaar approached the creatures, hands held out to either side in what he hoped was a recognizable symbol of peace.

"That's far enough, human," said a goat-men carrying an ax. This one was taller than the others, and wore a set of tattered, warped chainmail. Its voice was deeper than Lathaar expected, and far more intelligent. Jerico had told him all about his fights against the wolf-men, and how clever they could be, but hearing it in stories and hearing it in reality were two completely different things.

"Welcome to our home," Lathaar said, standing in the middle of the gap between the Citadel and the surrounding army. "A shame you didn't give us notice beforehand. We could have prepared a more proper welcome."

The leader's eyes widened, and it panted in what was either laughter or anger.

"Our king has sent us to destroy you," it said. "You may choose how."

"Your king?" Lathaar asked, not liking the sound of that.

"The King of the Vile!" the goat-man cried, and it hefted the ax above its head. The rest joined in, deep, trembling roars akin to vicious bulls. Lathaar let the sound wash over him, and he had to clench his fists to keep them from trembling. He would not show fear, not to his enemies, and certainly not with his students watching.

"You said we have a choice in our destruction," Lathaar said calmly, as if they were discussing the weather. "Care to tell me what those choices are?"

The goat-man leader stepped forward with a rattle of chainmail.

"No one will come save you. All the lands fall to our king. Come out. Fight us, and die like warriors. Or stay in your stone home and starve. We will not attack. We will not throw away lives on your doors and steps. Come to us and die, or stay within and die." The creature's lips pulled back to reveal thick yellow teeth. "Your choice."

The goat-men chanted, swinging their weapons or stomping their feet. "Fight! Fight! Fight us!"

Lathaar let them go on for a bit, forcing the smile to stay on his face. If the creatures of the Vile Wedge had crossed the Gihon united under a king, then hope for aid was painfully low. Thousands of soldiers had marched east with King Antonil, and though the angels still protected the land, they were spread far too thin. With King Bram invading from the south, pressing Mordan from both fronts, which direction would the angels even choose to defend?

"A fine offer," Lathaar said when the commotion died down. "If you'll give me a moment to discuss it with my friend, I'll come back with an answer."

The leader gestured to the Citadel. "Go. We wait."

Lathaar turned his back to them, keeping his walk calm and his back straight. He wouldn't let the creatures think him fleeing. When he reached the doors, Jerico stood leaning against the jamb, his arms crossed.

"I heard every word," he said. "Get in here."

Lathaar entered, Jerico shutting the door behind him. Lathaar leaned against the wall and sighed.

"Well?" Jerico said.

Lathaar shook his head. "I don't know. If they attacked us we could hold, killing their numbers advantage with both the doors and the stairs. But out there, in open fields, we'd have no chance. There's too many, Jerico. It's not worth the risk. I say we wait it out."

The King of the Vile

"Wait it out," Jerico repeated. "While paladins of Karak march alongside Ker's soldiers toward Mordeina?"

"What other option is there?"

Before Jerico could answer, they heard footsteps on the stairs. Both turned to see several of their older students coming down in a group. They held their weapons, swords and maces and shields. The weapons' glow was so soft, so faint in the daylight. The weakness of their faith bothered Lathaar terribly, and he felt the blame lay solely on his shoulders.

"We want to fight them," said the eldest student, a tall, dark-haired boy named Mal. "All of us. We're not scared."

The cracking of his voice said otherwise. Jerico looked back, and Lathaar shook his head.

"No," he said. "We're not sending children out to die."

"We're not children," Gareth said from behind Mal. He was one of the few who wielded a glowing shield like Jerico, and he lifted it up before him. "We can fight."

Jerico leaned in closer, lowered his voice.

"Perhaps it is time," he said.

"No." Lathaar clenched his jaw, and he held his ground. They were too young. Too lacking in training. "You and I, we'll stand together against them. It's time we showed these beasts how badly they've erred in coming to our home and threatening those we've sworn to raise and protect."

There was no hiding the disappointment on the faces of the younger paladins, but Lathaar knew it was better they be disappointed than dead. None of them had ever faced a real opponent in battle. To handle hundreds at a time, and those of a bestial nature like the goat-men? No, he would not have those deaths on his conscience.

"Bar the doors after we leave," Lathaar told Mal. "If something happens to us, you'll be in charge of the defense. Stay inside, ration food carefully, and keep the youngest in their rooms until you're certain the beasts won't attack. If Ashhur is kind, help will come from Mordeina. Is that understood?"

Mal nodded, looking relieved as well as disappointed. Lathaar turned to his friend and drew his swords.

"At my side?" he asked.

Jerico patted his glowing shield.

"Always and forever."

Together they exited the doors of the Citadel. The gathered army cheered at the sight of them, and they stomped their hoofed feet eagerly. Lathaar approached their leader, and calm slowly spread through his body. This was it. Not since the second Gods' War ended had he drawn his blades with death in mind, but the anticipation of battle, the heightening of all his senses, came back to him as familiar as his own reflection.

"Come to die?" their leader shouted when the two paladins were halfway between the Citadel and the ring of goat-men.

"I offer this one chance," Lathaar shouted back, ignoring the question. "We have brought low ancient evils from when the world was first born. We have sundered armies of the dead and slaughtered demons of the air. We have faced down gods and not broken. You are nothing to us but rabid beasts to be put down. Retreat, and you will live. Attack, and you will face the fury of Ashhur." Lathaar grinned. "Your choice."

The goat-men slammed their hands together and let loose a communal roar of anger. Lathaar shook his head. He'd not expected them to listen, but at least he'd tried.

"You are but two against many," their leader spat. "We will stomp your bones into dust, and we will rip apart the children you protect." It pointed its ax toward them. "Kill them, kill them both!"

The creatures charged from all directions, roaring. Jerico smacked his mace against his shield and Lathaar clanged his swords together.

"Surrounded, outnumbered, and with no chance for retreat or surrender," Jerico said with a smile. "Just like old times."

"And come the end, we'll both remain standing," Lathaar said. "Just like old times."

Lathaar braced his legs as Jerico lifted his shield. The blue-white glow shimmered, growing stronger, brighter, as Jerico prayed to their god. Energy swelled within it, and right before the creatures overwhelmed them, the paladin stepped forward, his scream flooded with power.

"Be gone!"

The King of the Vile

Jerico thrust his shield forward, and from it flew a mirror image, only it grew as it traveled, widening out as if it were the shield of Ashhur himself. The light struck the goat-men like a physical force, slamming dozens to the dirt. The sound of their screams accompanied cracking stone and breaking bones. Only the leader endured, having remained back when the others charged, and even it was forced to one knee from the overwhelming power.

One direction cleared, Lathaar turned left, Jerico right, to face the remaining horde. Swords shining in his hands, Lathaar charged, unafraid. Despite their numbers, it was the beasts that should be afraid of *him*.

"*Elholad!*" he shouted, and the metal of his swords vanished completely, becoming blades of purest light. No weapon could resist it, no flesh could endure it. The first of the goat-men reached him, head ducked, horns leading. Lathaar side-stepped, short sword swinging in an upward arc. The blade decapitated the goat-man without the slightest resistance, its body stumbling several feet more before collapsing. Two more rushed in, swinging their long arms for his face, hoping to tear into him with their thick yellow fingernails. Lathaar cut the hands off of one, then met the other with his shoulder. Their bodies connected, Lathaar trusting his platemail to keep him safe. The goat-man tried to knock him to the ground, but Lathaar dug in his heels, braced his legs, and pushed back enough to buy himself separation. It was only for a heartbeat, but that was enough to swing both blades in a wide arc, cutting the goat-man in half at the waist.

More rushed at him in an overwhelming wave, and Lathaar steadily retreated, still swinging. With each step, the blood of his enemies splashed across his armor. Some tried to leap at him with their horns, others protect their bodies with their arms. It never mattered. Lathaar clenched his jaw and kept his focus razor-sharp. The dead were piling around him, but they had him surrounded. With no place left to retreat, he couldn't make a single mistake. The moment one scored a significant wound, or he fell to the ground, he'd be no more.

Back and forth Lathaar swung, feet never still for a second. He cut reaching hands, forcing them back. He cleaved off charging horns and the heads they were attached to. Multiple times he felt fists slam into him, and despite his platemail, he feared the blows might still break bones. Constantly turning, constantly swinging, he caught sight of Jerico from the corner of his eye. His friend faced off against the army's leader, absorbing blow after blow of its ax with his shield while his mace swung wildly to keep the others at bay.

"Enough!" Lathaar screamed, and he slammed his two blades together high above his head. Light flared from their contact as if a new sun were being birthed. The goat-men staggered away in all directions, lifting their arms and turning their heads against the painful brilliance. Lathaar prayed the reprieve would be enough. Dashing forward, he cut a path through the blinded goat-men, reached open space, and sprinted toward his friend. Jerico blocked another blow, saw him coming, and then leapt backward.

The leader moved to charge, but Lathaar was there, throwing himself in the way. The chainmail the goat-man wore might as well have been cloth when the holy blades sliced through its neck and out its waist. It dropped to the ground and shuddered.

Lathaar thought the rest might retreat with their leader's death, but it only seemed to spur them on harder. Again Lathaar met their charge, trusting Jerico to hold his own. As he fought, the air around him thickened and he felt a growing unease. He ignored the feeling as best he could as he slashed one of the beasts across its long face, sending horns and teeth flying.

A sudden surge of emotion nearly sent Lathaar to his knees. His arms shook, and he gasped for air as if underwater. Overwhelming rage poured through him. The light of his swords expanded, brighter, longer. The weapons cleaved through multiple goat-men with a single swing, their blood evaporating at the very contact with the light. Another swing, and several more fell. Lathaar' didn't hear their death cries, but a solid ringing deep in his head. Only one thing he was certain of, and it frightened him deeply.

Ashhur was furious.

That fury drove him on, the light of his swords like whips, trailing after each swing in curved arcs for a dozen feet beyond their initial reach. The beasts dropped, and before such a sight,

The King of the Vile

they howled in fear and turned to flee. Lathaar knew he should let them, but he chased after nonetheless. His swords sang the song of blood as the beast-men fell and fell until there were none left to chase. Turning about, he found Jerico equally terrifying in his frenzy. With each slam of his shield, a goat-man's body would shatter. Afterimages of the shield continued on, scattering dozens more. By the time Jerico swung his mace, his foe was often already dead.

Only a scattered few remained by the time Lathaar reached Jerico's side, and they were far out of reach. Lathaar sheathed his swords. Though the light vanished from the weapons, his anger did not fade so easily. Jerico let out a deep breath, and he flung his shield onto his back and clipped his mace to his belt.

"What in Ashhur's name was that?" he asked.

Lathaar shook his head.

"I don't know," he said. "The priests say Ashhur slumbers, but I don't think that is true any longer. He's awake, and he's furious."

"Furious..." Jerico looked to the dead around them, and he shuddered at the memory of battle. "That's one way to describe that. I could barely think, Lathaar. If you asked me my name, I doubt I could have told you."

Lathaar understood well what he meant. He still felt the lingering effects, and as time dragged on, he feared that burning sense of anger in his chest would never fade.

"Back to the tower," he said. "This isn't over yet."

☙❦❧

Lathaar and Jerico left the Citadel, weapons sheathed, shield on Jerico's back, and supplies hanging from both their belts.

"I'm still not certain it's wise to leave them alone," Jerico said as they walked the faded path toward the nearest village to the west.

"I'm not sure there *is* a wise choice right now," Lathaar said. He flexed his hands. Even an hour later, his god's fury still smoldered in his chest. "But if there's a reason for Ashhur's rage, it must be Karak's paladins, and we're not bringing untested youths to face them."

"But how will they gain experience if we don't *let* them be tested," Jerico argued. "Whether we like it or not, this is what we were training them for. You heard them back there. They wanted to fight. They wanted to help us. That has to mean something."

Lathaar froze in his tracks and turned to face his friend.

"Then tell me," he said, "should we fall, and our students be captured, which of them do you think could endure the torture that would follow? You suffered at the hands of the prophet and his paladins. You know their cruelty. Tell me. Give me a single name you believe with all your heart could endure those trials, and I will let every student who wishes to come with us do so."

"Jessilynn," said Jerico, meeting his gaze.

Lathaar shook his head.

"Jessilynn's not here. And you know as well as I we've failed our own students. You saw the glow on their blades, if there was any at all. For now, they must be on their own. The bodies of the dead surround our Citadel. Perhaps without us, they'll realize what Azariah always insisted: this world isn't safe, and neither are they."

"They'll learn that just as quickly at our side, facing down our enemies," Jerico said as the two resumed walking.

"Perhaps." Lathaar glanced over his shoulder at the building they'd worked so hard to rebuild. "But I'd rather they be here when they realize it, not dying on a battlefield. Give them time to grow, both in heart and body. We'll bleed and die like we always have to buy them that time."

"So be it," Jerico said, picking up his pace as they crossed the dying grass. "If Karak wants to rear his ugly head again, we'll cut it off and burn the pieces so we can return home. We were supposed to be done with all this, Lathaar. What happened? Where did we go wrong?"

Lathaar swallowed, thinking of Ashhur's rage burning so hot in his chest.

"Heavens help us, I don't know."

12

Jessilynn and Dieredon lurked at the forest's edge, observing the distant Castle of the Yellow Rose in the morning light. They saw dozens of sprawling camps, pastures, and gardens within the castle walls, likely tended by refugees fleeing to safety. The walls were short and thick, easily scalable with ladders, this opponent had no ladders, only sharpened claws.

"Maybe we should wait until nightfall," Jessilynn said.

"These creatures see better at night," Dieredon said. "No, we must go now. Follow me, and stay close. Should we be spotted, do not panic. If we are swift, we still might reach safety in time."

Jessilynn nodded, pretending his words were comforting. Spread out before her, in similar arrangements to how they'd camped back in the ravine in the Vile Wedge, was the growing army of the King of the Vile. Groups of bird-men, twenty to thirty in each group, dotted the flat grasslands between the forest and the wall. Most were still, possibly sleeping. Far more active were the groups of hyena-men that lurched about in greater numbers. Even from a distance she could hear their yips and snarls. Most gathered near the wood gate, the sole opening through the curtain wall, though several patrolled the surrounding areas, and Jessilynn spotted a second large pack guarding the rear of the castle, as well as the road that led in from the north.

But the wolf-men had the greatest numbers of all. They formed a single enormous pack, nearly a thousand strong, just beyond arrow reach of the walls on either side of the gate. Though they were many, Jessilynn knew that number was a fraction of the total forces the beast-men could muster. As for the goblins and the goat-men, she saw no sign of either.

"Why so few wolf-men?" Jessilynn asked.

Dieredon squinted at the throng.

"Manfeaster is yet to arrive. That's why the camps are so disjointed and uneven. This is only a pen to keep Arthur from fleeing, not the actual conquering force. Once Manfeaster comes, the beasts will assault the walls from all sides with far greater numbers. Come. There will be no better time to sneak past."

"Wait," Jessilynn said, grabbing his wrist. "What do we do when we reach the wall?"

Dieredon grinned at her.

"Do you think something as simple as a wall can keep us out? Now try to keep up."

Dieredon ran from the cover of the trees, quiet as a whisper. Jessilynn focused on keeping her head down and her body hunched as she raced after him. The faded grass was tall, reaching up to her thigh, and she prayed that the cover might be enough to keep the two of them hidden as they approached the western wall of the castle.

Dieredon led them on a path between two clusters of bird-men. They were so close, she couldn't imagine they might miss her, but she trusted Dieredon as they rushed along. At one point, when they were halfway to the wall, he dropped to his stomach. Panicking, Jessilynn did the same. He gestured for her to join his side, and she slowly crawled through the grass.

"Patrol," Dieredon whispered.

Jessilynn nodded to show she heard, then waited. The elf kept his head down, and it seemed like he was counting. After about a minute or so, he slowly rose on his hands and knees, peering over the grass. Shaking his head, he dropped back down, mouthed the words *'not yet'*. Jessilynn lay still, fighting off her rising panic. They were in the open, with no place to run should they be found. What if their scent reached the sensitive noses of the hyena-men and wolf-men? There'd be no outrunning them, no fighting them off.

Stop it, Jessilynn told herself, digging her fingers into the dirt. They would reach the wall, or they would die trying. Worrying about anything else was pointless.

Dieredon pushed off to his knees, peered over the grass, and gestured for her to follow. Jessilynn rushed after him in her painful back-bent stance. To her left she saw the patrol that had stalled them, a good twenty wolf-men loping lazily around the castle. As they ran, they drew closer to the bird-men, and Jessilynn saw that many indeed were asleep. *Good*, she thought. Maybe they might get a lucky break after all.

When they were several hundred yards out from the castle wall, Dieredon dropped back to the ground. Jessilynn settled down beside him. They were at the edge of the tall grass; the remaining space between them and the castle was wide open, more padded dirt than grass. There'd be no hiding as they crossed the final distance. She thought the elf waiting for an opportune time, but instead she was surprised to see him ready his bow, aim skyward, and release an arrow toward the wall. It went streaking past one of the soldiers stationed atop it, missing his head by several feet. Jessilynn couldn't decide which surprised her more, that the elf had attacked one of Arthur's men, or that he'd missed.

Embarrassment replaced her surprise as she realized it was neither. Dieredon glanced about to ensure none of the creatures saw, then fired a second arrow, again missing the guard. The guard braced his hands on the parapet and stared down, and Dieredon waved as if they were close friends. The soldier nodded in confirmation.

Now we wait, Dieredon mouthed to her.

The soldier they'd alerted wandered further down the wall, then returned with two compatriots. They moved unhurriedly, doing little to alert the besieging army that something was afoot. After a minute, another soldier arrived carrying a bundle of rope. Dieredon grinned.

"Time to go," he whispered.

He lurched to his feet, and this time there was no attempt at stealth, no hiding or keeping low. Dieredon ran as fast as his legs could carry him, and Jessilynn sprinted after him. The soldiers tossed the rope over the wall at their approach. After only a few seconds, Jessilynn heard a single high-pitched shriek. They'd been spotted. Several more animal sounds followed, then dozens. She pushed onward with strength born of fear, ears ringing.

Dieredon reached the rope and scampered up the wall with ease. Even though she knew better, Jessilynn spared a glance over her shoulder. Dozens of bird-men from each encampment were rushing toward her, and further away came the wolf-men patrol.

Run, she told herself. *Run, run, run!*

Lungs burning, she reached the rope and grabbed on. She didn't even bother to slow down, slamming into the castle wall.

"Hurry!" Dieredon shouted from above. Arrows flew from his bow, and she heard pained cries as the approaching bird-men dropped one by one. More howls, more shrieks. Soldiers up top had joined in defending her, bolts plunging into the vile army. A body of a bird-man rolled beside her, an arrow lodged in its eye. Jessilynn stared at it; panic froze her in place. She had to move. She had to act.

Jessilynn grabbed the rope and began to climb, but she was weighed down. Her armor, while light compared to the platemail Jerico and Lathaar wore, still had significant portions of chainmail. And then there was the matter of Darius's sword...

Though it pained her, she reached across her back and undid the leather clasp of the enormous sword's sheath. The sword slid free, landing below her in the dirt with a heavy thud. The weight no longer on her shoulders, she pulled herself up, all her concentration on putting one hand higher. As she neared the top, Dieredon leaned down and helped her over. She collapsed on her back, gasping for air.

The soldier they'd first alerted stood above her, grinning.

"Welcome to the Castle of the Yellow Rose, you crazy bastards," he said. "I hope you enjoy your stay."

The soldier escorted them through several refugee camps to the castle proper. Jessilynn winced at the sight of the frightened and hungry people, most sleeping on the ground or on shared blankets. Only a few of the young and the elderly had been given tents. Their arrival seemed to give hope to the people, and Jessilynn tried to smile and stand tall as the downtrodden greeted her. Even as they cheered, or shook her hand, she felt like she were a living lie. They thought she symbolized the arrival of an army come to save them. They were wrong.

Once past the camps, they reached a well-worn dirt road leading to the keep. It was a tall but plain structure, four square

The King of the Vile

sides of even length. Its only real decoration was the impressive yellow rose painted across the front, the flower dipping with a single petal falling free. Vines grew from either side of the castle doors, coming together to form the stem of the rose. The yellow rose was the symbol of the Hemman family, who had ruled the North for decades.

"We've already alerted Arthur to your arrival," their escort said as they climbed the gentle rise. "I'm sure he will be happy to greet such distinguished visitors."

"I'm sure he will," Dieredon said. "I doubt he'd received too many visitors lately."

"Quite the opposite, actually," the soldier said, waving a hand toward the refugee camps behind them. "We have far more visitors than we can feed and protect."

Dieredon smiled grimly. "True enough."

The castle doors opened, and the soldier bid them to enter. Unescorted, Jessilynn followed the elf inside to find the lord of the castle waiting for them beyond the entrance.

"Greetings," said Arthur Hemman, "and welcome to my home."

He was an older man, though his perfect posture and sparkling green eyes seemed like that of a young soldier. His hair and beard were carefully trimmed, and both contained a significant portion of gray. He wore a thin suit of chainmail over his clothes, and over it, a tunic bearing the yellow rose.

"Greetings, Lord Arthur," Dieredon said, and he bowed low. "I am Dieredon, Scoutmaster of the Quellan elves. With me is Jessilynn of the Citadel. We've come to pledge our aid."

"The Citadel," Arthur said. "It still makes me smile knowing it was rebuilt. You continue a proud tradition, Jessilynn. Jerico once crawled through mud-filled tunnels to bypass a siege of my castle, and now you sneak through an army of beasts to do the same."

Jessilynn blushed. To be compared to Jerico in any way seemed ludicrous. All she'd really done was run for a bit and then climb a rope. Did he have to make it sound so…valiant?

"Thank you," Jessilynn said, not sure of what else to say.

Arthur smiled, gestured for the two to follow him.

"The situation isn't quite as dire as it seems," he said as he climbed a set of stone steps. They exited at the third floor, into a wide room filled with a rectangular table and dozens of chairs. Spread across the table was a worn map of northern Mordan. Scattered about the map were sheets of parchment, and when Jessilynn glanced at them, she saw symbols marking extensive catalogs of provisions, weapons, and numbers of soldiers.

"It seems dire to me," Dieredon said as the lord took a seat before the map.

"I said not *quite* as dire, not that things were pleasant," Arthur said. "Our food should last several weeks, and our water all winter. We've culled fighting men from the refugees as they arrived, and so far the primitive beasts out there have shown no capacity to build something as simple as a ladder to bypass our walls. Even if they tried, I have five hundred manning the walks. We'll spill our share of blood, but we'll hold them back."

Jessilynn thought of the thousands upon thousands of strong, fast creatures the King of the Vile commanded. Only five hundred? Arthur thought he could hold them off with only five hundred? It seemed Dieredon had the same fears as her, and he was not afraid to speak it aloud.

"Your men will not be enough to hold back the tide," he said. "What you see out there is but a shadow of Manfeaster's full power. When they arrive…"

"When they arrive, they will find elves and paladins to stand against them alongside us," Arthur said. At their awkward silence he paused, and leaned back into his chair. "Reinforcements are coming, are they not?"

Jessilynn stared at the map, and the Citadel that seemed so close on paper, yet so far away.

"No," Dieredon said. "The only reinforcements will be soldiers for Mordeina, though I cannot say when they will arrive."

"A cruel jest this is, isn't it?" Arthur said, sighing as he drummed his fingers. "Representatives of both elves and the Paladins of Ashhur arrive at my doorstep, yet you come alone in offering aid? Forgive me for saying this, but you two are not enough."

The King of the Vile

"We were never meant to be," Dieredon said. "Nor should we *need* to be. Where are the angels? Have you not called for their aid?"

"I have," Arthur said. "Again and again I shine light from the little cylinder they gave me, lighting up the night sky like a thunderstorm, yet nothing. No message. No reinforcements."

Arthur stood, and he picked up one of the parchments detailing their provisions.

"I haven't been rationing as carefully as I should," he said quietly. "I wanted to keep my soldiers strong and ready to fight. Once aid came, we'd scatter them with ease. Once..." He looked up at Dieredon. "I've talked with the various refugee groups as they arrived, and it's clear we're being converged upon from all sides. You said this...Manfeaster commands them. I believe you, if only because it explains why the different beasts are working together to lay siege to my home. Tell me, how many of these creatures does Manfeaster command?"

Dieredon did an admirable job keeping his expression passive.

"Fifteen to twenty thousand, by my estimate."

"Twenty thousand," Arthur said. He slumped in his chair. "Ashhur save us all. I only have five hundred, Dieredon. Five hundred against twenty thousand! Even with the aid of my walls, it won't be enough. And if they find a way to break through the doors, it'll be a massacre."

The lord's words left Jessilynn more and more unnerved. She'd thought being inside the walls would allow her to feel safe, but now she only felt trapped. Why had they come? Why had she thought she might accomplish anything against such numbers? She'd seen the army for herself. She knew the numbers Manfeaster commanded.

Dieredon put his wicked-looking bow atop the table and stared at Arthur with the confidence of an elf who had never once suffered defeat.

"You lose faith," he said. "With Jessilynn and I guarding your walls, your five hundred will fight like five thousand. No matter how well organized they might seem, no matter how strong their king might be, these creatures are still primal beasts that will turn on one another in enough time. All we have to do is survive, so that is what we'll do. Help will come, from the Citadel, or Mordeina, or the angels. This threat is too grave to be ignored."

Arthur rose from his seat, leaned his arms atop the table.

"I know the reputation you carry, Scoutmaster," he said, meeting the elf's gaze. "And I watched Jerico stand against waves of enemies like an immovable mountain. Even if that little girl over there is capable of doing the same, it won't be enough. You've not come to save us, only die with us."

That was it. Jessilynn could stand no more, especially to hear herself belittled so insultingly.

"There were once two Kings of the Vile," she said, "until this 'little girl' killed one of them, alone and surrounded by dozens more of the creatures. I didn't give up then, and I won't give up now. If we die, we die, but we'll die protecting innocents from the evil of this world. It's not our fault so many others refuse to do the same."

Arthur turned her way, and it took all her willpower not to wilt under his gaze.

"When the end comes, I will be out there with my soldiers, bleeding and dying with a sword in my hand," he said. "And after I fall, the people I swore my life to protect, those not already slaughtered on their flight here, will be torn to pieces. I have not given up, paladin. Do not misread my frustration for hopelessness. My fury is not for you, but those who would abandon us in our time of need. Now if you'll excuse me, I have work to do. You have my permission to explore the castle as you wish, as well as all castle grounds. Forgive me, though, for I have no rooms to offer. Right now, my castle is reserved for the sick and the dying." The lord shook his head. "Which is everyone behind my walls, if the south abandons us to our fate."

He turned from the table, and a moment later Lord Arthur vanished down the stairs. Jessilynn felt herself trembling in the cavernous room, overcome with anger, frustration, and fear. When she caught Dieredon looking at her, she bowed her head and crossed her arms behind her.

"I'm sorry," she said. "I didn't mean to snap like that. Jerico told us of Lord Arthur, and of how noble he was, but that dour old man was nothing like the stories."

"Do not judge him too harshly," Dieredon said. "Nothing is crueler than giving hope to a hopeless man and then immediately snatching it away. Now come with me. We need to see how much time we have."

Jessilynn kept quiet and followed the elf back to the stairs. Instead of going down, they climbed up until they emerged onto the roof of the castle. Jessilynn crossed her arms against the sudden chill of the wind. Dieredon walked to the parapet and gazed westward. From such height they had a beautiful view of the surrounding grasslands beyond the protective wall surrounding the castle grounds. Everything in the far distance was hazy, but Jessilynn knew Dieredon's sharp eyes would be the envy of a hawk.

"It's as I feared," Dieredon said as he shaded his eyes from the sun. "Pray angels come swiftly, Jessilynn. We have two days, maybe three at most, before we're out of time."

"Why? What do you see?"

Dieredon shook his head and grabbed his bow as if needing its comfort.

"The wolf-men," he said. "And their king."

13

"So how goes your studies?" Roand asked as he stepped through the door.

"Wonderfully," Tarlak replied. He sat at his desk in the room that doubled as both his residence and study. On one side was his bed, mattress stuffed with down so soft it hurt his back upon waking. Near it was a dresser with what few clothes he had, mostly black robes. Tarlak hated the color, for it reminded him too much of Karak's priests, but it was hardly the highest entry on his list of daily things driving him insane. There was also his entrapment in the tower and Cecil's constant presence. The worst, though, was the burning, itchy pendant sticking to the skin around his neck.

The vast majority of Tarlak's room was dedicated to the study and practice of magic. Three shelves lined the walls, each filled with notes, tomes on random, obscure topics such as astral projection and polymorphism, and various alchemical ingredients and spell components. Roand had given him complete freedom to choose studies, so long as he shared his results with the rest of the tower.

Tarlak pointed at Cecil, who sat in a chair opposite him.

"Tell me, does that hair look natural to you?"

Roand crossed his arms and looked over Tarlak's assigned apprentice and servant. Cecil sat hunched in the chair, face and neck flushed from anger and embarrassment. On his face grew a red beard that hung a foot below his neck.

"Natural as in to him, or as in real hair?" Roand asked. "Because it clearly does not match Cecil's blond hair."

"Real hair," Tarlak said.

"Of course it looks like real hair," Cecil muttered, scratching at it. "It itches like mad, too."

The King of the Vile

Tarlak slapped at his apprentice's hand.

"Don't scratch. Wait, go ahead and scratch. Does me no good if it falls right off the moment someone gives it a good tug."

"I take it this endeavor is of a selfish nature?" Roand stated.

"That's right," Tarlak said, patting his own burned face. "Need to replace what you and your ilk took from me. Two weeks now, and not a whisker. Clearly magical interference will be required to look like my dashing self again."

He waved his fingers through motions he'd learned from one of his books. Cecil's beard thickened the tiniest bit, the hairs losing some of their curl.

"An illusion spell would be easier," Roand said.

"I don't want illusion spells," Tarlak said, frowning as he examined his work. "I want the real thing. I want to feel the wind blowing through my hair. I want to tug at my beard as I think deep thoughts, such as 'how does one escape an inescapable collar of disintegration?' Speaking of beard, Cecil, yours is clearly not red enough." He snapped his fingers. "Hrm, too much red now, and it's still too long. Each tweak's just making it worse. We need to start all over. Go back to your room and give yourself a good shave. I'll wait."

Cecil glared as he rose from his stool. The combination of his mop-top blond hair and reddish beard made him look ridiculous, and Tarlak grinned ear to ear as his apprentice left the room. Cecil's constant presence was annoying, true, but it did allow occasional moments of entertainment.

"So," Tarlak said, swiveling on his stool to face the lord of the tower. "I've been giving some thought to this pendant of yours. Would a transitional state of matter do the trick?"

Roand frowned, the fire in his hair rippling.

"The moment you left a physical state, the spell would vaporize the substance you did become."

Tarlak clapped his hands as if disappointed. After he'd been inducted into the Council, Roand had brought him to his room and attached the pendant he currently wore about his neck. It was a chain of thick gold, with the front containing seven rubies of varying sizes. The rubies stuck to him like honey, and no matter what the time of day, or the temperature of the room, they remained uncomfortably warm. He tried shifting it up and down his neck as much as possible to keep the discomfort minimal, and every time he revealed thick red blotches on his skin. The purpose of the pendant was incredibly simple: should Roand ever desire it, for any reason, he could activate the magic of the pendant, turning Tarlak into dust.

"What if I teleport?" Tarlak asked.

"The pendant would travel with you," Roand said.

"Polymorphed myself into a mudskipper?"

"The pendant would resize itself to match your new size."

Tarlak tapped his lips.

"Waves of dispel magic?"

"Automatic activation prior to any detrimental effects."

Before Tarlak could ask again, Roand sighed, interrupting him.

"That pendant is the finest product of my lifetime of work," he said. "Four men have worn it, and all four have died attempting to remove it after varying lengths of time. No spell, no trick, no method possible will remove that pendant from your body or protect you from its disintegration. But let us presume otherwise. If you *did* discover a method to safely remove the pendant, what makes you think I would tell you?"

Tarlak grinned.

"What makes you think if I discovered a method that actually worked, I'd ask you?"

"You are amusing, Tarlak," Roand said, chuckling. "I am glad you did not die during Antonil's defeat."

"Same here," Tarlak muttered as Cecil returned, his face cleanly shaven. "Ah, welcome back, baby-face. Are you ready to grow a beard?"

"No," Cecil said, kicking over the stool he'd been sitting on. "I will not endure another beard, or change of my nose, or turning my hair into that bloody awful shade of red."

Tarlak wagged a finger at him.

"You're my servant, mister Towerborn, which means you'll aid in my experiments in any non-lethal way I see fit."

The King of the Vile

"No," Cecil said, a feverish look in his eye. "I'm not your servant, not anymore. Tarlak Eschaton, I hereby challenge you for your seat on the Council. Do you accept?"

Tarlak raised an eyebrow as he peered over Cecil's shoulder to the bemused-looking Roand.

"Do I have a choice?" he asked.

Roand's subdued laughter was answer enough.

Tarlak and Cecil stood on opposite ends of the bridge connecting the two towers, Tarlak before the Masters' door, Cecil the Apprentices'. Wizards and apprentices watched from windows of both towers. Their judge, Roand, stood to the side of the bridge on a floating disc of flame that swirled beneath his feet but did not singe a single thread of his orange shoes. It felt like a spectator sport, including cheers from the onlookers as Roand announced their names.

"Cecil Towerborn, you have claimed a seat on the Council," Roand said, his voice booming with melodramatics. "Tarlak Eschaton, it is your seat he has claimed. You must defend it with your life, or surrender your magic forever."

Tarlak beckoned over the Lord of the Council.

"Just for curiosity's sake," he asked, "how is it you will enforce such a punishment should I decide to surrender and vacate the premises instead of fighting that loon over there?"

"Dead men cast no spells," Roand said.

"Fair enough," Tarlak said. "Then I'm keeping my seat. Sorry, Cecil. Better luck next time."

"There won't be a next time," Cecil shouted from the other side. "Your corpse will float upon the Rigon before this day is through!"

"Sure it will," Tarlak muttered as Roand floated back to the center of the bridge on his burning disc. "Overeager little brat."

Roand resumed his little speech, with Tarlak convinced it was more for the onlookers than him and Cecil.

"The rules for the duel are few, and handed down to us by Turock Escheton in the early days of the founding. These rules will be enforced by myself, and by others of the Council if necessary. Whoever leaves this bridge, be it of your own accord or at the hands of your opponent, forfeits the duel. Though the bridge is protected with many ancient runes; anyone attempting to destroy the bridge immediately forfeits the duel. Once the duel has begun, it shall continue until a winner is established, halting only by my direct intervention. You may use any magic at your disposal, so long as you do not violate either of the first three rules. Is this understood?"

"Understood," the two said in unison.

Roand raised his right arm and glanced back and forth between them. "May this duel be one of honor, skill, and courage." His arm dropped. "You may begin."

Cecil immediately took the offensive, just as Tarlak thought he would. Twin lances of ice shot from the apprentice's hands, arcing over the bridge only to collide with the magical shield Tarlak summoned to protect himself. As the ice shattered, the shield rippled and distorted his sight of Cecil on the other side. The apprentice laughed.

"I've watched you, you know," he said, several more lances streaking in. Tarlak grunted as he poured more power into the shield. The ice struck, then broke, the shards scattered across the red and black brick before plunging into the Rigon River far below.

"Have you now?" Tarlak asked. "I should have guessed you were into that."

Just to annoy the petulant apprentice, Tarlak flicked a ball of fire no larger than a beetle toward Cecil's head.

"Joke all you want," Cecil said as he ducked beneath the attack, the fire striking the tower and fizzling into white smoke. "I watched you perform your experiments. I've seen how you struggle." Fire swelled around his hands, bright and golden. "You're weak. You're soft. You're pathetic."

He punctuated each sentence with a ball of flame. Tarlak dropped to one knee, his fingers dancing. Ice swelled before him, rising up to form a wall. The fire struck its smooth surface, filling it with cracks but failing to penetrate.

"Oh stop," Tarlak shouted over his ice wall. "You're making me blush."

The King of the Vile

"Enough!" Cecil screamed. The apprentice slammed his hands together, and a wave of forced shattered the ice wall and sent Tarlak rolling. He hit the door with a thud and let out a gasp. It seemed he'd struck a nerve.

"I am tired of never being taken seriously!" Cecil said as lightning crackled around his clenched fists. "I am tired of being everyone's joke!"

Lightning crashed against Tarlak's revived shield. He gritted his teeth as the lightning slammed in again and again, vanishing mere feet away from his body against the invisible protection.

"No jokes then," Tarlak said when Cecil finally stopped. The apprentice doubled over, gasping for air. He'd overextended himself, and Tarlak had no doubt a pounding headache would soon follow. Cecil had potential, but no control, no subtlety. The only problem was, he wasn't exactly wrong when he mentioned how weak Tarlak felt...

"No jokes, just wisdom," Tarlak continued. "Surrender now. This isn't worth your life. I've fought prophets and gods, Cecil. You don't compare."

Instead of calming him down, Cecil was enraged further. Dozens of red arrows shot from his palms, each one shimmering with heat. Tarlak slammed his hands together, summoning a powerful gust of wind perpendicular to the bridge. It shoved the arrows off course, and then with a thought, Tarlak adjusted the wind so it blew against Cecil as well. He hoped the apprentice would go toppling over the edge, ending the duel before anyone was seriously hurt.

He wasn't so lucky. Cecil planted his feet and pushed a hand toward the wind. Arcane words of power poured off his tongue, countering the spell. The wind died, having mussed his hair.

"I've spent years learning from the masters," Cecil said, steadily approaching with his hands out at either side. "Years reading texts, memorizing spells, practicing the movements and incantations. But you...you never stepped foot inside these walls. You don't *deserve* to claim a seat on the Council."

He pushed his wrists together, and a massive stream of fire rolled forth like from the mouth of a dragon. Tarlak summoned another shield and the fire wrapped around him, unable to penetrate, but the shield wasn't nearly as strong as Tarlak preferred, and sweat trickled down his neck. It seemed Cecil had a thing for fire. Having Roand as a mentor for so long probably had something to do with that.

"Texts?" Tarlak said, ignoring his growing headache. "Practice? I've fought real battles while you stuck your nose in a book, Cecil. Forgive me for being unimpressed."

Pride pushed him to ignore caution and counter Cecil's spray of fire with one of his own. His shield dropped, replaced by a deluge of flame. The spray was brighter, wider, and it pushed back Cecil's as if it weren't even there. Cecil panicked, dropping the fire to summon a shield. Tarlak watched the fire swarm about the apprentice's body. If he pushed harder, he could break through, reducing the man to ashes, but he didn't. Cecil was in over his head. If Tarlak could convince him of that, there'd be no reason for anyone to die.

Tarlak killed the spell. Cecil fell to one knee, gasping for air.

"You're right," Tarlak said softly. The two were only several feet apart, each having approached the other while unleashing their spray of fire. "I've not recovered all my strength, but I've recovered enough. I once matched spells with Celestia's daughter of balance, a woman who could level a mountain with her mind. Do you really think you could do the same, Cecil?"

"I don't care what you've done," Cecil said, voice growing louder and louder. "I don't care!"

He slammed an open palm to the bridge, and blue mist rolled off in waves, forming writhing tentacles that ended with dozens of sharp spikes.

That's a new one, thought Tarlak as he backed away. Tentacles lashed at him, and he ducked one, then sidestepped another. He dodged a third too late, and the blue tentacle ripped through his robe, leaving a shallow wound across the ribs. Pushing his wrists together, words of magic raced off Tarlak's tongue. An invisible shockwave knocked Cecil to his rear. The tentacles shimmered, the power holding them together broke. The mist wafted into the air and faded.

Tarlak held his wounded side and checked the hand to see blood coating his fingers and palm.

"That's just rude," he said, turning his attention back to Cecil. The apprentice had risen to his feet, wavering unsteadily. A smile was on his face.

"I drew blood," he said. "Did Celestia's daughter ever accomplish that?"

Tarlak chuckled, thinking of the dangerous, unpredictable Tessanna.

"She didn't draw blood," he said. "She *used* it."

He flung his hand toward Cecil, flicking the blood off his fingers. Taking a trick from Deathmask, Tarlak snapped his fingers just before the drops splashed across Cecil's robes. The blood exploded into flame, tearing holes in fabric and blackening skin. Cecil dropped to the bridge and rolled perilously close to the edge before stopping. A low moan escaped his mouth. As he pushed to his feet, there was a feverish look to his eyes.

"A neat trick," he said "Mind if I try?"

Tarlak realized too late what Cecil was planning. The apprentice pointed one hand toward Tarlak, magic rolling off it, while the other twisted into a few quick shapes. Then Cecil snapped his fingers and blood on Tarlak's side exploded, the impact knocking him over. Tarlak caught himself before the edge of the bridge, and he screamed at the horrible pain wracking his body. Where he'd been cut was now a blackened mess.

Gods damn it, thought Tarlak. *Haven't I been burned enough?*

Tarlak's strength was already waning, and after such a hit, he struggled to focus through the pain. He knew Cecil was approaching and he had to react. Rolling onto his back, he began to cast a spell. Cecil's boot pushed down on his throat, silencing it. The apprentice leered down at him.

"Is that all you have?" he asked, fire burning about his hands, the beginnings of another spell on his lips.

Tarlak's fingers danced as he focused his mind elsewhere. Cecil laughed, nearly ecstatic with joy. He pulled his boot off Tarlak's neck to kick the wounded side, and it took all of Tarlak's concentration to keep his fingers moving. The heel then pressed back down on his throat, denying him breath.

"Go ahead," Cecil said. The fire on his hands became daggers, and he held them ready to throw. "Try. Try to cast a spell."

Tarlak tried to answer, but the boot prevented him. Cecil acquiesced, lessening the pressure so a few words could escape.

"I already did, you asshole," Tarlak said.

From far beneath the bridge, a chunk of earth flew from the riverbank. Before Cecil could realize what Tarlak meant, the boulder slammed into him, lifting him into the air and flinging him over the side of the bridge. Tarlak lunged after him, hanging half-over the bridge as he waved a hand. Ice spread from the side of the bridge, forming a swirling tendril that caught Cecil where he flew. The ice wrapped about Cecil's body, trapping him.

As cheers roared from both towers, Tarlak slowly rose to his feet. His head pounded, and he struggled to breathe.

"I think I won," he said as Roand floated closer on his fiery disc.

"Not yet," Roand said, voice low, just for the two of them. "These duels are to the death, Eschaton. It's the only way to keep the apprentices from wasting the time of masters."

Tarlak did his best to keep his face passive, not wanting anyone else watching to know the purpose of their discussion.

"He doesn't need to die," Tarlak insisted.

"No," Roand said. "But if I'm to believe you've cast aside your foolish beliefs in Ashhur, he does."

Tarlak glanced at the trapped Cecil. The apprentice looked like he'd been knocked unconscious by the hit from the boulder, his head drooped and his eyes closed. Just a foolish man, Tarlak knew, warped by his time in the towers.

"And if I refuse?" Tarlak asked.

Roand shrugged.

"Then I'll activate the pendant around your neck."

Tarlak shook his head, hardly pleased with that potential outcome. An idea struck him, and he did his best to keep his expression passive.

"Sorry, Cecil," he said. He snapped his fingers, spreading ice all around Cecil's body, sealing him inside like a cocoon. When it was finished, he stomped a foot against the icy thread attaching the cocoon to the bridge. It shattered, and the cocoon fell to the river, landing with a loud splash.

Tarlak turned to the Masters' Tower and bowed low.

"Have I proven myself satisfactory?" he asked, projecting his voice as loud as his wounded side allowed.

Their applause was a definitive 'yes'. Roand floated off the disc and onto the bridge, and he spared a glance down to the Rigon River.

"It seems you're in need of a new apprentice," Roand said. "I'll assign you one shortly."

"Thanks," Tarlak said, clutching his side as he walked toward the door of the Masters' Tower. "Let's hope this one doesn't suffer a similar fate."

Roand chuckled, and he smiled as if it were the funniest thing.

Laugh, you lunatic, Tarlak thought as the tower door opened, and several other wizards greeted him with enormous smiles. *Laugh, each and every last damn one of you.*

As the door shut behind him, wizards shaking his hand and slapping his healthy shoulder, Tarlak tugged at the burning pendant about his neck swore that when he finally escaped the towers, he would be the last one laughing.

14

"Admit it," Aurelia said as she walked through the marketplace, little Gregory's hand in hers. "It feels great to get out of the castle."

Aubrienna bounced atop Harruq's shoulders, legs wrapped around his neck, hands gripping his hair.

"It's also slightly painful," Harruq said. Aubby tugged hard on his hair to stay upright as if to prove his point.

"You've been beaten, stabbed, and smacked around with magic," Aurelia said. "I think you can handle a little bit of hair-pulling." She stopped at a stall selling assorted necklaces. Aubrienna leaned forward, straining to see, while Gregory stood on his tiptoes and eyed the nearest few sets.

"Handle it? Sure. Like it? Nope. That's more your thing."

Aurelia smacked his shoulder.

"Behave. We have children with us, and in public."

"Would the little king like a necklace?" asked the squat lady running the stall. Her face was caked with paint, her lips a powerful shade of purple. Gregory shied away, and Harruq winced. The boy was still young, but acting so timid would not help the strained trust the people held in him.

"Go on, Gregory," Harruq said, hoping to coach the child out from his shyness. "Pick one you like."

Gregory peered around Aurelia's leg, giving the strange lady a wary look that would have amused Harruq under most circumstances.

"I'm not sure yet," he said.

"I like that one!" Aubby shouted from above, lunging forward and pointing. The act nearly sent her tumbling off

Harruq's shoulders, and he had to grab her by the legs to keep her stable.

"I'm sure the necklace is very pretty," Harruq told his daughter, "but let's not go diving headfirst to the ground for it, eh?"

Aubby laughed, kicking her feet together beneath his chin. Harruq grinned; he had to admit, being in the open air, surrounded by people, did help his spirits. Sure, they gave him wary looks, and the crowd would grow chilly when an occasional angel flew over, but overall it was fun to pretend things were back to the way they'd been in Veldaren, when the only responsibilities he had were to his family and not to an entire nation.

A scream from far down the road jolted his thoughts. The market was built into the side of the hill leading up to the castle, and he saw a gathering crowd of men and women farther down the way. Shouts grew louder, more numerous. From within the crowd, Harruq spotted the white feathers of an angel's wings, but nothing more than that.

"What's the matter?" Aurelia asked.

"I don't know," Harruq said. "But whatever it is, it's going sour fast."

He pulled Aubrienna off his shoulders and placed her before his wife.

"Get them to the castle," he said. "I'll find out what's going on."

"Are you sure you don't want to come with us?" Aurelia asked.

"I'm supposed to be in charge of this city," Harruq said. "I might as well act like it."

"What about your swords?"

Harruq shrugged. He'd left them in the castle, along with his armor, figuring neither would be needed.

"I got my fists," he said. "If need be, I'll improvise."

He hugged his wife, kissed his daughter on the forehead, and started jogging down the hill. Behind him, he heard the telltale hiss of a portal opening, and he breathed easier. The gathering crowd filled the entire street from side to side, and he heard cries for guards. People were flooding in from all directions, and Harruq sensed the rumblings of a potential riot as a lone accusation echoed like a chant.

"Murderer, murderer, murderer."

The crowd's numbers had swelled to well above a hundred when Harruq heard another shriek of pain pierce through the streets, the stalls, and the people. The reaction was both immediate and terrifying. Those in the outer ring fell back, scattering in all directions. Harruq used his size and strength to shove his way through. One young man tried to push Harruq aside, and when he failed, he swung at his jaw. Harruq caught his fist and held it in the air. The frightened man gaped, his anger quickly replaced with fear.

"I'm…I'm sorry," he stammered.

"Sure you are," Harruq said, tossing him aside. The crowd spread out, about fifty now screaming and throwing stones from a wide ring. In their center, enormous mace held before him, was Judarius. At his feet lay the dead body of a man whose face was crushed to a pulp. Two others lay nearby, sobbing, one with a crushed arm, the other a knee bent completely the wrong direction. The crowd refused to get any closer, and they hurled their accusation along with their stones.

"Murderer!"

Judarius kept his mace raised and his body hunched, letting his armor and weapon reflect the projectiles.

"Get back!" the angel shouted, not that any listened. Harruq pushed through the ring, and he screamed Judarius's name until the angel lifted his head.

"What are you still doing here?" Harruq shouted. "Get to the castle!"

Judarius spread his wings and he jumped into the air. Before he could fly, the crowd surged toward him. One brave woman lunged ahead of the others, her arms wrapping around Judarius's leg. Two others grabbed hold of his arms and neck. Still baffled by what was happening, Harruq tried holding back those near him to keep Judarius from being overwhelmed. His efforts were in vain as Judarius took his mace and swung, smacking the woman in the face. Blood blasted from her nose and mouth, and she collapsed

The King of the Vile

to the street with an aching cry. Judarius dropped to his feet, swinging his mace in a wide circle and screaming.

"I said get back!"

With his free arm he grabbed the man holding his neck and tossed him aside like a rag doll. Harruq elbowed someone in his way, pushed a woman aside, and then grabbed the last person hanging onto Judarius.

"Enough!" Harruq screamed, rolling the man across the ground. Judarius hefted his mace, and seeing no one charging, again unfurled his wings. Screams followed him, accusations of murder and butchery, but Harruq knew that'd have to be settled another time. The angel soared into the sky.

"Leave him be," Harruq ordered as their hatred turned toward him. "Do you want to die?"

"They murdered my son!" an older man shouted back. "We saw it, we all did!"

Harruq looked to the dead body. Blood and gore was all that remained of his face.

"He must have done something wrong," Harruq said, but there was no conviction to his defense.

Others quickly shouted him down. From all around him, Harruq heard more shouts of murder, and just as worrisome, he heard the flutter of angel wings. Amid the unrest, most began to flow toward the castle, but the older man approached Harruq, recognition in his eyes.

"You," he said. "You're the steward. You can do something about this. You have to. You have to."

Harruq opened his mouth, but no words came out. Nothing made sense. He didn't know what was happening, what was true, what promises he could make. The older man grabbed him by the shoulders, crying now, hands trembling, voice shaking.

"They murdered my son," he said. "My son, don't you hear me, my poor son..."

"I hear you," Harruq said as he looked to the castle. Accusations spread like wildfire, the pent up rage releasing in a sudden, violent fury. Not two hundred feet away, a stall was smashed to pieces by four men, and an angel landed, attempting to prevent the theft. Before the four men could retreat, one lay dying, and two others bleeding. Already smoke began to rise from throughout the city.

The grieving father looked to the corpse of his son, then cried into Harruq's chest.

"I hear you," Harruq whispered again, having never before felt so weak and useless in all his life.

※

Several hundred people gathered before the closed gates of the castle, chanting for a trial. Harruq had to shout and wave at the guards until they noticed him, then rush through the opening they made with their shields. Once inside the entryway, he found Sir Wess waiting for him, looking pale and nervous.

"I'm glad you've returned safely," Sir Wess said. "We've received reports of riots from all four quarters, plus the outer ring. I've sent out squads to confirm our guard stations are still secure, but beyond that, I've been waiting for your orders."

"Get them out there," Harruq said. "Every soldier you have, get them onto those streets ordering people to their homes. We've got to keep them from burning this whole damn city to the ground."

"What of the angels?"

Harruq stopped halfway toward his throne. "What of them?" he asked, turning to glare at the knight.

"The angels think they're helping to calm the riots, but they're not," Sir Wess said, not backing down in the slightest. "You need to get them out of Mordeina immediately."

"How?" Harruq asked. "By ordering them?"

"You're steward, and act in the name of the king."

"Don't you get it?" Harruq shouted. "I'm king, but I'm not *their* king. I have no authority over them."

"They live on our lands now," Sir Wess said, voice dropping as he stepped closer. "Which means they must obey our laws even as they enforce them. You do have authority over them, Steward. Now act like it."

Harruq's jaw tightened, but before he could respond, he heard the flapping of wings. He glanced up to see two angels flying through the tall window of the throne room: Azariah and Judarius.

The King of the Vile

"See to your men," Harruq told Sir Wess as the angels landed. "You have a long day ahead of you. Do whatever you can to protect the lives of the innocent."

"As you wish," the knight said. He bowed low, and glared at the angels as he exited the throne room. Harruq spun in place, gesturing to the other guards.

"All of you," he shouted. "Out. Now."

Once they were gone, Harruq marched up to Judarius, and it took all his control to keep his fists at his sides instead of pounding them into the angel's face.

"What in Ashhur's name happened out there?" he asked.

"I dispensed justice," Judarius said, as if it were obvious.

"Justice?" Harruq asked. "I watched you smash a woman's face in for grabbing your leg. Was that *justice?*"

"I was defending myself," the angel said, growing angrier. "I have that right."

Harruq flung up his hands. "Perfect. Just perfect. It's bad enough your kind stormed into homes in the middle of the godsdamn night to slaughter those you once forgave, but now you perform your executions in broad daylight? Do any of you, *any of you*, have a clue how precarious our peace has been?"

Harruq stopped as a third angel flew in through the window and landed beside the others.

"The riot has spread throughout the entire city," Ahaesarus said. "For now, my angels are focusing on maintaining the fires. Anything else is proving too dangerous. I have never seen the people so angry before." He looked to Harruq. "Do you know the cause?"

Harruq waved a hand at Judarius.

"They say your commander here killed a man without reason, and in full view of a market crowd, no less."

Ahaesarus's face reddened.

"That is preposterous," he said. "We have sworn our lives to mankind's protection. Surely they do not think—"

"Have you seen the fires?" Harruq interrupted. "Heard the chants for trial? Yes, Ahaesarus, they do. They think it very much so, and we need to do something about it before the entire nation descends into anarchy!"

"They are spoiled children," Judarius said with contempt. "I witnessed sin and performed my duties accordingly. We are Ashhur's divine wardens, yet they treat us like miserable sinners no different from them."

"Talk like that isn't going to help," Harruq said, grinding his teeth. "The people want a trial. They need to believe your kind will be held to the same standards as you hold them."

"But we don't hold ourselves to the same standards," said Azariah. "We hold ourselves to a *higher* standard."

"Then you have nothing to worry about! Let me show the city that you aren't above them, that an angel cannot kill a man and get away with it without at least a trial. If Judarius is innocent, then there's nothing to be afraid of."

"This is preposterous," Azariah argued. "What angel would commit murder? We do not kill without reason. We are this city's protection, its guardians in the sky. We endure their scorn, their fear, their unjustified hatred, all in hopes of spreading Ashhur's teachings, and now you would have them drag us down to their level through pretty ignorance? To put Judarius's fate in the hands of frightened children?" The angel stomped his foot into the stone, cracking the floor of the throne room. "No. We will not allow it. If you insist upon a trial, then *we* will be the ones to hold it. That is the only way we will agree to such a farce."

"You are not the one to make such a decision," Ahaesarus said. "Our city is in chaos, armies invade from both north and south. We cannot afford such distractions. Give humanity their trial. If Judarius is innocent, he has nothing to fear."

"To submit ourselves to mankind's courts will forever alter how we may serve Dezrel," Azariah argued. "You're right. I am not the one to make such a decision, and neither are you. We have already summoned a conclave of all angels for three days hence, so we shall put it to a vote then to decide who shall judge Judarius—mankind, or our own tribunal. Once these matters are concluded, and the city has regained some semblance of order, then we may look into other threats."

"Listen to me," Harruq said, fighting to remain calm. "I am telling you this for your sake. The people need to feel like humanity still controls its own fate. They need to believe we have

The King of the Vile

the capacity to govern ourselves. If they come to view you as their jailors, and not their protectors..."

"We are their guardians," Azariah said. "With all the responsibilities that entails. We will at least discuss allowing them a trial, Harruq. It is far more than they deserve."

He nodded at Judarius, and the two spread their wings to fly away. Ahaesarus grabbed Judarius by the shoulder, keeping him still.

"Wait," he said. "Tell me you did not murder that man. Let me hear the truth. That is all I ask."

Judarius pulled his shoulder free.

"That man deserved death, and I gave it to him. Now let me go. I have work to do."

With a gust of wind, he soared to the ceiling window. Azariah bowed and followed after. Harruq shook his head as he watched them go.

"Did he lie?" he asked.

"No."

Harruq laughed. It was the only reaction he could give.

"That's not much comfort," he said.

"No," Ahaesarus said softly. "It isn't."

"Azariah mentioned you were already preparing a conclave," Harruq asked. "Does that mean you'll finally decide to fly north to help?"

Ahaesarus sighed.

"I hope to address that concern, but that is not the real reason," he said. "The conclave was actually called so we may hold trial."

"A trial for who?" Harruq asked, face twitching.

"Given your prior relationship, we did not wish to tell you until the day of the proceedings. Azariah felt this would prevent you from taking rash measures. The trial is for the man responsible for the fall of Avlimar. Before the entire conclave of angels, he will be judged and sentenced."

"The fall of Avlimar?" Harruq said. "You mean—"

"Yes," Ahaesarus said. "The man who calls himself Deathmask. We found him at last."

15

Avoiding the road made his travel all the more arduous, but with the Kerran army so close, Alric knew he couldn't afford the risk. The tall grass slapped his thighs, and bugs constantly buzzed in his ears, but at least insects wouldn't imprison him.

There were still several hours left in the day when he reached a slender stream he had to cross. Alric stopped walking. He was exhausted, and the thought of trying to sleep in wet clothes set him ill at ease. He'd cross in the morning so he had the while day to dry off.

He unrolled the thick blanket he'd purchased with the coin Beatrice had given him and collapsed, staring at the distant army. After leaving Beatrice's cabin, he'd traveled west for several days until he found the main road north out of Scatterbrook. Not long after, he'd spotted campfires. He'd kept ahead of them for a while, but day after day of checking the distances and avoiding scout patrols had worn on him. As he leaned back and closed his eyes, he decided it best to let them pass. He could always travel to Mordeina in their shadow.

The sound of footsteps through the grass awoke Alric from his nap. Stirring, he reached for his rucksack. When he looked up, he was surprised to see it wasn't soldiers of Ker that stepped into his little campsite but a woman. Her hair was stark black and hung down to her waist, her dress plain and brown, clinging to her slender form. Despite the scars all across her arms, despite how her eyes looked like solid black orbs, she was undeniably beautiful. Alric started to apologize even though he had no idea what he was apologizing for.

"Oh," Tessanna said as she spotted him. "I see we're not the only ones wishing for some privacy."

The King of the Vile

"It's nothing," Alric said, confused by her mention of 'we' since he saw no one with her. He stumbled to his feet, slinging his pack over his shoulder. "I'll go."

"No, please stay," the strange woman said, and she crossed her legs and sat on his blanket. "It will be nice to have company other than boring soldiers and fanatical paladins."

Alric looked past her. The army was less than a quarter mile away, their camp filling the road and the clearings beyond. The proximity filled him with unease, but so far he had no reason to run. He sat back down.

"So, you're traveling with them?" he asked.

The woman nodded.

"For now."

"So are you, uh, a follower?" Alric said, trying to be tactful and failing miserably. The woman raised an eyebrow at him. "You know, a camp follower."

At that, the woman laughed, and she seemed genuinely amused.

"Many of them wish, I do not doubt," she said with a smile. "Why do you think I am one of the prostitutes?"

Alric's face flushed red. How in the world could he answer that question without making himself look like an even bigger jackass?

"I don't know," he said, picking burrs off his blanket. "You're beautiful enough to be one."

The woman giggled as if she were a little girl.

"I'm flattered. No, I am not a camp follower. I travel with my husband, who is very important to King Bram." She offered him her hand. "Tessanna."

"Alric," he said, accepting it and softly shaking once. The name sounded familiar, and though he tried not to, he found himself staring at her strange eyes.

"So," she said, "I have told you why I am here, but why are you?" She leaned in closer. "Are you hiding from the big, bad men from Ker?"

It was his turn to chuckle.

"In a way, yes," he said. "I'm traveling to Mordeina, and would prefer to avoid any...complications."

"King Bram is certainly a complication," Tessanna said, and she looked over her shoulder at the camp. "Though for good or ill, I cannot decide."

She fell silent, and Alric steadily grew uncomfortable. Something about this Tessanna felt otherworldly. He decided it was because of the eyes, those eyes whose irises looked blacker than coal. Just a strange gift at birth, he told himself. Nothing to be afraid of.

"Would you like something to eat?" he asked, unable to handle the silence any longer. He opened his rucksack and started leafing through its contents, trying to be polite. "I don't have much, and what I do have certainly isn't the most pleasant to the tongue, but it's still food."

Tessanna shook her head.

"I don't eat much," she said. "Go ahead if you wish, though."

"Oh." He closed the rucksack and settled down onto the blanket, fighting for anything casual to discuss with the most beautiful woman he'd ever laid eyes on.

"So where are you from?" he asked.

"A little village outside of Veldaren," she said. She leaned over, and her hair fell so that it was like she'd drawn a curtain across her face to hide. "After that, Veldaren, then a little cabin in the woods outside Veldaren, then Mordeina, and then in Ker, a house not far from the Corinth River. We...we never seem to keep a home for long."

"I'm sorry," Alric said. He'd met several refugees from the east since the war, and all of them had worn a sort of hollow expression. The war, the death, the destruction; it'd been like it scooped out an important piece of them that remained empty no matter how much time passed. Tessanna's shoulders shuddered, and he realized she was crying. Immediately he felt guilty and incompetent. Asking a simple question? He couldn't even get that right! He cleared his throat, ready to say he was sorry.

"Don't apologize," she said, her voice cold and lethal. "I have only myself to blame. I tore open the gate. I brought forth the war god. Every home I have lost, it has always been my fault. At least I found vengeance in the end. At least together, my lover and I burned the prophet to ashes. That's something, isn't it, Alric? That must mean something."

No more confusion as to how he knew her name. Alric stared at the daughter of the goddess, suddenly terrified. This was the sorceress who had ripped open the portal allowing Thulos to march into Dezrel alongside an army of war demons. Because of her, all lands east of the Rigon had fallen. Because of her, hundreds of thousands had died.

She looked up at him, peering through her dark hair with those black eyes. Tears ran down them, but whatever sorrow she felt didn't reach her voice.

"So where are you from?" she asked, chipper, smiling so sweetly.

"Greenbrook," he said. "It's one of the border farm towns in Ker."

Tessanna bobbed her head. "You've traveled far. Why go to Mordeina?"

Alric couldn't wrap his head around the situation. The dark angel of Celestia wanted to know why he traveled to Mordan's capital. Could he tell her? *Should* he tell her? Alric had heard tales of her and her lover redeeming themselves and pledging to Ashhur, but he'd heard other tales as well, of a more vicious sort.

"I'm not sure you'd believe me," he said, nearly laughing at the ludicrousness of it all.

Tessanna slid her fingers along the pale gray cloth of his blanket, fingernails scratching the rough fabric.

"I have seen the breaking of the world," she said. "I have glimpsed the stars in the abyss and heard the whisper of the goddess. There is very little I cannot believe."

Alric sighed. For such a powerful, storied person to stumble upon him while he slept, he had to assume at least the possibility Ashhur had sent her his way. So he swallowed down his nervousness and told her.

"I go because Ashhur wants me to go to Avlimar," he said.

Tessanna didn't even bat an eye.

"How do you know?"

"Dreams," he said. "Every night, always the same one."

"How do you know they're from Ashhur?"

"I just...do," Alric said. It was a question he'd never considered.

Tessanna slid closer on the blanket, and she pushed away her hair from her face.

"If you'd let me, I can see them," she said. "If you want me to. I won't make you. It won't hurt, I promise."

Alric chewed on his lower lip. The few people he'd told of his dreams had always assumed him delusional, or troubled, or flat-out lying. To have someone able to see them as well, to understand the overwhelming anger come the end when the shadow king put on his crown...

"You swear it won't hurt?" he asked.

Tessanna smiled shyly at him.

"I promise."

Alric nodded.

"Do it."

She reached out with thin, pale fingers, settling them against his temples. She closed her eyes, and Alric felt a strange tingling travel up his spine and into the base of his neck. Wisps of black smoke wafted from her fingers. Her grip on his head tightened, her tiny mouth locked into a frown. Alric grew more and more nervous as the woman's whole body began to tremble. He didn't dare touch her, didn't dare break her concentration. In the realms of magic, he was a babe, while she a master.

And then, just as quickly as it began, Tessanna pulled away. Her eyes opened, and he saw startling clarity in her gaze.

"You see them too," she whispered.

"Too?" he asked. "You mean..."

"I have," she said. "Glimpses and echoes of the future you will set in motion."

Tears ran down her cheeks as she looked upon him with a mixture of sadness and pity.

"I'm sorry," she said. "I could have spared you. I could have prevented this if I wasn't such a coward. If I'd only been the angel of destruction Celestia wished me to be. But Qurrah begged me not to, Alric. He begged me, and I couldn't refuse him, not after all he'd sacrificed for my sake. Because of it, now you must suffer in my stead."

Alric sat before her, and he felt so confused, so helpless.

"I don't understand."

"You don't need to," Tessanna said, smiling sadly at him. "Just follow the dream to its end."

"But why? What am I, Tessanna? How do I matter in all this?"

She gently stroked his face.

"Ashhur will awaken in a blaze of fire," she whispered. "And you're to be the spark."

They both turned at the sound of someone clearing their throat. Alric's entire body tensed at the sight of the half-orc in faded robes. His face was a soft gray, his hair a brown so dark it approached black. He carried blankets in his arms and a sack over one shoulder.

"Am I interrupting?" he asked.

"Not at all, Qurrah," Tessanna said, rising to greet her husband. Alric stared at the couple as she kissed his cheek. First Celestia's daughter, and now the great traitor of Veldaren? Perhaps he should have endured the wet clothes and crossed the stream when he had the chance.

Qurrah set down his blanket, unrolling it so he and Tessanna had a place to sit. All the while he kept an untrusting eye on Alric. It seemed fair enough. Alric didn't feel ready to trust him, either.

"So who is our guest?" Qurrah asked as he sat down.

"This is Alric," Tessanna answered. "He's on a mission from Ashhur."

"Oh really?"

Alric chuckled.

"She makes it sound silly when she puts it that way."

He'd expected Qurrah to scoff, but instead he leaned closer, resting his chin on his fist.

"I thought Ashhur slumbered," he said, his brown eyes sparkling with intelligence. "Isn't that what the priests and angels say?"

"I'm not one to contradict them," Alric said. "All I know are the dreams he sends me."

"Dreams?"

"Dreams. Visions. Whatever you want to call them. I see them every night, leading me to Avlimar."

"Avlimar has fallen," Qurrah said. "Your dreams lead you to a graveyard."

"Hush now," Tessanna said, cuddling against him. "Don't be so harsh. Can't you see he is troubled?"

She spoke about him as if he were a child, and it angered Alric more than it should.

"I can't explain it," Alric said. "And I won't try to. Ashhur wants me to go to Avlimar, and so I will."

Qurrah stroked Tessanna's hair as he stared at him.

"Some would call you a man of great faith," he said. "And some would label you a self-deluded fool. Both tend to mirror one another. How do you know which one you are?"

"I don't," Alric admitted with a sigh. "And that's what terrifies me every night when I lay down to sleep. It, and the dreams."

The half-orc stared at him. Alric kept his head up, refusing to wilt before that gaze.

"Ashhur gave me back my life," Qurrah said after a moment. "I owe him everything, yet I now dwell in his silence. I envy you, Alric. To hear his voice, even in a whisper, even in a dream, is a gift denied to me. I only pray that in the days to come, I find no reason to pity you instead."

Such an admission, even one tinged with warning, was unexpected from such a dark figure, and Alric struggled for the right words to respond with. Before he could, a female rider casually loped toward them on a spotted brown horse. Alric pointed over the couple's shoulder.

"Someone's coming," he said.

Qurrah and Tessanna both looked. Upon spotting her, Qurrah swore softly.

"Do you know her?" Tessanna asked.

"I don't need to," Qurrah said. "Do you see those robes? She's from the Council. That's all I need to know that I'm about to become very annoyed."

Alric stood there dumbfounded as the rider closed the distance and came to a halt. She had an unfriendly face, nose too long, eyes narrow, mouth locked in a permanent frown. Long silver earrings dangled far past her neck, jangling from the ride.

"Qurrah and Tessanna Tun?" she asked.

"We are," said Qurrah.

"I am Anora of the Towers," she said, "and I come at behest of the Council to offer my wisdom and guidance to this campaign."

Qurrah raised an eyebrow.

"I did not think King Bram was in need of counsel."

"I had heard that too," Anora said sharply. "But my opinion differs. You are his current counsel, are you not? That is why I came to greet you, but you seem so very far from the king to hold such a role."

Qurrah's right hand tightened into a fist, and Alric feared a confrontation would break out. Tension filled the air.

"Why have you really come, Anora?" Qurrah asked.

"I told you," said the wizard, "I have come to offer my guidance to King Bram and his invasion. The Council has eyes everywhere, and surely you can understand our preference that all of Dezrel not become a theocracy. I would think we would be allies, Qurrah Tun, not enemies."

Alric could tell that was certainly never going to happen. Tessanna slid between her husband and Anora and stared up at the wizard.

"My lover and I would like some peace," she said. "It gets so bothersome surrounded by soldiers and noise all day. You'll understood soon, I'm sure."

Anora tugged on her horse's reins.

"What bothers me are those who do not understand their place," she said. "Bram does not need you anymore, neither of you. If you were wise, you'd go home, and leave things beyond your understanding alone."

Tessanna rose to her feet, and she smiled so sweetly at their uninvited visitor.

"Remember who you threaten," she said "If you are not careful, I may have to unfurl my wings."

Anora smiled right back, and Alric thought the expression looked wrong on her face.

"I will remember that," the wizard said. "But before I go, you might want to return to the camp. Karak's paladins have captured a few prisoners I believe you'll be interested in."

"Why tell us?" Qurrah asked.

"How many times must I tell you?" Anora asked. "I am here for guidance, not confrontation."

With that she rode off. Alric was baffled as to what had just transpired. Qurrah and Tessanna seemed to understand more, and they shared a look with one another.

"Forgive us, Alric, but I fear we must be going," Qurrah said, rising to his feet.

"It's no bother," Alric said.

Qurrah hesitated, and him a look Alric couldn't read.

"Since you travel to Mordeina, would you deliver a message to my brother for me?"

"I suppose."

"Thank you," Qurrah said. "Please, tell him...tell him I'm not his enemy. No matter what he hears, I will always be there for him."

"Sure, sure, I'll try," Alric said. The half-orc hurried away, seemingly embarrassed. Tessanna blew Alric a kiss goodbye and joined her husband in returning to the camp.

Alric lurched to his feet the moment they were gone, pushed through the stream, and rushed north, the coming cold be damned.

16

For three days, Lathaar and Jerico had remained just ahead of the invading army from Ker. It was on that third day, when the sun was high in the sky, that a rider came thundering down the road atop a black horse. There was nowhere to hide, the nearest village several miles ahead and the surrounding fields had already been harvested ahead of the coming winter. The two paladins stood tall and greeted the approaching paladin of Karak with the respect they felt he deserved.

"Come to die?" Lathaar asked, swords crossed before him, naked steel glowing with light.

"Or maybe get your ass a solid spanking before running home to Karak?" Jerico added, his shield raised. The dark paladin pulled back on the reins, stopping beyond the reach of their weapons. He was a younger man, his freckled face lined with scars, either side of his neck sporting a roaring lion. Strapped to his back was an enormous ax. He stared at the two as if surprised by their comments.

"I expected something more...noble from the two of you," said the dark paladin.

Lathaar chuckled.

"You're part of a doomed invasion soon to be crushed by angels. Perhaps you should get used to disappointment."

"Or perhaps I should expect only the worst when it comes to Ashhur's followers," the dark paladin said, sitting up taller. "My name is Umber, and I come at behest of my master, Xarl, high paladin of the Stronghold."

Lathaar found this hard to believe.

"I question how your master would even know we were here," he said. "We've seen no one of your kind during our travels."

Umber grinned at them.

"No, but we have seen plenty of *your* kind."

Jerico softly swore.

"You lie," Lathaar said, more hoping than believing.

Umber shook his head and backed his horse up a step.

"Where the mother duck goes, the ducklings tend to follow," he said. "And trust me, Lathaar and Jerico of the Citadel, those ducklings broke very, very easily."

The ugly amusement on his freckled face was almost enough to send Lathaar lunging at him, ready to tear him to pieces with his blessed blades, but Jerico's hand on his shoulder kept him still.

"What is it you want with us?" Jerico asked.

"It's simple enough," Umber replied. "Come greet my master. We'll be awaiting you to the south, traveling in King Bram's vanguard. I trust you'll come, because otherwise, well..." Another sick grin and shrug of his shoulders. "Otherwise, we'll have to amuse ourselves with the little paladins instead."

Umber turned his horse about and snapped the reins. Neither Lathaar nor Jerico said a word as he rode away, up and down the gentle slopes toward the distant gray mass that was the Kerran army.

"What do we do?" Lathaar asked.

Jerico buckled his mace to his belt and flung his shield over his shoulder.

"We go," he said.

"There's only two of us, and they have an entire army behind them. What do you think we'll accomplish?"

"I don't know," Jerico said. "But we won't leave our students there to die."

"As you wish," Lathaar said. He sheathed his blades. "We'll go, and pray for a miracle."

"This is the land of miracles, after all," Jerico said, and whether he intended it or a not, a hint of sarcasm colored his words.

Lathaar stared at the smoke drifting on the wind above the approaching army. "Perhaps once, but it's hard to believe it still is."

The two followed the road south, each step seemingly heavier than the last. The distant army of Ker grew clearer as the minutes passed. Though they had thousands of soldiers, Lathaar wondered how they intended overcome Mordeina's great walls. *Perhaps that's not their goal.* If it was angels they wanted to kill, then the winged protectors would no doubt come right to them.

And if paladins of Karak had joined the army of Ker...

It should have been a ridiculous thought, given Bram's distrust of the gods, but the ten paladins waiting at the forefront of the vanguard proved it true. Their black armor shone in the sunlight. Kneeling before them, hands bound, mouths gagged, were four of their oldest students from the Citadel. Their faces were bruised, eyes swollen, hands cut. Lathaar's chest filled with sorrow and rage.

A dark-skinned paladin with long brown hair stood among the bound youths, and he stepped out from the line and rubbed a hand lovingly through young Gareth's hair.

"That's close enough," the paladin said. "For now, we only need to talk."

Lathaar and Jerico halted in the center of the road. Beyond the paladins, Lathaar noticed how the army of thousands had stopped as well. Did the dark paladins commanded that much power in King Bram's army?

"We're here," Lathaar said, keeping his voice calm. About thirty feet separated him from the dark paladins, and the urge to cross that distance with blades drawn was nearly overwhelming. "I assume you are the Stronghold's new puppet master, Xarl?"

"I am," the man said. "I must admit, it is so *exciting* to finally meet you two. The mighty paladins of Ashhur, towering men of might and power, stories of whom have reached even our walls over the passing years." He smiled. "To be honest, Jerico, I expected your shield to be bigger, but I guess you're used to hearing that, aren't you?"

"Especially from the ladies," said Umber beside him.

The rest of the dark paladins laughed.

"I'm going to kill him," Jerico muttered.

"Get in line," Lathaar whispered back.

Xarl patted the top of Gareth's head, then playfully slapped his face.

"Gareth here was kind enough to tell us they were trying to catch up to you," he said. "So now that you're here, let's lay things out nice and simple. No lies, no insults, no posturing or making grand speeches. Just the truth."

"And what would that be?" Lathaar asked.

Xarl drew a long sword from his hip. Black fire roared to life around the blade, and he slowly put it atop Gareth's right shoulder. The boy screamed into his gag as the fire burned through his bloody shirt and into his flesh.

"Lay down your weapons, fall to your knees, and accept your deaths," Xarl said. "Otherwise the children will die in your place while you watch." The fire burned deeper into Gareth's shoulder. "The choice is yours, now make it."

Lathaar's vision ran red as he watched Gareth slump over, tears running down his face as he whimpered. Xarl pulled free his blade and stalked behind the other three prisoners. His violet eyes never left theirs. Without even looking, the dark paladin stopped behind Mal, whose normally thin face was lumpy and swollen from bruises.

"Maybe hearing their screams will help you decide," Xarl said as he pressed his blade against the back of Mal's neck.

Mal howled as he burned. Lathaar's feet remained rooted in place, his whole body shaking with rage. Xarl grabbed Mal by the hair to hold him still, the grin on his face full of white teeth and sick pleasure. Lathaar had felt that fire firsthand many times, and he knew it didn't burn like normal fire. Skin blackened far slower than it should have, all so the pain one experienced could drag on and on.

Jerico shifted closer and lowered his voice. "We have to surrender."

"We surrender, they kill our students after we die," Lathaar said.

"If we don't surrender, they die anyway!"

Mal's screams pierced Lathaar's mind. He'd give his life to save the boy, to save any of the three. But to offer himself up to the dark paladins, to die after all he'd done? Was that how his life must end? They'd crushed Karak's army. They'd defeated the prophet. The times of sacrifice were over...weren't they?

"Lathaar," Jerico said. "We have no choice."

That was the worst part of it. They did have a choice. One meant cowardice, and one meant death.

"Still not come to a decision?" Xarl asked. He pulled the blade away from Mal's neck and moved down the line until he hovered over Samar. He patted the youngster's, then skipped both him and Elrath to return to Gareth.

"Maybe you think I'm lying," Xarl shouted as he kicked Gareth in the stomach to make him roll onto his back. "Let's put that to rest right here and now."

Before they could say a word, before they could realize what was happening, Xarl plunged his sword into Gareth's neck. The steel hit bone and slid to one side, ripping open the throat further.

Lathaar screamed and the dark paladins laughed, some cheering, others calling for Lathaar to come fight and die. He almost did. Jerico leapt in his way, shoving him in the chest.

"We have no choice," Jerico said, grabbing Lathaar's face with his hands and forcing their gazes to meet.

"I can't," Lathaar said.

"We give ourselves over, and the other three live," Jerico said. "What else can we do?"

Lathaar felt tears building in his eyes.

"You don't understand. I can't. I can't bring myself to give him that victory. We can kill him, Jerico. You know that. You know we can, if given the chance."

Jerico swallowed hard.

"The moment we attack, they'll execute our students," he said. "And if we don't attack, then we'll stand here and watch them die. Are you willing to do that, Lathaar? Are you willing to endure that horror just so you can one day meet them on the battlefield? Because I'm not."

"I want a decision, paladins!" Xarl shouted, pacing and smiling like a serpent about to strike. "Three lives for two, that's more than a fair trade. It would have been four, if you'd not been so tardy in making a decision."

Three lives for two, thought Lathaar. *Three lives for two*. He'd risked his life for others a hundred times before, how could he not do it again?

Xarl kicked Samar in the spine, knocking the red-haired boy onto his stomach. Putting a boot on the small of Samar's back, Xarl lifted his blade up for a thrust.

"You're running out of time," the dark paladin shouted.

Lathaar opened his mouth to answer, to beg for Samar's life, but a loud *crack* silenced him. A burning whip wrapped around Xarl's blade. The dark paladin spun around, looking as shocked as Lathaar felt to see Qurrah Tun and his bride Tessanna approach.

"That is enough!" the half-orc shouted. Lathaar was stunned by the power in his voice, raw anger overwhelming each word. Seeing the couple allied with the army of Ker soured Lathaar's mood even further, but at least it seemed like his students might have a chance.

"This matter doesn't concern you," Xarl growled. "Go roll in the grass with Celestia's whore while we deal with Ashhur's faithful."

The way the man said it, so calmly, so pleasantly, made him seem all the more vile. Shadow swirled about Tessanna's hands, and he wondered if Xarl would ever get the chance to speak again. Xarl pulled his sword free of Qurrah's whip, and the other paladins readied their weapons. The soldiers who'd been watching rapidly retreated, wanting no part of such a potentially deadly battle.

"Insult her again," Qurrah said, and though he whispered, it sounded as if his words traveled for miles. "Call her a whore, just one more time. Give me reason to rip the bones from your flesh while you scream."

The paladins tensed as magic flared around both Tess and Qurrah's hands. Lathaar shot a look at Jerico, and his friend nodded. Should battle begin, they would race into the melee to save their students.

"Is it permission you seek?" Xarl asked, pacing before Qurrah with a smile on his face. "If so, then you have it. If you wish me dead, then try. Let us see the power of the greatest traitor Dezrel has ever known. Karak will exalt me for eternity for sending him your soul to burn."

Before it could come to blows, a man pushed through their ranks. His skin was tan, his face scarred along the right eye, and he wore a crown. King Bram, Lathaar assumed. The man certainly commanded the respect of a king as he roared for everyone to stand down. Beside him, observing silently, was a frowning woman with a long nose and dangling silver earrings.

"What is going on here?" Bram demanded.

"Matters of the gods," Xarl said. "Of no concern to you."

"Ever since armies of the gods started invading sovereign lands, such matters concern me greatly," Bram said. He gestured to Gareth's body, then turned to Lathaar and Jerico. "What is the meaning of this?"

"A ransom," Lathaar said before the others could answer. "Our deaths so the children might be spared. Gareth was killed as a show of force."

Qurrah put himself between Xarl and Bram, his whip curling about his shoulder like a living snake, the fire that surrounded it fading down to a whisper of smoke.

"We do not invade at Karak's behest," Qurrah said. "The dark paladins serve you like any other soldier, do they not? Then make them follow your rules. Let the young be treated as prisoners, not tortured and executed in a gruesome display. Overthrowing the angels accomplishes nothing if you simultaneously establish Karak's authority over you."

Bram's miserable mood only worsened. Stepping past Qurrah, he addressed Karak's paladins directly.

"The young paladins are my prisoners, and they will be treated as such," he said. "Not tortured, not maimed, and not executed without reason."

Before Xarl could protest, Bram turned to Lathaar and Jerico. "As for you two, the time will come when Mordan finally fights, be it with angels or soldiers. Should I see you at their side, I will execute your students. This war we fight, you are no longer a part of it. Is that clear?"

Lathaar swallowed down a mouth full of razors. "Perfectly."

"Good." King Bram spun about, glaring at every party involved in the tense gathering. "My army's stalled long enough. It's time to march out. Sir Ian, bring the prisoners to my tent so we can set up more long-term accommodations."

"Yes, milord," Sir Ian said, gesturing to the three young men. Soldiers grabbed them from the dark paladins, who watched with weapons still drawn.

"Forgive us for letting our passions overwhelm reason," Xarl said, and he bowed low to the king.

"Don't let it happen again," Bram said, vanishing back into the sea of soldiers. With his departure, Xarl turned to Lathaar and Jerico, and he saluted with his sword.

"I pray we meet again," he said. "Even if the war between Mordan and Ker ends, I'm sure we'll still have much to discuss."

The dark paladin shot a look at Qurrah that Lathaar couldn't interpret, and then ordered his paladins to move out. They marched into the heart of the army. Tessanna finally released the dark magic about her hands. She kissed Qurrah's cheek and headed out to the grasslands adjacent to Bram's army.

"Why march with them?" Lathaar asked before the half-orc could leave. "It was Ashhur's forgiveness that granted you new life. Why now turn against his angels?"

"I never turned on them," Qurrah said, shaking his head. "They came for me, seeking to revoke that forgiveness and take my life. If you want to cast blame, cast it at their feet, not mine. Grace enforced at the edge of a blade means nothing, paladin. There is no redemption in murder, no forgiveness in executions. If this is what it takes for Tess and I to live a free life, then this is what we will do."

Jerico put a hand on Lathaar's shoulder.

"Come on," he said. "We need to put distance between us before nightfall."

Lathaar gave him no answer. His friend walked away, leaving him alone with Qurrah on the road.

"I was ready to exchange my life for theirs," Lathaar said. "If they die..."

"I will do what I can to keep your students safe," the half-orc promised. "I am no friend of Karak, nor his paladins. In that, you can trust me."

"Karak doesn't need your friendship to burn the world anew," Lathaar said, shoving his swords into their sheaths. "He just needs you to stand aside and do nothing."

Lathaar turned his back to the half-orc, head hung low, and offered a prayer to his students as he left them in the hands of his foes.

17

It had been a long three days, and despite the impending assembly, Harruq feared they had not seen the last of the unrest.

"Aubby's asleep in Gregory's room," Aurelia said, returning to find Harruq preparing. "There's enough guards to stop a small army, so they should be safe while we're gone."

"Good," Harruq said as he adjusted his collar. The shirt was blue, the sleeves ended in ridiculous poofs, and the collar felt painfully tight. His fingers tugged, and tugged, until the material ripped. Harruq froze, checking to see if he'd damaged the shirt.

"One of these days I'll learn to wear my armor everywhere," he said, sighing. The thread around the high collar had only torn the tiniest bit, and shouldn't be noticeable.

"If you go into that conclave dressed for a fight, then a fight will be what you get," Aurelia said. "You're effectively a nobleman now, so you're going to dress like one."

Aurelia helped him button the rest of his shirt and put on his outer jacket. She wore an elegant blue dress, with streams of silver swirling about it from top to bottom.

"Can I at least bring my swords?" Harruq asked.

"What'd I just say about dressing for a fight?"

Harruq grinned at her.

"That it's better than looking like this?"

She kissed his nose.

"Cute. You ready to go?"

"I am," Harruq said, offering his arm. "Are you going to open us a portal there?"

"Just outside. I think it'd be best for us to walk into Devlimar. With how much the city changes daily, and how many

The King of the Vile

people are swarming about it, I'd hate to kill someone with an errant teleport."

"You can do that?" Harruq asked.

Aurelia slipped from his grasp, her fingers waggling as she began to cast her spell.

"Reappearing inside matter, particularly living matter, causes a fusion of both, as well as rapid bodily expansion of the unlucky person in the way of the teleport."

"Sounds like a lovely way to die," Harruq said.

"There's worse. If you're really unlucky, neither person dies, and you live a life fused together, looking like something Qurrah would create while in a particularly foul mood."

She vanished into the swirling blue portal. Harruq paused before it and swallowed.

"Some things are better off not knowing," he said, then stepped through.

Harruq felt an immediate distortion. The room vanished, the ceiling replaced by stars, his carpet now pale grass. Though he took but a single step, deep down he knew he'd crossed a large distance. Aurelia waited for him.

"It took you a moment," she said. "Did I make you nervous?"

He kissed her cheek.

"Never."

Aurelia had taken them beyond the outer wall of Mordeina, to a field perpendicular to the main road leading out the city gates. Normally those gates were shut at night, but Harruq had ordered them to remain open. The people would only find other ways outside the city if he tried to prevent them. The road was filled with people, many carrying torches and lanterns despite the bright starlight. Hand in hand, Harruq and Aurelia walked to the road, joining the many others traveling to Devlimar.

The earthbound city of the angels sparkled, its outer buildings lit by dozens of evenly spaced torches. The progress the angels had managed in a relatively short time was remarkable. Harruq saw several towering spires, and at least thirty buildings stood in a small cluster within the enormous field beside the wreckage of Avlimar. It was still a pale imitation of the original, but Harruq figured a few more months would fix that.

Devlimar's beauty was marred by the ugliness taking place just outside its limits. Over a thousand people gathered to protest, the number swelling with each passing minute as the steady flow from Mordeina continued. A wall of soldiers held them at bay, Harruq placing them at Azariah's request. Judarius's fate would be decided by the collective will of all angels, which meant none could remain outside on guard duty to prevent the looting of their newly built home.

"Azariah says Judarius slew the man for stealing from Avlimar's ruins," Harruq said as they walked, voicing something that had been bothering him all day.

"Thomas," Aurelia said. "His name was Thomas."

"Right," Harruq said. "Well, Thomas didn't have a single scrap of gold, silver, or pearl on him when the guards found his body."

"That doesn't mean anything," Aurelia said. "Whatever he stole might have been taken by someone else during the riot."

"Or Judarius is lying."

Aurelia grabbed Harruq's hand and pulled him off the road, away from the few travelers nearby.

"Never say such a thing out loud," she scolded. "The people's trust in the angels is as thin as a blade of grass. If they start believing the angels capable of lying and murder..."

"But what if they *are* capable?" Harruq asked. "What then?"

Aurelia fell silent. Her grip on his hand tightened.

"What reason would Judarius have for such a killing?" she finally asked. "Thomas was just a carpenter. Why murder him in full view of witnesses? It's insane."

"I don't know," Harruq said. "But we need proof of Judarius's claims, and a public trial where the people can hear it for themselves. The people need to believe we're still in charge of our own fates if this madness will ever end."

"You're hoping the angels will voluntarily surrender power to mankind's courts, subjecting themselves to potential imprisonment and execution," Aurelia said. "You're hoping for a miracle."

The King of the Vile

Harruq sighed.

"They say we're living in the age of miracles. Let's hope there's still a few more left."

The noise of the crowd grew as they approached Devlimar. Soldiers stood locked shoulder to shoulder, shields raised to keep back the crowd. The hatred Harruq heard screamed all around him was stunning. People called the angels murderers, butchers, slave masters, and worse. Some cursed Ashhur, others called the angels traitors to the god's name. Harruq and Aurelia stood near the back of the crowd, watching as several people flung stones at the soldiers, which plinked off their shields and armor.

"They're frightened, and hurt," Aurelia said. "Whatever happens tonight, I do not think it will heal this wound."

"At least we can make a start," Harruq said. He slowly pushed his way through the crowd, attempting to be as gentle as possible. When he reached the front lines, the soldiers recognized him and Aurelia, and they parted so they might pass.

"Bring him to justice," a man near the front shouted. "Justice for all!"

The crowd took up the chant, the cry rising tenfold in volume as Harruq and Aurelia walked down the streets of the golden city.

Justice for all. Justice for all.

Despite how impressive the angels' progress was in rebuilding, the city was still fairly small, and it took them little time to reach the grand auditorium, built of marble and lit by a ring of hundreds of torches. The enormous structure was open to the sky, allowing angels to fly in from all directions. It was shaped much like a bowl, with row after row of benches circling the center. The only ground entrance was a tunnel carved through the marble. He stood at the end of the tunnel, nerves wavering at the sight of so many angels flying about. For a second he thought it might be wise to stay there instead of trying to find a seat.

"Stay calm," Aurelia said, tugging on his hand to pull him along. They stepped out into the center ring, and immediately the murmurs increased. Harruq felt his neck redden. Why would the angels care that he attended? He was there only as a witness, with no actual intention of addressing the conclave.

Ahaesarus stood in the center of the auditorium, and when he spotted Harruq and Aurelia he came over to greet them.

"Welcome," Ahaesarus said. "I have kept a seat reserved for you two at the front."

"Thanks," Harruq muttered. The two took their seats along the innermost ring of marble benches. Angels sat on either side of them, towering above their heads.

"There's Deathmask," Aurelia whispered in his ear.

Harruq followed her gaze, and sure enough he saw Deathmask sitting on a bench opposite them in the auditorium. His hands were bound behind his back and he lacked his iconic gray mask. He sat hunched over, dark hair falling over his scarred face. The powerful man rarely moved, and Harruq wondered if he were drugged or perhaps had a spell of some kind cast over him. The Deathmask he knew would be mocking and insulting angels all the way to the very end, not sitting there quiet and dejected.

The auditorium steadily filled with angels. Harruq rested his head in his hands as he stared at the angels in the center ring. Ahaesarus and Azariah stood side by side, patiently waiting. They were the only two not seated, and Harruq expected them to be the ones to lead the conclave. From their earlier arguments, he knew Ahaesarus would argue in favor of turning Judarius over for trial. Given how he was their leader, his words would carry enormous weight, but something about Azariah unnerved Harruq. He looked too pleased, too confident.

When all had gathered, Ahaesarus stepped forward and addressed the entire assembly.

"Angels of Ashhur," he said. "Wardens of mankind, I greet you. We come with purpose tonight, the first of which is to judge the man responsible for the destruction of our beautiful home of Avlimar. Ezekai, would you please bring him forward?"

A white-haired angel grabbed Deathmask by the arm and pulled him to his feet. Ezekai dragged him across the ring and flung Deathmask to his knees before returning to his seat. Ahaesarus paced before the man, arms behind his back.

"We are Ashhur's chosen, the last to have heard his voice," Ahaesarus said. "Know that any words you speak, we will know if

The King of the Vile

they are truth or lie. Answer with honesty, and without deceit. Do you understand?"

Deathmask looked up at the angel. Harruq saw deep black circles underneath the man's eyes, and when he spoke, he sounded exhausted.

"Yes," he said.

Ahaesarus gestured to Azariah, who took over the questioning.

"Then let us not delay any longer. Deathmask, are you responsible for the destruction of Avlimar?"

Harruq leaned forward, eager to hear for himself. He'd never believed it, not once, so he prayed this would be the moment his trust would be vindicated. Deathmask steadily rose to his feet, careful to keep his balance given his bound hands, and then looked the angel in the eye.

"No," he said.

The answer was like a shockwave traveling through the assembly. Harruq looked side to side, wishing he could sense what the angels sensed.

"Did he lie?" Harruq finally asked the angel to his left.

"No," said the angel. "He did not."

Azariah seemed flustered when he continued his questioning.

"Did you aid in the city's destruction, even if you were not directly responsible?"

"No."

"Did you ever set foot on Avlimar?"

"No."

Azariah stared at Deathmask for a long moment, slowly shaking his head.

"Foul magic," he whispered, then spun to the crowd, and he began to address them as well. "Many times you, Deathmask, were spotted within Avlimar, contradicting your words. My brethren, if you witnessed his presence, stand so you might be counted."

Harruq saw over a dozen angels rise to their feet. Damning evidence, certainly, but he knew there could be more going on. Surely Deathmask would bring up the possibilities of illusions and magic, but it seemed he had no interest in speaking. Worse, Harruq realized there was no one to speak for him, no one to defend him. The angels were the final word, and given their abilities to sense truth and lie, there had never been need for someone to defend the accused.

"I see my brethren, and I see you, a lowly thief and murderer," Azariah spinning back to Deathmask. "I know who my faith is in, and it is not you. Magic hides your words, deception protects your tongue. You are guilty of Avlimar's fall, and no spell will save you from our judgment."

Those words caused a stir among the angels, and Harruq was glad that at least some sounded upset. The rumble ceased as Deathmask's entire body shuddered from a fit of laughter. There was an air of madness to it. Harruq shifted on his bench, unsure of what to do.

"The glorious angels of Ashhur," Deathmask said, a feverish grin on his face. "The final judges of truth and lie. No man can lie, no innocent man be punished...unless you don't like the answer. Then it's *foul magic*."

Ezekai rushed forward when Deathmask spat at Azariah's feet.

"No lie, yet you condemn me," he said. "No lie, but you will execute me. Look at yourselves, damn it. Can't you see how blind you've become?"

Ezekai grabbed Deathmask by the front of his shirt, yanked him to his feet, and then shoved a gag in his mouth to silence him.

Aurelia pulled on Harruq's shoulder so he'd lean close enough for her to whisper.

"You have to do something," she said.

"Like what?"

"I don't know, but Deathmask is clearly innocent. They can't convict him with so little proof."

He looked about to the thousands of towering angels, each bearing swords, spears, and maces on their belts and backs.

"Yes," Harruq said. "I think they can."

"All of you have heard his words," Azariah said. "You have seen the witnesses. Do you find the man known as Deathmask innocent or guilty of Avlimar's fall?"

Hundreds rose to their feet, all shouting 'guilty'. Only one angel in four kept seated, and it sickened Harruq's stomach. This

The King of the Vile

was their justice? This was their trial? It was a sham, a bad joke, and Harruq leapt from his bench, unable to control himself anymore.

"I will not allow this," he shouted as he approached Azariah. "You have no proof, no evidence, and your own ears cannot hear a lie, yet you'd kill him anyway?"

"This is not your place," Azariah said, spinning to face him.

"I am steward of this realm, and that man is one of my subjects," Harruq said. "How is this not my place?"

Angels began to protest, some questioning the same. A divide between them was growing, Harruq had no doubt. Ahaesarus stepped before Harruq, and he gently held him back.

"Stay calm, my friend," he said.

"Calm?" Harruq asked. "I am calm. You want to see me pissed? Drag Deathmask off to die instead of handing him over for trial. A *real* trial."

Azariah shook his head.

"His crimes were committed against us," he said. "Not your people, but Ashhur's servants. We will judge him, and as you can clearly see, he has been found guilty." The angel spun to Ezekai, and he nodded. "Do what must be done."

Ezekai grabbed Deathmask by one arm, and a second angel came to join him. A swift blow from Ezekai's free hand knocked the dangerous man unconscious. Harruq moved to stop them, but Ahaesarus intercepted, pushing him back with an enormous hand.

"This matter is done," Ahaesarus said quietly. "But another matter lingers. Save your strength. Deathmask is only one man, but this coming divide will affect thousands..."

Harruq peered over Ahaesarus's shoulder as Ezekai and the other angel lifted into the air, flying off with Deathmask's limp, unconscious form. Beyond reach of human hands. Beyond justice.

The peoples' chant echoed in Harruq's ears, and it felt all the more troubling.

"We have a second matter now to address," Azariah said, stepping away from Harruq and Ahaesarus. "The matter of mankind's desire to hold a human trial for one of our own, Judarius."

Harruq drifted toward his seat but refused to sit. Having so many eyes on him made him nervous, and he felt sweat trickling down his neck, but after witnessing Deathmask's supposed 'trial' he knew he could not let things proceed without him. Just like there was no one to speak for Deathmask, there were none to speak for the dead Thomas. The angels saw themselves as perfection. Perfection meant no doubts, no questioning. Harruq needed to remind them the world was not as black and white as they saw it.

"Judarius, would you please stand?" Azariah asked.

Judarius rose from his seat along the front and crossed his arms over his muscular chest. Azariah gestured toward Ahaesarus, who took over the questioning.

"The man named Thomas," he said. "Did you murder him?"

Judarius shook his head. "All I have done was justified. I committed no murder. I am guilty of no sin."

Harruq didn't need to ask this time if he spoke the truth or not. The looks on the angels' faces was one of overwhelming relief.

"I consider this proof enough," Azariah said. "To hand Judarius over to trial only risks that an innocent life is judged guilty by imperfect hands. We cannot allow it. Let this matter be settled and forgotten."

"Except there is more at stake here than that," Ahaesarus said, stepping into the very center of the auditorium and turning to address the assembly. "If Judarius is innocent, then we need fear no trial. We must let the people we protect feel they are our children, not our slaves. If they believe angels may commit crimes without punishment, they will rebel against our aid."

"To acknowledge their request is to acknowledge we are capable of crimes," Azariah argued. "That alone would invalidate all our efforts."

Enough of this, Harruq thought. He stepped forward, joining Ahaesarus's side.

"Witnesses saw him cut down Thomas," he said. "Witnesses no different than the angels who just condemned Deathmask to death. Yet here you give them no voice. You feel no need to question them, or bring them before the assembly to describe what they have seen. Judarius was innocent before he ever spoke a word, no different than Deathmask was guilty before he even opened his mouth to answer."

Harruq's words were like wildfire to the assembly. The murmurs intensified. Azariah shook his head as if Harruq were a child.

"We have given so much to mankind," he said. "We bled and died for you twice over, first as Wardens, then as angels. We spend our waking days serving you, healing you, protecting. We ask for so very little, only a home we might call our own, and even that is called into question as mankind picks away at it piece by piece in the name of greed. Our lives are not our own, but Ashhur's. We are the slaves, not the people we protect. And yet you stand here. You point your finger at us, calling our justice into question. You do not understand our sacrifices, sacrifices we could never make if we were not perfect beings. For you to then repay this wonderful service with doubt and accusation is insulting."

The neck of Harruq's shirt continued to itch from sweat, and unable to take it anymore, he grabbed at it and yanked on the fabric. The shirt ripped, and he tore it free, stripping himself naked from the waist up. A quiet rumble traveled through the angels as Harruq turned, letting them see his many scars. His wrists and neck were burned, some from Qurrah's whip. His arms and chest bore dozens of long white slashes from swords and spears, and several purple splotches were the faded remnants of dark magic rupturing his flesh. Greatest were the matching scars across the center of his chest and back, left from when Thulos had run him through with his blade.

"Do you see the scars?" Harruq asked the assembly. "Do you see the torture I've endured? I have bled. I have screamed. I gave everything, I gave my *life* to the people of this land. You speak of your sacrifices as if they are unique. You act as if mankind is forever in your debt. *I* slew the war god. *My brother* burned away the prophet. Not you. We did what you could not. Have we anointed ourselves as gods above mankind? No. All we did, we did for those we loved."

He pointed an accusing finger at the crowd.

"You are servants of mankind, not masters. You are protectors, not executioners. Let Avlimar's fall be a lasting reminder that you are *not* above the people you serve. You do not lord over us from the skies, but walk among us in the dirt. If you would claim yourselves above our justice, if you would declare mankind inferior and undeserving of treatment equal to your own, then you bear no love for us. You don't *deserve* the place you once held. You cannot be our guardians. You cannot be our protectors. Be gone from us, each and every last one of you."

Harruq had expected an uproar. He'd expected to have his words drowned out with dissention. Instead he was met with chilling silence. All eyes were on him, far too many flooded with cold rage. Azariah slowly rose from his seat and stepped into the center of the auditorium.

"Do you give voice to those who throw stones at our homes?" he asked. "Do you speak the hidden thoughts of every thief and murderer within Mordeina's walls? Each day, we perform Ashhur's will. Each day, you loathe us for it. You are the sick telling the physician all is well. You are thief claiming no doors need locks. You are the murderer saying all men should lay down their blades."

Azariah stepped closer, his wings spreading, his entire presence seeming to grow so that each cold, calculated word thundered throughout the assembly.

"Ashhur would bring paradise," his voice boomed, "yet you would tear it down out of greed, selfishness, and cowardice. The way we demand is hard, but mankind does not want perfection. It fears it. It fears the sacrifice. It fears the day each man or woman will look into a mirror and see through their lies and justifications to the wretched being beneath it all. Mankind fears us because we cannot be fooled with their lies. We cannot be bought with their gold, for we do not share in their greed. We cannot be crippled with compromise, for we do not share in their doubt. I once walked through the golden lands of eternity, and I will do so again. Mankind was given to *us*, half-orc. We are to protect it, nurture it, and above all, force it to grow. The past cannot be accepted. The wretchedness of sin must be turned away at all costs. You think we act harshly, but in truth, we coddle your people. Let that end

The King of the Vile

today. Let us stand tall against their pitiful attempts to drag us into the dirt. We are to judge mankind, *not be judged by them!*"

Harruq felt the peace he'd bled for crumbling away, and there was nothing he could do to stop it. Ahaesarus rushed the center, but before he could speak a word, Azariah turned his way.

"No!" Azariah cried. "We will hear no more of this. I call this matter to a vote. Those who believe we should hand over Judarius for trial, rise to your feet so your vote may be counted."

Ahaesarus raised his fist into the air to show himself in favor. Harruq spun, scanning the thousands, begging for what he knew would never be. Angels stood, slowly, scattered. A third at best. The sight sank Harruq's heart into his stomach. The angels returned to their seats, and Azariah addressed the conclave again.

"Those who believe we are the only judges to whom we must answer, and refuse to hand Judarius over for trial, rise to your feet so your vote may be counted."

Azariah's fist shot into the air. All throughout the auditorium, angels stood up, hundreds upon hundreds of them. The rustle of clothes and feathers were war drums to Harruq's ears. Two thirds of the angels stood with fists raised, an easy majority. Azariah bowed to the assembly, then turned to where Judarius sat on a front row.

"I have heard Judarius's words, and I sense no lie in them. I declare Judarius guilty of no crime. Let this matter be forgotten."

Applause followed. Harruq rushed to Azariah's side, unable to contain himself.

"The people will not accept this," he said. "The riots, the looting..."

"Will be addressed," Azariah said. "Humanity may have abandoned us, half-orc, but we have not abandoned them. Hold faith in us. It shall be rewarded in time. Ashhur's voice is silent, so we must cry all the louder in his place."

The angel patted him on the shoulder, then moved to join Judarius, who had a crowd growing about him. Congratulating him, Harruq realized. The sight of it was sickening. Aurelia waited at the exit of the auditorium, and he made his way to her.

"Get us out of here," he said once he reached Aurelia's side.

"They don't understand," she said softly. "They've only made it worse."

Harruq glared over his shoulder to the assembly of angels. "They understand all right. I just don't think they care anymore."

A swirling blue portal ripped open before Aurelia. She kissed his hand and pulled him through, away from the city of angels to the city of man.

That night, the riots resumed, far worse than ever before.

18

Roand's room was the highest in the Masters' Tower, and climbing up the many steps left Tarlak winded. He doubled over before the door, gasping for air. Had his injuries taken so much out of him that a few stairs could defeat him?

Yes. Yes, they had.

"One day," he muttered as he knocked on thick oak door. "One day soon, you'll..."

"I'll what?"

Tarlak froze. The voice hadn't come from the door, but from behind. Slowly turning around, he found Roand standing two steps below him with his arms crossed. Tarlak swallowed as his mind reached for a lie.

"You'll be impressed with how much my studies have progressed," he said smiling lamely.

The master of the tower chuckled.

"I have had many people plot my doom in hopes of achieving power, fame, or revenge. I welcome you to try, Tarlak Eschaton. Killing you would sadden me, but your attempt on my life would certainly be an amusing one. I daresay it would be worth it."

"It's good to know all sins can be forgiven so long as I'm entertaining," Tarlak said as he stepped aside to let Roand pass. The wizard rapped the door once with his knuckles, and it opened. Tarlak followed him inside.

He'd expected something spacious and pretentious, perhaps carrying a vague fire theme, and he wasn't disappointed. The room was sparsely furnished, only a bed, a balcony closed off by glass doors, and a few chairs sitting in front of a fireplace. Seven wisps of fire burned in a circle just below the ceiling, like the flames of a candle only they hovered above nothing and released no smoke. The carpet was a radiating pattern of red, orange, and yellow, and the colors shimmered with each step Tarlak took. The furniture was painted black, and where it touched the carpet, tiny hints of flame flickered in and out. Tarlak shook his head, beginning to believe Roand's fascination with fire far surpassed scholarly focus and into the realm of deep-rooted fetishes. Oddly enough, the only thing not filled with fire was the actual fireplace, but a quick snap of Roand's fingers fixed that.

"So what is it you come to my room for?" Roand asked as he moved to one of the many shelves lining the walls between vast paintings of sunrises and sunsets. A bewildering array of liquor bottles filled the shelf, enough to leave Tarlak jealous. They had alcohol in the tower? Why had no one informed him of this?

"For starters, I came for a drink," he said.

Roand smiled at him over his shoulder. "A request I can easily fulfill."

Moments later, Tarlak reclined in one of the coal-black chairs before the fireplace. The cushions sank around him, surprisingly comfortable. He held a slender cup of onyx half-full of red wine in his left hand.

"What if I turned myself into an elemental being of fire?"

Roand stood beside the balcony door, swirling a cup of wine in his hand as he watched the sun set.

"I had someone try that," he said. "It was fascinating. Fire elementals are not native to our plane. Their bodies are held together with a liquid substance very much akin to flame, and it is constantly burning, but they are not just flame, as one might presume. And that liquid is very capable of disintegrating if the magic is strong enough. A wonderful day that was, witnessing a being of living fire burn to death."

"So that's a no?"

The master wizard laughed.

"That is, indeed, a no."

Tarlak grunted. He'd actually thought that one might give the fire wizard pause, but clearly not.

"Interesting, but how about this one?" he said, taking another sip of wine. "I guarantee you no one thought of this, not even yourself. What if I killed myself, then had a necromancer resurrect my body after removing the pendant?"

"The pendant activates upon your death. He will have nothing to work with."

"All right. Then how about he raises me as a ghost so I can haunt your ass from here to eternity?"

Roand grabbed the bottle from a little circular table beside him and refilled his cup.

"You are welcome to try," he said. "A few of my fellow wizards, Drasst in particular, specialize in necromancy, and they would love the chance to test a few of their more unique spells on a troublesome ghost haunting the towers."

"So even in death you won't let me win?" Tarlak lifted his glass. "A toast to the man who ruins the fun in all things, even dying."

Roand started the laugh, but abruptly stopped. His gaze locked on something outside the glass doors, and after a moment, a grin spread ear to ear across his face.

"You are wrong," he said. "I am not averse to fun, something our new friend is about to discover in a most unpleasant way."

Tarlak scratched at his scarred face, wishing he'd perfected his polymorph attempts so he could have an actual beard to stroke. New friend? Who might that be? Another renegade wizard? Traders, come to the towers hoping to make a fortune? Or perhaps Harruq had sent a scout to investigate the disappearance of their army?

No matter how many guesses he might have given himself, Tarlak never would have gotten it right. Two angels landed on the balcony, an unconscious prisoner carried between them. Roand set aside his glass and flung open the doors, allowing in a sudden burst of cold air.

"Greetings, master of the tower," said one of the angels. "We come bearing a gift from Azariah."

They tossed their prisoner into the room, where he rolled across the carpet before coming to a stop on his back. Tarlak choked down his surprise. Lying there unconscious, scarred face exposed, was Deathmask. Roand stared at the man, eyes wide, and the grin on his face was horrifying.

"Excellent," he said. "Most excellent. Tell your high priest that this is an acceptable gift, one I am most grateful for."

The two angels bowed in unison, then spread their wings and flew away. Roand shut the doors to his balcony, still eyeing Deathmask's body.

"Angels?" Tarlak asked, not sure how to correctly broach the subject and not particularly caring. "You're working with angels? Why in Karak's hairy codpiece would the lord of the council be working with the angels?"

"These are desperate times," Roand said as he knelt beside Deathmask. "Sometimes desperate measures must be taken in the name of preserving mankind's freedom."

The wizard slowly rubbed his finger across Deathmask's lips, covering the unconscious man's entire mouth with a waxy substance. Within moments, the substance hardened. Tarlak guessed it'd take a knife and a lot of time to pry open Deathmask's lips. An effective method to prevent spellcasting, something he swore to remember himself should the need ever arise.

"You've had associations with this man in the past, have you not?" Roand asked.

"You could say that."

The wizard nodded.

"Excellent. Stay where you are, Tarlak. I want you here when he wakes."

A quick spell, and invisible hands grabbed Deathmask's body, hoisting him off the ground. Instead of moving to the door, as Tarlak expected, Roand walked to the wall opposite the fireplace. With another wave of his hand, the wall rotated as if on hinges. The bookcase vanished, and replacing it was a black wall littered with chains, manacles, and hooks. Tarlak winced. The stone, it wasn't black, not naturally. It was literally charred that color.

Suddenly, Roand's fascination with fire made a lot more horrible, terrible sense.

The hovering Deathmask pressed against the wall, arms sliding between two manacles, which promptly shut of their own accord. Roand looped chains about his waist and bound Deathmask's ankles as well. Next he positioned a large hook

The King of the Vile

beneath Deathmask's jaw. It dug into the skin, drawing thin drops of blood as it held the unconscious man's head. Last was the delicate process of imprisoning Deathmask's fingers. Beside the manacles were two gnarled tangles, like a briar bush of metal. Roand pulled chains from the tangle, looping them about multiple fingers. Into bleeding fingertips he inserted sharp hooks, like those used by fishermen.

When Deathmask was firmly attached to the wall, Roand lovingly ran a hand down the side of the scarred man's face.

"Time to wake," he whispered.

Blue sparks arced from his touch, digging into skin. Deathmask flung himself forward, stretching the chains to their limits as his eyes shot wide open. His scream was muffled by the waxen gag, his nostrils flared as he breathed in and out. The hook in his jaw swung with him, firmly lodged in place.

Roand stood before Deathmask, their faces so close they nearly touched. There was no fear in his stance, no worry in his smile. Just pleasure.

"Welcome back, banished one," he said.

Deathmask attempted to respond, his words an unintelligible grunt due to the wax sealing his mouth shut. Roand *tsk'ed* at him.

"Not yet," he said. "It's time for you to listen. You are in my tower, my room to be precise. The position of the hooks in your body has been carefully chosen. They will bleed you, and prevent any casting of spells, but you will not die, not from them, so do not bother to try. I will sear shut any wounds you cause to yourself, and trust me when I say the reopening of them from another attempt will hurt far worse than the initial tearing. I have seen it enough times to know."

Deathmask settled down, glaring at Roand with mismatched eyes that steadily grew in awareness. Roand crossed his arms and took a step back.

"There. You seem more yourself. I'm unsealing your mouth, so I expect you to behave."

He brushed Deathmask's lips again, and the wax bubbled as it dripped down his chin. Deathmask hacked and spat bloody saliva onto the floor.

"Fuck you," he said.

Roand shook his head.

"Such crudeness. You weren't this way when you lived here."

Deathmask grinned like a caged animal.

"It's amazing what life outside these tower walls can be like," he said. "You should try it sometime. You'd learn just how little of the world revolves around your two little spires of stone."

"That the outside world is chaotic compared to the order of our towers is not something to gloat about," Roand said. "Nor is it something I'd wish to embrace."

The wizard spun and addressed Tarlak. "What name do you know him by?"

"Deathmask," Tarlak answered. "I've always known him as Deathmask."

"Deathmask?" Roand said, turning about with a frown. "A bit too theatrical, don't you think?"

"You stole my name," Deathmask said. "So I took a new one."

"I stole your name hoping to teach you humility. Instead, it seems to have inspired even greater hubris. You were never one to learn from your betters, were you, *Deathmask?*"

Deathmask laughed at the attempted insult.

"You don't get it," he said. "Whoever I was, no one beyond a few old, worthless men inside this tower grieved his passing. No one outside these walls ever knew I existed. This name you mock, the name you forced me to take, is known from every corner of Dezrel. Even the rumors of your power you so carefully leak are nothing compared to my own underworld legend. Banishing me was the best moment in my life, so thank you, Roand. Thank you oh so very much."

This was clearly not the way Roand had expected the conversation to go, and he looked deeply displeased.

"A vain, prideful man," the wizard said. "It is good to finally have you back so you may suffer for all the crimes you've committed against us."

"My crimes?" Deathmask asked. "What crimes have I committed against you, other than practicing magic despite my exile? I see a yellow wizard over there who did the same. I suffer, yet you let Tarlak live in your halls? Forgiveness for him, but not for me? Why is that, Roand? Is it because you're a gods-damned hypocrite?"

"Tarlak is currently atoning for his transgressions, all performed when he was not yet part of our council. You, though...you spat in my face by disobeying a direct order to stay out of Veldaren's affairs. You always thought you were the smartest and most clever of us. You weren't. And then out of some childish need, or a vain sense of pride, you had to go and insult us by enacting those same plans we shot down."

"That's shit," Deathmask said. "All of it, complete shit. You'd have strung me from this wall years ago if not for how many would have protested. You were a coward then, and you're a coward now."

Roand resealed the wax across Deathmask's lips, shutting him up. He then gently touched the disgraced wizard's burn scars.

"I merely took your name. That I didn't take your life was my parting gift to one who showed such promise. But instead of traveling to some remote corner of Dezrel to die in obscurity, you rebelled. You sought power, and practiced magic without our sanction. We even heard rumors of you teaching others our secrets. No matter how simple the spells, how base the cantrips you taught your guild members, you know that is something we do not allow."

Roand beckoned Tarlak to join him. Tarlak stood, his stomach suddenly cramping.

"I've witnessed you fight before," the lord of the council said. "You've a penchant for fire, though you don't seem willing to specialize in it. Perhaps you should reconsider. Flame is more than heat. It is the perfect method of destruction. It purifies. All matter, all substance, broken down to ash and dust while giving forth light and warmth. If carefully wielded, it can shape stone, twist steel, even remake entire kingdoms if left unchecked." He gestured to Deathmask's scarred face. "What you see is a crude, skill-less application. I would show you true art."

Tarlak didn't know where this was going, but he knew with absolute certainty he wasn't going to like it. He consoled himself with the knowledge that Deathmask was going to like it even less. *It's all about perspective*, he told himself. Perspective, and patience.

"Summoning elemental fire is child's play," Roand said. "But if you focus it on an incredibly narrow spot, igniting what you touch with a flash, you can burn flesh faster than the mind can recognize the pain."

The wizard placed a single finger on Deathmask's left cheek. Words of magic slipped off his tongue, rapid and short. Tarlak saw a brief flash of red, heard a pop, and then smoke rose in a thin gray trail. Deathmask flinched, clearly expecting pain, but when he opened his eyes he seemed unhurt. Roand pulled back his finger, revealing a single mark on the scars, burned so deeply it matched the blackened skin of a piece of meat left over a fire for too long.

"No pain," Roand said, smiling with smug satisfaction. "That is, until you want them to feel it."

As if brushing away a tear, he wiped his thumb across the black mark. The burned skin peeled away, revealing pale pink skin beneath that reddened from a sudden onset of blood. Deathmask screamed into his wax lips, his entire body tensing as he rocked back and forth against the chains. Tarlak shuddered.

"Do you see?" Roand said. "Perfectly smooth in its searing, fully controlled in its placement. A proper application of the art. Now you try."

Tarlak clenched his jaw tightly as Roand stood aside. Standing before Deathmask, Tarlak wished he could apologize, but he knew doing so would risk Roand's displeasure. Gently, Tarlak put a forefinger on the other cheek.

"The incantation is the same as a fire burst?" Tarlak asked.

"Perfectly similar. Use your thoughts to shape its flow. Pour out the power, and then cease it completely, as fast as your mind will allow. A flash, Tarlak. You are creating a flash of fire, so intense nothing may endure."

Tarlak swallowed down his nerves, his shame, and began the words. He felt the power building in his hand, power that he could unleash in a great torrent to impress a dragon, but he narrowed it down, imagining it coming out from the tip of his finger. The moment he felt the release, he ceased his words and cut off the spell. Smoke rose, and Tarlak felt uncomfortable heat on his fingertip. When he pulled back, a black mark similar to Roand's was burned into Deathmask's cheek. Tears ran down the captive man's face as he shuddered in his chains.

"Good," Roand said. "Very good. Not quite as focused as it needs to be, as you can tell by Deathmask's pain. To release magic, and then cease it in such rapid secession, is a skill one can only learn with practice."

He ran his fingers through Deathmask's hair, pulling it back from his face.

"Lots and lots of practice."

Hour after hour, Roand had Tarlak practice, until the night was deep, and every inch of Deathmask's scars had been replaced by Roand's art.

19

Each day that passed exhausted Jessilynn further. With eyes drooping and head hanging she walked the walls of the Castle of the Yellow Rose. The night was young, and she had four more hours before she might sleep again. The walls could never be left unguarded. They were too wide, too long, and it seemed every hour one of the beasts dared test the defenses.

"Looks like tonight might be a quiet one," one of the soldiers said as Jessilynn passed him by. He remained stationary, spear in one hand, shield at his feet. Part of Jessilynn was envious he didn't have to walk the entire length, but she also knew standing in one place would result in her falling asleep on her feet.

"I pray it is," Jessilynn said, smiling at him despite her exhaustion. Her presence inspired hope, and she tried her best to act the part expected of her. The soldier dipped his head, appreciative.

"Climber!" a soldier several hundred yards ahead shouted. Jessilynn felt her heart spike, and she sprinted down the wall in the direction of the cry. Any normal besieging army would have needed ladders, ropes, or siege towers to reach the ramparts, but with their incredible strength and sharp claws, the wolves and hyenas were capable of climbing to the top unaided. It took a bit of time, but if they weren't spotted by a patrol, a single beast could wreak havoc before being brought down.

Jessilynn raced past several soldiers, all who kept at their stations. At first they'd swarmed any attempted climber, but ceased when a group of four hyena-men reached the top after using another of their own as a distraction. The lesson had cost the lives of twelve good men. Now a handful of soldiers were placed on active patrol specifically to combat climbers, and

The King of the Vile

Jessilynn was the nearest. She watched as the man continued to shout. He held a bow, and twice fired arrows down the length of the wall. Jessilynn leaned between the crenulations and spotted a wolf-man scaling the wall at frightening speed.

"Climber!" shouted another man.

"Climber!" added a third, then a fourth. Jessilynn fought down panic as she pulled her bow off her back. This wasn't the true invasion, just another testing of their defenses. If it was the true attack, she'd have seen the massive swarms encamped beyond the wall surging toward her, but instead the several hundred yards between them and the wall remained empty. Telling herself to remain calm, she lifted her bow and sighted the climbing wolf-man beneath her. The first archer scored a hit on its shoulder, but the thing kept on coming. Letting out a soft breath, Jessilynn released an arrow of shimmering light. It hit the wall just left of the beast, blasting chunks of stone free. The wolf-man tensed, its head turning away from the bright flash, then resumed climbing.

You're better than this, Jessilynn told herself as she pulled back the string. An arrow of light materialized between her fingers, resting on the bow's sight. The wolf-man put a hand on the top of the wall, claws digging in. Before it could pull itself up, she released, and this time the arrow hit beneath its extended arm. The shot ripped a hole through its side, smashing the bones of its ribs and making a mess of its innards. The beast fell, blood and gore showering the dirt below.

Jessilynn spun on her feet, already pulling on her bowstring. The last soldier she'd passed had his spear ready, but she gave him no time to use it. The moment another wolf-man flung itself atop the wall, she let loose. The arrow struck its head, shattering its skull. The force of the hit flung it sideways, where it hit the stone and then lay still.

Bow still in hand, Jessilynn raced as fast as her legs could carry her, dancing around the bleeding body of the dead wolf-man. Far down the wall she saw several soldiers locked in desperate combat. One, the man she'd greeted, kept his climber along the side of the wall, his spear thrusting so it couldn't climb up. The angle of the wall kept her from seeing the creature. Jessilynn dropped to her knees and braced herself against the low wall. Half her body hanging over the side, she had a clear shot at the wolf-man. Her first hit was low, breaking the bones in its left leg. Her second broke its spine, dropping the creature.

Back to her feet, back to running. The air in her lungs burned, and she urged herself on despite soreness in every part of her body. She saw one last attack, only instead of one climber, it was three. The first wolf-man accepted a blow to its shoulder so it might reach the top, and it then dove upon the soldier with claws raking, teeth bared. The sounds of his screams were nails in Jessilynn's spine. She lifted her bow and aimed shakily.

She fired three glowing arrows in rapid succession. The nearest wolf-man died, two different arrows striking its back and punching through to strike the others. Its body erupted in an explosion of blood and bone. The others howled as the arrows struck, one losing an arm, the other collapsing from a hit to the side. The trapped soldier cut one down, then shoved against the other with his shield. Jessilynn drew a regular arrow from her quiver, not wishing to risk harming the brave man. She pulled back the arrow, but had no need to fire. The soldier shoved the injured wolf-man off the side of the wall to fall to its death.

"Please let that be the last," Jessilynn said as she collapsed onto her back and slowly caught her breath.

The thunderous cry that came from the wolf-man camp seemed to mock her request.

"Children behind the wall!" roared a voice Jessilynn instantly recognized. "I bring you gifts!"

Jessilynn groaned as she pushed herself upright and stared out across the field toward the swelling camp. At the forefront walked Manfeaster, black fur shimmering in the moonlight. The only break in color was around his long hands and claws, which were a deep red, like dried blood. Manfeaster stood tall as his pack gathered.

"Gifts!" Manfeaster cried. "Gifts from a king! Do you not want them?"

Jessilynn's grip on her bow tightened as she saw a crowd of people pushed through the wolf pack. There were at least forty of them, men, women, and children looking haggard and frightened as they were herded before Manfeaster. Their cries reached the

The King of the Vile

wall, and glancing over her shoulder, Jessilynn saw the frightened populace inside the castle stir with unease. They could hear the prisoners. They could hear Manfeaster's mockery. Jessilynn wondered how many out of the captured were family or friends of those within.

Soldiers steadily made their way to the wall, those asleep quickly roused and sent to retrieve their armor. Jessilynn waited, surprised by Manfeaster's patience.

"I know a lord hides within," the wolf-man shouted. "Let him face me. Let me hear his words. Or is he a coward?"

More soldiers on the wall, including a rather alert looking Dieredon. Given how he'd been resting for less than an hour, Jessilynn felt rather jealous.

"What's he planning?" Dieredon asked as he joined her side.

"I don't know," Jessilynn said. "Maybe he just wants to frighten us?"

The elf squinted into the darkness and shook his head.

"The goblins are building battering rams. It is only a matter of time before they attack. With their combined strength, they will break the gates with ease, removing our only advantage."

"Then we kill them before they get close," Jessilynn said. "What choice do we have?"

"What choice indeed," Dieredon said as his eyes narrowed.

Jessilynn followed the elf's gaze, but saw only blackness. Something didn't seem right. "What are they waiting for?" she asked.

"For the goblins to finish," the elf said. "That must be it."

"Then what is all this about?" she asked, gesturing to the distant prisoners. "Will they hand them over?"

Dieredon shook his head.

"I do not believe that will be the gift Manfeaster offers. I pray to Celestia I am wrong."

Manfeaster's patience steadily faltered until he was pacing before the prisoners, who he'd had lined up shoulder to shoulder.

"Will you ignore me?" he cried. "Will you ignore me even as I rip the flesh from your throat? So be it. I see the eyes on the walls. I know you watch."

Manfeaster reached out a hand. Jessilynn cried out, surprised and furious, as she saw one of the wolf-men offer him an enormous blade. Darius's sword...

"Do you see this blade?" the wolf-man cried. "Long I heard stories of its magic. My father could not withstand the power of the sword. We could not cross the river so long as the paladins stood against us. But the paladins are dead. The river is free. The sword is mine."

He took the weapon in both hands, turned to the nearest prisoner, and swung. It cleaved the woman in half at the waist. She died screaming, and those nearby joined in as wolf-men grabbed their arms and shoved them to their knees. One after the other, Manfeaster swung the blade, ripping open their throats, their chests, their stomachs. With each swing, he grew more accustomed to the weapon, more accurate with his executions.

Jessilynn lifted her bow, using her forearm to wipe tears from her eyes. She could not endure to see Darius's blade used in such a way, to slay the innocent. She could not sit back and do nothing. The distance was great, but she knew her blessed arrows could cross it. Light shone upon her as she pulled back the string.

"Don't," Dieredon said, grabbing her elbow.

"Why not?" Jessilynn asked.

"Because what we need more than anything is time," he said. "Manfeaster is willing to wait for the goblins to finish. Let him. Every minute that passes is one minute closer until angels from Mordeina arrive."

"If I kill him, they might scatter," she argued.

"Or they'll attack at once," Dieredon said. "I know this is hard, but you must put down the bow."

The light of her arrow stood out upon the dark wall, and it seemed it didn't go unnoticed.

"Little girl?" Manfeaster said after he finished killing the last poor soul. "Little paladin girl, is that you?"

"I am here," Jessilynn shouted, keeping the arrow drawn so its light might shine upon her. "Have you come to die like your brother? I killed him in his hunt, shot him dead like the dog he was. The same fate awaits you if you do not leave this place."

Manfeaster bared his fangs and panted laughter.

"I will taste your blood upon my tongue so very soon. Spare me your frightened words. They are feathers against my flesh."

I'll show you feathers, thought Jessilynn as she pulled back her arrow for flight.

"Don't," Dieredon said quietly. "Your time will come. Trust me, Jessilynn, please."

Jessilynn swallowed down the foul taste in her mouth and lessened the pressure on her drawstring.

"We refuse your gift," she shouted to the wolf king. "And we deny your crown."

"That wasn't the gift," Manfeaster said. "I will give you my gift."

He snarled something to the wolf-men around him. They bent down to the bodies and tore off their heads. Some broke easily, some needed to be twisted and pulled. Jessilynn shivered at every *crack* and *snap*. Forty wolf-men then rushed forward, each carrying a head. The moment they were close enough they flung the heads toward the walls. They could not reach the top, but flesh-covered skulls smacked all across its lengths. The wet crunching sound made Jessilynn want to vomit. The soldiers manning the wall looked equally horrified.

"This land is mine!" Manfeaster roared. "It belongs to the King of the Vile. I will chase you from it. I will break every head upon this wall. You rule no longer. The prison you made for us shall never be our home. This is our home now. Our land. Our nation. You will enter only as food for our bellies. Do you hear me, children behind the wall? Do you hear the bones breaking? Do you hear us feast?"

The wolf-men rushed back to the army and feasted as the soldiers watched. They tore into the bodies of the villagers, ripped them into pieces to be fought over. Tears ran down Jessilynn's face as she looked back to the hundreds of people gathered behind the wall, all relying on Arthur's soldiers to protect them.

"I don't care if they have battering rams," she said as the entire horde of creatures bellowed, shrieked, and roared. "I don't care how many they send, or how strong they are. We won't let this place fall. We won't let that fate befall those looking to us for salvation."

Dieredon placed a hand on her shoulder.

"You are more and more like Jerico with every passing day. That is his spirit I hear. Those are his words. Whether we live or die from this, I promise you, you will make him proud."

Jessilynn glared at Manfeaster, still holding the stolen greatsword.

"Not Jerico," she said, thinking of when Darius had come to her in her greatest time of need.

Dieredon's grip on her shoulder tightened, and when she turned back she saw the elf staring into the night sky.

"At last you arrive," he said to the air. Jessilynn spun around, searching the stars. It took her a few moments, but she caught sight of Sonowin's white body shining silver in the moonlight, great wings spread wide.

"Does this mean Mordeina's finally sent help?" she asked.

"We'll find out soon enough."

The two of them climbed down and made their way through the crowded encampments. Sonowin looped once above the castle before landing at the steps. Only two soldiers stood guard, and they raised their weapons. Jessilynn feared there might be a misunderstanding, but before they could even interfere she heard Sir Daniel Coldmine roaring at the two men.

"Put away your damn blades. You think orcs and wolf-men ride flying horses?"

The men obeyed, looking embarrassed. Dieredon sprinted across the grass and flung his arms around the neck of his horse.

"Welcome back, friend," he said.

Jessilynn jogged the last few steps, and she smiled at the touching sight. Sir Daniel saw them and bowed.

"My nameless saviors," he said. "I'd hoped to find you here. I'm glad to see you didn't die in some forgotten wood."

"I'm sure I will one day die alone and forgotten," Dieredon said, patting Sonowin's neck. "But not yet. What word do you bring from Mordeina?"

Daniel glanced at the two soldiers, who stood awkwardly nearby.

"Is Lord Arthur still in charge?"

"He is," Dieredon said.

The King of the Vile

"Then I'll save my words for him. Care to lead the way?"

"Rest, and eat if you must," Dieredon told Sonowin, pointing toward the fields. He turned to Daniel. "And follow me. I will show you the way."

Jessilynn joined them. She tapped Daniel on the shoulder after a spell, figuring it time she introduced herself.

"It's Jessilynn," she said. "Jessilynn of the Citadel, and that is Dieredon, Scoutmaster of the Quellan elves."

Sir Daniel cracked a smile despite his obvious exhaustion.

"Well then," he said. "I'm glad the two who saved my ass both have such impressive pedigrees."

They entered the castle and climbed the stairs to Arthur's room. Dieredon knocked twice, soft and respectfully, but Daniel appeared to have no patience for such things. He banged his fists on the door until he heard movement from inside, then stepped back. The door flung open, revealing a frowning Arthur dressed in loose bedclothes.

"Who the bloody abyss are you?"

Daniel bowed.

"Sir Daniel Coldmine, master of the Blood Tower," he said. "Well, I *was* master until those damn beasts overran it. I come bearing news from Mordeina."

Whatever sleep had been in Arthur's eyes quickly vanished.

"Come in," he said. "All of you."

They crammed into Arthur's spacious room. The walls were decorated with landscape paintings of the northern region, the blankets of his bed thick and colored crimson. Arthur returned to his bed and sat on the side.

"I don't care if the news is good or bad," Arthur said. "Just tell it to me in the plainest words possible. Now is hardly a time for pleasantries."

"That's good, because I've not come bearing pleasantries," Daniel said. "The southern lords mustered an army, but they're sending them south to counter a supposed invasion by King Bram."

"What of the angels?" Jessilynn asked, leaning against the door of the bedroom.

Daniel glanced her way. "They're not coming."

"They would leave us to our fate?" Arthur asked, mouth agape.

"It seems so. I don't know what's happening. I wish I did. It seems like politics of some kind, though damned if I can wrap my head around any of it. Just being in Mordeina...it's hard to describe, but it's like everything's rotten to the core, but no one wants to admit it."

Arthur sank into his bed and stroked his gray beard.

"That's it then. We've been abandoned to die."

"There is still hope the angels fly north to our rescue," Daniel said as he crossed his arms behind his back. "But for now...yes. We are on our own." He gestured to Dieredon. "This elf here saved my life, and I've come to repay the favor by returning his magnificent steed. My place is here in the north, protecting my people. The Castle of the Yellow Rose has withstood besiegement before, and by the gods or without them, she'll withstand this one, too."

Sir Daniel's words had meant to inspire, but Arthur dropped his head into his hands and sighed.

"Leave me be," he said. "I must digest this unfortunate news."

Jessilynn bowed along with the other two, and together they left Lord Arthur to dwell in private. The shutting of the thick door echoed through the stone hallway. Daniel stood before them, looking flustered and ashamed.

"I did what I could," he said, as if still needing to defend his actions. "I told Harruq, the lords, and the angels of the thousands of beasts swarming across the river, but it did no damn good."

"Do not be troubled," Dieredon said. "I have witnessed the stubbornness of humans for centuries. Sometimes mountains are easier to move than prideful hearts."

"How many times have you witnessed the stubbornness of angels?"

The elf's mouth twitched. "Not quite as often."

"Either way, it is good to meet the two of you again," Daniel said with a half-hearted salute. "Now if you don't mind, I need to find myself a bed. I expect I'll be here for a while, so I might as well settle in."

The King of the Vile

Jessilynn and Dieredon let him go, then exited the castle.

"Your, uh, horse went that way," a guard said, gesturing to one of the few somewhat empty stretches of grass close to the castle.

Dieredon thanked him and went after his horse. Jessilynn walked a few steps behind, wondering why the elf did not discuss this new development. A lack of aid coming from the south? But why? And how did it change their plans? She received no answers to these questions as they approached the place where the majestic Sonowin grazed. Dieredon put hands on either side of Sonowin's face and pressed their foreheads together. Away from the wall, and the many encampments of refugees, they finally found a measure of silence, and it hung heavy in the air. The elf seemed somber, which made Jessilynn nervous.

"We won't survive this," Dieredon whispered. "Not if we stay. Their numbers are too great, and ours too few. Our only real hope was to delay until rescue came, but that hope has been torn from us. Remaining here means death, nothing but death."

To hear such hopelessness in the skilled elf's voice was a thorn to Jessilynn's heart.

"What choice do we have?" she asked.

"We fly," he said, patting Sonowin. "We spread news of Lord Arthur's fall, and the massacre that took place within these walls. The outcry will give the angels no choice but to answer the threat."

Jessilynn's lower lip trembled, and she clenched her hands into fists. "You'd have us flee?"

"Rather than die here, yes. We accomplish nothing by throwing our lives away. It won't save a soul. The destruction awaiting us is complete, Jessilynn. Only a miracle will keep that army from smashing through the gates or climbing over the walls, and right now, I fear this world has no miracles left."

His words hurt her worse than if he'd pierced her with one of his arrows. She looked to the distant wall, mind haunted by images of villagers being slaughtered by Darius's sword. She felt tears building, and she hated it, hated feeling like such a little girl. She remembered Darius's words and clung to them.

Despite our terror, despite our fear, despite our doubts and sorrow, we fought anyway. Even when we thought it hopeless. Even when we knew it would cost us our lives.

"No," she said. "I'm not running."

She pulled her bow off her back, and she held it tight. "I was given this gift for a reason, and *this* is that reason. I've always feared I wouldn't live up to the legends that came before, the undead Jerico destroyed, the mad priest Darius brought low. *This* is my chance. You can go, but I'm staying. We told the people to flee here, and I won't abandon them. I will stand upon that wall, and I will hold those creatures back until they spill the blood in my veins. You say we need a miracle? Then so be it. I'll loose arrow after arrow until one arrives. Ashhur will save us, Dieredon. He will. I believe that with all my heart, and I want to be a part of it when it happens."

Dieredon stared at her with those guarded brown eyes of his. She waited for him to judge her, to call her a fool and insult everything she believed. Slowly he took the bow from her hands, set it on the grass, and knelt down. He cupped her hands in his and peered up at her in the moonlight.

"You are a lost child seeking light in a very dark world," he said. "And I would be honored to stand at your side upon that wall."

Jessilynn tried to smile, but she let out a sob instead as she flung her arms around the elf's neck and held him close.

20

Harruq watched the sun rise, the crisp morning air welcome against his skin. He stood on one of the upper balconies of the castle, drinking a bitter tea meant to chase the exhaustion from his mind. Fires had burned throughout the night, his soldiers having captured dozens of looters and arsonists. They'd all need to be judged, and Harruq would see to that. Then would come the merchants, the businessmen, all demanding reparations for their damaged homes and shops. Inevitably fingers would point toward Avlimar, seeking payment in the form of silver and gold. Payment he could never force the angels to hand over.

A long day of screaming and headaches, basically.

"I hope wherever you are, you appreciate this, Antonil," Harruq murmured as he leaned against the balcony rail overlooking the city sprawl. Smoke lingered in the air, making the skyline look like it was covered in dirt. "When we meet in the hereafter, I expect a damn handshake for handling all this mess."

He sighed. It was selfish to think that way, of course, but so what?. So many days spent bending over backwards to keep people happy, and failing anyway, had left him scraped raw. For all the good the angels had done, the sight of their white wings circling the distant Devlimar now filled his stomach with bile.

As his eyes lingered on the earthbound city of angels, he realized one of those distant pairs of wings was flying straight toward the castle. Harruq drummed his fingers on the railing and waited. The angel soared over Mordeina, never slowing, and as he approached, Harruq saw the enormous sword strapped to his back, as well as the angel's overall size. It seemed Ahaesarus was coming for a chat. Harruq was hardly surprised. An apology might be nice, too, but no apology would undo the damage of the angry riots.

The moment Ahaesarus landed, Harruq knew this was about something much direr than riots.

"Good morning," the angel said, bowing low. Harruq frowned, not liking the worry lines covering Ahaesarus's face one bit.

"Morning," Harruq said. "Come to join me for an early drink?"

"I wish the reason were that pedestrian."

The half-orc downed the rest of his tea and proceeded to twirl the cup on his forefinger. "Of course not. It never is. What's the matter, Ahaesarus? You look about how I felt after going blow to blow with Thulos."

The angel chuckled and joined Harruq in staring out at the city. For a long while he said nothing. The silence made Harruq even more nervous.

"We failed," Ahaesarus said softly.

Harruq caught the cup, ceasing its twirling.

"That's bloody obvious," he said, careful to keep his tone light. "Care to elaborate?"

The angel shook his head.

"Little good it will do. How did this happen, Harruq? Did we lose our way all at once, or was it a gradual slide? I thought we'd learned. I thought, after that horrible excursion into Ker for your brother, I could guide us to a proper path. But then Avlimar fell. I think, deep down, the hearts of many of my brethren fell with it."

"Tell me what's going on," Harruq said. He wasn't nervous anymore. He was terrified.

"Our place was never to rule," Ahaesarus said. "Nor to fight wars and anoint kings. We were to heal, to guide, and to use our blades to protect the innocent. I pray there is still time to make this right." He turned to Harruq. "In what comes next, know that I tried my best and was shouted down. Those who still heed my words are flying north with me, to the Castle of the Yellow Rose."

"How many?" Harruq asked.

"Three thousand," Ahaesarus said. "Little less than a third. Again, that is my shame to bear. Innocents die in the north, and I have done nothing but debate. Such fools are we. Such proud fools."

The angel offered him a hand, and when Harruq took it, Ahaesarus wrapped his other arm around him in an embrace.

"Azariah awaits you by your throne," he whispered. "He speaks for those who remain, and they are many. Do not keep him waiting."

"Sure thing," Harruq said, still confused, still frightened.

Ahaesarus stepped away, and Harruq was surprised to see tears running down his chiseled face. With a flourish of wings, the angel took to the air, flying northward. Hundreds more joined him from Devlimar, traveling in a great flock. Harruq watched, dread building, until he flung his cup to the balcony floor. The porcelain shattered, and he stared at the shards as if they were Mordeina herself.

Azariah indeed awaited him when he descended the stairs and made his way to throne room. Also accompanying him was an angel Harruq recognized from the previous night's trial, the one named Ezekai. The larger angel carried himself with the air of a bodyguard. *Why would an angel need a bodyguard in a guarded throne room?*

The only reason Harruq could think of made the twisting pain in his gut that much worse.

"Greetings, Harruq," Azariah said, dipping his head in respect.

"Pleasant mornings and all that," Harruq said as he plopped down onto the cushioned throne. "After last night's nonsense, I hope you've come with something approaching good news."

The thin smile on Azariah's face seemed to mock him.

"I come bearing truth. For some that is good, for some not, but it does not change my words. Do you have a moment of time?"

"I do."

"Then please banish your guards. These words are for your ears only."

Harruq sighed. Why come to his throne room if they wanted such private talks?

"Fine," he said, raising his eyes to his men. "Leave." Once the soldiers were out the doors, Harruq slumped in the throne. "We're alone. Care to share what's so important?"

"We angels held another conclave just before sunrise," Azariah said, the gold tint in his green eyes sparkling with life. "After the hatred we faced during the night, the calls for violence, the senseless burning and looting, we felt there was no choice. This ugliness had to be addressed, this thorn pulled from mankind's flesh before it could fester any longer."

Harruq raised an eyebrow.

"Are you talking about leaving?" he asked.

"Quite the opposite," Azariah said. "We have applied Ashhur's guidance and forgiveness to the people, but we apply it over an archaic system of laws and punishments. It is a bandage atop a broken suit of armor, unable to reach the wounded flesh beneath. If we are to perform Ashhur's will, then we must perform it upon a populace totally open to us, without artificial constructs of sinful mortals obfuscating the way."

Harruq wondered if maybe he should have kept his guards in the room after all.

"That's a lot of fancy words saying nothing," he said. "Care to tell me what's really going on?"

"In simplest terms, we will enforce Ashhur's will above all else," Azariah said. "Without fear of sinners' laments. Without questions from faithless doubters. We have walked the streets of eternity. We have beheld the face of Ashhur. With his voice now silent in this world, we ourselves will be his voice. I have been elected to bear this responsibility, and I will not shirk from such a burden."

Slowly Harruq rose from the throne, and he felt as if he wore a heavy suit of plate instead of his thin tunic.

"Above all else," he said with dread. "You're declaring yourself king."

"If that term aids your understanding," Azariah said. "This is a new age, Harruq. Dezrel has seen the truth of Karak's treachery, and they have seen Ashhur's faithful protecting the innocent. There is no more excuse for doubt, not in a world forged in the

The King of the Vile

ashes of the second Gods' War. Let us build a new kingdom from the dust, one ruled by Ashhur's angels, his edicts, and his voice."

"Your voice," Harruq said, ice swimming in his veins.

"The voice of the elected," Azariah said. "The voice of the one closest to Ashhur's wisdom. I was his greatest priest, and in Ashhur's absence, my role has only grown in importance. Have faith, Harruq. I will bear this crown with no more joy than you currently bear yours."

He nodded to Ezekai, who offered Harruq a rolled scroll. Harruq grabbed it, broke the wax seal, and read.

I hereby call for all to travel to Devlimar before the setting of the sun. During its descent, Ashhur's announcements will be given, along with a ceremony of great importance.

"Read that to the people of Mordeina," Azariah said. "It is vital that as many as possible attend."

"Devlimar's not near big enough to hold all the populace," Harruq said as he crumpled the scroll in his hands.

"Then let them stand outside and listen," Azariah said. "The important matter is that they come."

Harruq heard fluttering wings, and several more angels landing entered through the high windows. They perched on the sills like deadly birds bearing armor and weapons.

Harruq tossed the crumpled scroll at Azariah's feet. "Am I a prisoner?"

"Of course not," Azariah replied, smiling as if all were well between them. "So long as anyone accepts Ashhur's dominion over them, and commits no crime, then they are free. We will create a blessed land, Harruq, a re-creation of the Paradise from long before Karak and Ashhur warred with one another. Free people, worshipping with open hearts, no more slaves to us than the people are to you." He gestured to the side doors of the throne room. "So call your guards, call your advisors. Give them your message. As for myself, there is still much to do, and so little time to do it."

Azariah and Ezekai flew away, and Harruq called for his guards.

"Find Sir Wess," he told them, glancing at the angels who remained behind, lurking at the windows. "I've an announcement to make, and for that, I need an audience."

Thirty minutes later, Sir Wess had brought several thousand people before the castle entrance. Harruq stood on the steps before them, the scroll Azariah had given him smoothed out best he could. Ignoring the people's shouts, confused looks, and angry glares, he read aloud the words, each syllable a knife to his tongue. When he finished, he fled to his room.

"I heard your announcement," Aurelia said. She stood at the window, watching the crowd below disperse. Aubrienna bounced atop the bed, a stuffed doll of a knight in hand. "What news of theirs is so important they want the whole city to hear?"

"Azariah's declaring himself King of Dezrel," Harruq said. "That's what."

Aurelia turned from the window, walnut eyes widening.

"Surely not."

"Yes," Harruq said, slumping down onto the bed. Aubrienna promptly attacked him with the knight, but he had no heart for it. The stuffed toy thudded against his chest in vain attempts to stab him with a wood stick. Aurelia sat beside him, and she grabbed his hand and held it.

"Maybe it's not as bad as you think," she said. "With all the violence, maybe they want to start over. And even if Azariah tries, the other angels won't allow him to take a position he was never meant to have."

"I heard him," Harruq muttered. "I know. This isn't good. And the angels will let him, Aurry. There's...there's something wrong with them. They're lost, broken, different. You've sensed it too."

"You're afraid," his wife whispered, and leaned her head on his shoulder.

"I am," Harruq said. "They're not our protectors anymore. I was talking with Deathmask in Avlimar's ruins, trying to find out if there was truth to the claims of his involvement in destroying the place, when two angels found us. I had to...I had to kill one of them. I ordered him to stand down and let Deathmask leave, but he refused. You should have seen it, Aurry. The sheer disgust on his face at the thought of taking orders from a mere mortal."

"Why did you never tell me?"

He shrugged.

"I've managed to dance around the issue, but I figured it was only a matter of time before I slipped up and they caught me in a lie. Last thing I wanted was to land you in trouble, too."

"You get in trouble, then *we* get in trouble, you dumb ox," Aurelia said. She kissed his cheek. "As if I'd sit and wring my hands while the angels held you for trial."

"No, you'd probably blow a gigantic hole in whatever dungeon they tried to hold me in," Harruq said, laughing. "It'd almost be worth it to see the terror in the eyes of the angels who tried to stop you."

Aubrienna, having failed to get her father to play, slid off the bed to where several other dolls waited. As his daughter fought a dragon carved from wood and painted red, Harruq lowered his voice

"We can't bring her with us tonight," he said. "Same for Gregory. We need to find a safe place for the two of them should things turn ugly."

Aurelia slid off the bed and free of his grasp.

"Then let's get started."

The day passed swiftly. Harruq made sure to spend much of it with Aubrienna and Gregory, roaring like an idiot as he pretended he was a dragon. Several times guards interrupted, bearing news of the growing line at the castle doors. Every time, Harruq sent them away. No matter how loudly the people protested, there was little he could do. Even now, angels hovered over the castle, keeping watch. Azariah wanted the ears of the city, and in his glittering home, he would get them.

Finally, when the sun was just beginning to dip, Harruq rustled the young king's hair and kissed his daughter goodbye.

"Guard them well," he told Sir Wess, who awkwardly held the children's hands.

"It seems a foul plan that would have such youngsters hiding in a filthy dungeon," he said.

"There's nowhere safer," Harruq said. "Make sure no angels see you on the way. And avoid all the windows, is that clear?"

"Perfectly."

Aurelia kissed Aubby on the cheek, wished her well, and then watched the knight lead her and Gregory down the hall.

"Fucking angels," Harruq muttered.

They returned to their bedroom. Aurelia slid on a vibrant green dress, and Harruq realized it was similar to what she'd worn when he first met her all those years ago in Woodhaven. When he reached for his own fine silk shirt, Aurelia stopped him.

"No," she said. "Not that."

He sighed in relief and dressed in plain clothes, then pulled his leather armor off the stand in the corner. He concentrated on tightened the buckles even though it was a task he could do in his sleep; he didn't want his thoughts to drift into made-up scenarios of what might happen over the next few hours. Buckle after buckle, strap after strap, he fastened the armor granted to him by Velixar, armor baptized with the blood of dark paladins, war demons, pillaging orcs, shattered undead, and even a god.

The blood of the innocent, too. Before all else, he'd massacred a little village whose name Harruq couldn't remember, if he'd ever known at all. A thousand times he'd heard his brother be condemned, and yet here Harruq stood, steward of the realm. For whatever reason, forgiveness clung easier to Harruq than it did Qurrah, but they'd both bathed in innocent blood and given their lives to atone for it. And now before Ashhur's own chosen wardens, he wondered if he must give his life again.

"Ready?" he asked Aurelia when he finished dressing. His wife held a staff she'd magically summoned, and she leaned upon it while observing him.

"Almost," she said. Setting aside the staff, she knelt before the chest at the foot of their bed, opened it, and pulled out Salvation and Condemnation. Harruq hardened his jaw at the sight of them. Angel blood. He'd forgotten the angel blood that also stained his armor and blades. Would Shoa's be the last?

Harruq tried to ignore his fears, to grin and joke as he always did.

"I thought dressing for a fight might cause one," he said.

The King of the Vile

Aurelia buckled the ancient blades around his waist.

"That's what I'm praying for."

She kissed his lips, and then hand in hand they left for Azariah's crowning ceremony, to be held at twilight in the fallen city of angels.

21

"There they are," Tessanna said. She stood beside Qurrah atop a hill, overlooking the road. Camped and waiting for them, dozens of tents scattered throughout the valley, was the army of Mordan.

"They've come to face us at last," Qurrah said, frowning. King Bram's seven thousand were evenly matched in number by Mordan's forces, which meant Bram was doomed once the angels joined the fight, except the skies were clear of white wings.

"Where are the angels?" he wondered aloud.

Tessanna shrugged.

"Perhaps Bram was right, and they fly north to deal with the beasts crossing the Gihon River."

"Perhaps," Qurrah said, watching Bram's men scramble about, their march temporarily halted so they could sharpen their blades, ready their armor, and put every last man into formation. Bram would want Qurrah and Tess at the front of the battle, fighting alongside the dark paladins to crush Mordan's forces. The idea soured his stomach worse than curdled milk.

"I need to speak with Bram," he said. "Will you wait here for me with our things?"

"If you insist," she said.

"I do," Qurrah said. He wrapped his whip around his arm and trudged down the hill.

Bram's tent was packed with advisors updating their king on the preparations and discussing strategy and formation. Xarl was with him, a fact Qurrah was hardly pleased about. No one seemed to notice his entrance, so after failing to gain their attention by clearing his throat twice, he finally shouted.

"My king, if I might have a word?"

The King of the Vile

Bram glanced up from his table, and his initial glare cooled the blood in Qurrah's veins. Bram usually played the most noble of gentlemen, treating Qurrah like he were a precious friend. That glare, though...that glare said something very much the opposite.

"Go, and prepare as I've told you," Bram ordered his men, and they reluctantly filed out. "Not you," he added before Xarl exited. Qurrah bit his tongue. He didn't want the dark paladin there, but it seemed he didn't have an option.

"I assume preparations are going well?" Qurrah asked.

"They are," Bram replied. "I was wondering where you were off to. I was hoping to speak with you before the battle."

"About what?" Qurrah asked even though he was certain he already knew.

"I'd like you to stay back and protect Queen Loreina," he said.

Apparently Qurrah did not know the king as well as he thought.

"You don't want me in the fight?" he asked.

"I want you guarding what is most important to me," he said. "Which is my wife. The dark paladins will be more than capable of tilting the battle to our favor."

Qurrah narrowed his eyes. The king was diminishing Qurrah's importance to the overall campaign, but why? Did he know of Qurrah's growing reluctance to fight alongside him? Or perhaps the dark paladins had requested it, and Bram was all too eager to appease so long as it earned him his victory? Qurrah would have liked to say he didn't care either way, but he did. He cared immensely, for this was no normal opponent. This was his brother's army. Even worse, with Qurrah's role diminished, it meant dark paladins had that much more influence over the king.

"Do you know who leads them?" Qurrah asked warily.

"Based on the banners, I'd say Lord Aerling," Bram said.

Not Harruq, was all Qurrah heard. A bit of hope kindled in his heart.

"There's no angels," he said. "And Harruq does not lead them. We have no reason to fight them, Bram. Parlay. These lords are surely as tired of the rule of angels as you are. You might even win yourself some allies with your silver tongue."

Bram laughed at him. Just a soft chuckle, but there was no denying the dismissal.

"These men have marched against me to preserve their own power," he said. "Don't you see, Qurrah? The power of angels is already fading, and who will fill the void? I shall. My rule. My crown. Those lords you see up there? Those private bannermen? They're all fighting for a chance at the power I would take for myself. There will be no winning them to my side, only scattering them out of my way before continuing our march to the capital."

"And how do you know that with such confidence?"

"Because I have eyes where you do not," Anora said, slipping into the tent with them. She sneered, her long, pointed nose, giving her the look of a grinning weasel. The woman was already a distasteful presence, but to have her also gloating pushed her to new levels of unpleasantness.

"Then those eyes should see a clear lack of angels," Qurrah said. "This fight bears no meaning. Crushing a few stubborn lords is irrelevant to your goal."

"They stand in my way," Bram said. "And they will challenge my right to rule. I have every reason to see them scattered, angels or no angels."

Qurrah took a step back and tried to remain calm. He should have seen it earlier. He should have listened to Tess.

"This was never about overthrowing the angels," he said. "Never about protecting Ker. You want to rule both nations."

Bram looked frustrated while he rapped his knuckles on the table in the center of the tent. Xarl, meanwhile, just looked amused.

"Tell me, Qurrah, do you know a better way to overthrow the rule of angels than to become their king?" Bram asked. "Do you know a better way to protect Ker than to conquer the enemy that threatens you? Right now, Mordeina is ruled by a boy and a half-orc steward, both clearly in the pockets of the angels. If left unchecked, humanity will lose all control over her fate, and so I do what we must. If you can't accept that, if you can't agree that my battle is the righteous one, then leave my camp and return to your home in the woods. Enjoy the freedom that the blood of my soldiers will earn you."

The King of the Vile

Qurrah remained silent. He could see Bram's point, but he could also could clearly see Xarl and Anora on either side of the king, the Council of Mages and Karak's Paladins both eager to dive on scraps as King Bram marched into Mordeina. It wasn't about removing mankind from the prison of angels. It was about replacing that prison with one of Bram's making.

"If you wish me to stay at the rear of the army, then I shall," Qurrah said, and he bowed.

"Try to stay alert," Xarl said. "An ambush might come at any time."

He was mocking him, of course, but Qurrah smiled as pleasantly back as he could manage.

"Wise advice. I'll keep it in mind."

And then he hurried out, unable to stand their presence any longer. Qurrah rushed through the chaos of the army. When he reached the hill, he found Tessanna lying in the grass, beautiful as ever. She took one look at his face and knew at once what had happened.

"They don't need us anymore, do they?" she asked.

"Not with Anora and the dark paladins offering their aid," he said.

"I thought so." She rolled onto her back. "Anora, the paladins...they're predictable, you realize. What they want. What they're hoping for, power and wealth, things Bram can understand. Us, though? He can't understand us, can't trust us, and therefore he can't control us. Of course he'd push us aside."

"It's not just that," Qurrah said as he knelt before his pack of provisions. "This war against the angels...it's all a lie. Bram believes in what he's doing, he truly does, but if it wasn't angels, it'd be something else he was protecting the nation of Ker from. Bram seeks power, no different than anyone else. I never should have believed otherwise."

With the pack open, Qurrah pushed aside a few scattered belongings until he found the robes that lay on the very bottom. Qurrah brushed his fingers against the white fabric, which seemed to shine in the daylight. It was so smooth, so wonderful to touch. Despite the blood and gore that had fallen upon them, no stain seemed capable of finding purchase. Qurrah thought to when he'd first received the robes, a gift given by the angel, Azariah.

Show the world who you really are, Azariah had said. Perhaps it was time to do so again.

Tessanna saw the robes and rose to her feet. Qurrah hovered over the pack, frightened to remove them from within.

"Do you know what Lathaar told me?" he said. Tessanna wrapped her arms around his shoulders. "Karak does not need my help to burn the world anew, nor does he need yours. All he needs is us to stand aside and do nothing."

Tessanna nuzzled his neck. "Do you truly think we are such a threat to Karak's delusional goals?" she purred.

Qurrah remembered his stand on the bridge, the war demons he slaughtered in the sky, the waves of undead he tore down as he protected King Theo White and his soldiers. Yet still that paled compared to Tessanna when her black wings bloomed in full.

"Yes," he said. "I think we are."

He stripped down and slipped the white robes over his body. The fabric clung to his skin, and it felt so soft, so comfortable, he wondered why he ever stopped wearing them. Rising to his feet, he took his wife's hands and pulled her close.

"If we entered Mordan to protect mankind's freedom, then we start right here and now," he said. "Let us become everything Karak has ever hated. Let us become chaos."

"Where have *you* been these past few months?" Tess whispered, kissing his lips and giggling like a child.

"Sleeping," he said. "Are you ready?"

She squeezed his hands.

"My magic's weak," she said. "I'm not sure how much help I will be to you. My power came only from slaying angels. That's what Mommy wanted from me. I don't know if she wants this."

Qurrah shook his head.

"The wings are yours, Tess. Demand them. Leave the goddess no choice but to give you the power you need."

Tessanna pecked his cheek.

"We'll see."

A bellowing communal roar rolled up the hill, and the ground seemed to shake beneath Qurrah's feet. He looked to

The King of the Vile

Bram's army and saw them charging in formation toward the lines of soldiers from Mordan, the paladins of Karak leading them with flaming swords held high.

"Let's go," Qurrah said. "I have a promise to Lathaar to keep."

The three captured paladin trainees were kept near the back of the encampment, with two guards on watch at all times. When marching, the guards chained them together, but when not, they were attached to stakes pounded deep into the ground. Taking care of two guards would be easy enough, though the close proximity to Loreina's tent might prove troublesome. They needed to get in and out before the battle ended.

"Once I get the prisoners, hurry back to our campsite," Qurrah told Tess, trying to act calm in case they were spotted. "From the hill's vantage point you should have a clear view of the battle. Do what you can to influence it in Mordan's favor. I hold no love for Mordan and her nobility, but it's better they win than Bram."

"If you insist," she said.

Qurrah kept one eye on the battle as they neared the Bram's pavilion. Two armed soldiers stood at the entrance, but Qurrah gave them no reason to think anything was amiss. Other than his robes, of course, but he doubted a simple change in garment would elicit an attack. Qurrah led Tess around the back of the pavilion, toward the imprisoned paladins.

"The battle's already starting to swing Bram's way," Qurrah said as the enormous tent blocked sight of the conflict. "And that's with Anora yet to join in."

"You're asking much for me to sway this battle," Tessanna said, but despite her doubtful words, she sounded exited.

"Don't let Anora frighten you," Qurrah said. "You can defeat her with your eyes closed."

Past the pavilion were a few more rows of tents, and then a gap in the camp where the three posts were nailed. As expected, the four guards who watched over the chained paladins drew their weapons when he and Tess approached.

"Stay back," one of them said. "We've orders to allow no one to speak with the prisoners until the battle has ended."

"And I have new orders," Qurrah said. "*Sleep.*"

Darkness like mist floated from his hands, branching into streams that flowed into the soldiers' mouths and nostrils. One by one they dropped to their knees. Only the nearest fell asleep immediately, but Tessanna walked among them, whispering as she gently touched their faces. Their combined magic plunged the men into a sleep so deep that not even a bath of ice-cold water would wake them for several hours.

It'd have been easier to kill them, but Qurrah preferred to kill as few as possible. Even if Bram were in the wrong, the soldiers under his command didn't deserve to suffer. Qurrah himself had followed Bram, why should he condemn others for the same?

"Are you here to save us or kill us?" asked red-haired Samar as Qurrah knelt beside him. He seemed the most together of the three young paladins, his jade eyes watching Qurrah's every move.

"Have a little trust for once," Qurrah said as he grabbed the chain attached to the manacles about the boy's wrists. "We're here to save you. If I wanted you dead, I'd have kept my mouth shut while Xarl made a spectacle of you before your teachers."

Shadow swallowed the chain, weakening it. With a pull, Qurrah snapped the metal in half. He examined the chains wrapped about the paladin's waist and chest, locking them to the post. Extra precautions for the battle, it seemed. Had Xarl predicted his attempt?

"Qurrah?" Tessanna said. He glanced up, his innards freeze. At least twenty soldiers rushed toward them from Queen Loreina's pavilion. Had they hidden in wait? Even more worrisome was how several others rushed toward the front lines, no doubt seeking reinforcements.

"Shit," Qurrah murmured. The captured paladins squirmed with fear.

"Look out!" one of them shouted.

Qurrah saw movement from the corner of his eye, and he rolled as a sword struck the dirt where he'd knelt. When he came up to his feet, fire flared about his hands. A young dark paladin faced him, thin wisps of fire, barely more potent than the whiskers on his chin, burning about his blade. He must have hidden in one

The King of the Vile

of the nearby tents, otherwise Qurrah would have seen him approach.

"The soldiers are mine," Tessanna said, fire blazing about her hands. Qurrah put his back to her, trusting her completely. Even if Tess wasn't at full strength, she was potent another to combat men with mere armor and blades.

The dark paladin had his eyes fixed on Qurrah. "Xarl thought Ashhur's cowards would attempt to flee during the battle," he said. "But never did I think you would be there to aid them."

"Karak and I don't get along," Qurrah said, lashing the whip at the grass between them. "How long until you and your god get that through your thick skulls?"

Qurrah heard screams from the soldiers behind him, and he chose that moment to strike, hoping the young paladin would distracted. His whip wrapped about the man's right leg, the burning leather blazing so hot it burned through his armor and scored flesh. The dark paladin hollered in pain as he charged forward, weapon raised for attack. He took two steps and swung, a high arc meant to cleave Qurrah in half from shoulder to hip, but such clumsy brutality would never suffice, not against him. Qurrah had fought the Watcher in his prime. He'd faced his own brother when at his greatest fury. This brat was nothing compared to them.

Shadows swarmed around Qurrah's open hand as he sidestepped the attack. He dove past the paladin and yanked his whip upward as he rolled back to his feet. The burning leather slid against the dark paladin's chestplate before reaching his throat. The man let out a choked cry as it burned the flesh about his neck. Sword limp in his hand, he stepped back, flailing desperately at the whip. Qurrah gave him no chance. Shadow flew from Qurrah's palm, a solid bolt of force that struck the paladin's chest. The metal crunched inward, blood flowing through the newly opened cracks.

The dark paladin collapsed to his knees, all strength leaving him. Qurrah grabbed the young man's face with his free hand, using his heel to trap the wrist holding the sword. A word of magic, and fire blazed from his fingers, setting the dying man alight. Qurrah shoved him to his back, his screams lasting but a moment before he fell still.

"I expected better," Qurrah spat at the smoldering corpse.

"And so you shall have it."

Qurrah turned. Anora approached through the encampment, a smug grin on her face. His worry returned. A dark paladin in training was one thing. A master wizard from the Council was another. He braced his legs, summoning all his power from the well deep within him. This would be no easy task. Sparing a glance, he saw Tessanna dancing through the soldiers, and to his surprise, she was smiling. Fire looped about her, an impenetrable tornado. From within, she flung arrows of shadow, against which their chainmail meant nothing.

"The moment I saw you I had a feeling we'd find time for a duel," Qurrah said, releasing his whip and banishing its flame.

"I too hoped I would be given the privilege of killing you," Anora said. "The great traitor and his whore of Celestia? Such accomplishments will have me remembered forever at the towers when I return."

Qurrah looked over her shoulder, saw the battle still raging. At least with Anora engaging him, she wouldn't be aiding the larger fight. Not much consolation there. Shadows sparking from his fingertips, he grinned at the woman, telling himself to enjoy the challenge. It'd been ages since he faced a spellcaster of any repute.

"When you return," he said. "How cute. You think you'll win."

He gave her no chance to respond. Twin bolts of shadow flung from his palms, their edges sparking with white electricity. Anora extended a hand, fingers splayed. A translucent shield shimmered into existence and the bolts slammed into it with a *crack* like breaking stone. The shield rippled but did not break. Qurrah flung three more, giving her no reprieve. The bolts broke against the shield, but each one would take a tiny piece of her strength, slowly sapping her. To be fair, Qurrah was likely weakening quicker, but he had to trust that his power was greater. If Tessanna would join in...

"Is this all you have?" Anora asked. She stomped a foot, and the ground shook as if she were a giant. Qurrah stumbled, his next spell ruined, and the woman took the offensive. Her shield vanished and two long blades of concentrated lightning formed in her hands. They appeared made of concentrated lightning, crackling at her touch. She swung one, and despite the distance between them, the blade grew until it were nearly twenty feet long. Panicking, Qurrah summoned his shield, and he grunted as the lightning crackled against it.

"I'm just getting started," Qurrah said as the second blade struck. The brightness of both blades hurt his eyes, but he dared not look away. His best advantage now was that with her hands holding her unique weapons, she couldn't react as quickly against his attacks. Flaring power into his shield, he took a step forward. The lightning blades bowed as he shortened the distance, and through the newly formed gap he let loose a burst of flame.

A flame that vanished into nothing as the woman pressed her wrists together and muttered a word of power. Qurrah went to cast again, but she pointed a finger at him. A barrage of colors flashed before his eyes. Disoriented and suddenly queasy, he staggered backward, hands flailing to re-summon his shield. He more felt than saw the lightning blades strike against it. Thrice more they hit, then pulled back.

Desperate, Qurrah flung invisible waves of weakness and disorientation right back at her, hoping to force her to relent.

"Curses?" Anora said as her earrings shimmered with sudden energy. "Do you think I'm not protected against something so quaint?"

Qurrah shrugged.

"One can hope."

She lashed him with her lightning as if punishing him for his petulance. The magical blades grew again, and this time they wrapped around him like Qurrah's own whip. From all sides of his shield they crackled, tearing into his magical protection, wearing him down. Qurrah felt his mind breaking from the strain. He'd never fought such a weapon before, one that seemed designed solely to break through his magical protections. Lances of ice and blasts of flame he could scatter with ease, but this damn electricity? It didn't hit just once, nor at a focused point, but everywhere, over and over in constant pressure.

He retreated, hoping in vain for space. Anora matched him step for step. They drew closer to the chained paladins, who cowered in terror at the battle playing out before them.

"Tess!" screamed Qurrah. Damn his pride, and the stupid soldiers. He needed help.

Almost at once fire surged toward the sorceress, and she had to cross her wrists to counter. Tessanna approached, black tendrils growing from her back like the wings of a demon. They snapped at Anora like snakes that swayed side to side. The spellcaster's lightning blades grew to absurd lengths and sliced through the shadow, banishing them. But Anora's focus was split now, and Qurrah kept up the pressure. Bones ripped free from the dead paladin of Karak's corpse, shimmering with magic as Qurrah controlled them with his mind. They lashed against Anora's exposed skin, slicing and bruising her. A gust of wind rolled out from her in all directions, blowing back the floating bones.

A blade of lightning crashed against Qurrah's shield as she spun, attacking both he and Tess at once. Qurrah pushed himself through the pain. Most of the bones might be gone, but the body still remained close, filled with the leftover energy that collected after a soul's passing. Words of magic dashed off his lips, and he poured his own power into the corpse. With a clenching of his fist, it exploded. The larger bones that lingered, particularly the pelvis and skull, proved the most damaging. Anora staggered, and finally those damn blades of lightning faded away as she summoned a proper shield to protect herself.

"Even outnumbering me, you will not win," she said, though it sounded like she was trying to convince herself and not them. "I've trained with masters. I know spells you can only dream of."

"And I have walked the chaotic spaces between the worlds you call dreams," Tessanna said. A wave of her hand, and a ring of fire exploded outward from her waist. Anora protected herself from it with her shield, but the remaining two soldiers Tessanna had been fighting were run through, their armor melting and flesh burning away. Their innards spilled across the ground as they collapsed. Clenching her fingers, Tessanna ripped their spines

The King of the Vile

from their bodies. The bloodied bones swirled about her, each vertebrate snapping free as they orbited in three long ovals.

"Masters," Tessanna said, her voice echoing as if two people spoke, not one. "Who are they compared to a goddess?"

Anora pressed her hands together and unleashed a crimson beam of raw magical power. The beam hit the swirling bones with a sound of thunder, but it was the beam, not the bones, that broke. Tessanna waved a hand, and bone pieces flung toward Anora, black shadows swirling about them. They struck the woman in the chest and stomach, each hit sounding more painful than the last.

Anora screamed, and she pulled a gem from a pocket and clutched it tightly. At a word, the gem shattered. Qurrah sensed the power within it, and it poured into Anora accompanied by a rushing sound of air. Tessanna struck again, and Qurrah joined in, firing bolts of shadow alongside her shimmering bones. Both hit Anora's renewed shield and dissolved.

"Two decades I poured my strength into this gem," Anora shouted. "Two decades of preparing to overthrow Roand, and you've made me waste it on you!"

Qurrah might have felt more proud if he wasn't scrambling to stay alive. A barrage of fire and ice exploded out of Anora. Her eyes and mouth unleashed flame, her fingertips shards of ice. Every hit on his shield was like a punch to the gut. Tears filled his vision. Anora's entire body shimmered, magical power arcing off her like lightning. Poor Samar was so close he had to close his eyes and turn away lest his face be burned.

That lightning blasted toward Qurrah. Instead of blocking, he ripped open earth before him and created a wall. The beam smashed into it, blasting through stone and tearing into Qurrah's body. He rolled along the ground, heart hammering, ears ringing. A similar blast flew toward Tessanna, but she handled it better. The bone shield swirled, magical protection shimmering like a shadow before her. The lightning continued on and on, and Tessanna screamed from the pain. Despite the power required for such an incredible display, Anora refused to relent. Beads of sweat ran down her forehead, blood trickled from her nose, yet it seemed the reserve granted by the gem provided her with endless power.

"I will drag you to the towers," she shouted. "I will let you suffer for an age in rooms where time is but a dream. You'll bleed, and scream, and beg..."

Her words died as Samar extended his leg as far as he could and kicked her directly in the crotch. She doubled over, the lightning about her hands flickering for the slightest moment.

Qurrah dove toward her, word of power on his lips.

"Hemorrhage!"

His power flooded into her, and she could not counter in time. Her face exploded, blood rupturing from her nose in a torrent. The rest of her flesh peeled back, caving in her teeth and sending her eyeballs flying in opposite directions, the connecting nerves trailing with them. An aching death rattle escaped her throat as she collapsed to her knees, then slumped to one side, a pool of blood collecting beneath her head.

"Thanks," Qurrah said, slumping beside the kid.

"Welcome," the paladin said. His eyes lingered on the dead body, and he looked an inch away from vomiting. "Please don't tell Jerico. I doubt that counted as fighting honorably."

"Forget fighting honorably," Qurrah said. "Fight to live. Everything else is vanity."

Rising to his feet, he looked at Tessanna. She was tired, beaten, and bruised, but alive.

"Remind me to never make enemies of the Council," Qurrah told her, and he laughed. Bodies surrounded them, dozens of dead soldiers, plus a dark paladin and a sorceress of the Council...and they weren't safe yet.

"Let's get you free," Qurrah said, circling around to the back of Samar so he had easier access to the chains.

"There's someone coming," said Mal, the tall kid bound between Elrath and Samar. Qurrah groaned, and he peered over the post. Sure enough, someone did walk toward them through the rows of tents, someone Qurrah recognized rather well.

"Take the paladins and go," Qurrah said to Tess as he started for Xarl.

"I can help you," she insisted.

The King of the Vile

"There's no time! If Xarl's here, then the fight is nearly over. Escaping now means nothing if Bram marches to Mordeina unopposed."

Tessanna clearly disagreed, but she quickly began undoing the chains of the three young paladins. Qurrah stepped in front of her, trusting himself to be enough of a distraction that the others could escape in time. Xarl slowly circled him, his long sword and short sword blazing with fire.

"First I kill Anora, and now you," Qurrah said, stalling. "It seems today is a day of answered prayers."

"The great traitor," Xarl said. "I should have expected such behavior from you. You're only following your nature, after all."

"You throw that title at me as if it were an insult," Qurrah said. "But I betrayed Karak above all else. He gave me power, and with it I slew his prophet. I swore him my life, and now I deny it to him with every breath I take." The half-orc pointed at Xarl, whip writhing on his arm like a furious serpent. "Call me traitor. Say it a thousand times, and a thousand times I will thank you for the honor."

"You think your life is no longer Karak's?" asked Xarl. "You think Ashhur will protect you? It is not 'traitor' I should call you, Qurrah Tun. Fool, I label you. Blind, deluded fool. That Karak ever gave you his power is a mystery I'll never understand. What promise did he see in you that a hundred others could not have also fulfilled?"

Qurrah grinned, and as the excitement of battle pounded through his veins, he dared think himself similar to his brother. Let the conflict fuel him. Let the danger thrill him, adding strength to his tired limbs.

"Ask Karak for your answer," he said, taking the handle of his whip into his hand. "I'm about to send you to him."

He swung the whip, hoping for another surprise hit like before, but Xarl was much faster. His longsword plunged toward the ground, and the whip wrapped about its blade. Xarl pulled, and Qurrah had no hope of matching his strength. The whip flew from his hand. The fire vanished when it landed.

Even though the fight with Anora had drained him, Qurrah dug deep within himself, pointed both palms to the grass, and blasted out a wave of purple fire. The fire rolled forward, steadily rising in height. Xarl clanged his swords together and flung them into the dirt. An invisible shockwave spun outward from the god-blessed weapons, creating a ring around him and banishing the fire. Yanking the weapons free, the dark paladin rushed forward. Black fire burned about the steel, hungry for flesh. Qurrah retreated, hands dancing.

"Hemorrhage!" he shouted, frustrated by how weak his voice sounded, and even more so at the weakness of his spell. Xarl crossed his arms, the spell opening a wound on his forearm beneath the gauntlet. It didn't so much as slow him down. About to be run through, Qurrah dropped to the ground, crossed his arms, and summoned a wall of shadow about himself.

The flaming swords struck the shadow wall, bounced off. Xarl hesitated, looming above him, visible as a black and white version of himself. Qurrah detonated the shield, and the blast flung Xarl into the air. Maddeningly, the paladin landed on his feet.

"How many tricks do you have left?" Xarl asked as he charged.

Qurrah pointed toward Anora's body, and her arm reached out to grab Xarl's ankle. The paladin lost his balance and fell, and Qurrah flung a frustratingly small bolt of shadow at him. The bolt struck the armor across his shoulder, crunching it inward. Xarl leapt back to his feet and screamed as he slammed his weapons together. Karak's power washed over Qurrah in another shockwave. It sickened his stomach, and he vomited.

Xarl took two steps forward and swung. Qurrah fell back, but not fast enough. A burning blade sliced through his white robes, the very tip digging into his left side for a brief, painful moment. He dropped back to the ground, rolled, and then bounded to his feet. Blood dripped from his chest and it hurt to breathe. He was too weak, too drained to fight. So he ran toward Loreina's pavilion—or more specifically, the shadows the huge tent cast. Qurrah could create portals leading from shadow to shadow, sometimes crossing miles if given enough time. Words of magic flying off his tongue, he focused on a specific destination. The shadows before him deepened, and with a hissing of air, a portal ripped open. Wind roared out of it, blowing against his robes.

"Coward!" shouted Xarl as he raced toward him, legs pumping, platemail rattling.

Qurrah slowed down and allowed the sprinting dark paladin to draw closer, focusing on keeping the portal open. He had no intention of being a coward, no intention of fleeing.

The portal wasn't for him.

Xarl lunged toward Qurrah, two swords leading. The moment Qurrah saw the paladin leap off his feet, he stepped left and spun. The burning swords stabbed into the portal. Grabbing Xarl's wrist, Qurrah pulled, adding to his already impressive momentum. The dark paladin went headfirst inside, but before he could enter completely, Qurrah killed the spell. The portal slammed shut. Xarl's upper half teleported to a shady grove within a distant forest, the lower half plopping to the ground and pouring blood.

"Good riddance," Qurrah muttered.

Qurrah ran past the pavilion to the distant hill where he'd sent Tessanna. He saw the three young paladins waiting there, but not his lover. Frowning, he pushed himself on until they were within earshot.

"Where's Tess?" he asked.

"There," Samar said, pointing skyward. Tessanna hovered above the battle, a beautiful dark angel flying on ethereal wings. A dress of midnight covered her body, its fabric sparkling with stars. Clouds formed about her, hanging low in the sky, so dark they seemed more like smoke than cloud. Shadows fell across the valley, and with the darkness came a chill wind that made Qurrah hug his arms to his chest. Whatever exhaustion Tessanna had felt, it was gone. Whatever her limitations, they appeared to no longer exist.

"Is this what you want?" Tessanna screamed at the top of her lungs, neck arched heavenward. "Then here I am. My hands are yours, my life yours, and my wings!"

It seemed Celestia heard, and she answered. *My power came only from slaying angels,* Tessanna had told him. Perhaps there was truth to that. Perhaps Celestia desired the angels to fall, and that was why Tessanna's dwindling power had returned during her battle against them in Ker. If that were the case, then based on the power Qurrah watched his beloved unleash, Celestia didn't desire Bram's army to lose.

She desired them blasted off the face of Dezrel.

Tessanna whirled her hands, and ropes of flame lashed out from the sky, each one the length of the battlefield. They slammed down among the front rows of the army, charring dozens dead. Those who chased the fleeing Mordan army found their skin peeling away and their clothes catching flame. A wave of Tessanna's hand, and clumps of shadow swelled throughout the valley, oily black tendrils emerging to slam into nearby soldiers with enough strength to dent armor and shatter weapons held up in defense.

Fire fell like rain from her hands. The clouds thickened, the first of many strokes of lightning blasting into the heart of the army. Wind knifed through the ranks, carrying shards of ice that ripped exposed flesh. Qurrah watched in awe as Tessanna pushed herself higher, beams of shadow blasting craters into the ground. The earth split and molten rock flowed out in thin rivers. Soldiers collapsed in the heat and were swallowed by the steady flow.

Qurrah's fear outweighed his awe. He'd asked her to influence the battle, but now she looked like she could conquer armies with a thought. That power carried shades of her past self, when her mind was fully broken, and the connection was not a pleasant one. Worse, though, was how the power continued to grow. It wasn't controlled. The storm, the fire, the magic...it spiraled wildly into chaos, and with such power, he feared Tessanna was not alone in the sky.

And then she spoke, each word confirming his fear.

"How much death must your race witness before you are sated?" his beloved cried, but the voice was not hers. *"Why thirst for power yet never crave peace? Why love so weakly your fear conquers mercy? Should I show you that same love? Should I scar your kind the way it scars my own creation?"*

Bram's army was completely scattered, soldiers fleeing in all directions from the fury of the goddess. The ground shook beneath them, yawning wide, snapping limbs and tearing open the flesh of those who fell. The gathered clouds struck with lightning, again and again, the thunder like the beat of a celestial drum.

"Tess," Qurrah said, struggling to remain on his feet as he watched. "Tess!"

He was losing her. Her eyes were throbbing beacons of white, her hair a wild nest of snakes that billowed in the storm. What could he say to her? Would she even hear?

"You are wild animals fought over by gods that refuse to see they deserve better. I am tired of playing the intercessor. Must I act the butcher instead to bring peace to my realm?"

Fire exploded from the growing cracks in the ground. Lightning lifted bodies into the air and incinerated them before raining down ashes. Shadows grew claws and spilled blood. Despite the wind, despite the thunder, the terrified sounds of the dying still reached Qurrah's hill. The destruction showed no preference now; the armies of both Ker and Mordan were assaulted by Celestia's power.

"Tess, please," Qurrah whispered, slumping to his knees as he witnessed such a fearsome display. "Come back to me. Don't leave me here alone."

The dark angel in the sky turned, and her glowing eyes fell upon him. The rumble of the storm hesitated, and Tessanna curled her arms and legs inward like a frightened child.

"No!" she shouted. Her voice echoed over the valley, loud as thunder. "No more killing, no more death. No more slaughter! Leave...us...be!"

It seemed the world held its breath. When the voice of the goddess spoke, it echoed across the valley from no discernable source.

So be it.

The ground ceased its shaking, fire seeped back into earthen cracks to intermix with the living shadow. Clouds scattered, streams of sunlight piercing through with growing intensity. Tessanna floated above the carnage, her starlight dress fading away as her black wings took her to the hill. Gently she landed, her wings dissolving like morning mist. Qurrah flung his arms around her. It seemed her legs held no strength, and she crumpled to the grass.

"She's hurting," Tessanna said, tears streaming down her face. "Mommy, she's leaving us, all of us. Her back is to our world, Qurrah." She clutched her forehead with her fingers. "I'm alone in here, all alone, no more voices, no more reflections. A dead mirror, a dead mirror..."

"Shh," he said, holding her close. "Not alone. I'm here. We're here. Let her turn her back on our world. That means it will be ours now, and not the gods'."

"We won't rule a world," she said, shivering against him. "We'll rule an empty shell."

"What of Ashhur?" asked freckle-faced Elrath, the shortest of the three paladins, and Qurrah started. He'd forgotten the youngers were there. "Has he turned his back on us as well?"

Tessanna sniffled as she pulled away from Qurrah.

"His eyes are open, but do not rejoice. Your god's gaze is no longer one of love, but of fury. His anger comes, and the goddess will not hold him back. We will all suffer come nightfall."

Qurrah took her by the hands and helped her back to her feet.

"One problem at a time," he said. "We need to flee while Bram's still reeling from his losses. I have no heart to fight more soldiers and dark paladins."

"Neither do I," Tessanna said, laughing despite her exhaustion. "And telling Mommy that made her so very, very angry."

A half-orc, his half-insane lover, and three inexperienced paladins of Ashhur raced away from the burned and broken valley, the corpse-strewn reminder of the goddess's rage. Qurrah urged them on, wishing to cover as much distance as possible before nightfall, before whatever fury Tessanna foretold came about with the setting of the sun.

22

The hour was late. Roand stood in the center of the bridge connecting the two towers, arms crossed against the biting wind. Tarlak had insisted he meet him there after the sun had begun to set and the various members of the towers were settling down to sleep. The whole process felt thoroughly unnecessary, but the unusual wizard had proven himself to be surprisingly adept at spellcasting. Maybe, just maybe, he'd found a way out of his imprisonment pendant.

A gust of wind filled Roand with shivers, and he cast a simple spell to warm his robes. Adept spellcaster or not, if Tarlak didn't show soon...

Tarlak stepped out of the Masters' Tower. To Roand's distaste, he carried a set of robes colored a vibrant yellow.

"I hope you've brought those to toss off the side of the bridge," Roand said.

Tarlak grinned wide as he made his way to the center. "Actually, I consider these robes part of a wager."

"A wager?"

"Yes, a wager." Tarlak stopped just before him, and he set the robes down on the checkered red and black brick. "I'm about to show you how to escape this inescapable pendant you've stuck around my neck. In return, I expect to be allowed to wear my yellow robes. Surely that's a simple enough reward, given how I'm pointing out a flaw in your greatest creation without an audience."

Roand rubbed his smoothly shaven chin. Nearly every mage had some sort of eccentricity to be dealt with. Anora feared the sight of running water. Adjara needed the company of young boys every few months, not to mention Viggo's crimleaf addiction. Compared to that, what did an ugly yellow robe matter?

"If you succeed, and you show discretion when it comes to revealing the nature of your escape, then I will allow you to wear your yellow robes," Roand said. "And if you fail, well..." He shrugged. "If you fail, I will leave them here as a reminder to everyone not to doubt my abilities."

"Deal!"

Tarlak stepped away from the robes made a show of stretching his arms and back. Roand retreated a step or two as well, wanting to be a safe distance away. Tarlak was obviously nervous, which was strange. Roand couldn't help but wonder why he'd bother with the attempt at all. After a few years of loyalty, Roand wouldn't need such a show for him to remove the pendant. Tarlak's work on Deathmask alone had nearly convinced him of the man's dedication to the craft. In time, Tarlak's mastery of fire could rival his own.

"I've thought about this a bit," Tarlak said as he hopped up and down on the bridge. "Lots really, perhaps the most attention I've ever given any sort of problem. Take it as a compliment. So, how does one remove a pendant that is absolutely, completely, thoroughly unremovable?"

"Pray tell," Roand said, unable to keep a hint of sarcasm from his voice.

Tarlak's grin returned.

"That's the trick. You ready to see?"

Roand nodded. Tarlak gave a clap, then let out a deep breath.

"All right," he said. "Remember, no interrupting. This is a delicate process, and if you interrupt me, then I will never tell you how I can remove it...well, at least, not until I've told everyone *else* how I removed it."

"Spare me the petty threats, Tarlak. You have my word, so stop wasting my time. I'd like to be in my bed, where it's warm."

"Right." Tarlak waggled his fingers. "Let's do this."

The odd wizard started his spell. Roand listened to the words, curious. Tarlak's hands weaved through the somatic components of a spell, and combined with the verbal, Roand realized that whatever spell he cast, it dealt in some way with the manipulation of ice. The wizard sighed. Ice? Tarlak's solution involved ice? The heat the pendant could create rivaled that of the sun. No ice, no matter how cold, would withstand.

He almost told Tarlak this, to spare his life, but the wizard had absolutely *insisted* there be no interruptions, so Roand held his tongue and watched. Tarlak's spell ended, and strangely enough, Roand saw no ice anywhere.

"There's part one," he said. "I guess I should have mentioned this had two parts. You ready for part two?"

"I wait with bated breath," Roand grumbled.

Tarlak winked.

"Trust me. You'll like this one."

He started up a second spell, and its makeup was far more intriguing. Roand recognized a few of the ancient words, enough to know that it held at least some connection with translocational magic. Still, Roand had enacted dozens of safeguards against portals, teleportation, and the like. What did Tarlak think he might do that Roand had not thought of? The spell slipped off Tarlak's lips, faster and faster, as his hands shimmered a dark purple.

Then all at once, the spell ended.

"Perfect," Tarlak said.

He grabbed the pendant around his neck and pulled it free. The gem within it flared to life, and before Roand could turn away to protect his eyes, the magic activated. A blinding flash of light, a roar of heat, and Tarlak's body blackened to ash. Even his bones broke apart from the intense heat. It took only a second, and then the dust that had once been Tarlak Eschaton drifted away on the wind.

"Hrmph," Roand said, lowering his arms. "How disappointing. You were fun, Tarlak."

Roand stepped over the robes, leaving them there as promised, and returned to the masters' tower.

When Tarlak opened his eyes, he vomited uncontrollably. The motion nearly sent him plummeting from his ice cocoon and into the Rigon River flowing quietly beneath him.

Damn that's cold, he thought. His entire body shivered, and the ice touching his bare fingers was painful. Still better than falling to his death, of course. Tarlak glanced about, assessing the situation.

He hung from the bottom of the bridge connecting the two wizard towers, the ice dangling from a thread like a hornet's nest. Climbing up from the heart of the ice cocoon didn't seem possible, which meant a bit of magic would be required. Given his current predicament, that posed multiple interesting problems.

"Here goes nothing," Tarlak said. He pulled his hands free of the ice, shaking them a few times for warmth. He put his fingers through the quick motions to summon more ice. To his relief, it sprayed from his palm without fail, building a makeshift bridge from the exit of his cocoon to the bridge above. He put in a few ridges, like steps, to aid in the climb.

"Glad to know I've still got it," he said. Slowly he crawled along the ice, lifting himself up at every step, doing his best to touch the ice with his robes instead of his bare hands. When he reached the top, he rolled off the ice and onto his back. And then he laughed. He laughed, and laughed, until tears ran down the sides of his face.

"I beat you," he whispered, pretending that pompous ass Roand was looking down at him. "I beat you, I beat you, I godsdamn beat you!"

So much for inescapable amulets. Once he finished laughing, he rolled onto his stomach. He was pleased to see his yellow robes where he'd left them. Roand was a man of his word. Stripping off his old wet robes, he put on the new ones. He almost felt like his old self, and with a grunt he rose to his feet. The robes were nice and warm, for which he was grateful.

"One down," he said, thinking of Deathmask strapped to a wall in Roand's multi-purpose bedroom and torture chamber. "One to go."

Tarlak had quickly learned during his stay at the towers how arrogant everyone was. The apprentices thought themselves better than their masters, and the masters better than the entire world. That arrogance dripped from the walls itself, including their protection wards. The front doors down below were carefully guarded and protected, but the two doors up top, connected to the bridge? No one could scale the perfectly smooth sides of either tower. No one without magic, anyway, and if someone had magic, why would they need to break into the towers in the first

The King of the Vile

place? They could use the front doors, for what user of magic would not be a member of the towers? Surely not someone posing any real threat.

There were no locks, no bars, no guards. Tarlak walked over to the door of the masters' tower, pushed it open, and strolled right on in.

Tarlak had to pass through the Grand Council room before he reached Roand's room at the top of the tower. He climbed fifteen steps and entered the circular hall. It felt like a lifetime ago he'd stood before those arrogant pricks, awaiting their judgment. As if those nine members could lay claim to the entire spectrum of magic. Practicing spellcasting without their consent was the crime they'd wanted to execute him for. Such arrogant cocks. Such assholes.

"Calm down," Tarlak muttered. "You're almost free of the place, so let's keep a clear head until then, eh?"

It was harder than he expected. Fearing an occasional mind-reading or slip of the tongue, he'd guarded even his thoughts while performing his experiments. But now, for better or worse, there was no more hiding. Either he'd escape, or die freeing Deathmask. There'd be no more of the farce.

Tarlak crossed the hall to a set of stairs deceptively hidden behind one of the walls. He climbed the steps to Roand's door and hesitated. This was it. Had Roand gone directly to bed? And if so, had he already fallen asleep? Of course, there was also the worry about alarms and traps. The Lord of the Council was the highest position one could attain. Roand might be arrogant, but he wasn't stupid. All it'd take was a quiet dagger in the night, and suddenly there'd be a new Lord of the Council.

Tarlak stroked his chin, but his red goatee wasn't there. His mood went foul, and deciding it could all go to the Abyss, he cast a wave of anti-magic to dispel any wards and alarms. When none seemed to activate, he pushed the door open and stepped inside.

The room was red and fiery as ever. Roand's bed was empty, and it looked undisturbed. Wherever he was, Tarlak hoped he stayed there for a good long while. Deathmask hung from the wall, still firmly shackled and chained. His head hung low, dark hair covering much of his face. Either asleep or unconscious, by

Tarlak's guess. Hopefully the former and not the latter. He wouldn't mind slapping the unpredictable rogue awake, but dragging his unconscious body out the tower was a different matter.

First, Tarlak scoured the wizard's desk, pulling open drawers. When he found what he was looking for, he slid it into his pocket and turned his attention to Deathmask.

"No time for sleeping," Tarlak said as he hurried across the room. "Wakey-wakey."

He gently removed the hook lodged beneath Deathmask's chin, figuring that was the best place to start. The motion caused Deathmask to stir, and he muttered something unintelligible.

"Easy now," Tarlak said as he turned his attention to the mess of hooks and slender chains that kept Deathmask's fingers from moving. "I'd hate to hurt you worse than you already are."

"Not...possible," Deathmask said. He lifted his head and peered at Tarlak with bloodshot eyes. His face bore the scars Tarlak himself had put on him, but several new ones formed lines across the man's forehead. "Who in the bloody Abyss are you?"

"That's hardly how you should address your potential rescuer," Tarlak said as he pulled a pulled a fish hook from Deathmask's forefinger. "And check the robes. Who *else* would I be?"

"A disguise," Deathmask said. "But why?"

"Not quite a disguise. I'll explain later, once we're very, very far away from this horrible asylum for the mentally deranged."

After a minute, he had Deathmask's left hand free, and he moved on to the right. The man's fingers were swollen, puffy bruises growing from where the hooks had been embedded in the soft flesh of his fingertips. Thankfully no bones appeared broken. Roand probably considered such basic tactics as beneath him.

Once both his hands were free, Tarlak turned his attention to the chains, which were easy enough to slide around Deathmask's body until he was free. He got a good look at the many more burns that covered his chest and legs in the process. Apparently Roand had gotten bored with only assaulting the face. Scars were visible through burned gaps in his clothes, and a few looked incredibly recent.

The King of the Vile

Tarlak removed the last of the chains. "At least he left your genitals alone."

"What?" Deathmask asked, still sounding delirious.

"Don't mind me," Tarlak said. "Just talking to myself to keep the nerves calm."

The only thing left were the manacles. Magic had closed them, so Tarlak had a feeling magic would be required to open them as well. He cracked his knuckles and waggled his fingers. He'd feared everything would feel foreign and weird, and in the back of his mind it did, but so far his motor skills seemed to function perfectly. Given the intricate movements required for spellcasting, this was an incredible relief.

Tarlak touched the manacle holding Deathmask's left arm and murmured a basic unlocking spell. The metal sprang open the moment he finished.

"All right," he said. "We'll have you out of here in..."

The door opened behind him, and Tarlak's shoulders dropped as he sighed and turned about.

Roand stood in his doorway, a comical look of bafflement on his face. He held a silver plate with a wedge of cheese and a few thin slices of bread. *A midnight torture snack?* Such a mundane act made the wizard seem all the more demented.

"Cecil?" asked Roand, cocking his head to one side.

"Not quite," Tarlak said. "I told you I'd escape, didn't I?"

Roand calmly entered his room and he set his plate on a small table. His surprise was quickly replaced by amusement.

"You transferred your consciousness to a new body, letting your old one be destroyed," he said. "I must admit, I never anticipated such a strategy. You are to be commended."

"By 'commended', you mean 'allowed to go free without repercussions', right?"

Roand shook his head.

"Disrespectful humor to counter fear while in my presence," the Lord of the Council said. "What did I tell you I felt about that?"

Tarlak cracked his knuckles.

"That I should instead act like a proper wizard," he said. "So to follow your example, that'd mean burning your body in a hundred places. Let's start with that, shall we?"

Attacking a wizard whose nickname was 'the Flame' with a fire spell might have been crazy, but Tarlak was cranky and at the end of his rope. Roand would think it little more than an insult, which was exactly the point. Fire burst from Tarlak's palms, a thick beam that swirled with smoke. Roand clenched a raised fist, a whisper of magic escaping his lips. A shield shimmered around him, orange in color. When the fire beam hit, it dissipated as if it'd never existed.

"Cute," Roand said.

He countered with his own beam of fire, this one thrice the size of Tarlak's. Legs braced, hands outstretched, Tarlak summoned a magical shield against the blast. When it hit, he let out a cry. His entire body shuddered and an immediate ache filled his head. Karak help him, the heat, the *power*...

At last the beam ended, and the moment it did, Tarlak dropped to one knee, hands a blur. A thick sheet of ice spread from wall to wall. It lasted a mere moment before a blast of pure, invisible force punched straight through its center. Shards of ice shattered against another of Tarlak's shields. With Deathmask behind him, he couldn't dodge, lest the captured man be burned or impaled. A terrible predicament, really.

Tarlak shifted to one side, hoping to reduce the risk of potential collateral damage. The rest of his ice wall melted away and Roand stepped forward. Fire seemed to burn from every inch of his body. It set his carpet aflame, but did nothing to his skin and clothes.

"It need not end like this," Roand said. A circular shield of flame swirled into existence before him, holding firm against the several bricks Tarlak ripped out of the walls and flung at him. "You're a stubborn man used to following his own will. Adapting to the towers will take time, time I'm willing to give you. You're not the first to attack me, and if you stand down, I will pardon you of this crime."

The King of the Vile

"I'd rather you curse me and call me foul names," Tarlak said, mind racing. He needed to slow Roand's approach before he ended up a blackened husk. "Must you remain so boringly calm?"

He slammed his hands together, fingers interlocking. A sudden windstorm shoved Roand backwards. The wizard struggled to remain where he stood, but Tarlak only increased the power. At last, Roand countered by sending a barrage of fire bolts that Tarlak had to end his spell to block.

"I speak no insults because I have no desire to inflame you," Roand said as he regained his balance.

"Is that another pun?"

At last it seemed he'd inspired a bit of anger in the Lord of the Council. Roand opened his mouth and let out a thunderous cry. Fire roared from his gullet as if from the belly of a dragon. Tarlak summoned another barrier, but the fire forked, fully surrounding him, and then collapsed against his shield. Tarlak clenched his teeth as he fought to keep the flames at bay. Not just the carpet burned now, but the paintings and shelves as well. Despite his shield, Tarlak felt the heat on his skin, felt sweat beginning to run down his neck and face.

As quickly as it began, Roand ceased belching fire. Before Tarlak could recover, he hurled molten balls of stone from his palms. Tarlak's shield barely held. The impact created a shockwave, one that cracked Tarlak's mind like glass. He rolled across the floor, coming to a stop at Deathmask's feet.

"A new age approaches for Dezrel," Roand said. The fire surrounding his body vanished, and he straightened the sleeves of his robes. "You could have ruled with us instead of dying without reason."

"Ruled?" Tarlak asked, rising on unsteady legs. "Ruled what? These two little towers? What do I want with a few piddly apprentices under my thumb?"

"Not these towers," Roand said. "An entire nation, granted to us by Azariah himself."

Tarlak froze. "An entire nation?" he said. "And Azariah would give you this...why?"

"Because I have personally trained him in the arcane arts. Because I helped him bring Avlimar crashing to the ground. And mostly because he knows he cannot accomplish his own goals without allies such as myself."

Tarlak felt like he'd been hit in the head with a club. Azariah arranged Avlimar's collapse? But why? How did that make one lick of sense?

"So you help Azariah, and in return he gives you...parts of Mordan?"

Roand shook his head.

"Mordan will remain under the angels' rule. The nation of Ker, however...their entire army marches north toward Mordeina, leaving her so very vulnerable. Ker, whose queen believes we will protect her. When their army crumbles, we will finally leave these towers as we should have decades ago. We cannot yet save the entire race, not the poor souls trapped in Mordan, but at least we might create a new kingdom. Azariah has promised us freedom from the angels, from Ashhur's rules, and from Karak's meddling inanities. Two kingdoms, each bettering mankind in their own way. It harkens back to Dezrel's earliest days, if you think about it."

"Yeah," Tarlak said. "Because that went so well the first time."

"We need only to be patient," Roand said, shaking his head. "The angels cannot procreate. Their numbers will steadily dwindle, and once they are too few, we will invade. At last, humanity will be free. No gods. No kings. Just the rule of the wise. Under our guidance, we will forge a paradise beyond anything Karak and Ashhur ever created. It is a goal so noble, a future so inevitable, I cannot fathom how you don't see it as well."

"Maybe because he's not an idiot," Deathmask called from the wall. His free hand weaved through the air, and a single bolt of shadow flew across the room. It was small and weak, but surprise was on his side. Roand's shield came up too late, and the bolt hit him in the chest. The impact sent him stumbling back a step. Jumping on the opportunity, Tarlak pressed his hands together and let loose a torrent of lightning.

"*Enough!*" Roand cried, arms whirling. A funnel of flame surrounded him, and when the lightning hit, it swirled into the funnel, becoming part of it. A terrifying mixture of fire and lightning now his shield, Roand flung fireballs from within, which Tarlak detonated with a focused burst of magic. The flame enveloped the room, licking the stone walls and consuming the bookshelves. Smoke covered the ceiling, growing thicker by the moment. Tarlak flung a single shard of ice at the glass doors before the balcony. They shattered, and fresh air blew into the room as smoke poured out.

"I offer you power, and you respond with insults," Roand said. Tarlak caught sight of a ripple in reality, and he blocked too late. It flung past him, an invisible force smacking Deathmask in the forehead. The power drove his head against the wall with a sick, wet sound. Praying the man was still alive, Tarlak made his new fingers dance. Ice flew in thin, pointed shards, but they could not pierce the swirling barrier. Attempting a new tactic, he cast a spell to polymorph Roand into a mudskipper, but as expected, the wizard had protections in place within his rings and necklaces.

Damn, thought Tarlak as he dove to the floor to avoid a spear made of solid flame. It hit the wall and exploded, adding more fire to the already burning room. Tarlak coughed up smoke, the heat becoming torturous.

"I offer you a home, and you attempt to destroy it."

The funnel around Roand broke apart, becoming a wave that rolled toward Tarlak. Panicking, he flung his arms up and summoned the strongest shield he could manage. The magic slammed against it, and immediately Tarlak knew he'd made a mistake. The strain to keep it intact broke him. His knees turned to water, he went momentarily blind. He kept the fire back, but some of the lightning pierced through, lashing his skin. His body shook with random muscle spasms as he collapsed to the ground. The carpet beneath him burned, and he rolled onto his back to smother it.

"Such a pity," Roand said. He kicked Tarlak in the face. Tarlak groaned, blood spilling from his nose. He rolled back onto his stomach and he received another kick to the neck for his efforts. Coughing and gagging, he dragged himself closer. Roand frowned down at him, looking like a disappointed parent.

"You had great potential," Roand said, shaking his head. "A shame your stubbornness and morality pushed you away from a wiser life."

"You're right," Tarlak croaked, hand dipping into his pocket. "Such a damn shame."

Before Roand could step away, Tarlak shoved the object he'd taken from Roand's desk against the wizard's ankle: one of his precious ruby imprisonment pendants. As the gemstone touched Roand's skin, the chain looped around and clasped shut of its own accord. Warmth spread against his palm as the magic within the ruby activated. Tarlak heard Roand cry out, knew he prepared a spell, but Tarlak gave him no time. Just as quickly as he'd applied the pendant, he ripped it off with all his strength. The silver clasp broke. The pendant flared. With a sound like thunder, Roand's body vaporized, his body turning to brightly glowing embers that faded into ash and dust.

Tarlak collapsed onto his back. His limbs were sore, his ears rang, and he bore a myriad of burns, but that didn't matter, not in the slightest.

With the room still burning around him, Tarlak laughed his ass off.

"I'm still here, in case you've forgotten," Deathmask said from the wall. He sounded groggy but otherwise fine.

"Right, right," Tarlak said. He rolled onto his stomach, then pushed himself to his feet. "I think it's time for a hasty retreat, Deathmask. What do you say to that?"

Deathmask grinned as the last three manacles opened one after the other.

"To that, I say amen and hallelujah, let's get the fuck out of here."

"Amen indeed," Tarlak said, grabbing Deathmask by the shoulder and opening a portal far, far away.

23

Jessilynn looked to the orange sky, but she saw no wings.

"Where are you?" she whispered. They were out of time. The goblins had finished their battering rams, and the rest of the beasts roared and cheered from beyond the wall, whipped into a growing frenzy. The attack was about to begin. Despite the walls and the hundreds of armed soldiers rushing across the ramparts, Jessilynn feared they would not last the night.

"Where will you make your stand?" Dieredon asked. Together they overlooked fields swarming with beasts of the Vile Wedge.

"Here at the gate," Jessilynn said. She pointed to where the goblins were lining up the battering rams. "So long as they have to climb the walls, we'll maintain our advantage. If we have to fight them on open ground..."

"Then we'll defeat them on open ground," Dieredon said. "We've committed to battle, so do not waste time doubting. Our strength will lead to our victory, and their defeat. That is all that matters."

Jessilynn grinned, pretending she wasn't scared for her life. "You make it seem so simple and easy."

"It is," Dieredon said, patting his bow. "Stick the sharp end of the arrows into the bodies of our enemies. Repeat until they're all dead or dying."

"You sound like Jerico," Jessilynn said, laughing.

The elf shrugged.

"I was thinking Harruq," he said. "Truth be told, I wouldn't mind having that idiot half-orc with us right now. If *he* was standing before those gates..."

A communal shout shook the air, the thousands of beasts roaring, shrieking, and howling. It washed away whatever little relaxation Jessilynn had gained, and she spun about anticipating a charge. None came.

"Soon," Dieredon said, removing his bow from his shoulder. "Very soon."

Soldiers lined the entirety of the wall surrounding the castle, which left them painfully thin given the lengthy distance they had to cover. A mere ten men joined Jessilynn and Dieredon above the gate, all ten wielding bows. Soldiers continued to slowly filter in, those who'd slept now woken and sent to the wall. The only large grouping of soldiers was right before the gate, a collection of forty, half of which weren't soldiers at all, but volunteers who'd fled to the castle for protection. Daniel Coldmine stood among them, already hoarse from hollering orders.

"Nothing gets through!" he shouted. "Moment that door starts to crack, you start shoving your blades in the gap. Between your swords and the archers above, we'll have them terrified to come near this damn gate!"

Jessilynn was thankful for his fire. Though she knew she should be an inspiration to the defenders, she didn't know what to do or say. She just wanted the fight to begin.

"I watched these beasts tear down my towers," Daniel continued. "Again and again, they cross the rivers, terrorizing innocent folks, and it's about time we bloodied their noses for it. Ten die for every one of you, you hear me? Any less, and I'll hunt you down in the Golden Eternity to berate you for not giving it your all. You hear me, soldiers? You want me haunting your ass for the next million years?"

"No, sir!" cried those below and above the gate, and Jessilynn found herself shouting it as well. His confidence warmed her heart. It wasn't that Daniel wasn't afraid. She'd bet plenty that he was. It was that he didn't care. Mind on the task at hand, with anger and pride overcoming weakness and fear. Her own confidence grew.

"They'll struggle to get their ten," Jessilynn shouted down at Daniel. "Not enough beasts will reach the wall, not with my arrows stopping them."

"Will they now?" Daniel shouted back. "That's a sight I'd love to see!"

Jessilynn smiled. Seeing the kindled hope in the soldiers' eyes urged her on. "You're right," she shouted. "How about I show those monsters what they have to look forward to?"

She drew back the string of her bow, and as an arrow of light materialized between her fingers, the soldiers let out a cheer. Aiming blindly into the distant horde, she let the arrow fly. A flash of light marked its passing, and the cheers grew louder.

"Two dead with one shot," Dieredon said, making a show of peering into the distance with his elven eyes. "And at least five more nearby that just shit their fur."

Jessilynn laughed and fired three more arrows. It felt good to be on the attack for once, to believe that her enemies should be afraid of her and not the other way around. Shimmering, ethereal arrows slammed into the distant enemies, their impacts marked by tiny explosions of light.

Her laughter died as the horde roared back. The stampede began, thousands barreling toward the wall in a gigantic wave of feathers, claws, and fur. The ground shook.

"Focus on bringing the battering rams down," Dieredon said before putting two fingers to his mouth and whistling.

"Where are you going?" she asked. She could barely hear herself over the growing commotion.

"To keep them off of you," he said.

Sonowin flew down from the sky. The elf hopped over the wall, landing on the winged horse's back as she zoomed by.

"Until the rising of the sun," he shouted over his shoulder.

The horse rose into the air, Dieredon's arrows already flying toward the charging army. Jessilynn readied her bow, and she saw that the other archers atop the flat space above the gate were staring at her. It took her a moment to realize they were waiting for orders. Her orders.

"Keep them off the walls," she told them, an arrow of light glimmering in her hands. "Leave the battering rams to me."

"Are you sure you can kill so many?" an archer with a milky right eye asked. "Any beasts carrying it will be replaced by more as they die."

Jessilynn sighted the nearest of the four battering rams, each carried by a dozen of the vile creatures.

"I'm not aiming at the ones carrying it," she said.

Her arrow sailed through the air, the holy projectile slamming into front of the first battering ram. Upon contact the carved face of a snarling wolf exploded into shrapnel. The two wolf-men nearest the front cried out, one falling to the side and clutching its eyes as it bled. Jessilynn did not relent, firing three more arrows at the ram. The wood broke further, long cracks spreading along its entire length. Switching aim, she fired two more along its upper half, right into those cracks. The final shot broke it completely, the battering ram splitting into three pieces. The beasts holding it let it drop to the ground, howling as they charged the wall empty-handed.

The archers beside Jessilynn let out cheers at the battering ram's destruction, but Jessilynn didn't share their jubilation. It'd taken six shots to destroy the ram, and three more rams remained, each racing toward the front gate with reckless abandon. Six shots, without distraction, without having to defend herself. As the first of the vile creatures reached the wall, she feared taking down the other three would not be so easy.

"On the walls," the archer with the milky eye shouted. "Shoot only the ones on the walls!"

The archers plunged arrows straight down into the faces and shoulders of the climbing beasts. It was the wolf-men that were focused on the front gate, hundreds of them colliding with the stone, thick claws digging in as if climbing a tree.

From her peripheral vision, Jessilynn saw bird-men rushing the length of the wall north of the gate. She assumed the goat-men to be along the south, but wondered how they planned to climb the wall without.

Screams and howls of pain joined the angry cries of the attackers. Soldiers with swords and spears remained at ready along the farther reaches of the wall, hacking down at the beasts who'd reached the top. Jessilynn saw one wolf-man shrug off a spear to the shoulder, fling itself into the soldier, and send them both tumbling off the other side of the wall. Praying both died quickly from the fall, Jessilynn fired arrows as fast as her arm could move.

The King of the Vile

A second battering ram splintered from her barrage, with several of the wolf-men dying with it as her arrows ripped through them.

As Jessilynn brought her aim to the third, another wolf-man made it to the top of the wall. An archer screamed as claws dug into his legs. The wolf-man swung its arm while still clinging to the wall, sending the man tumbling down to the swarm below. He struck ground headfirst, and for that, Jessilynn was thankful, for a trio of wolf-men ripped him apart the moment he landed. Two other archers plunged arrows into the beast's neck. It fell, but the diversion allowed another to leap to the top, snarling with hunger.

Jessilynn turned her attention away from the battering rams to assist the other archers, but before she could fire, an arrow sailed down from the sky and pierced the wolf through the throat. Sonowin banked low, and Jessilynn heard Dieredon shout at her even as he loosed more arrows.

"The battering rams, Jess! The rest are mine!"

Sonowin swooped over the invaders. Dieredon twisted sideways and fired arrow after arrow into the backs of the climbers making their way up the wall. Jessilynn berated herself for losing focus; lifting her bow, she gritted her teeth as the nearest battering ram reached the gate and slammed into it at full speed. She heard a deep thud, felt the gate rattle beneath her. Jessilynn fired three arrows in rapid succession, making sure each shot also passed through one of the wolf-men. The ram dropped to the ground, the remainder unable to heft its weight and therefore sparing the gate a second hit. Jessilynn gave them no chance to recover, three more arrows hitting the same spot, breaking the ram in half.

A scream spun Jessilynn around. Two wolf-men ascended the wall simultaneously, one howling with victory, the other diving atop an archer and ripping into her chest with such ferocity Jessilynn saw rib bones poking through flesh and clothing. Both had Dieredon's arrows embedded in their fur. Jessilynn pulled back the drawstring as one leapt toward another of the archers. Her arrow caught it mid-air, ripping off an arm and blasting it over the side of the wall. Jessilynn turned to the other, but she never had to fire. Two arrows from Dieredon pierced the beast's in the spine.

Another heavy thud as the next battering ram connected with the gate.

Persistent dogs, aren't they? Jessilynn thought as she spun back around, needing no reminder from Dieredon as to what her task should be. Only one battering ram remained, and once it fell, the soldiers on the ground could rush atop the wall to aid in the defense. Jessilynn held her breath as she blasted into the ram again and again. Ignoring the cries of the dying, the hail of arrows all around her as Dieredon kept her safe, she let Ashhur's power fuel her. The ram fell to pieces, having managed only three good hits on the gate.

Jessilynn's excitement lasted only long enough to see the wolf-men abandon the rams and instead begin raking their claws against the gate's thick wood. It'd take time before they'd make any progress, but they'd get through eventually.

Jessilynn ran along the wall, weaving through corpses of both men and beast in search of a better angle. So few soldiers remained, and with each death, the way grew that much easier for the rest of Manfeaster's army. Bodies piled up at the base of the wall, providing steps for the next wolf-man that moved to climb.

A hundred feet down the wall, Jessilynn had her angle. Two soldiers fought alongside her, stabbing with long spears at beasts attempting the crest the parapets. Trusting them to keep her safe, she blasted into the wolf-men hacking at the gate, careful to aim so she didn't hit the gate itself. The last thing she wanted was to open the way for them. Jessilynn's arm ached, but she refused to relent, even when one of the two guarding her was yanked off the side screaming.

Not yet, Jessilynn thought as the wolf-men dragged their muscled bodies over the wall. *We don't die yet!*

Dieredon landed between her and the nearest beast, wielding his enormous bow like a staff. The string had vanished, and two long blades jutted out from either end. The elf leapt about, a whirling storm of death against all who tried the climb.

"Arrow after arrow!" he cried as he cut open a fur-covered belly, leapt two steps back, and then flicked the bow into an upright position. The drawstring reappeared, and he buried an arrow into the wolf-man's bleeding guts. "Arrow after arrow!"

The King of the Vile

Jessilynn prayed Ashhur continue to give her the strength. Wolf-men surged toward the gate, and so she built a second gate with their dead. They had no way to hide, no way to protect themselves. Arrow after arrow, she destroyed them. Arrow after shimmering arrow, she killed those who would slaughter the innocent lives beyond the wall.

Dieredon was a wonder as he spun about her, with no fear of the claws that swiped toward his leather armor and no difficulty in piercing their flesh with his long blades. Anytime he had a moment to breathe, he snapped the blades in and lobbed arrows along the length of the wall. It never seemed to be enough. For every beast they killed, three more rushed to its place.

"Come on," Dieredon shouted, suddenly grabbing her wrist and pulling her toward the stairs. "The walls are lost!"

He was right, no matter how much she didn't want to believe it. Of the soldiers who had held the walls, maybe a tenth remained. Jessilynn followed Dieredon down the stairs, snarling wolf-men at her heels. They raced toward Sir Daniel's men, who had formed a line alongside the twin sets of stairs on either side of the gate, battling the wolf-men who descended them. Several of Daniel's soldiers saw their approach and rushed to defend them, shields up, swords swinging. Jessilynn vanished into their numbers, falling to her knees and gulping in air. From beyond the wall, the wolf-men let loose a victorious howl.

Jessilynn looked to the red sky, but she saw no wings.

"The gate's been weakened, not that it matters much," she heard Daniel shout to Dieredon. "They'll be through in moments."

Jessilynn staggered to her feet and grabbed Daniel by the arm. "Then open it."

"You want me to do *what?*" Daniel asked, looking at her as if she'd lost her mind.

"If the way is open, they'll rush through instead of risking the climb," she said. "Let them come to me instead of all across the wall. Give me clean shots, and I'll make them pay."

There was no time to argue. Either Daniel trusted her, or he didn't.

"Fine," he said. "We've lost anyway, might as well take as many as we can with us." He shouted the order to a soldier beside him, who pushed through the ranks and ran toward the weakened gate to pass along the message.

Jessilynn pushed her way to the front of the remaining throng of soldiers. On either side of her men and beasts died; she trusted Daniel's soldiers to hold. Dieredon stepped up beside her, just a moment's pause before leaping into the fray on her right.

"Make your teachers proud."

The gate creaked, then burst open. A seemingly endless swarm of wolf-men rushed the opening. Jessilynn drew back the drawstring and felt a sudden calm overtake her. Her arrows were her god's will manifested, his weapon against the darkness, his rage against the evils plaguing his beloved creation. They were not bound by physical limitations. Jerico had once formed a shield hundreds of feet wide to protect Harruq and Aurelia at the battle of Mordeina, when the angels first appeared. A hundred times she'd heard that story, and a hundred times she'd pretended it was her wielding the shield instead of Jerico.

There was no pretend any longer. Jessilynn watched the wolf-men surge toward her, claws out, mouths open, howling in bloodlust. Thousands of lives were at stake. Shivers running through her body, Jessilynn pulled back the string, felt soft feathers brush her cheek. An arrow shimmered into existence, swirling with light. Its power grew, its brightness overwhelming yet not at all painful to her eyes. A lump in her throat, tears blurring her vision, Jessilynn whispered a word she'd never dared speak before.

"Elholad."

When Jessilynn released her arrow, it was a like a bolt of lightning striking from the heavens. The projectile appeared as a single beam that punched through flesh and bone like they were dust. The shockwave that followed was a god's thunder, shaking the stone walls and opening a crack in the earth. Those caught in its path flew aside from its power, bones shattered, flesh ripped open. The arrow pierced through the army, decimating hundreds. Trees collapsed once it reached the forest, their trunks blasted out from beneath them.

The King of the Vile

Jessilynn dropped to her knees and gasped for air, feeling like she'd run a hundred miles. Her heart hammered in her chest, her hands shook. She couldn't even lift her bow. Bones and gore littered formed a bloody trail that exited the archway and traveled through the field beyond. Despite the open gate, no wolf-man dared approach. Up the walls they went, preferring the arduous climb over the risk of being caught in another such blast.

Dieredon's hand fell on her shoulder.

"We need to retreat to the castle," he said. "They're everywhere."

Jessilynn rose to her feet with his help, and she did not argue. The walls were completely overrun. She'd killed so many with a single shot, and still it was not enough. Sir Daniel rallied his troops toward the castle and the sprawling camps of refugees that filled the space between. Men, women, and children fled their campfires and ran toward the castle. The beast-men descended on them, wolf-men ripping into their necks with their teeth, hyena-men slobbering and yipping as they shredded flesh with claws sharp as knives. Everywhere, terrified people screamed. Everywhere, innocent lives ended.

Twenty soldiers armed in platemail guarded the entrance to the castle proper, Lord Arthur among them. Refugees fled up the hill and through the huge doors, cramming into the safety of the castle. This was their first respite, as the invaders were taking time to devour their prey in the fields before reaching the castle.

"I saw an arrow do what ten ballistae could never hope to achieve," Arthur said, bowing before her. "It's almost enough to convince me Ashhur is with us."

"Ashhur *is* with us," she said.

"No, *you* are," Arthur said, drawing his sword. "If *he* were with us, his angels would descend from the skies to stop this massacre. Instead we must hold this hill on our own."

Jessilynn bit her tongue and turned from the lord to watch the people fleeing up the hill, their numbers rapidly dwindling as Manfeaster's army closed in from all sides. Her head pounded, and the fingers of her right hand were raw from the constant drawing of the bowstring, but she was not done. Even if her hands bled, she would still let loose her arrows. Dieredon joined her side, his clothes soaked with blood. He put a hand on her shoulder and squeezed.

"Stay strong," he said as Sonowin landed beside him on the hill. "I'll do what I can from above, thin them out. Make sure you retreat into the castle before all is lost."

"We need to buy time," Jessilynn said, trying to be brave. "The angels will come, I promise they will."

The elf gave her a sad look before he left. Jessilynn's inner fire was stoked, and she lifted her bow and pushed to the front of the line.

"My arrows will funnel them to either side," she said. "Cut them down. Not a single one of those creatures reaches the castle door, do you hear me? Not a one!"

Their cheers were half-hearted, but her words weren't for them. Jessilynn felt anger growing in her breast, hot and wild. Hundreds of evil creatures dead by her god-blessed arrows, and yet Dieredon and Arthur would claim them abandoned? No. She refused to believe that. They just had to hold on a little longer. They had to bleed, to fight, to push beyond the breaking point. They hadn't been abandoned. Not yet.

Sir Daniel took up position beside her. "Here they come!"

Jessilynn saw two women and a man running hand-in-hand, a hyena-man chasing after. Jessilynn breathed in, breathed out, and fired her arrow. The hyena-man ducked low, snarling as the bolt sailed over its left ear. Jessilynn tried to force herself to focus, to push through the exhaustion that clawed at her eyes and pulled down on her limbs. She sighted again, but could not deny the relief she felt when one of Dieredon's arrows came down from the heavens to kill the beast. The three who'd been chased entered the castle. They were the last that would survive; beast-men of all races brought down the rest, and afterward rushed the last defenders of humanity.

Bow raised, Jessilynn told herself it wasn't yet over. Between Lord Arthur's personal guard and the remainder of Sir Daniel's men, they had a total of fifty gathered in a tight formation before the castle door. Fifty against the remaining thousands. Not hopeless, she told herself. Not if they stood strong. This was when Ashhur would come to their aid. This was when their strength

The King of the Vile

would be rewarded. Tales of their bravery would be told over cook fires for years to come. Readying another ethereal arrow, she shot it down the hill, killing two hyena-men who ran one after the other.

Before her string had even ceased vibrating she pulled it back, releasing another arrow through the heart of a bird-man that shrieked at the top of its lungs as it climbed the hill. Jessilynn felt a spike of pain as she drew back for a third. Blood dripped from fingers rubbed raw. Knowing there was little she could do about it, she gritted her teeth and endured the pain. Her arrows could not slow, not for a heartbeat, or all was lost.

The vile creatures dropped by the dozens as her glowing arrows punctured their bodies, broke their bones, spilled their blood. Dieredon circled overhead, raining down arrows so fast they seemed fired two at a time. The dead littered the hill, but what had once been a scattered trickle of beast-men was now a massive wave. The entirety of Manfeaster's army converged on the castle. Hyena-men raked at the shields of the soldiers, wolf-men snarled and crunched armor between their jaws like walnut shells. Jessilynn barely had need to aim, the night was so thick with enemies. Each shot killed at least two, sometimes many more as the arrow traveled down the hill, connecting with body after body and wrecking incredible damage.

"Into the castle!" Sir Daniel screamed at Lord Arthur as the soldiers steadily retreated.

"Like the Abyss I will," Arthur retorted. "I will die in battle, not cowering behind doors that won't hold!"

Jessilynn tried to delay such a fate, but the beasts veered to either side in an attempt to avoid her shots. The mass of soldiers blocked her aim; the shielded wolf-men leapt upon the defenders while she stood there helpless. The best she could do was kill the beasts once they were upon them, but in her heart, she knew it a shallow gesture.

Scores of bird-men raced up the hill, letting loose with shrill shrieks that were horrific to the ears. Lord Arthur surged ahead to greet them, blade swinging. He took down three of the beasts, his sword hacking through their thin, feather-covered limbs. Jessilynn killed two more, but it was like scooping a bucket of water out of a river. Lord Arthur fell, claws ripping his exposed flesh, strange beaks plucking out his eyes as he screamed.

The line began to break, and no amount of arrows Jessilynn fired seemed to help. They were down to ten men, all of them beaten and spent.

"Get inside!" Dieredon screamed at her as Sonowin flew low overhead.

"You heard him," Sir Daniel said, shoving her with his free hand. Jessilynn stumbled, a word of protest on her lips that would go unspoken. "Fight from within the castle, girl. It's our last hope, now go!"

Jessilynn ran through the open doors, sparing a glance over her shoulder to see Sir Daniel impale a pouncing wolf-man with his sword. The creature swung as it died, thick claws tearing open the brave man's throat. Jessilynn turned away, choking down a sob. Another soldier slammed the door shut and flung the bar in place.

Jessilynn stumbled through the cramped castle foyer, pushing through wounded men, crying families, and children lurking in every corner. When she reached the stairs she ran up them two at a time despite the burning in her legs. She had to get up. She had to get to the top. Motion kept her tears at bay. Action kept her thoughts on anything but the dead and dying.

When she reached the ladder that led to the high turret, she climbed up, flung open the trap door, and scrambled onto the rooftop. She then ran to the front of the castle, just above the main door, and gaped. The army of the vile covered the horizon, swarming like so many ants.

Jessilynn looked to the purple sky, but she saw no wings.

"You," she whispered when she brought her gaze back down and saw Manfeaster approaching the hill, escorted by ten of his strongest warriors. The distance was great, but her arrow would span it. Ignoring the goat-men slamming their horns against the castle doors, she pulled back a glowing arrow and aimed at the King of the Vile. If their leader died, then maybe, just maybe the army could still break into disarray. The bow shook in her hand, and she struggled to keep it still. When she fired, the glowing bolt sailed wide, killing a few random beasts. Jessilynn hurried two

The King of the Vile

more shots, each missing. Her vision grew blurry. Manfeaster stayed where he was, wisely coming no closer, and he lifted Darius's blade above his head, howling in mockery.

Jessilynn was ready to fire a hundred more arrows until she dropped the bastard, but then she heard the splintering of wood. Turning her attention back to the castle door, she saw that the combined might of the goat-men had broken it down. They rushed inside amid shouts and terrified screams.

"No, no, no," she said, firing arrows straight down. *It can't end like this.* This was their last stand, their final battle. They couldn't fail. All those people crowded inside, fearful, begging for safety, and she'd let them in? The soldiers inside weren't enough to last even a few minutes. Bird-men, goat-men, wolf-men, they all died as she blasted the entrance, but for every one she stopped two more rushed through. The screams of the dying grew all the louder.

It didn't matter. She couldn't stop. She had to keep going, had to keep fighting. Jessilynn heard the beating of wings above her, and she glanced back to see Sonowin land atop the castle, the horse settling atop the trap door to keep it closed. Dieredon hopped down and slowly approached.

"Come help me!" she screamed at him. "We can still hold them off!"

The elf didn't ready his bow or draw an arrow.

"You have to help me!"

"Jessilynn..."

"No," she said, shaking her head. "No, it's not..."

"Jessilynn, enough. It's over."

Tears ran down her face, her lips quivered. Jessilynn kept firing, the mechanical motions seemingly happening on their own, and it wasn't until the third releasing of her drawstring that she realized she held no arrows. She fired no shimmering manifestations of her faith; just an empty string thrumming impotently. Falling to her knees, she dropped her bow and stared at the carnage. Fields in all directions were filled with corpses, the beast-men feasting until their stomachs were ready to burst. The sounds were overwhelming; crunching bones, slurping tongues, ripping muscle and flesh. A few wounded screamed, not many, for it seemed cries of pain only attracted attention and subsequent death.

Jessilynn leaned over the side of the castle and vomited. The sounds, the sights, it was all too much. She prayed she never witnessed the horrors of the Abyss, but if she did, she felt it would look and sound similar to the disgusting display assaulting her senses. She vomited until her stomach was empty and her chest hurt, then slid back to a sit, entire body numb.

Broken, hopeless, Jessilynn looked to the starry sky and saw the beating of white wings.

It felt like a cruel joke. They would come now? They would fill the night sky with their wings now the battle was over and done, and thousands lay dead or dying? Jessilynn slowly rose to her feet as the angel army split into multiple streams, surrounding the wall and gathering in larger numbers were the gate was broken. She thought to grab her bow, then left it there. What point was there? She carried no regular arrows.

A trio of angels split from the rest and landed on the turret. Jessilynn recognized one of them as their leader, Ahaesarus. She'd met him before, in her early days in the rebuilt Citadel. It'd been just once, a mere checking up on how Lathaar and Jerico were doing, but Jessilynn had never forgotten. Ahaesarus had looked so divine, his perfect face chiseled from marble, his hair spun gold, his wings softer and whiter than those of a swan. Now she only saw a weary face with long hair covering his eyes like a shroud.

The angel said nothing, only stared at her. The sound of feasting seemed to have stunned him silent. But Jessilynn wouldn't remain silent. Slowly she stepped toward the angel, her voice quivering, an inch from breaking completely.

"Why weren't you here?"

He opened his mouth to say something, then closed it. Nothing? All he could offer her was guilty silence?

"Why didn't you come for us?" she asked, stepping closer, hands clenching tight. "Why'd you leave us to die?"

Her fists struck his muscular form. Her face buried into his chest, slathering his armor with her tears. Over and over she hit him, flailing and sobbing uncontrollably. She screamed the word at

The King of the Vile

him, the only word she had left. She didn't know if it were a question or a condemnation, and truth be told, she didn't care.

"Why? Why? *Why?*"

"I'm sorry," the angel whispered. His heavy arms wrapped about her. "The blame is mine, and I will bear this guilt unto eternity. We failed you, Jessilynn. We failed you all."

She ceased her flailing and weakly leaned against him as she sniffled. She had nothing left, nothing at all. "What happens now?"

Before Ahaesarus could answer, Jessilynn felt the angel shudder as if he'd been stabbed. She opened her mouth to ask, but a sudden terror slammed her chest harder than a hammer. Panic flooded her body as if she were still within the thick of battle. She wanted to run. She wanted to hide. Even in Ahaesarus's arms, she did not feel safe.

A voice spoke in her mind, each word an indictment.

There will be death. There will be bloodshed. But it is not in my name.

Jessilynn struggled to remain standing. She'd already cried her tears, yet fresh sorrow washed over her dulled mind. Vainly trying to gather herself, she wiped her face and stepped away from Ahaesarus. The angel had appeared heartbroken upon his arrival, but now he stared south with abject horror. When she glanced to the other hovering angels, she saw that they looked equally terrified.

"Azariah," Ahaesarus whispered. "What have you done?"

The words chilled Jessilynn to the bone. "What do you mean?" she asked. "What's going on?"

"Where is their leader?" the angel asked, placing his hands on her shoulders.

"Leader?"

"Of the creatures. Their ruler, their king."

Jessilynn pointed past him to where Manfeaster lurked amid a group of his most powerful wolf-men. He was one of the few not joining in the gluttonous feast the bulk of his forces partook in, with only those near the edges of the walls fleeing to the inner fields from the line of angels brandishing weapons forged in the smiths of eternity.

"There," Jessilynn said. "The one wielding Darius's old blade."

The angel saw, and kissed her forehead.

"Forgive me, Jessilynn," he whispered. "But we must have an army for what is to come."

With a mighty flap of his wings, he lifted into the air. More and more of the creatures looked up from their feasting to see the angels, and fearful murmurs spread throughout their army. Jessilynn walked to the edge of the castle tower. Ahaesarus flew straight at Manfeaster, landing with his enormous weapon drawn. Manfeaster cowered, Darius's sword held clumsily before him. The rest of his wolf-men backed away, frightened by the angel's presence.

"Are you Manfeaster?" Ahaesarus asked, his voice thundering across the field. "Are you their king?"

"I am," Manfeaster growled.

Ahaesarus sprang forward, batting aside Darius's sword as if the huge wolf-man was but a child. A single swing and Manfeaster's body split in half, blood and innards spilling across the already gore-soaked grass. Frightened howls shook the army, and many turned to flee, only to cower again as more and more angels landed, sealing them in. Jessilynn wondered if the angels would slaughter them all. Such death should have made her sick, but she was so broken, so tired, a large part of her wanted to see the vile beasts banished from Dezrel for all time.

Ahaesarus stabbed his golden blade into the dirt. Bending down beside Manfeaster's remains, he grabbed the hilt of Darius's sword. At his touch, the blade shimmered a soft white.

"I am unworthy of wielding the blade given to me by Ashhur's hands," he said, rising once more. His voice echoed in the night, and Jessilynn held no doubt that every last one of the beasts heard. "But this...this sword I will carry. This burden, I will bear. The sword of a man who sought redemption, and then found it. The sword of a man who died so others might live."

Ahaesarus's wings spread wide, and he lifted off the ground.

"I was there!" he cried. "I was there when your kind was given mind and form, elevating you beyond your beastly nature. I was there as you warred for the brother gods. Since the day you

The King of the Vile

walked on two legs, you were meant to serve in battle. You bled and died, nothing more than a weapon we wielded without guilt or conscience. And then for your reward, we banished you from our world. We imprisoned you in the blasted remains of Kal'Droth between the rivers to starve. To prey upon one another, regressing, returning to your savage beginnings."

He spun, sword pointing down at them all.

"You wish for a kingdom of your own. You fight for a land with plentiful game and grass that does not wither and die at the lightest heat or softest frost. Your sins are many! The death I cast before your feet is great, and will be atoned only at a mighty cost. The bones between your teeth, the blood you taste on your tongue, condemn your generation. But to your children, I will give a kingdom! I will grant them a land where they may grow to adulthood feeling not hunger, not fear, but hope. All you must do is serve. All you must offer is your lives to protect those you once butchered."

Every last one of them was enraptured by his words, Jessilynn included. She couldn't fathom what she was hearing. She didn't understand it. Ahaesarus flung his sword to the dirt, and the impact seemed to make the ground quake for miles in all directions.

"Bow before me, you vile creatures!" Ahaesarus shouted. "For I am now your king!"

They fell by the thousands to their knees, burying their faces to the dirt and crying out their allegiance.

Jessilynn dropped to her knees as well, not out obedience, not out of respect, but from pure shock. Dieredon took her hand, quietly offering whatever comfort he could as they watched the display.

"Ahaesarus?" Jessilynn whispered. Fresh tears ran down her face. "What have you become?"

24

Alric Perry approached Mordeina's walls with a chill in his heart. The past few days he'd convinced himself he neared the end of his delusions. He would come upon the capital city and see only empty sky where Avlimar once hovered, and there'd be nothing left to believe. How could he set foot in a city that did not exist? His dreams would be proven as lies and he could return home, assuming he had a home left to return to. Rosemary might have already moved on, and if she had, he prayed it was with someone better than himself. Ivan Buckhart had always lingered about Rose a bit too closely when the ale flowed freely during the harvest festivals. A good man, Ivan, and from a far better family. It hurt thinking of his wife moving on from their five years of marriage so easily, but better that than her waiting for him to return home when he knew he never would.

For to the west of Mordeina was a glittering city of gold and silver. Alric knew right then that his dreams were true, realized that place would be his grave.

A merchant wagon rolled down the road away from the capital. The driver, a chubby man with a goatee, cheerfully greeted Alric as he passed.

"I thought Avlimar fell?" Alric asked him as he turned around to keep pace with the wagon.

"It did," the merchant said. "They rebuilt it. Devlimar, the glorious home of uptight angels eager to get their wings into a twist about every little damn thing." He spat over the side of the wagon. "They're preparing themselves an announcement, and like the smart person I pretend to be, I'm getting out while there's still a chance. Whatever they've got to say, it won't be anything good, I promise you that."

The King of the Vile

Pieces of Alric's dreams hovered before his vision, and he had to agree.

The merchant slowed his wagon a bit, and he leaned down, beady eyes squinting. "You've any business in Mordeina? I'd not mind a bit of company on the ride south, and I'm telling you, stranger, right now the city's not a wise place to be."

Alric badly wanted to take him up on the offer. What good would he accomplish in Devlimar? What would he say? His dreams always ended before he spoke. The idea that words spoken by a lowly farmer from a foreign nation would carry any weight in a city whose very streets were paved with gold was ludicrous. He could go. He could climb aboard that wagon, turn his back to Devlimar, and forget the whole business.

Except when he returned home to Rosemary, it wouldn't be as a fool who believed too much in his dreams. It'd be as a coward too frightened to chase them. Alric could endure having his faith lead him to embarrassment, but he couldn't abide to betray it and never know the reason Ashhur brought him all these hundreds of miles to the home of his angels. Despite every bone in his body wishing otherwise, he shook his head and waved goodbye to the merchant.

"Perhaps I'll see you on my way home," he said, not believing a word of it. "But for now, I'm needed in Devlimar."

"Needed?" the merchant asked, guffawing. "The only thing needed in that shogging city is a good kick in the pants. Hope you're not trying to peddle anything, stranger, because whatever you're selling, I assure you, the angels aren't buying."

No, he had nothing to peddle, only words to speak. He turned away from the wagon and continued on the road toward Mordeina. The hours passed, and when he reached the crossroads, he found the way toward the city of angels increasingly crowded. People of all ages trundled down the road, a climate of fear hanging over them, their words tinged with dread. Alric listened in on conversations when he could, and all of the speculation focused on a single topic: what announcement would the angels make?

Alric heard dozens of guesses, from Ashhur's return, the angels' departure, and war with Ker, to more troubling ideas such as stricter laws and executions, an overthrowing of King Gregory, and the formation of a new ruling class bearing white wings. Alric joined the flood of humanity steadily flowing toward the city of silver and gold, gloriously invisible, an unnoticed speck among his race, and he tried to take comfort in that. One of thousands, that's all he was. Insignificant. Unimportant. He told himself he could remain silent as the angels made whatever announcement they wished to make. He never had to open his mouth. He never had to say a word. After all, in his dreams he never had.

That thought was cowardice, of course, no different from fleeing with the merchant. To continue on toward Devlimar required a little courage, and to stand before a host of angels and declare the supposed word of Ashhur would take a whole lot more.

The closer to Devlimar he got, the more Alric wondered if he'd even have the *chance* to speak. Crowds surrounded the city, thousands of people cramming together in an attempt to enter an amphitheater designed to hold several hundred. Alric couldn't even enter the city itself, let alone the amphitheater. The sun slowly set, the first of many stars starting to wink into existence, and what should have given him peace only showed him how little time he had left.

Wonderful, thought Alric. *Am I really going to travel hundreds of miles only to be stopped a few hundred feet away?*

A rising commotion surrounded a squad of soldiers bearing torches. The soldiers escorted a couple through the waiting throng. The lady was an elf, her long, beautiful dress green and gold. Beside her, was a gray-skinned man who looked incredibly familiar. The traitor's brother, Alric realized, and his eyes widened with realization. Harruq and Aurelia Tun, come to attend the proclamation. If anyone could get him inside...

Alric shoved and elbowed his way toward the group. Plenty of people were shouting, asking questions of the man who ruled in King Gregory's stead while the boy grew, which meant Alric had to shout even louder to be heard.

"I met your brother!" he cried to Harruq. "I met Qurrah, do you hear me? I bring word from your brother!"

He shouted it over and over until Harruq's eyes flicked toward him. Alric pushed aside a man to stand before the halted soldiers. Harruq pointed him out, beckoned him closer. The guards parted a step so Alric could approach.

"What about my brother?" Harruq asked, nearly shouting to be heard.

"I met him on my travels here," Alric said. "He gave me a message to tell you should we meet."

Neither the half-orc nor his wife seemed too confident, and Alric could hardly blame them.

"Well, let's hear it," Harruq said.

"Not here. Inside."

Harruq shrugged.

"All right," he said. "Let's go. You're coming with us."

Alric joined the couple within their circle of platemail and swords, the hairs on his neck standing on end. Attention had turned to him, onlookers curious why he was given such an honor. He kept his head down, focused on putting one foot in front of the other instead of looking at the tall buildings of crystal and glass, buildings hauntingly familiar to those from his dream.

They slowly made their way to the amphitheater. Neither Harruq nor Aurelia said anything to him, only held each other's hands. The simple act left him feeling even more a trespasser. He begged Ashhur to give him a sliver of confidence. Seeing Harruq's towering form so close, arms big as his head, ancient blades swinging from his belt, left him feeling pathetic and small. Why could Ashhur not deliver such a message from Harruq's lips? Surely people would listen. Harruq was a hero, he was no one.

The amphitheater was crowded with angels and humans alike. The soldiers remained near the entrance as an angel guided the three of them to seats waiting on the very front row. Harruq sat on the marble bench, wrapped an arm around Aurelia's shoulders, and then glanced at Alric from the corner of his eye.

"Well, we're inside," Harruq said. "Care to share my brother's message?"

Alric cleared his throat. Murmurs washed over him. It made him antsy having so many people nearby. He felt like a bull trapped in too small a pen.

"It's...it's not much," Alric said. "I met Qurrah and his wife, Tessanna, as they were traveling with King Bram's army."

A frown tugged on the corners of Harruq's mouth.

"That so?" he said. "I'd heard rumors he was with him. Never wanted to believe it. So what was his message?"

Alric coughed. His throat felt dry, his face flushed.

"He said to tell you he wasn't your enemy, and that no matter what you hear, he will always be there for you."

Harruq grunted. "He marches toward the capital I protect with the army who would besiege it, then tells me he is not my enemy? That make sense to you, uh...what was your name again?"

"Alric," he said. "Alric Perry, from Ker."

"You've come a long way, Alric. Care to tell me why?"

"You'll see soon enough," Alric muttered, but a commotion swept through the crowd, drowning him out. Four angels descended from the sky, each holding a long steel chain connected to the foot of a throne. Its base was made of interlocking gold and silver weaves, and red cushions bearing the symbol of the Golden Mountain were its padding. The throne settled into the center of the amphitheater atop a waiting red dais. The sight made Alric want to vomit. A throne, just like the one in his dreams.

The four angels took positions beside the throne. Two bore long blades, a third had an enormous mace strapped to his back between his wings. The fourth held a small gold chest tucked underneath his arm. One of the four, an angel with white hair and bronze eyes, stepped forward and addressed the crowd with a booming voice.

"People of Dezrel," he shouted. "I present you Azariah, high priest of Ashhur."

Azariah flew over the high walls of the amphitheater. The angel bore white robes so clean and pure they seemed to reflect the light of the torches that lined the walls. His brown hair was cut short about his neck and interspersed with silver and gold lace. He smiled at the gathered crowd, a smile that was surely meant to be benevolent but to Alric seemed arrogant. The angel moved his fingers in a few quick motions, and then he spoke. His words carried despite him showing no effort to project his voice, and Alric wondered if some sort of magic was involved.

"Men and women of Mordeina, I thank you for coming," he said. He stood before the throne with wings folded behind him now his voice. Hear my words, and know they are Ashhur's. Look upon me, and know you look upon the face of your savior. Just as Ashhur reigns in the golden hereafter, so too must he reign here in Paradise, and I shall be that king in his stead."

Alric remembered his guilt for the life taken at his hands. He remembered the message of repentance he'd heard, the moment he'd fallen to his knees and given over everything of himself, all that was good, all that was evil, and received only love in return. As Alric watched the white-haired angel set the silver crown upon Azariah's head, rage pulsed through every vein in his body. Like Alric, the people of Dezrel would kneel in search for the grace of Ashhur, but all they'd see was Azariah's smiling, haughty face. They would pray for forgiveness but receive hatred. They'd see a crown that demanded love and gave none in return. They weren't individual beings to be saved, but cattle to be herded from green pastures to gold.

Azariah was the highest ranking priest bearing wisdom of the centuries, and Alric but a lowly farmer, but he understood Ashhur better than the angel did. Vision turning red, he rose from his seat. Before Azariah could speak another word, Alric stepped out from the crowd to address the new king of Paradise.

25

Harruq listened to the angel's proclamation, shocked still as stone. He'd feared Azariah would declare himself king, but this...this was madness. Azariah was demolishing everything mankind had ever created, replacing human courts and laws with those solely dictated by the angels. People would have no say, no control. They were at the mercy of angelic feathers, with death awaiting all who strayed. It was madness. It was insane. Butchers pretending their swords carried salvation. This was what he'd bled for? This was what Haern, Delysia, Brug, and countless others had died fighting for? This...this perversion?

"This is wrong," Aurelia whispered. "People will die before they submit to such measures."

Harruq knew that was true, too. The riots, the midnight fires...they would only be the beginning. Bloodshed was coming, and Harruq felt helpless to stop it. Whatever power he'd had was gone. The angels had stripped him of it, and with the lords' army facing King Bram in the south, his two twin blades were all he had to fight back. Two blades against thousands. What would he accomplish other than his own death?

Alric suddenly leapt from his seat and into the open space before the red dais. The man was unarmed, his clothes covered with dirt and stains. The angels surrounding Azariah reached for their weapons, but they hesitated. The king of the angels leaned forward in his throne, eyes narrowing as he listened.

"My ears burn from such holy lies," Alric shouted. "You say Ashhur is silent, and that you speak for your god. You say he is absent, and it is your place to fill the void. But he is watching, he is listening, and I tell you now, he is *angry*."

"They're butchering them," Harruq said, a flash of anger finally pushing through his shock to wake his limbs and mind. "Butchering them like animals."

How many had gone out to bear witness to the proclamation like Azariah had demanded? Five thousand? Six? A terrifying number of dead, but it seemed it wasn't enough. A legion of black wings took to the starry sky, flooding out from Devlimar in all directions like bats exiting a cave.

"Let's go," Aurelia said, opening another portal. "We need to get Aubrienna somewhere safe."

"You want to flee?" Harruq asked his wife as the swirling blue tear in reality appeared before them. "We're to leave everyone to die?"

"What else are we to do?" Aurelia asked. She pointed to the sky full of black wings, darker than the night itself. "They'll be here any second. There's no time to warn anyone. No time to muster defenses. We have to act now, and as best we can."

Harruq slammed a fist against the side of the wall. "They're rabid dogs! And now they're coming here!"

"You want to fight them?" Aurelia asked. She grabbed his hand, which pulsed with pain from striking the hard stone.

"I do."

"And so do I. But we'll fight when our child is safe, and not a moment before."

She leapt through the portal, and after a moment's hesitation, Harruq followed. He reappeared at the steps of the castle, the portal swirling shut behind him. Two soldiers on guard duty snapped to attention at their sudden arrival..

"Run to your families, both of you," Harruq ordered. "Protect them the best you can."

"Protect?" asked one of the guards. "From what?"

Harruq pointed at the black wings in the sky. "The angels."

They didn't seem to understand, but Harruq feared they would soon enough. He turned from them and ran down the steps, silently wishing them luck before barging through the castle doors. Aurelia easily kept pace as they raced down a side hall toward the dungeon entrance. It was in the far back of the castle, well-guarded with two separate doors, each one locked and operable from the outside only. Most importantly, there were no windows. They passed by the occasional servant or guard, and Harruq shouted the same warning to them all.

"Get to your rooms and lock the door. It's not safe!"

They were almost to the dungeon when Harruq heard the first screams. A shattering of glass, certainly of a breaking window, punctuated the death cry. Harruq winced but continued on toward the entrance of the dungeon. The soldier on guard sprang to attention, nearly knocking his helmet off with his frantic salute.

"Steward?" the soldier asked.

"Get the doors open," Harruq ordered. "We're under attack."

He'd thought he'd have to explain, but anger sparked in the soldier's brown eyes.

"It's the angels, isn't it?" he asked as he spun about and jammed a key into the lock. "Sir Wess warned us this might happen."

Good for him, Harruq thought as the door opened. Two more soldiers stood within, and they began unlocking the second door when they saw Harruq dressed in his armor. The sounds of death and destruction echoed down from above. After a moment of fiddling with the key, the second door opened, and Harruq led them all inside.

The dungeon was empty of occupants, a side effect of having angels in charge of justice instead of far slower courts. A small round table was near the entrance, and a trio of soldiers stood at ready, weapons drawn. They visibly relaxed when they saw it was Harruq who entered.

"Did the announcement not go well?" one asked.

"That's putting it mildly," Harruq said. "Where's the kids?"

"Asleep."

The guard pointed to a corner where a dozen bright-colored pillows had been tossed together to form a bed. Gregory and Aubrienna slept side-by-side underneath a thick white blanket. Under normal circumstances Harruq would have found it adorable, but under normal circumstances they wouldn't have been hiding from insane angels inside a damn dungeon. Harruq scooped Aubrienna into his arms. The little girl groaned and

The King of the Vile

turned, fighting to stay asleep. Harruq shifted her onto his left arm and shook Gregory with his right.

"Come on, up, up, the both of you," he said.

"What's going on?" one of the guards asked.

"Ashhur turned his back on the angels," Aurelia explained. "They've gone mad and are slaughtering everyone. We need to flee to safety."

Both children reluctantly woke, muttering incomprehensible sentences as they rubbed at their eyes. Harruq hefted them both onto his shoulders while Aurelia ripped open another portal.

"Inside," she ordered. "All of you."

The soldiers looked between each other, uncertain.

"You heard her," Harruq barked, his patience worn thin. He stepped on through himself. His surroundings changed within the blink of an eye; he now stood atop a thick layer of leaves, staring up at pleasant starlight. The leaves crunched beneath his heavy boots as he stepped away from the portal to allow room for the soldiers who followed. They were at the edge of a shallow pool of water surrounded by a copse of trees with thick, sprawling branches. The moon reflected off the water, which rippled gently from whatever life existed beneath the surface.

Aurelia appeared last, and the blue portal vanished back into nothingness.

"Where is this?" Harruq asked, looking around.

"Two miles north of Mordeina," Aurelia said. "I go here sometimes when I need to get away from you."

"Wonderful. You'll have to show me sometime when it's daylight and we're not running for our lives."

Harruq set both children down beside the nearest tree. Despite his efforts, neither looked ready to wake, and he wished he'd grabbed a few of the pillows before dashing inside the portal. Brushing Aubrienna's hair away from her face, he kissed her cheek and whispered goodbye.

"Let's go," he said.

Aurelia frowned. "We're not leaving them."

"Those angels are slaughtering everyone," Harruq said. "We have to go back and save those we can."

"Do we?" Aurelia asked, staring at their sleeping child. "We have to protect our family, Harruq. We do that here, not back in Mordeina."

Harruq reached out for her hand, squeezing her slender fingers tightly. "We can't abandon the people. Not when we can help so many."

"But what if we make a mistake? What if I lose you, Harruq? What if they lose us? Would you have Aubby grow up without her parents?"

"And how many little girls are dying right now?" he asked, a knot in his throat. "How many children are losing their parents? We have to do something. We have to save who we can."

Aurelia grabbed his shoulder and leaned against him. He'd always seen her as strong, often stronger than him, so he was surprised by her sudden shiver.

"I know," she said softly. "But why must it be us?"

Harruq kissed the top of her head.

"Because we're the only ones who can," he whispered.

She shed a pair of tears, which fell upon the shoulder of his leather armor. "This burden will break us," she whispered.

"Maybe someday, but not tonight. Tonight, we make those murderers pay."

The group of soldiers had stood awkwardly at the spot where the portal vanished, waiting for their decision. Harruq sniffled as he pulled back from his wife, and he wiped at his eyes to banish evidence of his lingering doubt.

"Two of you stay here with them," he told the soldiers, who were still waiting awkwardly by the spot where the portal had vanished. "Keep out of sight until we return. And if we don't..."

"If we don't, flee north, toward the Castle of the Yellow Rose," Aurelia said. "Find Ahaesarus. He's the only other ally I know you can trust."

The two oldest of the six stepped aside, and they bowed.

"We'll protect them with our lives," one of the soldiers said.

"You'd better," Harruq said. "The rest of you, you're coming with us. We have some psycho angels to kill."

Aurelia began casting another portal, which tore open with a *hiss*.

The King of the Vile

"Where are you taking us?" Harruq asked.

"To the castle steps," she said. "If we're to push through the city, we'll need every soldier we can find. I figure we start from there and work our way south to the gates."

Harruq glanced back at Aubrienna, and the soldier standing protectively over her. He couldn't shake the fear that he might never see her again.

"Sounds like a plan," he said, and forced himself through the portal before his second thoughts betrayed him. He reappeared at the top of the castle steps, stumbling across wet, unsteady footing. Blood, he realized. He stood in a pool of blood. The other four soldiers cheered and saluted, for Sir Wess had organized a defense at the castle doors. He and his twenty men appeared to have killed four of the angels. Their bodies lay crumpled at the bottom of the steps, their blood trickling across the stone.

"Glad to see you're alive," Sir Wess said. His sword, his armor, even his gray mustache were spotted with blood. "And better yet, armed. We'll need your swords and magic if we're to live through the night."

"Let's not celebrate until we see the sun rising," Harruq said. "We need to get away from the castle. If you'll follow me, I'll lead."

"Away from the castle?" one of the soldiers asked. "But we can fortify our positions here."

Harruq grabbed the man by the top of his breastplate and pulled him close, trying to still his anger given how frightened the soldier surely was.

"You see those windows?" Harruq said, pointing to the enormous openings near the rooftops on either side of the grand throne room further inside. "Think of how many just like those are on every floor of the castle, and then tell me again how do you plan on defending this stone tomb. We've got Gregory safely out of Mordeina, so if you want to join him, you need to keep your sword ready and follow me, all right?"

The man swallowed and bobbed his head. "I will."

"Good man." Harruq patted him on the shoulder, then turned to Sir Wess. "They're strong and furious, which means there's no point staying defensive. Use their recklessness against them. If any come rushing at us, you rush them right back and hope for a lucky hit to the heart or throat."

"We'll do our best," said Sir Wess. "Lead on, Steward."

Harruq grinned. "I'd rather you call me something far more intimidating prior to going into battle."

"Very well," Sir Wess said with a grin of his own. "Lead on, Godslayer."

"Much better. Aurry, you ready?"

Aurelia twirled her staff, lightning crackling from both ends. "I am," she said.

"We make no turns, no delays," Harruq told the soldiers as he drew his swords. "Just a straight shot from here to the city gates. I don't know how many people will join us, but consider that an after-thought. The important thing is that we draw the attention of as many of those winged monsters as we can. Each one we bring down is one less that can kill an innocent elsewhere in this city. We don't stop for anyone, we don't hesitate, and we don't run away. You follow my lead. Me and Aurry will take the brunt of the hits, so focus on keeping the rest of the people safe."

Two pairs of circling black wings suddenly straightened out, the angels diving toward their group. *Damn...not even off the steps yet.* Harruq slammed his swords together multiple times, the ancient weapons showering sparks. Let the soldiers see the power he wielded. Let them believe, for even a moment, that he and Aurelia might save an entire city.

"Be glad you're not one of them," Harruq shouted to the soldiers. "Because their shitty night's about to get a whole lot worse."

Aurelia lifted her staff, and three bolts of lightning shot into the air. The two angels twisted and twirled, avoiding the first two. The third scored a solid hit, plunging head to feet through an angel's body. He fell limp to the city street, landing with the sickening crunch of breaking bones. The other angel barely slowed as he swung an enormous two-handed sword. Harruq countered with Condemnation and Salvation, grunting in satisfaction as the angel's blade rang loudly before bouncing off. The angel could not kill all his momentum despite his spread wings, and he continued forward, right into Harruq's waiting swords. The angel impaled himself up to the hilt, gasping as blood spewed out his mouth.

Harruq kicked the body off so it might join the others at the bottom of the steps.

Two down, he thought. *Couple thousand more to go.*

Except there wouldn't be as many as there should. When Harruq stood upon the wall, watching the black wings fly out from Devlimar, he'd seen hundreds flying toward Mordeina...and thousands more scattering in all other directions. They'd scour the entire countryside that night. How many miles might they cover? How many villages would they burn? Would they ever even stop?

Harruq shook his head. It'd do no good to dwell on such things, and even less if his fear became infectious. *Time to be the blood-soaked hero*, he told himself. *Time to flee yet another city as innocent life is devoured by the darkness.*

"Let's move," he told the soldiers.

They marched ahead, all of them keeping one eye on the sky. Harruq began to feel a little bit better, as each step toward the distant city gate seemed like progress. They passed by homes, the soldiers calling out to them repeatedly, the same offer each time.

"Come with us to flee the city!"

Shadows moved behind windows, and many doors creaked open, but remarkably few joined them at first. Harruq wondered how many were praying they would be one of the lucky ones that escaped the angel's wrath. *Probably a depressing amount*, he decided, and pushed it out of his mind. A home on his left had its door broken inward, and two soldiers rushed toward it as a fallen angel emerged from within, holding a bloody blade in his left hand and the corpse of a young child in the right. The soldiers swung their swords while shouting curses. The angel blocked one, batting the sword away as if it were nothing, and then flung the corpse at the other. The soldier stumbled backward, and the angel leapt after, bloody blade plunging for his neck.

Harruq flung Condemnation in the way before it could find purchase. His glowing red sword clanged against the angel's steel, easily able to withstand the blow. Pressing the advantage of surprise, Harruq leapt into the angel with complete abandon, thrusting with Salvation while punching with Condemnation's hilt.

The two blades collided amid the scream of the angel, Salvation piercing flesh. Harruq pumped his legs, pushing them to the front of the house. The angel slammed against the wall, the contact knocking the weapon from his hand as his head cracked against the wood. Harruq ripped Salvation free with a sudden gush of blood, looped both blades about, and cut off the angel's head.

"Thanks," said the soldier whose life he'd saved.

"Still not enough," Harruq said. He glanced inside the home, saw the bodies of a man and woman lying side by side near the door, and shook his head.

They continued down the street, weaving back toward the group of soldiers. A single angel dove from the sky, black wings curled behind his back like a hunting hawk. Two died when he crashed into their ranks, but then the angel was overwhelmed by a vicious rush of swinging swords. Another angel burst out of a ransacked home, only to be bathed in fire from Aurelia's fingertips. He dropped dead a blackened, smoking husk.

"Come on," Harruq shouted, growing frustrated by how few had joined them. Right now they had a mere seven, five of which were one family. Harruq saw plenty of wings circling, but so far their group had gone mostly unnoticed. Not quite the plan.

"Aurry," Harruq asked. "Think you can get their attention?"

Aurelia spun her staff once, then lifted it above her head, tip pointed toward the distant angels. "I believe so."

Lightning streaked across the sky, the accompanying thunder loud enough to rattle Harruq's teeth. The bolt struck two different angels, dropping them dead instantly. Harruq blinked against the after-image burned into his eyes.

"Yeah," he said, twirling his swords in his hands. "That'll do it."

The group continued moving, a scattering of people coming from either side of the road to join them. Three sisters ran screaming from an alley, an angel flying overhead in chase. Harruq pointed and shouted, but he had no need. Aurelia sent a barrage of ice lances, forcing the angel to dodge. Two found purchase, neither penetrating his armor deep enough to kill. Looping around from one side of the street to the other, the angel readied his spear and charged. Harruq stepped in front of the soldiers. His red

The King of the Vile

blades were a blur as they struck the spear from beneath, whacking it harmlessly upward. Momentum carried the angel past Harruq and into the soldiers, where it tumbled to the ground. Sir Wess himself cut the angel's throat with a single smooth stroke.

"Keep moving," the knight shouted. "More are coming by the minute!"

As were the people of Mordeina, Harruq was happy to see, and not all of them civilians. Soldiers, some in armor, some in civilian clothes, joined their ranks, Sir Wess quickly positioning them where they were needed most. The number they protected had grown from seven to over fifty. The soldiers formed a protective ring around them. Harruq patrolled the front, shouting and hollering like an idiot at the angels in an attempt to goad them his way.

"Harruq!" Aurelia shouted. Harruq gutted the single angel he fought, then stepped back so three soldiers with him could finish him off. He turned, felt his heart skip a beat at the sight of four angels approaching quickly from the rear. Fire and ice leapt from Aurelia's hands in an alternating barrage, but the angels were prepared, weaving left and right, avoiding the attacks. Harruq took off at a sprint, looking on helplessly as three soldiers leapt to her defense, shields up. Aurelia finally scored a direct hit with a bolt of flame when the angels were too close to dodge, and a burning corpse crashed into the soldiers like a living battering ram. Aurelia danced, her staff a whirling blur as it batted aside several slashes from two angels. The soldiers tried to recover, but they were quickly cut down, leaving Aurelia isolated.

"Over here, you bastards!" Harruq roared. Two ignored him, but one turned his way, lifting his enormous two-handed sword. Harruq charged straight at him, unafraid of the lengthy weapon. With such momentum, he merely had to put his swords in the way as the angel's attack swooped around, hoping to cleave him in half. Salvation and Condemnation flared, the angel's sword rebounded, and then Harruq was barreling into him. The angel was knocked to the ground, the bones in one of his wings snapping loud enough Harruq could hear. The angel screamed, and Harruq silenced him with a stab to the throat.

Twisting the sword free, he turned to Aurelia, who had built a wall of ice around herself. She unleashed a torrent of flame at the angels as they hovered ten feet in the air. Fire filled the sky above her, pushing both angels back. Harruq pumped his legs, then jumped. His red blades cut through the angel's knees, and he screamed as blood showered the street along with a pair of useless legs. Harruq landed poorly, dropped to a roll, and stopped only when he struck the side of a home.

Groaning, Harruq pushed himself back to his feet and staggered toward his wife. His aid, though, didn't seem necessarily. The ice wall shattered as the angel smashed into it repeatedly with his sword, only to be met by a beam of raw magical force. It struck the angel in the chest, caved in his breastplate, and then flung his broken body a dozen feet backward.

Aurelia dropped to her knees, holding her head. Harruq skidded to a stop beside her, but she pushed him away.

"Them," she said, gesturing to the crowd of survivors they'd collected. "Help them."

Five angels looped around them in circles, weaving in to slash at the soldiers before rising again. That they'd be so careful compared to the recklessness of the previous assaults worried Harruq to no end. The angels were superior combatants in every way. If they actually showed patience, and surrounded their group before they could escape the city...

"Am I not good enough for you?" Harruq shouted, trying to draw their attention. "Too scared to take on an out-of-shape half-orc?"

Two banked away from the soldiers toward him, and Harruq braced himself. Each angel held a long sword bathed in blood. Harruq pushed off just before they arrived, stealing the offensive. He ducked beneath the first's slash, then brought both weapons to bear on the other. His glowing blades rattled against the angel's sword but failed to find purchase. The other flanked him, forcing Harruq to split his attention. Feet spinning beneath him, he bounced between them, Salvation focused on one target, Condemnation the other.

"Try harder!" Harruq shouted. He could see the rage in the angels' eyes, held back by the flimsiest of control. "I'm not even breathing heavy," he said with a sneer.

The angel on his left lost control, using his wings to give him a burst of speed as he thrust with all his strength. Harruq sidestepped, slipping Salvation just underneath his chin and slitting his throat. He thrust Condemnation at the chest of the other angel, who had tried to follow. Before the angel could rip his sword free, Harruq was already spinning. One blade struck his neck, the other his waist. Blood and innards poured free.

Haern would be proud, thought Harruq as he stood over the two dead bodies.

A *boom* of thunder turned his attention back to their growing caravan. Aurelia had struck another dead from the sky, but it was like swatting a hornet's nest: it only seemed to make more appear, and angrier than ever. *We wanted their attention, now we have it.* All throughout the city, people would find themselves a reprieve, and if they were smart, Harruq hoped they'd make a break for the open city gates.

"By my side," Harruq shouted to his wife. Keeping the people safe would be impossible with how many angels now dove toward them, but if he and Aurelia remained standing, they'd inevitably draw their attention off the civilians. Though clearly exhausted, Aurelia continued to fling elements toward the angels, each lance of ice or ball of flame smaller than the last. An angel rushed at Harruq like a mad dog, on his feet instead of his black, oily wings. He threw his spear with incredible strength before chasing after with arms swinging. Harruq flung himself into Aurelia with his back, knocking them both out of the way as the spear sailed over them. Harruq rolled, bounced to his feet, and chopped with both swords. The angel died trying to dive on Aurelia, Salvation and Condemnation punching twin holes in his chest.

Harruq pulled Aurelia to her feet and there they stood, back to back. Up above, two fallen angels dove simultaneously. Harruq trusted Aurelia to hold her side, and he braced for impact from the other. His angel wielded a gigantic mace, and he pulled back at the last minute to swing with frightening strength. Harruq lashed out with his swords struck the mace. The jolt traveled all the way up his arms, seemed to make every bone in his body ache, but he kept the flanged head from crushing him like a bug.

The angel pulled the mace back for another swing, but Harruq was faster. A single hop forward closed the distance, his left arm extended to its limits so Salvation might thrust beneath the lower lip of the angel's chestplate. The blade pierced his abdomen, and when he reflexively doubled over in pain, Harruq looped Condemnation about, cutting off his head. The angel's mace hit the ground with a loud *clang*, the body fell with a dull thud. Harruq turned, relieved to see Aurelia had killed the other by ripping a chunk of the road up as a wall just before impact and letting the angel collide with it. The dead angel's spine was crushed, his eyes vacant.

"Keep going," Harruq said, taking Aurelia's hand. "All of you, keep going!"

Over a hundred had joined them, but Harruq saw hundreds more rushing ahead, taking advantage of their distraction. Good. If those people escaped the angels' wrath, then they'd done their jobs.

Not completely, he thought. He still had to get him and Aurelia back to Aubrienna safely, and given the constant harassment, he wasn't sure they'd ever get the chance.

Glowing red arrows shot into the air from Aurelia's palm as Harruq rushed toward the formation of soldiers. To his surprise, Sir Wess was already making his way to him. Harruq shouted to be heard over the chaos.

"It might be time to break and run."

"Not quite," Sir Wess said, gesturing down the road. "The men on the wall weren't so quick to fall as I feared."

Peering over the people, Harruq saw that a group of nearly fifty soldiers marched toward them, fighting off the occasional angel on their path. Harruq laughed, and he smacked the older knight in the chest.

"Seems you've trained them well," he said, grinning.

"About damn time someone noticed that."

The knight returned to his men as Harruq took Aurelia by the hand.

The King of the Vile

"Join the rest of the soldiers," he said. "Let them give you a moment to catch your breath."

"It's just a headache," Aurelia said. "I've suffered worse. I'm married to you, aren't I?"

Harruq kissed her lips. "Love you. Now get your elven ass surrounded by soldiers."

She didn't argue further, which only convinced Harruq she was as tired as he thought. The lengthy group of people traveled along the street, the attacks growing more and more scattered. Harruq returned to the front, wondering if they'd suffered the worst of it. When they reached the first gate that led through the twin walls surrounding the city, the attacks stopped entirely. Even the gap between the walls was empty. Some of the soldiers cheered, and the many people sighed with relief. Harruq's optimism lasted only until they exited the outer gate. Over a dozen angels hovered just outside, waiting. Harruq recognized one in particular, the sight of his ugly, jagged-toothed smile filling him with sadness.

"Judarius is mine," Harruq shouted to the soldiers at his back. "Take care of the rest."

The soldiers acknowledged his command and proceeded to shout taunts at the angels. Harruq stayed at the front, eyes locked with Judarius. Deep down, he knew the angel would relish the challenge. Ever since their very first duel, when Harruq brought the skilled fighter down, Judarius had sought a rematch. Now he'd get it, only this time it was for blood.

The angels dove in a single wave, Judarius leading them. Spells leapt from Aurelia's hands, balls of flame trailing black smoke soared over Harruq's head. The angels veered, breaking formation. Only Judarius kept straight ahead, like an arrow aimed for Harruq's chest. Black wings flared out, beating to kill Judarius's momentum. He dropped to the ground, his enormous mace leaving a deep imprint in the grass. Judarius's gray eyes glared at Harruq from a nearly unrecognizable, twisted face.

"You flee like cowards!" he screamed.

Harruq heard steel striking steel as the battle raged behind him. Praying Aurelia was safe, Harruq forced the fear from his mind so he might face his foe. He lifted his twin blades, trusting their powerful magic to keep him safe.

"You butcher sleeping women and children without warning, yet we're the cowards?" Harruq asked. "I think you need some perspective."

Judarius snarled like an animal, the image aided by the sharpness of his teeth and the blood of innocent people splashed across his armor. He stepped closer and swung his mace with enough power to shatter stone and topple buildings. Harruq ducked, rotating as he side-stepped so that he could emerge with swords swinging.

"Perspective?" snapped Judarius. His mace whirled about, easily batting aside the dual strike. He swung twice more, Harruq just barely managing to dodge each one. His legs felt made of mud, his arms were limp. He thrust once, the attempt easily parried, and then Judarius pulled back for another swing. It was too low to duck underneath, too close to leap away from, so Harruq dropped to one knee and put his swords in the way. The power of the hit jarred his arms, filling him with pain from his shoulders to his fingertips. The red glow about the swords dimmed momentarily, as if the steel itself were protesting.

"Perspective?" Judarius repeated, pushing harder against Harruq's block. "I watched as mankind was given life from clay. I guided them in their infancy, and now I suffer while their sinful race is elevated above us in the eyes of the god I served for centuries. Tell me, Harruq, what *perspective* explains such a betrayal?"

Harruq felt strength flooding back into his tired limbs, strength born from rage. He shoved aside Judarius's mace with a loud cry.

"Betrayal?" he roared. "You would slaughter those you were meant to protect, then cry betrayal?" He slammed both his swords down against the mace, which Judarius held parallel to the ground to block the blows. "You would bathe the streets in their blood, then cry victim?" He shoved the angel back, slashed open his thigh before he could protect himself, then launched into another barrage. His twin blades crashed into the mace again and again. His fury gave him strength, hid every hint of pain. Harruq hammered against Judarius until the angel fell to his knees, still struggling to hold back the blades.

"Betrayal, Judarius?" Harruq screamed. "You want to know what explains such betrayal? Look in a damn mirror! The answer's in the innocent blood you bathed in!"

Both swords swung sideways, shoving the mace aside. Before Judarius could step back, Harruq flung himself forward, slamming his forehead into Judarius's face. Blood splattered from his nose, and he lost his balance. Harruq pulled his swords back for another swing, but a quick flap of wings gained Judarius enough separation to avoid decapitation. A few more, and he rose into the air, safely fleeing toward Devlimar.

"And you called us cowards." Harruq spat blood, turned to see the rest of the angels dead or fleeing. He let his swords drop and gasped in air as his battle lust slowly faded.

"Damn fine show," Sir Wess said as the soldiers rushed past Harruq. "Remind me to never make you angry."

Harruq didn't have the heart to chuckle. Amid the sea of tired, bloodied people, Harruq saw his wife, just as bloodied and tired. He sheathed his swords and pushed toward her.

"We made it," he said, wrapping his arm around her waist.

"I need to get Aubrienna," she said after kissing his cheek.

Harruq looked to the sky. Though he saw many black wings hovering above the city walls, and the screams of the dying still reached his ears, no more angels made their way toward them. No doubt they wanted easier prey for their vengeance. Harruq clenched his teeth. They'd mitigated the carnage, but they'd not stopped it. No one could.

"Go on," he said. "We'll be here waiting."

Aurelia waved her hands, then vanished with an audible *pop*. Harruq walked among the people, his surroundings a surreal image carrying far too many echoing images from his past. The refugees walked south, away from the capital. Many looked to him for direction, to be the faintest spark of hope amid their misery..

Aurelia returned not long after, a portal opening ahead of them and dispensing two soldiers, one carrying Gregory. Aurelia held little Aubby. People murmured in surprise or relief at the sight of the boy king. Another victory against the angels. After such a horrible night of loss, even the tiniest blow against them felt sweet.

The portal hissed shut. Harruq hurried over and wrapped his family in his arms.

"Hi, daddy," Aubrienna said, rubbing at her eyes. "I was sleeping."

Harruq kissed his daughter's forehead as tears ran down his face. "Go on back to sleep, babe. We have a long way to go before morning."

She didn't answer, only nestled into his arm and closed her eyes. Harruq took Aurelia's hand, and together they walked among the people toward the land of Ker, and a land free of angels.

26

Lathaar knew something terrible approached as they lay down that night to sleep. He felt it in his bones, in the uncomfortable grass underneath his bedroll, in the way the night air hung perfectly still. Jerico had barely said a word to him during that day's travel, as if burdened by the same overwhelming sense of wrongness. It felt like any second the ground might erupt beneath their feet. They were only a few hours away from Mordeina, but they'd drifted off the worn road and camped instead of pressing on through the dark.

Lathaar stared at the stars, feeling like worms crawled in his veins.

"Something's wrong," Jerico said, sitting up from his bedroll on the opposite side of their dwindling campfire. "You feel it too, don't you?"

"Like Ashhur's crying out in warning for no apparent reason at all?"

Jerico sighed as he rubbed his eyes. "Yeah, that'd be it. Get your armor on. I've got a bad feeling we're going to need it."

Lathaar rolled up his bedroll, tied it, and then stuck it into his pack along with his blanket. Then he began the lengthy process of putting on the various pieces of chain and plate, which he'd wrapped in a separate blanket beside him on the grass. Once the chain shirt was on, he buckled together the breastplate, and then reached for his gloves.

He felt a sudden surge of emotion so powerful it was like a kick to the stomach. Lathaar dropped to his knees and braced his weight on his arms as he shivered. It felt like a fever had come upon him, sudden and vicious. Sweat rolled down his neck, and though the night was filled with soft blue starlight, his vision ran scarlet.

A single voice whispered in his mind, furious yet sad, determined yet exhausted.

There will be death. There will be bloodshed. But it won't be in my name.

Lathaar felt Ashhur's anger growing in his breast. The fury left him terrified, for he knew his own anger could never feel so raw, so powerful. It was beyond him, beyond his control.

"Jerico?"

Lathaar forced the word out as best he could. For some reason, he expected his whisper to go unheard. The night was quiet, yet a tremendous roar filled his ears with the cries of frightened and confused people.

"I'm fine," Jerico said, gasping in air as if he'd just run a dozen miles. "I'm..."

It hit them both at once. The fist of a god. The rage of the infinite. Neither paladin could remain upright, flinging themselves to the grass and burying their faces. Every part of Lathaar's body trembled. Every part of his mind blanked with fear. A single word echoed throughout his consciousness, devastating and simple.

Fall.

Tears fell from Lathaar's eyes, and then the moment passed and he felt like himself again. His heart pounded in his chest and light sparked from his fingertips without need of him to grasp one of his swords.

"What was that?" Lathaar asked, staggering to his feet.

"I don't know," Jerico said. "But we're not staying here. Waitsfield Village is a mile up the road, so let's get to it. I'll feel better once we're in some semblance of civilization."

Lathaar heartily agreed with. Out on the road he felt exposed and vulnerable, a rarity in all his travels. Something horrible was happening, and hovering over it all was that single command: *fall.*

They traveled side by side in silence. There was no way of knowing what had gone wrong, so Lathaar kept his mouth shut and tried to keep his mind from haphazardly bouncing from idea to idea. He failed, mostly, but the fear increased the clip of his walk. Jerico kept up with him, seeming of similar mind.

The King of the Vile

Waitsfield had no road leading to it, only a sign pointing west. The two paladins spotted the sign easily enough in the moonlight, and they turned off the road toward a long stretch of hills. In the darkness, the hills looked like frozen ocean waves; soft, gentle, unending. They melded into one another, with no real clear path between them, so Lathaar trudged straight ahead, cresting each hill in turn. After thirty minutes, Lathaar saw a single broad hill that covered much of the horizon, and Lathaar began to jog, determined to reach the village.

Waitsfield was nestled in the center of the valley beyond. To Lathaar's relief, he heard no signals of alarm or distant shouts, saw no sign of fire or distress. It was just a sleeping town surrounded by a simple wood fence to keep out nighttime predators. A single lit lantern hung from a post beside the closed entrance. Still unable to relax, Lathaar marched down the hill along a worn path in the grass.

"What do we do?" Jerico asked on the way down. "Wake everyone? Tell them we've got the shivers, so prepare for...something?"

"I don't know," Lathaar said. "Perhaps we'll play it by ear."

The wood fence came up to Lathaar's chest, just high enough he couldn't climb over with ease. In the light of the lantern he knocked, waking a man who slept in a rocking chair adjacent the gate.

"Ashhur help me, you gave me a scare," the man said, lurching out of the chair. He looked in his fifties, his skin deeply tanned, his smile missing half its teeth. "There's no inn here, if that's what you've come looking for."

"That doesn't mean there are no places to stay," Jerico said, smiling that charming smile of his. "Especially for a pair of paladins of Ashhur."

A bit of the sleep left the man's eyes. "Well I'll be." He quickly lifted the latch and swung the gate open. "Not sure your kind's set foot in Waitsfield in over a hundred years. What brings you this way?"

"The desire for a mattress softer than my travel-worn bedroll," Jerico said. "That and a warm meal come the morning, cooked by someone who knows what they're doing."

"Come in, come in then," the man said with a laugh "We might be able to scrounge something up. My name's Coy, and welcome to Waitsfield Village."

Lathaar stepped inside, and when the gate shut behind him, his hands drifted to the hilts of his swords. Whatever threat plagued his mind, it was located inside the village, of that he had no doubt. Jerico glanced at him over his shoulder, his look showing he sensed the same.

"I'm thinking the Codgers could spare you a room, so long as you two don't mind sharing," Coy said as he led them past several thatched-roof homes on their way toward the commons in the center of the village. "Their eldest son died on a hunt last year, Ashhur bless his soul, and they haven't seemed too keen on clearing out the boy's old things just yet."

Lathaar listened to their guide while searching for signs of life in the sleepy village. Just before they reached the commons, all three heard the sound of splintering wood, followed by a scream.

"Amanda?" Coy said, suddenly rushing off to the right. "Amanda!"

Lathaar and Jerico raced after him, readying their weapons. They passed a line of buildings forming the perimeter to the commons, then turned again to find Coy collapsed to his knees before a squat, rectangular home. The door was shattered. The occupant, a pretty lady no older than twenty, lay half on the porch, half on the single step leading up to it. There was blood everywhere Before either paladin could react, the intruder speared Coy through the chest with something long and sharp, twisting it once before ripping out the barbed head with a bloody explosion.

"Ashhur help us," Lathaar whispered as he readied his swords.

The creature before him bore the same carefully molded armor as an angel, the same flowing robes, the same grand wings. But this thing was pale and ugly, his wings black, and Lathaar understood, right then and there, what the proclamation of *fall* had meant.

"So our father abandons us," said the hideous thing, "yet still grants you power. You, who are pale mockeries of what we are. I can think of no greater insult."

The King of the Vile

"I can think of a few," Jerico said, lifting his glowing shield. "Do you want to hear them all, or just my favorites?"

The fallen angel readied his spear, bits of pink flesh clinging to its tip. "The shield-bearer," he said. "The coward who fled to the Wedge when the Citadel fell. Yes, come. Show me the bravery of one who lived among dogs while his brethren were butchered."

Jerico's face darkened as the glow of his shield dipped the tiniest bit.

"He's mine," he told Lathaar before lunging ahead. The fallen angel met his charge, leaping off the porch with wings flared and spear thrusting. Jerico easily positioned his shield in the way, sparks flying as the tip of the spear scraped across. His mace swung, striking only air as the angel turned to one side and slid past. Jerico followed him, shield leading. Twice more the spear jammed into the shield. The angel failed to find an opening, but his weapon's reach allowed him to attack while still retreating away from Jerico's counter with a leap of his long legs.

Lathaar ran down the street, hoping to put himself at the angel's flank so he could no longer retreat, but then he saw another pair of black wings soar over the commons and land on the opposite side. Praying for his friend, Lathaar sprinted across the commons, keeping his eyes on the home he suspected it'd landed before. Not that it'd matter if he lost sight. In his gut, he feared the screams of the dying would reach his ears before he arrived.

He was right.

Lathaar burst through the broken door of the home, swords leading. Surprise was with him, and he rammed both blades through the back of an angel who stood beside the fireplace. Ripping out his swords, he kicked the corpse to the side. At his feet was a young woman in a shift, tears running down her cheeks. The body of a young man lay in her arms, throat cut.

"Stay inside," Lathaar told her, wishing he could offer more comfort. "And find somewhere to hide in case more return."

She nodded, eyes still wide from shock. Lathaar wondered if she'd even move, or if she'd stay there clutching her dead spouse. He couldn't stay to find out. Rushing back out the door, he jogged across the commons, relieved to find Jerico walking toward him.

That relief was tempered by the sight of blood dripping down his left shoulder through a crease in his platemail.

"You all right?" Lathaar asked.

"Yeah, I'll be fine," he said. "Damn spear snuck past my shield, but at least it got stuck on my armor so I could finally bash that thing's brains in."

Lathaar toward Mordeina. It might have been his imagination, but dark shapes, darker than the night, moved among the stars above.

"More of them," he said. "Perhaps *all* of them."

"What happened?" Jerico wondered. He stared at the distant shapes, looking sick. "Did things truly become so terrible while we hid in our Citadel?"

"We weren't hiding," Lathaar said, a bit harsher than he meant. "We just didn't know."

"I fear there might be little difference."

Someone shouted at them, trying for their attention. Both turned to see several men headed their way, one of them carrying a torch. It seemed the sounds of combat had begun rousing people from their beds. All throughout the town doors opened, men and women peering out with simple weapons in hand.

"What the fuck is going on?" the first to near them asked.

"Your village is under attack," Lathaar said. "Get back to your homes, now."

"Attack?" the same man asked, ignoring his demand. "By who?"

Lathaar pointed to the sky. "The angels."

As if drawn by their glowing weapons, another black-winged angel dropped to the ground in the center of the commons, this one wielding a sword and shield. While they'd once been gold, the hilt and edges of the shield looked made of bone, making them that much more frightening.

"Hide!" Lathaar shouted at the villagers, who'd frozen at the angel's arrival. "Bar your doors and hide! The Abyss comes to your home this night!"

Finally they fled as the angel stalked closer. Lathaar met his approach, wanting to put himself between the angel and the injured Jerico.

"Heal your wound," he said, knowing that with a moment's prayer Jerico could seal the cut to prevent further blood loss.

The angel charged, shrieking in mindless rage. Lathaar blocked the clumsy chop with his short sword, wincing at the pain from the jarring force that traveled up his elbow to his shoulder. By Ashhur, the angels were strong. Lathaar swung with his long sword, hitting the shield. He then pressed closer, parrying away another thrust and beating into the shield with both weapons.

Jerico could endure a mountain falling on him so long as his shield stayed in the way. Could the angel say the same?

The blow of the two blades rocked the angel on his feet, allowed him no time to counter. Lathaar beat against it twice more, all his strength pouring into his holy blades. A crack ran up the middle of the shield, and the angel tried to steal the offensive with a wide swing that would have cut Lathaar in half if not for Jerico thrusting himself in the way. The angel's attack hit Jerico's shield, accomplishing nothing. Lathaar slammed his swords into the bone shield one more time, shattering it. His swords continued on, cutting off several fingers before slicing through the angel's lower jaw, down his throat, and into his chest.

Lathaar ripped his swords free, kicking the fallen angel's corpse for good measure.

"Thanks," he said.

"Glad you trusted me to jump in at the right time," Jerico said, clipping his mace to his belt.

Lathaar chuckled grimly. "Let's go with that instead of me fouling up. Sounds better."

More voices called to them in the sudden quiet after the battle. The paladins turned to see an older man wearing a leather hauberk rushing over, two armed men with him.

"Hey," he said. "I'm Kenneth, Waitsfield's mayor. Give the order, and we'll get what fighters we can to help you."

"Keep your fighters in their homes," Jerico told the mayor. "They're no help in this fight."

"Maybe not in fighting," Lathaar said. "But we can't be everywhere at once. Start bringing people toward us in the commons. Get them packed into the nearest homes, then lock the doors and hang tight until daybreak. Think you can get the people to do that?"

The mayor nodded. Despite how terrified he must've been, the man seemed remarkably together.

"I know I can," he said. "So long as you'll keep us safe."

The mayor bowed, and the men with him clumsily mirrored him. Lathaar watched them go until Jerico smacked his side.

"Got another," he said.

A fallen angel swooping down with sword ready. Lathaar drew his blades and joined Jerico in cutting him down the moment he landed.

The hours of the night past with a steady, bloody crawl. Jerico and Lathaar kept together, patrolling the commons with their glowing weapons always at ready. The blue-white light seemed to draw the angels toward them, inciting rage greater than any barb Jerico might throw with his words. The two paladins would cut them down, each one a challenge given their size and strength. Every bone in Lathaar's body ached, and despite healing their wounds after a moment's prayer, the toll wore on them.

In the gaps between attacks, Lathaar begged Ashhur to keep him going despite the long night, despite the exhaustion that clawed at his eyes.

"Is it dawn yet?" Jerico asked as he slumped against the wide trunk of one of the few oaks growing in the commons.

"Not quite," Lathaar said, grunting as he stretched his arms. He pointed skyward, to where an angel hovered in the air. "Another incoming."

Instead of attacking, the angel remained there, wings steadily flapping. He wielded no weapon, and based on his lack of armor, Lathaar knew him to be one of Azariah's priests. All priests, both angel and human, had lost most of their magical power in the years following the second Gods' War, but the ball of flame this angel flung toward Lathaar seemed to contradict that basic understanding. Lathaar had little defense against magic, so he did the intelligent thing and ran for his life.

The ball struck the ground and exploded, billowing fire in all directions. The second Lathaar heard the sound of its detonation he dove into a roll, tucking his arms and legs tightly against his body. He felt a momentary surge of heat as the flames licked his back, but then he was safely out of reach. Coming out of his roll, he leapt onto a porch and staggered farther away from the angel. Another ball of flame exploded, and Lathaar turned to see Jerico fleeing a similar attack. His friend kept his shield up as he looped around to the front of the home, momentarily blocking sight between him and the angel.

"What in blazes was that?" Jerico shouted as they huddled underneath porch awnings on either side of the street.

"What did it look like? A damn fireball."

"Yes, but why is *he* throwing one?"

Lathaar wished he had a better answer than the one he gave.

"Because he's trying to kill us."

The angel priest soared overhead, two more balls of flame leaping from his dancing fingers. Jerico sensed the attack before it ever arrived, Ashhur screaming a warning in his ears. The paladin crossed the road as the home he'd taken shelter behind exploded, fire easily setting its thatched roof alight. Jerico raced past Lathaar, who sprinted after.

"That's not fair," Jerico said as he glanced over his shoulder at the chasing angel. "You know that's not fair, right?"

Lathaar grimaced as another ball of fire erupted ahead of them in the street, forcing both to veer aside at the last moment.

"No," Lathaar said. "It's not."

Magic from the sky, and neither paladin had a way of attacking. Fair didn't even come close. Thankfully, either the angel's training hadn't been very extensive or he simply lacked imagination, since his attacks so far remained limited to fire. Plus he wasn't very accurate. So long as Jerico and Lathaar kept to their feet, they could avoid the somewhat slow projectiles...but the town burned around them, and any additional angels flying in would go unchallenged.

Lathaar glanced over his shoulder, and his eyes widened.

"Duck!" He grabbed Jerico by the shoulder and pulled him down. A ball soared over their heads, slamming into the front of a home and bathing it in flame. Lathaar heard a scream from within, and a window along the side smashed open as a man started letting his children out one by one. Whatever relief Lathaar felt at seeing them escape died the moment another angel swooped above and immediately banked around for a dive.

"Damn it!" Jerico screamed, turning about and lifting his shield. "That's enough. No more running."

He stepped toward the priest, arms out wide.

"Here I am," he shouted. "Send me your best shot, you black-winged bastard!"

Lathaar trusted him to know what he was doing, for he couldn't stay to help. The other angel was diving toward the children, and against such a foe the little ones had no chance to escape. Legs pumping, Lathaar clutched the hilts of his swords and begged Ashhur for speed.

"Look out!" he screamed at the children. Two dropped to their knees and covered their heads, but the third, a little boy with curly brown hair, tumbled as he fell from his father's arms out the window. The diving angel aimed his sword like a spear, slamming into the child and skewering him through the chest. Lathaar lost control. He didn't care that the angel continued on toward him at dangerous speeds. He didn't worry about any harm to himself. This sick, ugly caricature of Ashhur's servant would die.

Roaring mindlessly, he swung both his swords in an overhead chop while leaping into the air to meet his foe. His blades flared white, accompanied by a loud ringing sound. The angel twisted his blade to block, wings still flapping. His momentum should have blasted Lathaar over, but a shockwave unleashed upon contact with Lathaar's swords. The angel screamed as he smashed against an invisible wall, limbs twisting, bones shattering. Lathaar's feet touched ground and he swung again, the shimmering white steel slicing the angel in half.

Spinning about, Lathaar ignored the heart-wrenching cries of the father, who'd climbed out the window and collapsed over the body of his dead son. He couldn't dwell on that yet, had to let the rage carry him.

Across from him, Jerico faced off against the priest, blue-white mist lifting off his shield as blasts of fire slammed against it. Each explosion rolled across the sides, licking Jerico's arms. So far the paladin endured, but each hit caused his shield to flicker. How long might he last? Sheathing his long sword, Lathaar shifted the short sword over to his right hand.

"Elholad," Lathaar whispered. The blade vanished completely, becoming pure light that swirled and shimmered like mist. He took three steps to gain momentum, then flung the blade end over end with all his strength.

"Come down here, you gods-damned monster!"

It never should have worked, but it did. The blade twirled through the air so quickly it seemed less a sword and more a whirling circle of light. It cut through the priest's left arm, severing it at the shoulder, then continued on, ripping through the bones of his left wing. The angel cried out as he dropped, and Jerico allowed him no reprieve upon landing. Thrusting his shield, Jerico cried out Ashhur's name. A glowing image of his shield grew outward, smacking the priest across the face and chest.

Jerico readied his mace as he approached the wounded priest, but he was given no chance to finish him off. Down from the sky dove another fallen angel, greatsword swinging. Lathaar never saw the angel himself, and only with Ashhur's warning did Jerico get his shield up in time. The two collided, a rolling mess of robes, wings, and platemail. Jerico was first to his feet, swinging his mace at the angel, who blocked.

"I got him," Jerico shouted. "Get the priest!"

Lathaar sprinted after the priest, who had pushed to his feet and staggered away. A trail of blood marked his passing. It seemed his destination was the commons in the heart of town, and he flapped his lone healthy wing to gain what little extra speed he could. Lathaar pumped his legs, teeth clenched as he drew his longsword out of its sheath. He wouldn't let this creature escape. If people were dying all across Mordan, the least he could do is make the monsters that attacked this village pay.

Lathaar burst past the homes and onto the soft grass of the commons, the angelic priest mere feet ahead of him. He reared back with his longsword. The priest suddenly spun about, his hand a blur. Fire burst from his palm, painfully bright in the starlight. Lathaar panicked, abandoning his swing and diving to the side. Fire washed across his shoulder, heating his armor, and he choked down a pained cry. He rolled, avoiding a follow-up burst. Once on his knees, he lifted his sword, knowing it was meager protection but praying Ashhur's power within it might matter somehow. The priest grinned, appearing a crazed beast, blood dripping from his wings, shoulder, and teeth. Beneath the angel, shadows swelled like a pool.

"Ashhur should have left us with his power, not you," the angel said. Fire swarmed his hand. Lathaar opened his mouth to offer one last retort, but snapped it shut when tendrils shot up from the shadow pool beneath the angel, latching onto his extended limb and yanking it low. More tendrils wrapped about the priest's legs and waist, with a particularly long and thin one looping a dozen times around his neck. The angel strained, eyes bulging, scream trapped in his choked throat. The shadows quivered, convulsed, and then ripped the angel apart.

"I was never fond of their kind," said a voice. Qurrah Tun emerged from behind the dead priest, grinning despite the gore that covered him. Lathaar sheathed his sword and breathed out a sigh. For perhaps the first time in his life, he was thrilled to see the half-orc. He rose to his feet and offered his best tired smile.

"You certainly know how to..."

Lathaar's voice trailed off as Elrath, Mal, and Samar rushed past Qurrah. There they were, all three young paladins, bruised and tired but alive. They flung themselves against Lathaar, and he held them, unabashedly weeping. Was this real? He never thought he'd see them again, yet here they were, safe and free. It filled him with overwhelming relief.

"Forgive me," Lathaar said. "I should have given myself over for you. I should have..."

"We're fine," Samar said. "And we'd have never forgiven you if you did."

"All three of you are a sight for tired eyes," Lathaar said, pulling them tighter to him, grinning when he finally let them go.

Tessanna joined her husband's side, having arrived along with the young paladins. She tossed Lathaar's short sword at his feet.

"I'm glad you can watch over them now," the black-eyed woman said. "I swear, their constant optimism grates on the nerves."

The King of the Vile

Jerico came around the side of smoking rubble that had once been a home, mace hooked to his belt. "I think that might be the last of them," he said, then suddenly froze where he stood. "You...you're all right?"

Now it was Jerico's turn to rush the three young paladins. He strapped his shield onto his back and wrapped them in his arms, one after the other. Lathaar wiped at his face, trying his best to compose himself. The battle had dimmed, but that didn't mean the threat for the night was over.

"How did you escape?" Jerico asked.

"Tessanna and I broke them free of their chains during the battle with Mordan's forces," Qurrah explained. "Samar there even helped me kill a mage of the Council who attempted to halt our escape."

Jerico punched the red-haired kid in the shoulder. "Way to do us red-heads proud," he said, grinning.

Qurrah glanced to the gory remains of what had been the angel priest, his distaste clear as starlight.

"Lord Aerling wanted to hide in a forest when the first angel attacked our camp," the half-orc said. "Such cowardice would not do, not with my brother potentially in danger at the capital, so we left and began traveling through shadows northward. Lucky for you, Tessanna sensed your presence once we neared Mordeina."

People had begun emerging from their homes, rushing to find loved ones or attempt to put out fires. Lathaar watched them, a rock forming in his gut. He heard a steadily growing number of calls and shouts from the village gate, the commotion too far away for him to decipher.

"What now?" he asked. He turned to the young paladins. "You three, stay here where it's safe."

"Wait," Qurrah shouted, but Lathaar ignored him. He forced his tired legs to move. It didn't matter how exhausted he felt. He'd still fight on. Jerico kept pace despite his multiple wounds and dented armor. Only his shield remained in immaculate condition.

"Well," Jerico said. "That was a fun surprise."

Lathaar shook his head and forced himself to prepare for whatever new challenge awaiting them at the village gate. He saw no more angels marring the sky with their black wings, so what now? Traitorous soldiers? War demons? Perhaps hundreds of undead? He'd sworn to give his life to the people of Waitsfield to protect them, and his drained body was dangerously close to letting that happen. If only the sun would rise. He felt if he could just see the sun, and know that this awful night was over, then the nightmare would finally end. Yet despite how many angels they killed, and how many prayers he whispered, dawn felt so far away.

The closer they got, the more Lathaar heard. Shouting. Crying. People frightened, or in pain. Had a new battle joined theirs? Amid it all, he heard the rattle of armor, and sparing a glance at Jerico, he saw him readying his mace and shield for another fight. Picking up the pace, the two rushed past the final row of homes, only to skid to a stop at the open gate.

Lathaar saw soldiers, but none loyal to the fallen angels. Hundreds approached the village, and they were not undead, nor were they war demons, but instead tired, haggard people carrying little more than the clothes on their backs. At their head walked Harruq and Aurelia Tun, Gregory carried in his arms, Aubrienna in hers.

"I told you they were here," Harruq said to Aurelia, grinning despite the deep circles underneath his eyes and the dried blood across his face and armor. "Who else would be dumb enough to wield weapons so bright they'd attract attention from miles around?"

"Only this fool," Lathaar said. He smiled and embraced his friends.

Suddenly, the dawn didn't seem so very far away.

27

In the young morning, Azariah led his followers southward through the skies. To his left flew his brother, Judarius, his enormous mace safely strapped to his back. He'd spoken only a single sentence in Azariah's presence since the Fall, and that was to inform him of the half-orc's escape with his elven wife and the child king. To Azariah's right flew Ezekai, newly promoted in rank behind only Azariah and Judarius. A worthy reward for an angel that had remained loyal throughout all his doubts and struggles. Of all the Fallen, Azariah knew that Ezekai understood him best.

The rolling hills leading to Mordeina steadily passed beneath them. The light reflecting off the dew should have made the grass sparkle in the early sun, but Azariah saw only a dull gray with the faintest hints of green. Ashhur's betrayal not only robbed them of their beauty and grace but also the ability to enjoy beauty itself. What food Azariah had eaten tasted of ash. The world around him was a mess of interlocking grays and blacks, with what little color remained faint and diluted, as if he viewed it through a wall of smoke. The wind blowing against his skin used to fill him with peace, but now it itched like poorly weaved wool. His head ached from the unnatural bones growing from his skull to form his crown. To speak was a frustration. His broken teeth cut his tongue and lips. Azariah couldn't even close his mouth properly, for the teeth were broken in such odd angles that they would not rest upon each other but instead jab into his gums. At all times he tasted blood, and it was a cruel joke of Ashhur's that it was the only substance whose taste wasn't dulled.

"There," said Ezekai, the white-haired angel swinging closer and shouting to be heard. His outstretched arm pointed to the west. Azariah turned his head, scanning the distance. A gentle wood grew for a few miles along a minor creek. The leaves had already fallen for the coming winter. Through their gaps he saw intermittent tents.

"No campfires," Azariah said. "Do they hide from us?"

It was possible. Given the carnage of the night before, a few of his angels might have plunged recklessly into the army. Rational thought had meant nothing in those early hours of rage, nor the fear of death. *It doesn't matter.* Even if the humans had warning, it would not help them. Nor would the cover of trees. The people would either bow or suffer complete destruction. Azariah was tired of politics. He was tired of votes, and debates, and questions of morality. These miserable excuses of life could barely keep from killing each other, yet they still deluded themselves into thinking they grasped the concepts of eternity better than the angels themselves. It was like listening to a babe still at the breast telling their mother they were the wiser.

Azariah dove, those with him following. With all their wings spread wide, they were like a cloud, and their shadow crossed over the forest. Before Azariah's foot ever touched ground, the soldiers were scrambling for their weapons. It seemed the humans had encountered one of the fallen during the night. Azariah wondered which of his timeless brethren had died. The angels had scattered in all directions after the Fall, some flying for dozens of miles just to find a place untouched by bloodshed they might release their rage upon. They had trickled back into Devlimar throughout the morning, making it impossible to know who might have perished.

"Bring me your lord!" Azariah shouted, unafraid of their spears and swords. He kept his wings spread wide so all might see his black feathers. That was one benefit of Ashhur casting them aside: his current form inspired terror far more than his previous ever could. Given how they'd tried, and failed, to rule through grace and mercy, perhaps a frightening visage was more appropriate for the new world.

The men shouted as they formed lines, men with shields on the front, spears and archers in the back. Azariah shook his head, patience wearing thin, not that he'd had much to begin with.

"Your lord!" he roared. "Bring him to me!"

The King of the Vile

The very sound of his voice made the soldiers shake. Good. Perhaps they could conclude this meeting without bloodshed. He and his fellow Fallen had drunk their fill the previous night as they shattered the rotten foundation of the old, but now was a time for rebuilding. A new kingdom. A new Paradise.

Murmurs reached his ears, faint and distant. Always faint and distant. Even if Azariah had stood beside them the sound of their voices would have come from a distance. What point was there in such cruelty, Azariah wondered as the soldiers fetched their lord. Why did Ashhur not strike them deaf and dumb instead? Why rob them of their beauty? Why sap them of their ability to enjoy the pleasures of the world? He felt his god seeking to teach him a lesson, but it was far too late. Ashhur had turned his back to them. Ashhur's light had been replaced with emptiness and disgust. There would be no learning from such a teacher.

And besides, Azariah had far grander plans.

At last a chubby man stumbled to the front. Azariah recognized him as Lord Richard Aerling, master of the lands between Stonewood Forest and the Bloodbrick. His black hair was in disarray, his long mustache frayed and uneven. Just being in his presence was unpleasant. To Azariah's eyes, he was as disgusting as his own new form, yet had Ashhur cursed Lord Richard? Of course not. He was fat because he was a glutton, unpleasant because he was cowardly and covetous. Weakness led to his ugliness. What weakness had the angels shown, other than a desire for Ashhur's subjects to live by Ashhur's rules?

"I am in charge of the soldiers here," Richard said, puffing out his gut and trying to look intimidating. He failed miserably. "Three of your kind attacked my camp last night, and I demand to know the reason."

Azariah stepped toward the lord. The line of soldiers rattled with the sound of raising shields and drawing swords.

"You demand?" Azariah asked. "Who are you to make demands of me, cur?"

Richard's face turned a deep red.

"The man who has a hundred spears ready to throw into your gut, that's who," Richard said. "We have been attacked, and I will have justice. Once the crown hears of this..."

"*I* am the crown," Azariah said. Speaking the words made the bones of his skull ache. "We have cast down humanity's rulers. You have no stewards, no princes, no king. You lords will bow to Ashhur's law, or you will bow in anticipation of the executioner's blade. There is no other choice."

"That's preposterous!"

Azariah flashed the man a smile full of broken, blood-covered teeth.

"This world is preposterous," he said. "It is a land of insanity, wretchedness, and sin. I will fix it, Richard Aerling, with or without your help. You have no one to appeal to, no courts or leaders to cry to for mercy. Only me, right here before you, telling you to kneel. Now will you kneel, or must I have Ezekai remove your head from your shoulders?"

For the slightest moment, Richard seemed ready to accept. Then his pride overruled his cowardice. A poor choice.

"No!" he shouted. "We will not accept your rule over our nation."

"*We?*" Azariah asked, and he raised his voice so that it would carry throughout the forest. "You don't seem to understand, Richard, but you do not speak for these people anymore. I have stripped you of your authority. Every man beside you bears the same power, and they bear the same choice. Will you die, or will you kneel? My angels are ready, and your numbers few. Die if you must, but know you die in vain."

Richard was shaking now. He took a single step back, then pointed straight at Azariah.

"They're blustering," he cried. "Demons, evil creatures, all of them. Attack, attack now!"

No one moved.

Richard spun around, the red of his face draining out, replaced with a deathly white. "Do you not hear me?" His voice had already lost much of its gusto.

Instead of answering, one after another the soldiers dropped to one knee and dipped their heads. Just a few at first, a shield-bearer near the front, a few archers in the back, but each man or woman who kneeled convinced two more to do the same. When

The King of the Vile

the entire army knelt in respect, Azariah clapped his hands, pleased.

"They will not die for you," he told the lord. "They will only watch you die. Ezekai, reward Richard for his pride."

Richard fled, but he barely made it past the first rank of soldiers before the angel grabbed him by his collar and flung him to the dirt. The lord sobbed hysterically, all while hurling curses at his former soldiers. Ezekai drew his sword and cut him in half, putting a thankful end to the blubbering. Azariah pointed to Ezekai, though the act was hardly necessary. All eyes were already on the angel who'd slain their lord.

"The angel before you is Ezekai, a trusted servant of Ashhur," he said. "He will now command your forces. Mordeina is still a nest of filth, and we will need your help to flush out the rats."

Ezekai bowed to Azariah in appreciation, then ordered the humans to begin dismantling their camp. Pleased by the day's progress, Azariah turned to Judarius.

"Come," he said. "We have a second army to find."

Azariah had kept constant surveillance on the armies from Mordan and Ker, and he knew their clash had resulted in a stalemate that cost both sides dearly. Azariah expected King Bram Henley to flee to safety after such losses, but he'd had only a few days to gain ground on foot. Compared to their wings, it'd be a matter of hours.

They returned to the well-worn trade road and followed it south. Azariah used the time to dwell on the past five years, viewing things through newly opened eyes. The laws and practices of men had failed. Releasing the guilty regardless of their sin, so long as they repented, allowed a weak faith to blossom. Feelings of guilt didn't last, Azariah realized. It only prevented the appropriate punishment. Scars, death, those could never be undone. They'd let grow beneath their feet an unruly, ungracious nation where guilty sinners repeated their sins, spitting in the face of those who granted them mercy.

When Ashhur cast them into his shadow, Azariah had been on the verge of building a new kingdom that would have fixed this. It would have conveyed the serious nature of sin to the weak believers. It would have removed the thorns that grew among the flowers. He'd seen the flaws in the current system years ago, and begun planning accordingly. He'd learned magic from Roand the Flame, and made deals with the Council to procure their help. Mankind would never accept the rule of angels while they floated above them in Avlimar, nor would his fellow angels understand how great a divide existed between them and the mortals until forced to live among their kind. Crashing Avlimar to the ground, casting blame onto Deathmask, having Judarius execute Thomas, it all had been leading up to the eventually taking of power away from humans and placing it into the hands of far better, wiser rulers: themselves.

And then Ashhur betrayed them.

Azariah felt his rage blossom anew. They declared mankind not fit to rule themselves, and demanded they follow Ashhur's laws instead of their own. That was worth abandonment? That was what their god believed? Most angels were Wardens, and had been since the beginning. They were meant to guide mankind, to lead them...and then they were cast low for doing what they were made to do.

Azariah felt a shiver run through him as the land passed beneath in a gray blur. Both Karak and Ashhur were imperfect pieces of the whole god they once were. Perhaps once split, and lacking the balance and concepts of the other pieces, they could not fully understand the puzzle that was mankind. Such thoughts were beyond blasphemous, but it explained so much. It explained why Ashhur could not reconcile the wisdom of Azariah's path. It explained why Karak would sacrifice life itself to reach true order. Imperfect pieces, needing to be united...

Judarius flew closer, drawing him from his thoughts. The angel didn't need to say anything, for Azariah quickly spotted the army of Mordan marching upon the wide road like a winding snake. Banking upward to slow his speed, he spread his wings and took in the scene. By his estimate, King Bram had less than half of his original seven thousand soldiers he'd marched over the Bloodbrick with. A pitiful amount. Even at full strength, did the king truly think he could have assaulted the walls of Mordeina? Or perhaps he thought the people would rejoice and throw open the

– doors, eager for the man who had disavowed all gods to save them from Ashhur's control?

Sickness squirming in his stomach, Azariah felt that a likely possibility. Better to be ruled by a man desiring only obedience than a god that demanded improvement and self-sacrifice. Perhaps that was humanity's greatest flaw. They would willingly shackle themselves so long as the jailor told them their sins were not sins at all.

"Be ready," Azariah shouted to Judarius. "I will extend the same offer as before, but I do not expect the people of Ker to kneel, nor abandon their king."

"Will we kill them all if they refuse?" Judarius asked. "The Council will not be pleased."

Azariah frowned. He'd promised the Council of Mages they'd have a land of their own. When first working with Roand, he'd believed that achieving salvation for the people of Mordan was worth the loss of controlling Ker. Saving the entire world was impossible, so why not cede the loss to achieve some measure of good? That was just one of many compromises that had steadily eroded their dedication. The land of Ker needed to be subjugated just as much as Mordan. This meant her army, and her king, needed to pledge loyalty or be destroyed. The wizards would be dangerous foes, but they needn't know of their expendability yet. If asked, Azariah would say the destruction of Bram's army opened the way for the Council's takeover of the nation. There would be no lie in that.

"The Council is still one of humans," Azariah said. "And we are done fearing what humans say or do."

Azariah dove, slamming down on the road with a heavy thud. Judarius took position beside him. Soldiers rushed about, readying for battle, as the other fallen angels hovered around them in a circle.

"Fetch me your king, for I would have words with him!" Azariah cried.

The soldiers continued forming up shoulder-to-shoulder so they might not be ambushed from any side. Azariah expected the king and queen to be hiding among their numbers, and he wondered if Bram would have the courage to face him. The human soldiers whispered to one another, yet as a minute dragged on, it seemed Azariah was no closer to receiving an audience.

"Your king!" he shouted again. "Bram Henley, master of Angkar, come forth so we might discuss terms."

"I have terms for you," a soldier shouted from behind the front lines. Men shifted aside so an older man in shining platemail and sporting a gray beard pushed to the front. He held a spear in one hand and a shield in the other. By the markings on his chestplate, Azariah guessed him to be one of Bram's generals.

"And what might those be?" Azariah asked, annoyed.

"Just what my king has ordered me to tell you," he said.

"And what might that be?"

"In his words?" The older man grinned. "Fuck yourselves and die."

The man hoisted his spear and then threw it in a single, smooth motion. Azariah fell back a step, caught off guard and unable to defend himself. The spear sailed true, its aim for Azariah's heart, but it did not pierce his flesh. Judarius's mace swung with perfect timing, smacking the spear upward so that it careened wildly away. The nearby soldiers roared as they charged, but both Judarius and Azariah soared skyward, out of their reach. Arrows followed, ripping through the air on either side. Azariah's heart pounded as he flew faster, faster, ignoring how close the wild shots came. One even struck Judarius's armor, but it could not punch through the enchanted plate.

Without an order to attack, the other angels surrounding the army fled as well. Azariah spun about once out of reach of the arrows and glared at the bodies of several of his brethren lying bloodied in the grass. The soldiers cheered and struck their weapons and shields together, mocking them for their cowardice.

"How have you not yet learned?" Judarius asked him. "Humanity is never, ever to be trusted."

Azariah glared down at the cheering soldiers. "Destroy them all."

"They deserve no less," Judarius replied, smacking the head of his mace against his palm.

The angel reared back, sucked in air, and then bellowed his command to the entirety of the Fallen.

The King of the Vile

"Dive!"

The angels soared together, black wings and gleaming swords streaming toward the soldiers like rampaging floodwaters. They could have crashed through the outer lines of shields, but they had no need to. They were no normal army. Battle lines meant nothing. The angels flashed overhead, enduring another barrage of arrows, and then rammed into the archers. Man's blood flowed like a river. The footmen tried to turn their attention inward, but Judarius led a segment of two hundred angels from the inner ranks and back around to the outer. His mace smashed through armored men like they were naked children.

The sounds of death and battle echoed in Azariah's ears. Before, it'd been a sound that made his chest tighten and his head light. Now it was strangely muted and distant. Pleasant, Azariah dared admit, like chimes. Hands curling into formations, Azariah decided to join in the fight. Ashhur's priestly magic might have left him, but the arcane powers Roand the Flame had taught him remained.

A ball of fire leapt from Azariah's hands and slammed into a formation of soldiers rushing from the east flank in hopes of aiding against Judarius's push through the center. The men screamed as flames bathed them. Azariah felt satisfaction at the size of the explosion, and he sent a second toward different portion of the battle, careful to avoid injuring his own kind. After fire came stone; he ripped up boulders from the ground beneath soldiers so they fell into the holes, only to then have the stones settle back atop them, sealing them into airless tombs.

It all came so easily to Azariah, and always had, even back when the world was young and he called the Eveningstar his friend. He wished he'd studied more back then. He'd taken Ashhur's grace for granted, but now that it was gone, he finally realized the biggest difference between priestly spellcasting and the arcane. To cast such spells before, Azariah had to whisper words of prayers to Ashhur. He came as a beggar before his god, hands outstretched, hoping to have power given to him so he might destroy his foes or heal the flesh of his allies. But with the arcane, he wasn't a beggar, but a king. By his strength, he took the power he envisioned. Even the words and hand formations were not necessary. They only aided in the demand, for it was the strength of soul that mattered. Much of it was an art, and while the mages painted in rudimentary colors, Azariah had glimpsed the entire spectrum over centuries in eternal glory.

Rivulets of flame raced through the battle lines, guided by Azariah's weaving fingers. Cracks burst open in the ground, hands of molten rock grasped men and dragged them to their deaths. Besieged from all sides, some of Ker's soldiers tried to flee, but they could not run faster than the angels could fly. Some fell to their knees, begging for mercy or swearing fealty, but they could not take back their initial rebellion. Azariah swooped overhead, shards of ice flying from his palms like a hailstorm. He felt like Ashhur in the earliest days of Dezrel, when mankind was but dust in jars of clay.

The sounds of battle faded away. The carnage ceased, for there were no more soldiers to kill. Only a small group remained in the heart of the battlefield, and Azariah hovered over them warily. By their black armor and burning blades, they were clearly paladins of Karak. Eight of them gathered around King Bram, protecting him against any attack by the angels. Azariah knew he could stay airborne, casting magical attacks of fire and ice until the paladins lacked the strength to defend themselves, but he didn't.

Azariah's eyes had opened to many things over the past years, allowing him to see the paladins of Karak in a whole new light.

He landed before the group, keeping a safe distance in case they refused to listen to reason. The paladins readied their weapons, bunching tightly together in anticipation of battle. Azariah looked them over, surprised by their youth. In the times before the first Gods' War, when injury and disease were abolished by the Wardens' constant care, he'd have considered them nothing more than children. Yet here these children were, wielding powerful weapons bathed in fire as hot as their faith.

"Who among you may speak for the rest?" Azariah asked.

"I may, if we must," one said. He had a freckled, scarred face, and two lion tattoos on his neck.

"And who are you?"

The King of the Vile

"Umber," said the paladin. "And stay back unless you want an ax in your gut. You may be uglier than we remember, but you're still angels of Ashhur, bloodthirsty ones at that."

Azariah lifted his hands to show he meant no harm.

"I only seek words," he said. "Are you willing to listen?"

Umber glanced around at the thousands of angels hovering about, watching. Sweat trickled down his forehead and neck, but despite his obvious nervousness, he kept himself together well enough.

"If you bring words instead of swords, then we're willing to listen," Umber said.

Azariah nodded. He felt oddly hopeful, despite the supposed impossibility he knew he was about to propose. Ever since Karak and Ashhur warred, so had their followers. Centuries of conflict, all stemming from that defining moment when Celestia flung both gods into the eternal void, imprisoning them in their respective domains. But Azariah remembered the days when he'd been a mere Warden. He remembered when loving one god did not make you an enemy of the other's followers.

"There was a time when Karak and Ashhur were brothers," he said. "When they worked together in search of a way of life for mankind that would result in peace without slavery, happiness without perversion, and wealth without suffering. Those times may come again, if only you are willing to listen and learn just as we have allowed ourselves to learn."

Umber still seemed wary, but the ax in his hands wasn't lifted quite so high, nor clutched so tightly. "And what lesson might you angels have learned?"

What lesson? Only one, which he'd learned as he came upon a heartbroken Ezekai outside the remains of the slaughtered village of Norstrom.

"No matter the lessons we offer or how many laws we create, mankind will still be sinful creatures," said Azariah. "That sin wears on us like nails clawing the length of our spines. Sin is an act of selfish rebellion. A chaotic act against a natural order, Karak might say. My kind endured the sin out of need to save the sinner, but that cost us dearly. We need peace. *Dezrel* needs peace. And there is only one way to find peace in this broken world." Azariah smiled. "Emptiness. In absolute emptiness, we may find peace."

"And in absolute emptiness, we may find order," Umber said. He lowered his ax and offered his hand in friendship. "Perhaps you are right, and there is still wisdom we may share."

Azariah shook his hand, and he couldn't help but feel proud. In a single day, he'd healed the rift Ashhur and Karak had created. In a single day, he'd proven himself more capable than the gods they followed. The dark paladins stepped aside, making open the way to King Bram. The man stood tall, blade drawn, unafraid of his impending death. It didn't seem an act, either. *Impressive.*

"My wife yet lives," Bram said as Azariah approached. "Riding on my fastest horse toward Ker. She'll rally my people. Every man, woman, and child capable of lifting a weapon will tear at your wings and cut at your flesh. We will not submit to Ashhur, nor his abandoned followers."

Bram swung his sword. Azariah caught Bram's wrist before the blade connected. Azariah's other hand grabbed the king by the throat and lifted him into the air.

"They will submit, or they will die," Azariah said. "The same choice offered to kings and beggars alike. A fair offer, and a fair punishment. Let your nation resist, Bram. We'll burn it to ashes if we must and start anew. Time means nothing to us...and nor do your impotent threats."

Bram's free hand pulled at Azariah's, trying to loosen the grip enough to breathe, but he was too weak. Azariah stared into the king's eyes, never blinking, never relenting. He watched the life dwindle away, that precious spark fading into deathly stillness. A life of temptation and selfishness ending, an imprisoned soul breaking free of its tattered, sinful shell to find peace in the hereafter. Beautiful. Just beautiful.

Azariah tossed the worthless bag of flesh and bone to the ground.

"These are grand days," he told the paladins of Karak. "The future of Dezrel is in our hands. Let us rebuild Paradise like it was before war tore it asunder. Let us build it wiser, and stronger, so it may withstand the ages. A land ruled not by sinful creatures, but the gods and their servants. A righteous land. An orderly land."

Umber put his fist to his breast and bowed, and all other paladins bowed with him.

"To Paradise reborn," he said.

"To Paradise reborn," Azariah echoed, and he smiled.

A paradise reborn...and ruled by a crown of bone.

28

Tarlak's portal opened in the grasslands twenty miles away from the two towers, but it wasn't far enough. He'd prefer to be all the way in Mordeina, but that required energy he simply didn't have. Twenty miles was nothing to mages using locator magic. So as Deathmask lay on his back in the grass, Tarlak scrawled a few quick runes into the dirt with a stick, cast a spell over them, and then plopped onto his rear.

"What do you think?" he said. "Hide out here for a month or two, then go storming back and rip those damn towers to apart brick by brick?"

"Sure," Deathmask said, arm over his eyes. "I might need more time, though. The Council's going to the bottom of a very long list of people I need to skin alive, starting with Azariah."

Tarlak frowned at the mention of the angel. Roand had claimed he worked with Azariah to bring Avlimar crashing to the ground. He'd expected to miss a few things while trapped in the towers, but that one seemed like a doozy.

"Roand and Azariah working together," he said. "Care to help me make sense of that?"

Deathmask sighed and sat up. Black circles surrounded his eyes. Tarlak doubted he'd gotten any sort of restful sleep while chained to the wall. Still, given all Tarlak had done to get him out of there, it only felt fair to get a few answers before they both passed out for the night.

"It happened not long after Antonil's army was crushed," Deathmask said. "I have a feeling the Council had a hand in that. Would I be right?"

"Absolutely. Bastards bombarded us with magic as we approached the tower seeking aid."

The King of the Vile

"Why go to them for aid?"

Tarlak sighed.

"Because we had our asses handed to us by an orc army led by a war demon. When we reached Ker's border, King Bram refused to let us cross. At the time, I thought he was being an opportunistic jerk, but given Roand's plans of taking over Ker, I wouldn't be surprised if Bram was being manipulated by the Council in some way."

"That answers a few questions," Deathmask said, his eyes glazing over as he thought. "During Gregory's crowning ceremony, Avlimar came tumbling to the ground. Not an angel was there due to the ceremony, a convenient little fact I should have noticed far sooner. I always thought it was so whatever magic necessary to destroy it could be cast in secret, but obviously it was because Azariah didn't wish to lose any of his people."

Tarlak drummed foreign fingers against his kneecap. "You said Gregory's crowning ceremony. I'd feared Kevin Maryll would attempt to usurp the throne when the Council betrayed us. Did he?"

"Yes."

"And Queen Susan died in the attempt?"

"Unfortunately. Susan's death elevated Gregory to the throne, at least in theory." He chuckled, the glazed look vanishing from his eyes. "And yes, Harruq and Aurelia both survived just fine, in case you were worried about that. Harruq even cut off Kevin's head and tossed it out a castle window. You know, sometimes that half-orc knows how to do a display just right."

Tarlak let out a sigh of relief despite immediately feeling guilty about it. Susan had always been kind, and surprisingly accepting of Antonil's odd collection of friends. Losing her was terrible, but he couldn't deny his relief at knowing his friends had survived. Tarlak had lost enough people close to him to fill a dozen lifetimes, and the last thing he wanted was to add more to the list.

"I can piece together most everything else," Tarlak said. "Though I'm curious, why did the angels capture you?"

"Azariah blamed me for Avlimar's collapse."

"You? But why?"

Deathmask shrugged.

"I guess I have a guilty face."

"Yeah," he said, wincing. "Sorry about that, by the way."

The guildmaster chuckled, his smile stretching the worn, wrinkled scars across his mouth, cheeks, and jaw.

"At least my face is still my own," he said. "The same cannot be said of you."

Tarlak laughed. "I spent the past few weeks focusing on polymorphic studies just for such an occasion. Give me a few days. I'll be my old self again, or at least a fairly close approximation of it."

"Excellent," Deathmask said He settled down into the grass. "Speaking of a few days, that is how much I would like to rest. Wake me come morning so that doesn't happen."

"Will do."

Tarlak removed his hat to use as a pillow, and then lay down on his side. Not the finest of beds, and nothing compared to the ridiculous softness of his mattresses in the towers, but Tarlak felt himself relaxing better than he had in weeks. No burning amulet clung his neck, chaining him against his will. No more wondering when he might ever see his friends again. Come the morning, he'd rip open a portal to Mordeina, march right up those castle steps, and wrap the Tun couple in a gigantic bear hug.

Granted, he might want to explain his new form first...

Tarlak woke with a splitting headache and an aching stomach. Grimacing, he pulled his knees to his chest and tried to go back to peaceful dreams where he suffered neither ailment. Maddeningly, a toe poked into his back.

"You were supposed to be the one waking me up, remember?"

Tarlak groaned as he rolled over. His eyes fluttered open. Deathmask hovered over him, arms crossed, scarred lips locked in a frown.

"I beg your forgiveness," Tarlak mumbled. "By chance you find us anything to eat?"

"The sun's barely risen. Did you think I caught, killed, skinned, and cooked a rabbit for you during that time?"

The King of the Vile

Tarlak reached into an inner pocket, but the robes weren't actually his. This meant no hidden stash of topaz, which meant no whipping himself up a simple meal with a few wags of his fingers.

"Well, I know exactly where in Mordeina I'll be taking us," he said, envisioning the open air marketplace in the eastern district. Stumbling to his feet, he shook his hands and twisted his neck in an attempt to clear his head. Casting a portal over such distances wouldn't be easy, and the last thing he wanted was to make a mistake and send both them to a random location, or even worse, right into the middle of something solid like a mountain.

"Roand mentioned the angels ruling Mordan," Deathmask said as Tarlak prepared the portal. "Gregory might have already been overthrown. If that is the case, the city may not be safe for either of us."

"Caution may be your thing," Tarlak said as the portal ripped open before him. "But I'm more of a 'bust in and blow things up' kind of guy. The angels want to capture either of us, they're welcome to try. Besides, I'm hungry, damn it."

Tarlak stepped through. He'd focused on the rooftop of a home beside the market, a place he figured would be safely concealed and bereft of people. When he stepped out, he moved aside so Deathmask didn't bump into him, then turned toward the market. Before Deathmask could even appear next to him, Tarlak already knew something was wrong.

"What happened here?" he wondered aloud.

On any given day over two hundred people should have been walking through the lengthy street, browsing the dozens of tables. There should have been the smell of cheeses, pastries, and fresh bread, all arrayed on plates and cloths. The sun was low in the sky, and many would need to eat prior to heading off for their daily labors.

Only there was no one here.

"Clearly we missed something," Deathmask said. The portal hissed shut behind him. "A rebellion of the angels?"

"Perhaps," Tarlak said. He snapped his fingers and stepped off the roof, gently floating down to the center of the barren street. Deathmask hung from the side of the roof before dropping onto his feet. Tarlak wandered down the road, the pain in his stomach growing worse. Many of the tables were overturned the stalls trashed. A stone wall sealed in the market to the right, but on the left were many buildings tucked behind the stalls, and Tarlak saw a quarter of them were damaged in some way. A few had broken windows or holes smashed into their thatched roofs; almost every one of them had a door that hung off its hinges.

Most frightening of all was the blood. There were thick puddles of it, splashes of red on walls, and long streaks upon the road as if someone had been dragged along it.

"Tar, over here."

Tarlak turned to see Deathmask standing before the post of a particularly large stall that had escaped damage. He hurried over, eyes narrowing as he saw a thick piece of parchment nailed to the post. Tarlak ripped it free of the nail.

"What is this?" he asked.

"The Laws of Ashhur," Deathmask said. He glanced up and down the street. "I don't know if you sense it, Tarlak, but I do. The essence of death lingers about here like a plague, strong enough for a necromancer to get drunk on. Look at the blood in the streets. It's like the Abyss came to visit Mordeina in the middle of the night."

Tarlak read the first few laws. Do not steal. Do not rape. Do not worship Karak. At 'do not murder' he crumpled the parchment up and tossed it into a drying puddle of blood.

"Seems like someone's not paying attention to their own damn laws," he said. "This is bad, possibly very bad. We need answers."

Deathmask waved a hand to the cobblestones.

"Then we follow the blood."

The smeared tracks were easy enough to follow. Tarlak kept his eyes open for any sign of human life, but the market was home only to a few rats and buzzing flies. Surely if they moved closer to the residential districts they'd have better luck. The idea that a city of thousands could be dead was too mortifying to consider.

The market ended at a main street running north to south. The blood smears turned north. *So much blood.* Tarlak followed it, wincing at the pungent smell that assaulted his nose.

"That's what I think it is, isn't it?" he asked.

The King of the Vile

"I fear so."

It took another minute of walking down the eerily quiet street before reaching a junction. The smell grew stronger, nearly overwhelming in its power. The blood smears turned left, and Tarlak's fears were confirmed.

There had to be at least two hundred bodies piled atop one another in the center of the road. Those near the bottom were an indecipherable mess of gore and rot, while those at the top sprawled out, skin pale, eyes milky in death. A rickety cart was parked beside the pile, four bodies atop it waiting to be dumped. Several men stood beside the cart, working together to lift the corpses and toss them upon the pile. They wore cloths over their faces against the stench, but given how strong the reek was, Tarlak assumed it didn't help much.

"Hey," Tarlak shouted, giving the corpses a wide berth as he rushed around. "Hey, who did this? Who's responsible for this?"

The men watched his approach with dead eyes. It gave Tarlak the chills.

"The angels," one of them said. "How could you not know?"

"We only recently arrived," Deathmask said. "What caused this? Why would angels massacre so many?"

The men clammed up, their eyes lingering on something behind Tarlak, and he felt his chills worsening. Leaving them to their work, he turned about to see an winged monster standing atop one of the nearby buildings, arms crossed over his chest. His skin was ashen, his robes dull, his breastplate the color of bone, his wings dark as ink. His lips parted to reveal broken teeth sharp as knives. It was an angel...but it wasn't.

"Go about your work," the angel said. "If you are new here, heed the laws of Ashhur, for they are now..."

He paused, as if seeing Deathmask's scars for the first time.

"You," he said, drawing his sword from its sheath.

"Me," Deathmask said,

Several bruises swelled across the angel's exposed arms. They deepened in color, from green to purple, and then exploded with showers of blood. Tarlak knew such a spell could devastate a man if given enough power, but Deathmask didn't have that power to give, nor was the angel a normal man. Though he'd had a night to rest after his ordeal at the hands of Roand, Deathmask was still far from recovered. Spreading his black wings, the angel dove toward them, sword leading.

Tarlak shoved Deathmask to the side and rolled. The sword drove into the street, easily breaking the cobblestones. Coming up from his roll, Tarlak weaved his hands through the air, fingers hooking into the proper shapes. Ice flew from his palms in a flood, forming a curved wall between them and the angel. Tarlak prepared a blast of lightning, expecting the angel to fly over. Instead, he shattered the ice with a single swing of his sword and lunged forward with a burst of wings.

Panicking, Tarlak brought his focus back to the ground and enacted his prepared lightning spell. It struck the pale angel in the center of his bone chestplate with enough force to slow, but not halt, his momentum. Bleeding and screaming, the angel slammed into Tarlak with his shoulder. Tarlak hit the ground, head striking stone hard enough to make his vision swim. The angel towered over him, sword raised to swing.

Shadows swarmed up from the ground, taking the shape of six-fingered hands. They did no harm, only grabbed at the angel's legs and arms, holding him in place. Tarlak dared not waste his opportunity. He closed his eyes and prayed he said the right syllables. Fire leapt off his hands in a great torrent. When he opened his eyes, he saw the angel had slumped to his side, his pale skin burned and bubbling, his arms bleeding from the open wounds Deathmask had given him. Shadow hands clutched his wrists and ankles, preventing him from rising.

"Make it quick," Deathmask said. He knelt beside the angel, bracing himself with one hand while the other was outstretched and shimmering purple. "I can't hold him long."

Tarlak looked at the twisted angel, who writhed and screamed in pain. The image was so surreal, it felt like something from a dream. No. Not a dream. One of Karak's nightmares. Wishing to hear no more, he flung a shard of ice at the angel's head. It punched through his temple, immediately ceasing all movement. His arms went slack, his final death rattle rumbled through drooping lips.

The King of the Vile

Deathmask let out a gasp as he released his spell and banished the shadows. Tarlak saw that the men who'd been stacking the bodies had long fled. Knowing they needed to get out of sight before they were spotted, Tarlak grabbed Deathmask by the arm and pulled him to his feet.

"What in Karak's maggot-infested armpit is going on here?" Tarlak wondered aloud as they ducked into a slender alley.

"Is it not obvious?" Deathmask said, slumping against a wall. "Ashhur has turned his back on his former servants. Whatever we fight isn't angels, but the bitter, angry remnants of what they once were."

"Pleasant," Tarlak said, scanning the skies for more. "So what do we do?"

"I don't know what *you'll* do," Deathmask said, "but I know my path. Veliana was here in Mordeina when all this transpired. I need to make sure she's all right."

"Do you know where she is?"

Deathmask shook his head. "She's protected against scrying, which means I must find her the old-fashioned way. We had a few safe havens set up for emergencies, and I daresay this counts."

"Are you sure she's even alive?" Tarlak asked.

"I am," Deathmask said. "She survived this purge, I am sure of it. Sad as it is, we've endured worse."

Tarlak wished he could argue otherwise, but both men had suffered the flight from Veldaren. He offered his hand to Deathmask, who after a moment's reluctance, accepted it and shook.

"Are you sure you want to stay?" he asked.

"I will not abandon Veliana to this shit-hole," Deathmask said. "Besides, Azariah's pissed me off. He's about to discover I have a long history of being thorns in people's sides, and never before have I been quite so...motivated."

The way he said it gave Tarlak a chill. "Good luck then," he said, pulling back his hand. "I have my own friends to find."

Deathmask saluted with two fingers, then staggered down the alley on unsteady legs. Tarlak turned his back so he didn't have to watch him go. He had a bad feeling in his gut. Even though the leader of the Ash Guild had endured a thousand trials, Tarlak feared that in a broken city filled with broken angels, he might find his end.

Putting such somber thoughts out of his head, Tarlak focused on his scrying spell. It disappointed him a little bit how easily he located Harruq, somewhere fifteen miles to the south of Mordeina. Aurelia should have cast spells of protection against such a simple spell. Granted, she likely didn't realize the Council was allied with the angels. That, or she'd not survived the night...

Recasting the scrying spell for Aurelia, he quickly found her mere feet away from Harruq, and he breathed a sigh of relief.

"Need to stop doing that to myself," he muttered, then cast a teleportation spell, all too eager to put the city of Mordeina behind him.

When he reappeared, he found himself at the edge of a small village. Several hundred people gathered in tight groups throughout, a few still asleep. Their faces were haggard, their eyes red from crying. Directly before Tarlak was a burning campfire. All around it, sitting on cut logs or tall stones, were his Eschaton.

Harruq sat beside Aurelia, little Gregory bouncing on his knee. His twin swords leaned against the log he sat on, both sheathed. Aurelia's beautiful green dress was stained with blood, but she herself seemed unharmed. Jerico and Lathaar sat opposite them, wearing only their leather under armor, their plate lying on a blanket behind them. Qurrah sat on the grass beside his brother, head resting on his chin, burning whip dormant as it curled around his left arm. Next to him was Tessanna, little Aubrienna cuddling in her lap as the black-eyed woman softly sang to her. Tears swelled in Tarlak's eyes. All alive. All together. How long had it been since they gathered in such a way?

Of course, appearing out of nowhere behind them with a teleportation spell while looking like Cecil Towerborn didn't garner him the welcome he might have normally received. Harruq spotted him first, and he leapt off his log while grabbing one of his swords and ripping it out of its sheath. Poor Gregory rolled and fell onto his stomach from Harruq's frenzied reaction, and he began to cry.

"Who the abyss are you?" Harruq asked. He shoved the tip of his sword at Tarlak's neck.

"It's me, Tarlak," he said, lifting his hands in surrender.

"Tarlak?" Harruq asked, looking baffled. "Tarlak's dead, so if you're claiming to be him, you better have a damn good way to prove it."

"No one else is crazy enough to wear yellow robes like this," Tarlak said, and he pointed past the half-orc's shoulder. "And Jerico and Lathaar over there can tell you immediately that I'm not lying about being Tarlak, nor the whole 'wearing yellow' part, either."

Harruq spared a glance over his shoulder, and he visibly relaxed at the sight of the two paladins laughing.

"Praise Ashhur," Jerico said. "It's our crazy wizard, back from the grave."

Quick as he'd grabbed his sword, Harruq dropped it and wrapped Tarlak in an enormous hug that nearly strangled the air from his lungs.

"Don't you ever, ever do that again," Harruq said when he finally released him. Tarlak staggered a bit as he recovered his balance, and he grinned at the half-orc.

"I have no plans on it," he said.

Aurelia was next, gently wrapping her slender arms around his neck as Harruq scooped Gregory up and began calming him down.

"I assume you have a story to tell us?" she said.

"I'm sure you have one for me as well, but both can wait for now," Tarlak said as he kneeled down before Aubrienna. The girl pressed herself harder against Tessanna's breast and frowned at him from the corner of her eye. Realizing words would not convince someone so young as Aubby, he cast a quick illusion spell.

"I'll work on making this real later," he said as his voice changed. Aubrienna's eyes stopped seeing Cecil but instead saw Tarlak's old face and hair. "But until then, this should do. Recognize me now, Aubby?"

"Uncle Tar!" the girl shouted, flinging herself at him. Tarlak laughed as she buried herself in his arms, laughed even as he cried.

"Why were you wearing such a funny face?" she asked him.

"Uncle Tar was trying to be silly," Tarlak said, struggling not to sniffle. "He won't do it again, I promise."

He accepted another hug, kissed her forehead, and then let her go back to Tessanna. After embraces from both of the paladins, Tarlak slumped beside the campfire, cracked his knuckles, and addressed the group as if nothing had changed since their times together in his old stone tower outside Veldaren.

"So," he said. "What's the plan?"

"That's just what we were discussing," Qurrah said. "Before your...interruption."

"I do what I can. Made any decisions yet?"

Lathaar cleared his throat.

"Forming a resistance against the fallen angels shouldn't be difficult, not after the travesty they committed last night. Still, given Ker's invasion and the petty rivalries between lords, there's a risk it will devolve into a mad scramble to acquire power, splitting Mordan completely instead of unifying it into a single army."

"Which means little Gregory here may be incredibly important," Jerico added. "Gregory is still king, no matter what pompous statement Azariah makes. So long as he lives, we can focus everyone's energy on a single cause: the return of the rightful king to his throne. That's something we can rally people behind. It may even sway lords who have pledge allegiance to Azariah out of fear for their safety."

"It sounds sensible enough," Qurrah said. He wrapped an arm around Tessanna as she leaned against him. "It'll take time to discover everyone's loyalties, so we'll need to act quickly to learn who is friend and who is foe. My question is how do we protect Gregory? The angels will be hunting for him, and when assassins can come from the sky, I fear nowhere will be safe. Even those we consider friends may betray his location to the angels for potential reward."

"I know of one place," Lathaar said. "We bring him to the Citadel."

The moment he made the suggestion, Tarlak knew it'd come to pass. Hiding Gregory in the bastion of Ashhur's power, a thick-walled tower where the angels' wings would mean nothing and no

The King of the Vile

one within would betray or kill him? As close to perfect as they'd find in the insanity that was Mordan.

"I've got no objections there," Harruq said. "What do we do about the army of the vile that's crossed the Gihon and into the northern lands?"

"Ahaesarus flew out to fight them," Aurelia said. "Perhaps he and the angels with him avoided the punishment that befell the others."

"Wait," Tarlak said. "Army of the vile? Care to fill me in?"

The half-orc shook his head. "Another time, Tarlak. You still have your own story to tell."

"Fine," Tarlak said, and he clucked his tongue. "Be that way."

The two paladins rose to their feet, once more clapping Tarlak on the back and shoulder.

"We need to see to the wounded," Lathaar said. "We'll also do what we can to keep spirits high. Any rebellion against the angels is going to be bloody. We can't afford to lose a single soul to despair."

Tarlak waved at them, then turned his attention to Harruq.

"This won't be as simple as a fight against the angels," he said, lowering his voice. "The Council of Mages has been working with Azariah for some time now, teaching him magic in return for the promise that he would hand them Ker. I have zero doubt that they'll interfere with this war, finding some way to turn it to their advantage. At the very least, they'll take over Ker's government while King Bram is away."

Harruq rubbed at his eyes.

"We have enemies in the north, enemies in the capital, and now mages working with an army marching from the south. I'm not sure this could get worse."

"Sure it could," Tarlak said, grinning. "I could still be dead. That sounds way worse."

He plopped down beside Harruq and draped an arm over his broad shoulders.

"Think of it this way," he said. "We've killed prophets, gods, demons, and dragons. What chance do a few measly fallen angels have? We'll kick Azariah's ass, defeat whoever the abyss is in the north, and then stomp any mage dumb enough to challenge the trio of Qurrah, Tarlak, and Tess to a magical fight. War over. Crack open some wine barrels, it's time to celebrate."

Harruq smiled. He seemed to appreciate the attempt at cheering him up. Setting Gregory down, Harruq took the boy's hand in one and Aurelia's in the other.

"Come on, Aubby," he said. "Let's go grab something to eat now that everyone else has had a chance."

Aubrienna accepted a hug from Tessanna, then leapt to her feet and ran to Aurelia's side, taking her waiting hand. Tarlak watched the couple head into town, and he let out a sigh.

"Things are far more dire than you let on," Qurrah said once they were gone.

"Always the observant one, aren't you?" Tarlak muttered. "Any one of the masters at the Council is a dangerous foe. If they focus their collective attention on any one thing?" He shook his head. "Let's just say if that happens, I'll be glad to have a daughter of balance on our side."

Something about the way Qurrah looked at him worried Tarlak that his confidence in Tessanna might not be so valid.

"Perhaps," Qurrah said. He turned to his wife, who stared north, toward the distant speck that was the capital city of Mordeina. Her lips quivered, and her hands trembled in her lap. Tarlak frowned, confused, but it seemed Qurrah understood.

"You hear it, don't you?" Qurrah asked.

Tessanna slowly nodded her head.

"Hear what?" Tarlak asked.

The half-orc lovingly brushed Tessanna's face with his fingers, then brought his attention back to Tarlak.

"Not what," he said. "But who. Ashhur's entire creation has fallen. His attempts at peace have broken into warfare. His loving servants have slaughtered innocents in a night of black wings. Any priest or follower who speaks of Ashhur's love will have fields of corpses as evidence to deny that love."

Tarlak reached for the pendant of Ashhur he wore around his neck out of instinct, but it was gone, missing ever since he'd been nearly killed during the ambush at the towers.

"Ashhur," he said softly. "You hear him weeping."

Tessanna stood, dark hair falling about her like a shroud. She turned her deep black eyes Tarlak's way, and he felt naked before them, as he always had since she first set foot in his tower.

"No," she said. "Not Ashhur. I don't hear Ashhur. I doubt I ever will."

She stepped closer, brushing her hand through the illusion to touch the face that had once been Cecil Towerborn's.

"Hear for yourself," Tessanna whispered. Her magic flowed into him, and he saw the land turn to shadow, felt his ears open to a realm not of physical matter, nor of magic, but of gods. And in this echo of that world, Tarlak heard. The sound filled his heart with hatred and ignited his blood with a passion to prove every damn syllable wrong. To prove what they'd done had meant something. That it wasn't a joke. Wasn't a failure.

Karak, down in his Abyss, laughing.

Laughing.

Epilogue

Azariah soared over the quiet streets of Mordeina on his way to the castle, his mood remarkably improved since he last left it. The remaining army of Mordan had pledged allegiance, the capital city was solidly in their control, and a weakened Ker now lacked a king, and therefore any realistic chance of challenging them during the tumultuous early years of establishing Ashhur's rule. Even Karak's paladins seemed willing to work with him to cull chaos from the land. Such a momentous day, how could he not smile?

But Azariah didn't smile. Smiling stretched his lips across his jagged teeth and made them bleed. Still, it was a good reminder not to take joy in his accomplishments, not when so much remained to be done. Today alone still carried one last difficult task he must perform...

"May we talk?" Judarius asked, flying beside him.

"Of course," Azariah said. "Follow me inside."

He dove to the castle steps and lightly landed on his feet. Blood still covered the steps, but the corpses of both men and angels were gone. Judarius landed beside him, and he cast a disdainful look at the quiet stone structure.

"Why come here?" he asked. "Let us rule from Devlimar and make petitioners come to us."

"Mankind needs their symbols," Azariah said. "This castle has been the seat of power in Mordan since we were mere Wardens. I shall meet the public here, as well as release commandments and appoint advisors. This will ease the transition." The angel smirked. "Besides, I will not have mankind walking through the streets of glorious Devlimar. They are not worthy."

The King of the Vile

Azariah stepped through the grand doors, which were shattered from battle. Inside the castle was surprisingly peaceful. Azariah walked across the soft carpet, taking in the grandeur of the high columns, lengthy curtains, and open spaces. He'd thought coming here each day to manage the kingdom would wear on him, but now the prospect didn't seem so terrible. It wasn't that the architecture was impressive, not compared to the infinite spirals of silver and gold that decorated Devlimar. It was that the castle was his. Just knowing the structure belonged to him made it seem that much more welcoming.

"We will need to appoint many advisors to handle the coming challenges," Azariah said as he strolled toward the throne. On a normal day, there'd be lines of petitioners, a dozen guards, and several advisors, but now their muted footsteps were the only sounds he heard. "We'll also need to divide Mordan into districts and choose its guardians, but that all may wait. What did you wish to speak with me about?"

"Ahaesarus," Judarius said. "And his eventual return."

Azariah halted before the throne and turned around.

"His numbers are half ours," he said. "And how many more might he lose battling the beasts from the Vile Wedge? We also have an army of soldiers he does not, and allies in the dark paladins and the Council. What does he have? Why should we fear his return?"

Judarius crossed his arms over his chest and glared.

"Because he won't be alone," he said. "The Godslayer and his wife escaped, along with the boy king."

"Gregory is king no longer," Azariah said.

"By our word only, which the people will be eager to ignore. The same goes for the soldiers you think have sworn loyalty to us. They are loyal to their lords, and those lords only follow out of fear. They will betray us the moment they feel we are weak. You know that as well as I."

"Is that all?" Azariah asked, tiring of the warnings.

"No," Judarius said. His brother grabbed him by the front of his robe and pulling him close. "No, it's not, and I don't like how little fear you show of our opponents. I fought the half-orc and lost, Azariah. We may be angels, but Harruq slew a god. People will flock to him, especially if he protects the boy king. Aurelia's magic is not to be ignored either, or have you forgotten the power she wielded when we fought alongside her against Thulos? Even worse, I received a report from the Council. Roand the Flame is dead, presumably at Tarlak Eschaton's hands. Deathmask fled with him as well, giving us two more powerful opponents."

"My magic is stronger than any of them," Azariah grumbled.

"But all three combined?" Judarius asked. "And that doesn't count the half-orc's brother. Qurrah Tun was beloved by Karak for a reason, and neither he nor his lover were with Bram's army when we destroyed them. Celestia will not like what has happened today, which means the daughter of balance may soon bring her wrath against us. Should they meet up with the resistance, we will face a force of tremendous power. And to counter them, you'd use cowardly human lords and dark paladins of Karak, who were once our most hated enemy. Listen to me, brother. Your rule is not as strong as you think."

Azariah folded his wings behind his back and sat upon the throne. His fingertips drummed against the armrests. His body sank into the cushions. Looking out upon the crimson carpet, he realized it looked like a trail of blood that ran from his seat to the doors, and all who entered must walk through it. Another worthy symbol showcasing the inherent risk in petitioning one who held the power of life and death over every man, woman, and child. Power he needed to solidify against such resistance.

"We have suffered too much to let things slip from our grasp," Azariah said. "Too many have bled and died for us to fail. Ahaesarus, the Eschaton, the daughter of balance...let them come. We will crush their bodies to dust. They think themselves heroes, but they are only defenders of the sinful chaos that created a need of heroes in the first place." He rose from his throne and put a hand on his brother's shoulder. "Walk with me."

They crossed back over the crimson carpet and out the broken doors. On the steps of the castle, they overlooked the quiet Mordeina.

"How well do you remember Karak's siege of this city?" he asked.

Judarius shook his head.

"Very well, up until my death," he said. "Everything beyond is a blur, at least until Ashhur was imprisoned by the goddess."

Azariah outstretched his hands and began casting a spell. The words of magic flew off his lips, so easy, so comfortable. It was a familiar power, and given where they stood, it felt remarkably appropriate. In the earliest days of Dezrel, Karak had attempted to destroy all of the old Paradise and crush Ashhur and his people. Now they faced similar danger, and not just from Karak, but Celestia, and even misguided followers of Ashhur himself.

The power focused in his chest, vibrating, seeking release by the shouting of a single command word. Azariah let it build. The sensation was intoxicating.

"When you fell, I cried over your corpse," Azariah said. "I whispered to you the Treaty of the Fallen, asking your soul to be guided on to shining shores instead of this dull, aching existence. But do you know what Ashhur did?"

Judarius shook his head, and he seemed troubled by the question. "I do not."

Azariah smiled, willing to endure the shedding of blood it caused.

"He bid you to *rise*."

His word was a whisper, but it floated across the city. Azariah felt a tremendous pull upon his chest. His strength, his power, poured out of him. It sought the vacant vessels that lay throughout the city. No matter the broken bones, no matter the torn muscles and rotting flesh. There would be no mind to feel the pain.

All throughout the city, the corpses crawled free of the piles, organizing into neat rows and columns. They made not a sound, at least not from their lips. Their bones creaked as they walked, their footsteps heavy and wet from blood and pus. In his mind's eye, Azariah saw them all, and he commanded them with wonderful ease.

"The dead were made to serve, and by Ashhur's hand first," Azariah said, arms lifted in triumph as shadows swelled about his fingers. "They once fought to protect the people of this city, and now centuries later they shall do so again. There will be no rebellion, not here. In all places, I shall have eyes. In all corners, I shall have soldiers who will fight without doubt or fear. I will have an army that will never betray my command. Dezrel may kick and scream like a stubborn child, but we shall bring peace to this troubled land, and they shall be the blade I wield to do it."

He lowered his arms as the effort required to maintain the dead settled upon his mind. It was like a thousand needles digging into his forehead, but he would endure. Velixar had done it, after all, and Azariah had ten times the strength of that rotten lich.

"No matter the cost," he whispered. "For I have the strength to pay it."

Judarius said nothing, only watched as the dead streamed toward the outer walls, the perfect army for their perfect king.

Enjoy this novel? Want to let others know what you thought? Then please leave a review for me here: http://smarturl.it/amzkingofvile. I'd much appreciate it.

More series in the world of Dezrel by David Dalglish:

The Half-Orcs: http://smarturl.it/amzhalforcs
Shadowdance: http://smarturl.it/amzshadowdance
The Breaking World: http://smarturl.it/AMZBreakingWorld
The Paladins: http://smarturl.it/amzpaladins

You can also check out my Facebook page at http://www.facebook.com/DavidDalglish or my website at http://ddalglish.com to keep up on pretty much any of my updates.

Note from the Author:

First off, a quick warning. This note here is likely to ramble a lot, discussing ideas and alternate endings never used, as well as the origins of a few specific characters. Some of you may not care in the slightest, so just scroll to the very last paragraph if you'd rather hear about upcoming works. Hopefully there's a few of you that might find this interesting. So here we go. Oh, and trust me when I say that all this does eventually come together, and bear relevance to the book you just read.

In the summer between graduating high school and entering college, I wrote about sixty pages on an abandoned novel (abandoned as in 'a hard drive crash lost me everything'). Its working title was Demonworld. The idea was that a group of heroes from multiple dimensions were all captured and brought to this one world overrun with demons. These heroes would then be forced to battle in a gigantic arena for the entertainment of an assortment of demons, imps, and monsters. Imagine the coliseums of old, except with orcs and fire elementals. Fun fact: Haern's first incarnation came from this novel, as one of the main characters who were captured and brought into the Demonworld. He soloed a frost giant in the first chapter, because Haern is awesome. Oh, another fun fact: I originally planned on having Haern reveal that he was a woman underneath all those hoods and cloaks, a twist I *almost* used in the Half-Orcs when I shoved him into that series out of sheer impatience.

The plan for the Demonworld book was for the heroes to kill a few scary things, break out into this blasted ruin of a world, and flee. Eventually they would be rescued from the chasing demons by angels, who would spin them a tale about this ancient sword the heroes needed to go obtain from this super-secret area that only the foretold hero could go inside. Well, the twist was the angels were, in fact, also evil, they just hadn't spent the past century or so living on the ground but instead in the clouds away from the imps and lesser demons, which saved them from turning all ugly and demonic. The sword was actually imprisoning an

The King of the Vile

ancient evil god named Kaurthulos, slain by said sword, and the angels couldn't get to it because it was protected against evil.

I'll give you one guess as to the name of the lead evil angel. Hint: it starts with an 'A', and ends with 'Zariah'.

All right, so here I am, drawing the map of this Demonworld, and I'm trying to add in some unique stuff. Some flavor, if you will. And one of the things I added on a whim was a random tower labeled "Lich's Tower". Now at the same time, I'd been working on The Weight of Blood for The Half-Orcs, and I was struggling to decide where I wanted to take the series. But I knew the eventually fate of Qurrah Tun...he was to become a lich. And suddenly, I knew what I wanted to do. I would *merge* these two stories together. Harruq's swords would be the swords that trapped the ancient god, Kaurthulos. Qurrah would be the lich the heroes of Demonworld stumbled upon and learned some of its history. Tessanna would be the one who brought the demons into the world in the first place.

So all this is a very, very long way of saying that I have been planning for Azariah and Judarius to become fallen angels since their very introduction (for fun, take a look at the first thing Azariah ever says to Harruq in Shadows of Grace, or the kind of infamous traitor whose name is not all that well hidden within Judarius's name). Now what of all this Demonworld nonsense? Am I actually going to go through with that?

Nah. You see, I once wrote in a note that Qurrah's redemption didn't just save his life, but the entire world of Dezrel. I also wrote I had no clue it was going to happen. Both are absolutely true. Around the time I was writing The Death of Promises, I still had the (psychotic) plan of having the Half-Orcs Series end as a colossal failure, the world overrun with demons and fallen angels. My plan was to leap forward a good hundred years, introducing some new heroes, and having you readers meet a grown-up Aubrienna leading the resistance alongside her mother and father. When Qurrah knelt before Harruq at the end of Shadows of Grace, Harruq was supposed to slit his throat. Harruq was going to finally give in and do what everyone had been telling him to do, to deny forgiveness and instead kill his brother for all the pain he'd given him.

That moment of spite would doom all of Dezrel. Qurrah wasn't to die, but instead use Velixar's spellbook in his final moments to save himself by becoming undead. The ramifications are enormous. Suddenly Tessanna isn't trapped with Velixar, wishing to escape his control, but instead a willing participant in the carnage. Qurrah doesn't make his epic stand on the bridge with King Theo White. He doesn't burn Velixar at the battle in Avlimar. Originally, Qurrah was to escape Thulos's defeat with Tessanna dying in his arms (dying to Mira, no less, another character who totally went and got herself killed prior to my plans). Qurrah would go east, building his lich's spire from the bones of the elves he slaughtered as he burned the Dezren Forest to ash.

It all continues to spiral from there, in ways that'd be too lengthy to detail in full. I mean, I could, and part of me wants to. I've been writing in the world of Dezrel for nearly thirteen years, which allows for a bit of nostalgia when I look back to when everything was just a bunch of scribbles on a few sheets of paper. But to reward the sacrifices of so many characters with a demon world of death and shadow? No. I can't do that, not anymore. Perhaps that means I'm losing my edge, or maybe I'm no longer a crazy eighteen-year-old hoping to shock my readers by how I'm totally willing to do something so insane.

But there are still seeds, little ideas from the original Fall that I have used and still plan on using. Much of it has needed tweaking, for as I've written more and more of these books, fleshing out the world with series like The Breaking World and The Paladins, I keep finding new wrinkles in Azariah's original plan. And for once, I see a different future building for my silly little world, one where I can bring the series back to its roots, before it spiraled out from the adventures of the Eschaton into this sprawling war between gods. This means I'll be bringing this saga with the angels to a close come the next Half-Orc book, aptly titled The King of the Fallen.

For those wondering what happened with the orc army potentially led by a war demon: that's going to have to wait for another time. Given all the crap I had going on in this one, I decided a tighter focus was better than trying to add in a ninth

The King of the Vile

sub-plot. And as I said, I have emerging plans that go on for several more books, and in hopefully new and fun directions. This means the possibility of an orc empire led by a demon can be given its full attention instead of swiftly dealt with on the side.

After King of the Fallen comes Queen of the Faceless, and I'll let your imaginations run wild with what exactly that could mean. Not that it'll take that much to figure out some key elements. I mean, I've always had people asking me where Zusa, Alyssa, and Nathaniel ran off to during the events of the Half-Orcs...

To all of you who stuck with me, not grumbling too loudly during the long stretch between this book and The Prison of Angels while I both rewrote and then finished the Shadowdance Series as well as The Breaking World: thank you. To those wondering if there will be a similar lengthy wait: not a chance. As of right now, I'm scaling down my attention to two series, one with Orbit, one self-published. Bouncing between them should still allow one Half-Orc book a year, if not two, so settle in for the long haul. I'm not done with these silly Tun brothers just yet. If that's all right with you, well, then that's all right with me.

David Dalglish
December 15th, 2014